"Nicole Byrd has what

"A wonderful author."

D0194074

continued . . .

Titles by Nicole Byrd

ROBERT'S LADY
DEAR IMPOSTOR
LADY IN WAITING
WIDOW IN SCARLET
BEAUTY IN BLACK
VISION IN BLUE
GILDING THE LADY
SEDUCING SIR OLIVER

Seducing Sir Oliver

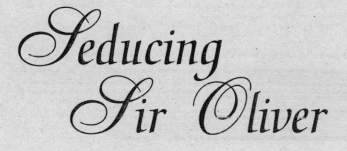

Nicole Byrd

BERKLEY SENSATION, NEW YORK

THE BERKLEY PUBLISHING GROUP
Published by the Penguin Group
Penguin Group (USA) Inc.
375 Hudson Street, New York, New York 10014, USA
Penguin Group (Canada), 90 Eglinton Avenue East, Suite 700, Toronto, Ontario M4P 2Y3, Canada
(a division of Pearson Penguin Canada Inc.)
Penguin Books Ltd., 80 Strand, London WC2R 0RL, England
Penguin Group Ireland, 25 St. Stephen's Green, Dublin 2, Ireland (a division of Penguin Books Ltd.)
Penguin Group (Australia), 250 Camberwell Road, Camberwell, Victoria 3124, Australia
(a division of Pearson Australia Group Pty. Ltd.)
Penguin Books India Pvt. Ltd., 11 Community Centre, Panchsheel Park, New Delhi—110 017, India
Penguin Group (NZ), Cnr. Airborne and Rosedale Roads, Albany, Auckland 1310, New Zealand
(a division of Pearson New Zealand Ltd.)
Penguin Books (South Africa) (Pty.) Ltd., 24 Sturdee Avenue, Rosebank, Johannesburg 2196,
South Africa

Penguin Books Ltd., Registered Offices: 80 Strand, London WC2R 0RL, England

This is a work of fiction. Names, characters, places, and incidents either are the product of the author's imagination or are used fictitiously, and any resemblance to actual persons, living or dead, business establishments, events, or locales is entirely coincidental. The publisher does not have any control over and does not assume any responsibility for author or third-party websites or their content.

SEDUCING SIR OLIVER

A Berkley Sensation Book / published by arrangement with the author

PRINTING HISTORY
Berkley Sensation mass-market edition / July 2006

Copyright © 2006 by Cheryl Zach.
Excerpt copyright © 2006 by Cheryl Zach.
Cover design by George Long.
Cover illustration by Leslie Peck.

ISBN: 0-425-21083-9

BERKLEY SENSATION®
Berkley Sensation Books are published by The Berkley Publishing Group,
a division of Penguin Group (USA) Inc.,
375 Hudson Street, New York, New York 10014.
BERKLEY SENSATION is a registered trademark of Penguin Group (USA) Inc.
The "B" design is a trademark belonging to Penguin Group (USA) Inc.

PRINTED IN THE UNITED STATES OF AMERICA

10 9 8 7 6 5 4 3 2 1

This book is for Sid,
who put the magic back into my life,
with all my love

One

*W*hen she first saw the man approaching, Miss Juliana Applegate hugged the upper branch of a gnarled oak tree. Her bare toes clinging to a lower limb, she wavered and almost lost her balance.

Before she spotted the solitary horseman, she had been playing a determined game of chase with a hen—the red hen, their best layer—but so far, the blasted fowl was winning.

It had evaded her first in the thicket. When it had flown to the lowest branch of the tree, Juliana swore and grabbed for the bird, but it fluttered to a higher fork and out of her reach. Still swearing briskly, Juliana kilted up her skirt and unlaced and pushed off her boots so that she could climb, too. This meant displaying an unseemly amount of limb, but she knew that old Thomas was safely occupied in the east pasture mending the last of the gaps in the fence, and there was no one else to see her.

The fence should have been mended earlier, but she had

thought the temporary switches would hold until the hay was in. If it rained before the hay was cut and dried and stacked, the animals would starve during the long York shire winter. So the hay had been harvested, but in the meantime, the cows had gotten out of the pasture. One had gotten mired in the bog, and although they'd pulled it to safety, the poor thing had broken a leg and had to be slaughtered. It was the second cow they'd lost this season. The other had succumbed to some ailment that even Thomas didn't know how to treat.

"You silly bird, do you want to be next?" Juliana glared at the hen.

Turning its head, the chicken watched her with beady eyes.

"If I don't get you inside the coop before sundown, a fox will snatch you. Then we'll have no eggs for Father's breakfast. Do you want to be fox food?" She reached toward it, but the irascible fowl flew to the next branch.

Juliana swore and prepared to follow, holding on tightly to the tree so that she didn't tumble to the hard ground beneath. The bark felt rough beneath her hands, even though her fingers were calloused from her daily chores.

Absently, she rubbed a healing blister on her palm, still tender from the hard work of haying. She tried so hard . . . tried to be the son her father hadn't had, tried to tend the estate since he had become unable to walk his small acreage, but she always seemed to fail him. Despite spending her whole life in this remote part of the shire, she wasn't wise enough about animals or crops or weather. Nor was she strong enough to do the haying without extra help—she had hired two lads from the village, as old Thomas was so bent with rheumatism that he, too, was not the most able.

The awareness of her shortcomings burned inside her, and for a moment, her view of the hen blurred. Juliana rubbed the back of her hand across her eyes. Every year seemed harder than the last. With their income from the estate shrinking, they had sent away the servants, all except Thomas and his wife, Bess, who had spent their whole adult lives on the Applegate estate.

When Juliana's older sister, Madeline, had explained gently that there was no longer money for salaries, Thomas had exchanged a glance with his wife. "Wages or no, nowheres else to go," he'd said. "No family left, and too old to be hired some'wheres else."

It was true. And even in this remote part of the kingdom, Juliana had heard how, in recent years, towns teemed with displaced farm workers, turned out by landowners converting crop acreage to sheep pasture in order to produce lucrative wool for the new machine-driven looms. And most of those now-idle laborers, unable to find work in the cities, ended up being driven to crime, begging on the streets, or quietly starving.

The elderly couple had stayed, and Juliana and her sisters—the always responsible Madeline, and even the twins, Ophelia and Cordelia, in somewhat sporadic bursts—had redoubled their efforts to stave off their creditors and hold on to the land her father's family had owned for generations.

So when she saw the man on horseback approaching this small, out-of-the-way house, Juliana's pulse jumped. Waving aside a bee hovering near her head, she narrowed her eyes to focus on his face.

He was not one of their neighbors; she knew them all well. Was he a courier, bearing dire messages about overdue debts? The man looked too well-dressed for that, and he rode too well to be a habitually desk-bound clerk.

The stranger rounded a bend, and she got a better view of him. Juliana gasped and almost lost her hold on the branch. She had seen this man before! Surely, this was the traveler who had come across a mud-soaked Juliana as she'd tried to coax her donkey out of the bog? That had been some time ago, and the man—the gentleman—had insisted on seeing her home. But—

She pushed aside a leafy twig and stared harder. It was the same man, she was sure of it. He was tall and dark-haired, amazingly good-looking, and dressed very fine. But why on earth was he here?

A sense of foreboding pressed heavy against her, and she tried to thrust it aside. There had to be some simple explanation. Maybe the man had lost his way. But her heart pounded as the horse and its rider drew steadily nearer.

As if aware of her lack of attention, the hen sidled a few inches closer along the branch. Juliana reached out and clutched the errant bird.

"At least," she said, "I have you!"

Burdened by the squawking hen, she climbed down as quickly as she could, scraping an elbow in the process, then slipped into her boots and hastened to put the hen safely into its pen with its sisters. She had just tossed several handfuls of grain inside the coop and barred it for the night when she turned to see her older sister rushing toward her.

"Jules! A stranger has come. Oh, and you are a sight!"

Madeline herself looked as neat as usual. Even though Juliana had last seen her sister in the kitchen, rolling out dough for shepherd's pie as she helped Bess prepare the meal, Madeline had shed her apron and showed not a hint of flour on her face. Every curl of her soft brown hair was in place, and only the small crease in her forehead revealed her anxiety.

Whereas Juliana herself . . . She looked down and shook her skirts back into place, then brushed at her faded muslin dress. A leaf clung to her bodice and a stray chicken feather adorned her collar. Tendrils of her own darker hair clung to her face, which was grimy after her struggle with the runaway hen. She shut one eye and rubbed the tip of her nose. At least she had donned her boots.

"Come quickly, you must wash your face and straighten your hair and your collar," Madeline told her.

"Why?" Juliana stared at her sister even as she matched her rapid pace toward the back of the house. "He didn't ask to see us, did he?"

"Of course not. Bess took him in to see Father. And they have the door shut. But . . . but I'm worried, Jules. I heard shouting."

"Shouting? At Father? How dare he?" Juliana broke into a run. Was Father in danger? But the stranger—when Juliana had met him before, he had seemed reasonable enough, even polite and helpful, insisting on coming to her aid and seeing her safely home. And from his speech and his dress, she had judged him to be a gentleman. So why would he yell at a man older and weaker than he? It made no sense.

She passed her sister, and it was Madeline this time who hurried to catch up. "Where are you going? Wait!"

"We must help Father!"

But when they entered by the kitchen door, and Juliana ran to the hallway to listen, she could hear only the faintest murmur from the study.

Her sister insisted that Juliana wash her face before going any farther. She obeyed, but with haste, splashing the water in the bowl and scrubbing her cheeks with a threadbare linen towel, then dashing down the hall to the sitting room. Madeline followed at a more ladylike pace.

Still, the study door remained shut. The interview inside seemed to stretch on for an eternity. With the heavy door firmly closed and the voices inside well muffled, Juliana could detect little of what was being said.

"I should go in to Father," she muttered.

Madeline shook her head. "No, if he wishes us, he will ring. We have no idea what this is about, Jules. He may not—may not wish us to know the business between them." Her tone was resolute, but she appeared pale.

"Then why do you look as if your whole world—our whole world—is about to come crashing down?" Juliana demanded. "What is it you suspect? Tell me, Maddie!"

Her sister shook her head. "I don't know. Only that I glimpsed the stranger as he walked down the hall, and he . . . he looks so much like Father."

Baffled, Juliana stared at her sister, who didn't seem to want to meet her eye. When she had first encountered this man, he had seemed oddly familiar, but she hadn't thought—

"Perhaps he's a cousin that Father has never mentioned." She did not care for the expression on her sister's face. "A distant cousin."

"Or perhaps more," Madeline murmured.

"What are you not telling me?"

Juliana felt a surge of frustration when her sister shook her head.

"I can't. I promised."

"Then I am going to see for myself!" Juliana bolted into the hall before her sister could stop her. She strode toward the door which led to her father's study, but when she reached for the doorknob, she hesitated.

The voices inside were still low, and perhaps her sister was right. Would her presence aid her father or only make this interview, whatever it was about, worse?

But why the shouting earlier?

As she lingered, not sure what to do, she heard footsteps from inside approaching the doorway. Unwilling to be caught in such a compromising position—the man might think she was trying to eavesdrop!—Juliana rushed away from the door and around the next corner. Breathing hard, she paused there and pressed her back against the wall.

Was he going into the sitting room? No, she heard the front door shut, and, faintly, the patter of hooves on the gravel drive. He was leaving.

She heard Madeline's voice. "I'm coming, Bess. Did you find Miss Juliana?"

"No, miss," the elderly servant answered. "I'll look upstairs for her."

Juliana gave the maid time to disappear up the staircase, then turned the corner to meet her sister in the hallway.

"Bess says that our father wishes to speak to us," Madeline explained. She was still pale, but her tone was resolute.

Feeling almost sick with fear, as well as a dreadful curiosity, Juliana nodded. She waited beside her sister when Maddie knocked on the study door.

A pause, then from inside, their father called, "Come in."

He sounded . . . defeated. Oh, dear Lord, what was this all about? Had the bank called in their debts, and were they to be turned out into the hedgerows at last? Surely that handsome, fashionable gentleman had not been an ordinary bank clerk come to deliver the bad tidings?

Her head whirling with unlikely ideas, Juliana followed her sister inside the room.

Behind the desk, Father stared at the bookshelf on the wall and didn't look up. When he raised his head, his expression was grimmer than she had ever seen it.

"Shut the door," their father said. "I have a difficult story to tell you."

~~~

As Lord Gabriel Sinclair rode up to a smallish country house built out of gray stone, bigger than the cottages the local farmers inhabited but smaller than the seat of the local squire, he discovered that his heart was hammering as if he were going into battle. Perhaps in a way, he was.

How long had he searched to find the man who dwelt here? In some ways, he thought, all his life. There had been long, empty years when he would have bartered his soul to find the missing part of himself . . . even before he'd understood exactly what was lacking. So why did he feel icy cold now?

He pulled up his horse and dismounted, tying the reins to a convenient post. No servant had yet appeared. The household seemed neglectful or perhaps understaffed. No matter, as long as the man Gabriel wished to see was at home.

Taking long strides to the front door, he rapped the brass knocker. It gleamed from a recent polishing, and the doorway had been swept.

He felt tense as if . . . The door opened, and he pushed the thought away. An elderly servant in a faded gown gazed at him in inquiry.

"I wish to see the gentleman of the house, Mr. Applegate," Gabriel told her.

She nodded. "Yes, sir. If you'll come this way. Who shall I say is calling, sir?"

"Just tell him Mr. Smith," Gabriel told her. She would not understand the irony of his lie, but the man he was about to see should.

She led him down the hall to a room toward the end and opened the door. He stood back while she announced, "A Mr. Smith to see you, sir," and then made her departure.

Taking a deep breath and trying to control his expression, Gabriel stepped inside the room. Getting his first good look at his host made Gabriel's chest tighten. It felt like a blow, seeing how similar to his own were the other man's features, only a little blurred and softened by several decades of time passing. But he had the same dark hair, the same unusual deep blue eyes and firm chin—all the features that women had so often deemed pleasing in Gabriel.

The man behind the desk had a quill in one hand and a ledger beneath the other. He looked up now but did not stand, and his expression of polite welcome froze as he took in the newcomer. For a moment, the air seemed charged with sudden emotion.

Yes, Mr. Applegate deserved an unpleasant surprise. Gabriel had had enough of them in recent years.

Gabriel met the man's astonished stare with a hard look of his own and waited. At last, the older man broke the silence. "Your name is not Smith, I think," he said slowly.

"No." Gabriel heard the curtness of his answer, but did not try to soften his tone. He had expected many feelings on seeing this man for the first time, had imagined he might feel affection or relief. But now, most of all, he felt anger blossom inside him, anger that could erupt out of control if he were not careful. He found his hands curling into fists and tried to relax his fingers.

"Society knows me as Lord Gabriel Sinclair. But you, of course, know that is not really a valid designation."

The older man's mouth twisted for a instant, then he had himself under control again. "I think the marquess owed you—and your mother—that much," he answered, his voice level. "My acknowledgment of paternity would have helped neither of you. In fact, it would have ruined her in Society's eyes, as you well know."

"How dare you even speak of my mother!" Without

conscious choice, Gabriel found that he was shouting. "You have no right!"

"I loved your mother, and she loved me," the man with his face said. The calmness of his tone only stoked the fires of Gabriel's long repressed anger. "I hardly think you can judge. You have no idea what the situation was."

"I know you, by your involvement with a married woman, made her life hell!" Gabriel snapped.

"Her life was already hell. She told me so, and she swore that I gave her the only solace, the only happiness she'd ever had the chance to grasp. I-I hope she spoke the truth." His tone remained even, though bleakness darkened the familiar hue of his blue eyes.

"If you had not taken advantage of her unhappiness, perhaps—" Gabriel paused, knowing too well what his titular father's character had been, and how unlikely it was, under any circumstances, that his mother's condition would have improved.

"If I had been older and wiser, I might have been more prudent. Yet, how could I not have come to her aid? My . . . involvement, as you call it, with your mother began the night I found her weeping, hiding in the corner of a London garden. The marquess had struck her, and she was afraid to go back inside to rejoin the rest of the party until the flush of the blow had faded from her cheek."

Gabriel winced. Growing up, he had suffered similar blows often enough, and he had no trouble crediting this tale, though it pained him to admit as much. He swallowed hard against the lump in his throat.

"But—"

"I was aware of the dangers our association held for her. But I loved her from the moment I saw the tears on her cheek, from the first time I touched her hand . . ." The man behind the desk looked away, and his forehead creased.

"She was a gentle spirit, your mother, beautiful and good to her core. She deserved a better life. The marquess had been charming and solicitous before the marriage, and not until she was his wife did she learn his real nature. She'd tried to run away once, before I met her, but he found her and brought her back. He threatened to kill her if she left again."

The words pounded him as a fist might. Gabriel found his chest constricted. Trying to push away the fog of pain that slowed his thoughts, he shook his head.

"She could have applied to Parliament for a divorce, but that is a slow and uncertain process," Applegate continued, his tone dogged. "She was sure the marquess would slay her long before the decree could be granted. I offered to take her away to the Continent—Napoleon had not yet tightened his grip over the whole of Europe—but again, she feared her husband too much. The marquess had wealth and power, and I . . . well, you see my situation." He gestured vaguely toward the neat but small room with its book-lined shelves and plain desk.

"I was a small landowner with barely enough resources to support a family. I would have given it all up for her, I swear to God I would have, but she was afraid to risk it. And besides, something else held her back. You know, of course, that she already had a baby. If she had left her husband, she would never have seen him again."

Gabriel pressed his lips together to hold back a groan. His older brother, John, the current marquess. Yes, it all made a dreadful sort of logic. Yet he held on to his anger, which he had nursed for so long. It was an old friend and had comforted him for years. How could he so easily accept this facile explanation?

But the older man was still speaking. "In the end, the marquess became so suspicious she told me we must part, forever. I did as I was bade, though it pained me more than I can tell you."

"And married very soon afterward, I see, and fathered more children." Gabriel knew his tone was accusing, but all his life he had lacked a father who cared for him. And this man had just walked away?

Applegate winced. "Yes."

"And you felt no responsibility? If not for me—enduring the marquess's hatred all my life, disinherited and sent into exile when I was barely grown—what about the other child you sired upon my mother?"

Applegate looked away. "That was not planned. I was in the south of England, and your mother had escaped the estate for a few days during her husband's absence. We met unexpectedly. I-it was not wise nor right, no. But I take the blame."

"As you should," Gabriel muttered. But despite his attempts to nurse it, his anger was ebbing. "The marquess threatened to kill the child, you know. My mother had to send her away. And then later my sister, Gemma, was left all alone. What about your duty to her?"

The other man's expression was contorted. "Yes, I failed her for a time. There were . . . complications, circumstances which distracted me. But I sought her out as soon as I could and saw to her well-being, even if from a distance. So you have found her, then? The solicitor I engaged to issue her allowance wrote that she had gone to London and was searching for her unknown family. I'm pleased that you are reunited."

"No thanks to you," Gabriel told him. "And why, after my mother died, after the marquess died, did you not come forward? Did you plan to ever tell me the truth? Can you not face the consequences of your actions? I call you a coward, sir!"

Applegate's features tightened, but instead of jumping to his feet or calling him out—could one morally, even with the direst justification, fight one's own father?—the man lowered his face to his hands.

Gabriel's anger leaped once again. He would not allow the man before him to evade, yet again, an accounting for all the suffering that his actions had caused. Gabriel took two quick strides and rounded the desk, ready to pull the man to his feet and shake him until his teeth rattled in his head—

And paused just as suddenly.

The chair Applegate sat in appeared to be specially made. Wheels had been added to allow it to slide smoothly, and a rug covered the man from his waist down. Despite the covering, Gabriel could now make out that his father's legs were wasted and strangely twisted.

Looking up to see Applegate raise his head, Gabriel recognized for the first time the veneer of pain that dulled the once handsome features. Stunned, he met the older man's gaze.

"As I said, there were complications," Applegate said, his voice low.

❧

"Come in, girls," their father told them.

Juliana drew a deep breath. The situation could not be as bad as she feared, surely, it could not. But the expression on her father's face, the sound of his voice, flattened with anguish just as if he were having one of his worst days— oh, dear heaven, what could this be about?

For a moment she hated the good-looking stranger who had disrupted their peaceful, if impoverished, lives, hated him with an intensity she had not suspected she was capable of. How dare he come here and say—say what, exactly?

Her father was speaking, slowly and almost painfully, and she pulled her attention back to his words.

"Perhaps it is natural to wish to spare the ones we love knowledge of our darkest sins," he said. "I told myself I wanted to save you the pain of knowing, but perhaps I was really thinking of myself."

Juliana shivered. Without thinking, she reached for her sister's hand as they stood side by side and clung to it as if it were an anchor. Madeline's fingers were icy to the touch; she must be as cold with fear as Juliana herself.

"At any rate, I had hoped to avoid telling you what I must tell you now. But perhaps it's better that all secrets are out, at last. I can only say at the start that I am sincerely sorry for all the sins I have committed," he continued, his voice rough with pain.

Juliana felt an answering ache deep inside her. "Father—" she began, but he waved her to silence.

She felt Madeline press her hand, and she heeded the unspoken admonition and was silent. Every word seemed to cause her father distress; better to allow him to say what he felt he must say, even though she both wanted desperately to hear it and feared the revelation.

"When I was a young man, I spent some time in London, among Society more elevated and more wealthy than I." He paused and sighed.

Juliana bit back the reassurances she wanted to offer him. Her father had always been a most good-looking man, and he was charming and intelligent and had a kind heart. Just because he was not rich . . .

"I had not enough fortune to make an advantageous marriage, and I always knew I would end up coming home again, but I was young and ready for adventure. I found it—and a deep if illicit love—when I chanced upon a lovely young lady weeping in a garden. She was a remarkable person, and I fell in love, even though she was already married. We met secretly for a time, and there was a child born . . ."

Juliana bit back a gasp. The stranger who had looked so like their father—

"Yes, the man who came here today is your half brother, although no one but his mother and I knew the truth. Her husband the marquess suspected, and after that he kept a tight watch on his wife."

He paused, and Juliana knew her eyes had widened.

A *marquess?* This was lofty heights of Society, indeed. Even though her father had been born a gentleman, such rank was far outside their usual social sphere. And a secret affair—for an instant she tried to picture her father as young and impetuous, then she pulled her attention back. He was speaking again.

"At that point we agreed that we must part, both for her sake and the child's. Deeply unhappy, I returned to Yorkshire and tried to focus on running my tiny estate. A young lady I had known all my life appeared to notice my malaise and was kind and understanding. We fell in love, married, and had wonderful daughters . . ."

"So you never saw her—the marchioness—again?" Madeline asked, her voice gentle.

He winced. "Only once. Some years later, traveling to Dover to purchase some sheep, I encountered her unexpectedly. She had come south to visit a lady friend while her husband was away from home. It was totally unplanned, but I regret to say that our scruples and our resolutions slipped away. We had two days together, only, but another child was the result, this time a girl. And it was almost the marchioness's undoing. After that, her husband kept her a virtual prisoner for the rest of the years she lived."

He stared into the distance, and his expression was so grim that although Juliana wanted to rail at him on her mother's behalf, she held her tongue.

"I know you will find it hard to forgive me—" His voice faltered.

Juliana forgot her outrage. She hurried around the desk to kneel beside his wheeled chair and take his hand. "We love you, Father. We will always love you."

He rubbed his eyes and swallowed.

She wanted to ask, Did our mother know? But she didn't have the courage.

It was her sister who spoke.

"So the stranger who came to see you today—" Madeline's tone was amazingly even. Was she not as shocked and astounded by these revelations as Juliana?

"He is Lord Gabriel Sinclair," their father said. "Your half brother."

"Did you write to him? How did he find you?" Madeline persisted.

Juliana felt a stab of guilt. It was her fault! After coming across Juliana and her donkey in the bog, he had escorted her home . . .

Their father shook his head. "He says he had been searching for me for some time. They, he and his brother the current marquess, found some clues in their late mother's effects that made them suspicious. He is angry at me, too, with reason, just as you have every right to be. But he also, well, he told me I had been lax in my responsibilities, and I agreed. I will live with those sins all my life, as well as other transgressions on which God will judge me. But I suggested that having sought out the knowledge of his kinship, he has, in effect, invited additional obligations. Blood is still blood. I suggested—and he has agreed—that he invite one of his half sisters to come visit for a time in London."

"What!" Juliana forgot herself totally. She found she had jumped to her feet. Trying not to shriek like a fishwife again, she lowered her voice, but it still sounded strange, even to her own ears. "This man—this lord—probably hates us, and we should pay him a visit? Why should he— or we—wish to do such a thing, Father?"

"He is family, and blood ties matter, even when they are not to be—we have both agreed—acknowledged openly."

"But—" Madeline protested.

Their father shook his head. "Girls, look about you. As much as it grieves me to admit, I cannot provide for you properly, you know that. Since my accident, and despite our best efforts, the estate has gone downhill. It was never terribly prosperous to begin with. With no real dowry and so few eligible young men in the neighborhood, you have no hope of a good marriage. Your sister Lauryn was extremely fortunate to fall in love with the squire's son, and he with her, and lucky as well that his father allowed him to offer marriage."

And the fact that their father had made over their best and largest pasture to the new bride, for her husband and father-in-law to make use of, had no doubt nothing to do with it, Juliana thought, then pushed away the cynical notion to pay close heed to her father's amazing words.

"But what about you two or the twins? No, if I have to face the results of my youthful transgressions, and rightfully so, at least some good should come of it. Lord Gabriel—"

"If what you say is true—I mean, I know it is, but—he's not really a lord," Juliana muttered, rebellious, but her father ignored her and continued.

"Up to now, we have had no closely connected kin able to sponsor you and allow you to meet a wider range of suitable nuptial candidates. For your sake, I will not waste this chance. Lord Gabriel has agreed to take one of you back south with him in two days' time. It really should be Madeline, since she is the eldest—"

"I will not leave you, Father!" Madeline's tone was firm, and her expression had reverted to the familiar stubborn mien that her sisters called "Saint Madeline."

Their father tightened his jaw. "One of you will go to London," he repeated. "You can talk it over between the two of you and decide who it shall be. But I shall not pass up this chance to allow you an opportunity to look about you. You deserve a decent marriage."

"But if we cannot even acknowledge that this man is our brother—our half brother—how will it help?"

"He can still sponsor you," their sire said. "We have agreed to say that we are distant cousins." His moment of firmness seemed to have passed, and he turned his gaze toward the ledger on his desk. "Now, I have some work to do, accounts to balance if we are to pay our bills this quarter; the harvest was meager enough. You may decide between yourselves which one shall journey to London."

"And the twins?" Madeline asked.

"You can tell them when—when you think they're ready." Their father sighed. "They're very young, and it may be a shock to them."

Since Juliana knew that little short of a volcano's eruption or a badly made dress—on the rare occasions when they could afford new clothes—would alarm the twins, that was the least of her present worries. But she saw that she and her sister had been effectively dismissed. Her father picked up his quill, and her older sister motioned to her.

Wishing she could stay and argue, Juliana reluctantly followed her sister out into the hall.

"I am not going to London with that man!" she snapped.

"Hush, don't let Bess hear you," Madeline said. "Come back to the sitting room."

Juliana pressed her lips together and hurried back to the front room where they could shut the door, although not before Bess appeared in the hall, her expression inquisitive as she rubbed her hands dry on her apron.

"Would you like a tea tray, miss?"

"Not yet, Bess," Madeline answered. She shut the door firmly and turned to face her sister. "You see, she is curious. We must not allow this news—"

"Is it news?" Juliana interrupted. "How can you be so calm, Madeline! Tell me the truth, did you know?"

"That we had a half brother—and, heavens!—a half sister, too? No!" Madeline dropped down into one of the chairs.

Juliana found she could not sit calmly. She paced up and down the threadbare rug. "But you knew something. Tell me!"

Her sister rubbed her temple. "I only know what Mother told me once, when she was ill and a little out of her head with fever. Later, when I asked her if it was true, she made me promise not to tell anyone else, not even you, dearest. Besides, you were very young at the time."

"Barely two years younger than you!" Juliana snapped, irritated by her sister's long held tendency to assume a maturity beyond her years. She shook the old exasperation away so she could concentrate on the present thunderbolt. "But what did she tell you? She knew about the other woman?" Horrified to think that their sweet, patient mother had had to live with such knowledge, Juliana bit her lip and stared down into the fireplace.

"She knew that Father had been in love with someone else before they began their courtship. He had told her as

much, though not the details. I didn't know that it was a
married lady, or that her rank was so high." Madeline
paused. "If she knew about the other transgression after
they were married, she never told me."

"I hope she did not," Juliana muttered. "When she could
do nothing, it would have been a dreadful blow. How could
he do such a thing?" She drew a deep breath, trying to calm
herself. "What else did Mother know?"

"That was all that she remarked upon. And she told me,
later, when she was more coherent, that it didn't matter, really. She said"—Madeline put one hand to her face—"that
she loved Father so much, and was so thankful for all he
had done for her, that she didn't mind being his second
choice, as long as she had him to sit across the dining table
from her every day, as long as he was the one who fathered
her children. And he was always an attentive husband. I do
not believe she was unhappy, Jules."

"Oh!" Juliana had to blink hard and look back at the
hearth. Their parents' marriage had seemed so serene and
so loving. How could . . . No, she must not allow all her
memories to be destroyed. Her mother had loved her father,
and he had loved her. Despite the other relationship, she
had to believe that was true. She shook her doubts away.

"Life is complicated," Madeline muttered. She seemed
to be thinking much the same. "And it's not for us to judge."

"I don't see why not!" Juliana retorted, turning to
glare. "We are certainly suffering the consequences of it,
just as much—or more so—than Father. At least Mother
did not have to see a stranger with Father's face ride up
the drive! Oh, Maddie, what if people guess? I mean, you
did, right away. If they look at this—this Lord Gabriel and
then at us—"

Madeline rubbed her temple again, and Juliana knew
that she was not the only one pained by these revelations.

But she was too distressed to think beyond her own inner turmoil.

Her sister said, "I only suspected because of the resemblance this man bears to Father. No one in London will have seen our father recently, and I doubt few remember him, a cash-strapped young man from the North visiting the city over thirty years ago. And you look more like our mother, really, except that you do have Father's eyes."

"Mayhap, but—" Then she frowned. "You are assuming that I shall go to London? No, Maddie, I refuse! I need to be here to keep an eye on the estate and help Thomas. And you're the eldest, you should go and look over whatever marriageable men our new half brother can introduce you to. Though without a dowry—and I cannot believe this—stranger—is going to provide dowries for four hither-to-unknown and quite illicit connections—I don't see how a visit to London is going to help us!"

Her sister sighed. "No, nor do I, but our father is grasping at any straw, I think. He is much concerned about our future and has been ever since his accident. And as for the estate—" She looked up to regard her sibling as if she guessed how much their father's comment about the estate going downhill had wounded Juliana's feelings. "I know how you have labored, far more than you should have. You have tried hard to be the son he didn't—or we assumed he didn't—have. But it's not fair to you, Jules. You should go, even if the trip proves to be only a pleasant diversion. I remember you used to talk of seeing London."

"Years ago," Juliana argued, looking away from her sister's sympathetic gaze. "And certainly not under these conditions. It's not as if I have any great beauty or charm to compensate for my lack of fortune! No, you should go, Maddie. I should be here. There's the south pasture to be resown, and—"

"The hay is in," Madeline pointed out, her voice soft. "The grain reaped, and most of the garden harvested. Thomas can dig the turnips and the beets and tend to the animals. There is little to do for the rest of the year. You've done your best. It's not your fault the estate is not more productive."

Juliana bit her lip. How could it *not* be her fault? She should have been able to do better, she should do better . . .

"But I need to be here to help out!"

"You will help by not being here. With your absence, we will have one less mouth to feed," her sister noted.

Startled, Juliana looked up. "Is it as bad as that?"

"Close enough," Madeline said. "Father does not tell me the details, but I have seen how closely he watches the household accounts. And he insists that someone accompany this—this so-called cousin. I will not leave Father. I promised our mother I would look out for Father, you know that."

The curse of being the oldest child, the oldest girl, Juliana thought. "That is hardly fair to you," she argued. "You are six and twenty, Maddie. If any one of us should go—"

"No." Madeline's voice was firm, and she shook her head, her chin set stubbornly so that for a moment, she looked quite like their mother. "I am a spinster already, and quite resigned to it, Jules. No, I promised I would look out for him; he has no one else."

"He has other daughters. Do you think I care any less than you do?" Juliana shot back. She folded her arms.

"Of course you care. But I swore to our mother, Jules, on the day she died. I cannot break such an oath!"

"So you, who are the most beautiful of us all, are allowed no other purpose in your life? I cannot believe Mother would have wanted that," Juliana tried to protest.

Her sister shook her head. On this matter she had never

listencd to hcr sister's counsel, and Juliana feared she never would.

"And you can hardly wish to send one—or both—of the twins, to London, without us to keep them in check."

"Oh, good God!" Truly aghast, Juliana put a hand to her mouth. She had not even considered such a possibility. The twins—or even one of them, though they were seldom separated—abroad in a big city? When they could get in enough trouble in the countryside?

"Of course not," she agreed. "We are lucky they are visiting Lauryn at the squire's home and not here to see the—our half-brother— appear out of the blue. I don't even want to tell them. Not yet."

"We shall have to tell them something. Father is serious, Jules. You must go. And anyhow—"

Her sister's voice wavered, and without thinking, Juliana braced herself. "What? Not more bad news?"

Her expression hard to read, Madeline looked up at her. "I didn't wish to tell you, but you will find out soon enough. Mr. Masham is coming home."

"Oh, hell's fire!" Juliana sank down, at last, upon the closest chair. What other disaster could bcfall her?

Two

"Are you certain?" Juliana asked her sister, trying to keep her voice from wavering.

Madeline nodded. "It was only to be expected," she pointed out, her tone gentle. "He has a home here, after all."

"Yes, but since he married a great heiress, and is now enriched by her father's wool mills, I thought he might stay in Lincolnshire," Juliana retorted, knowing that she sounded bitter. "I hear their estate is quite grand."

Her sister answered her thoughts rather than her words. "I know it is hard, after he courted you so openly, and our neighbors were whispering that he might make you an offer any day."

It was hard, and yes, she had thought herself that James Masham might very well propose marriage, despite her lack of funds. And she had considered accepting, which was the most bitter morsel of all. Not that she had been madly in love with him, thank heavens, but she had known

him since she was a child, when they had hunted birds'
nests and roamed the moors together. He was not slow of
wit—that she could never abide in a mate!—and he was
well enough looking despite a somewhat weak chin. They
had seemed congenial enough, even if he'd never stirred
her pulse. At least he had never labeled her eccentric for
tooling around the shire on her donkey when their one
horse was needed in the fields or for doing her best to over-
see the estate's property after her father's carriage accident
and the broken hip which had never properly mended.

But then, on a visit south to other relatives, he had met
the wealthy wool heiress. After a whirlwind courtship—
inspired either by the girl's beauty or her fortune—news
had drifted back about his wedding.

So now Juliana found herself in a very awkward position. With only a handful of gentry in their neighborhood,
she, as one of Mr. Masham's oldest friends, would be
expected to welcome his wife and help make her feel at
home in the shire. Their neighbors would throw dinner
parties and teas, perhaps even a small dance, and it would
be impossible to avoid the newly-wed couple. Mr. Masham
and his new bride would, no doubt, be billing and cooing
and flaunting their conjugal bliss for all to see, and everyone else would be watching them, and also observing
Juliana, to see how well she was bearing up under her
"disappointment."

She thought of her last visit to the village, and how old
Mistress Landry had inquired, with an arch look, about
what Miss Applegate thought of her old friend's sudden
marriage. "You being, as it were, the closest to him."

Oh, it didn't bear thinking of!

Suddenly, a trip to London did not seem so totally out
of the question.

But to stay with an unknown half brother, who must be appalled to discover that he had new and impecunious relatives he probably—certainly—didn't even want?

What a quandary!

Juliana gulped, and her stomach seemed as shaky as that bog where Lord Gabriel had first encountered her. "I think," she said, her voice weak, "we might require that tea, after all."

Madeline nodded and pulled the bell rope.

Aware that her face must be flushed, Juliana rose and went to stare, unseeing, out the window. The lane was empty, now, but she could still picture the handsome man who had ridden into their lives and turned them upside down.

If only he had never found them!

Perhaps some secrets should never be revealed. Behind her, she heard the door open as the maid answered the bell, and her sister's voice as she asked for a tea tray.

Juliana gazed beyond the trees that cloaked the turn at the end of the drive, as if she could see all the way to London. A chill ran down her spine, and she shivered.

~⊗~

In the best bedchamber that the inn in the village had to offer—not saying much since the only other room was situated over the stable—Lord Gabriel Sinclair sat at a small table and tried to compose a letter to his wife.

How in the name of heaven could he explain that he would be returning to town with a hither-to-unknown half sister? And one whom he could not acknowledge openly, but whom he had agreed to sponsor. It was insanity—he must have lost his wits.

Gabriel stared down at the grimy sheet of paper, which was the best the inn could furnish, and regarded the quill with a frown. He took out his pen knife to trim the quill's ragged point and also to stall for time as he tried to think how to explain his agreement to this preposterous scheme, when he did not in truth understand it himself.

He had been so angry, so ready to shout and pound his fists, even though he was generally restrained in his manner and icy in his rare moments of rage, never out of control like his—no, not his father, he had known that for some time. Like the late marquess, the man the world thought was his father, Gabriel corrected, his mouth set into a grim line.

Was it fair to blame his mother when her life had been so harsh, her husband so cruel? Did he have any right to judge? He rubbed his hand across his face, then picked up the quill and tried again.

My darling Psyche,
I have found my true father. And more.

More. Oh, that was indeed the problem. He had expected to confront a hale and hearty and unrepentant sire, some aging Lothario no doubt still jaunting about the countryside seducing respectable and otherwise virtuous ladies. To find John Applegate guilt-stricken and contrite was unnerving enough, to find him crippled from a grievous injury, which was beyond the doctors' skills to mend, even worse. Gabriel could not strike a disabled man, could not even rail at him properly as he'd planned. And then to observe that Gabriel had half siblings in need. . . .

What was he supposed to do for these half sisters, and why did he have to discover them so close to actual privation? And so many . . . One he might have provided for, but five—well, four; thank the Lord one of them was already married—he did have his own future children to think of.

Was it right to take away funds that he had hoped to lay up for his own descendants? He thought of his wife, Psyche, who had the right to agree to any possible acts of charity, even if she had not brought a great deal of their current fortune to their marriage. And then there was his brother, the current marquess, who had been bequeathed all the wealth and the estate that went with the title when the late marquess had cut Gabriel out of any inheritance; he had no connection of blood and thus no responsibility to these young women at all.

Did Gabriel? If he had not spent a good part of his life abandoned by his family, living by his wits alone, he might have felt less sympathy for them. But he knew the fear that stalked you, the musings that came in the middle of the night, when an uncertain fate lay ahead. And women—young ladies—had even fewer opportunities to help themselves than did young men.

He had been desperate enough, but he had survived his wanderings and his disinheritance and returned eventually to reclaim his place in Society. If his half sisters should attempt even one iota of his adventuring, they would be considered beyond the pale—such were the constraints Society placed upon females.

If the estate failed them completely—John Applegate had shared his debts quite openly, and his situation made Gabriel shudder to remember it—what would they do?

The only respectable occupation the young women could undertake would mean hiring themselves out as governesses, to be delegated to cold meals in the attic, scanty earnings, and long hours of often thankless care for other people's children. The less respectable alternatives were even worse and would render them social pariahs.

Did he wish to force his half sisters into that kind of life? Their father would eventually die, and without his

small lifetime annuity, their tiny estate would not be sufficient to support the girls, even if—as Applegate avowed
was a possibility—their debts had not already overcome
them.

Wishing that his father had not been so candid, Gabriel
rubbed his face once more. Perhaps he even regretted the
long search which had brought him here. If he had known
the answer to his long quest . . . but it was too late now. He
picked up the pen and dipped it into the inkwell.

> *My darling Psyche,*
>   *I have found my true father. And more.*
>   *I have discovered that I have half sisters, and their con
> dition is not prosperous. I have agreed to bring one of the
> young ladies home with me for a visit to London, in the
> hopes of putting her in the way of meeting young men more
> suitable than are available on this distant heath. Our real
> relationship, I will warn you, is not to be acknowledged,
> and only you and I will know the truth. The world will be
> told that they are distant cousins.*
>   *I will explain more when I return; I expect to leave the
> day after tomorrow. Thank you for understanding, my
> darling.*

He added a few more private words of love—God, he
missed her!—then, as he saw no blotting paper, blew on
the ink until it dried and then carefully folded the sheet.
Looking about him without luck, he crossed to the door
and called for a servant. When she appeared, he directed
the maid to fetch sealing wax.

This led to a long search, but Gabriel was resolute in his
demand. He hardly wished anyone else to read this letter!
At last, the servant located a lump of wax, which he heated
on the edge of the poker held over the hearth fire—there

was no proper wax jack to melt it—and he managed to seal the note, impressing it with his signet ring.

Then he sent the missive off at once and, waving aside offers of food, ordered his horse saddled. Not to return to his father's house, but simply to ride across the moor and work off some of his frustration, Gabriel told himself.

And God only knew what Psyche would think when she opened his letter!

Staring out over rooftops at a hazy London sky, Margery Lyon, Countess of Sealey, snapped open her delicate silk fan. The day was warm and the air heavy with the hint of moisture. A storm gathered to the west, but although the clouds darkened, so far the rain was only a distant promise.

Fanning herself, she sighed. She was not a woman given to pensive moods, but she had lost a dear friend and lover some months ago, and his loss still grieved her deeply.

Some might gaze at her silvery hair and the laugh lines around her mouth and eyes and say that at her time of life, loss was to be expected. But Margery had always lived life well, savoring the moment, relishing the sweet times and refusing to dwell on the bitter ones. She had never been one to weep and wail before the world. Twice widowed, she mourned in private, tucked her pain away into a private corner of her soul, put on her usual cheerful face and went on with her life.

But now there were the letters. . . .

Who could hate her so much?

Until now she had held her own counsel, but she wondered if she should confide in someone. She had good friends, both male and female, some she could trust to the death. Yet it seemed such a petty thing, these sordid little epistles, surely not serious . . .

While she wrestled with the question and considered whether to ring for a maidservant to ask if the next post had arrived, a footman appeared in the wide doorway of the drawing room.

"A caller to see you, milady. Lord Montaine."

Surprised and just as glad to have her train of thought interrupted, Margery turned and nodded. "Show him in, please."

The footman moved away. Within a few moments he was replaced by the familiar stocky figure of a man of medium height, with dark, slightly receding hair and pale blue eyes. Clad in a fashionably cut outfit of Continental style, he made her a graceful bow.

"Bernard, what an unexpected pleasure. When did you arrive in England? I haven't seen you since the Congress." She advanced to offer a hand for him to kiss with his usual European flair.

"*Mais oui,* and such a gossipy mix of old-style Royalists just back from exile and turncoat Bonapartists it was, *n'est-ce pas?* Every one of them eager to once again redraw the map of Europe." Shaking his head in cynical amusement, he waited for her to sit.

She directed the servant to bring them a tea tray, then went back to her chair. He sat down, too.

"We could hardly leave Napoleon's relatives on half the thrones of Europe," she pointed out, her tone mild. "And besides, Vienna did have lovely parties, with so many monarchs and diplomats there ready to be entertained."

"So why did you leave so soon? The balls were not half so much fun after you had gone, Margery, *ma belle.*" His pale eyes intent upon hers, the comte leaned closer.

She laughed. "Oh, really, Bernard, with so many beautiful

ladies to flirt with, how could you even notice my absence?"
She added more soberly, "In fact, I heard that a dear friend
was ill, so I returned home earlier than planned." And her
secret mission for the Foreign Office had been fulfilled, but
that, of course, she would not mention. Then, slightly belatedly, she added, "And how is Simone, your lovely wife? I'm
sure she must have enjoyed Vienna, too."

Something flickered in his face before he conquered the
emotion, and too late, she remembered she had heard a
mention, through her diplomatic contacts, of the comtesse's
recent death.

"I regret—" he began.

She held out her hand in an impulsive and sincere gesture of sympathy. "I am so sorry, Bernard, forgive my blun-
dering. I have heard of your loss. It must still be very hard
for you to talk about."

He nodded. "It was quite sudden, perhaps a bad dish of
clams, the doctor said, or simply a severe dysentery."

He pressed her hand again to his lips, holding it there a
few moments too long, in a way that reminded her that he
had never been particularly faithful to his meek little wife
and he had most obviously been open, years ago, to an *af-
faire d'amour* with the countess herself.

But she had never risen to his lures. Something about
him, something about the way his wife watched him when
Bernard was not aware . . .

Gently but firmly, Margery drew back her hand.

She was lonely, too, just now, but she was not sure this
was wise. When one was alone, it was easy to make the
wrong choice. She would have to think about this.

"Perhaps a change of scene was a good thing for you,
then. Or do you have particular business in London?" she
asked.

"*Comme ci, comme ca.* A little of this, a little of that,"

he suggested. This time there was a definite gleam in his eyes. Not a grieving husband, she decided, despite his polite pretense. An amorous man, however, just as always, beneath the facade of the sorrowful widower.

He took his leave soon after, perhaps knowing he had gotten as much from her as she was willing to yield, for now. He was interested in an affair, if she was. At least, she thought he only wanted an affair. Surely he did not seek marriage? She had wealth and position, already, and as a widow, she had much more control over her own resources than most wives ever did; so why would she want to marry? And if she desired the pleasures of lovemaking—and she often did; age had not dampened that desire, happily, but only strengthened it—she was sophisticated enough to know how to conduct discreet affairs of the heart . . .

And as for Bernard, he had money, too, and power, already. But did he want more? Did he desire her wealth, her power, to add to his own?

"And what do you offer me in exchange, Bernard?" she wondered aloud. "Love? Are you capable of love? Ah, we shall see."

The footman brought in the post, and amid the usual pile of invitations and notes she saw another piece of that grimy paper that made her heart beat fast, but not at all in a pleasant way.

And she thought that having someone always at your side, someone you could count on as you faced the evil in the world, might not be such a bad thing . . .

⮞⮜

The next day Gabriel's hired carriage arrived—he had had to order it sent to the village from Ripon—and on the following morning, when all the horses were well-rested, he rode his own mount in front of the carriage and led it to the small manor house occupied by John Applegate and his daughters.

This time he was formally introduced to the two eldest girls—he bowed over each lady's hand, in turn, with a somewhat wooden politeness—and found, to his slight surprise, that the eldest, whose Christian name was Madeline, was not the one who had been chosen to accompany him. Instead, his guest was to be the second daughter, Juliana, the somewhat unpredictable girl whom he had first encountered when her donkey had gotten mired in a boggy bit of heath.

Those who knew him in London and who called him suave and charming might not recognize him today, Gabriel thought grimly. But it was an unusual situation. Indeed, even John Applegate looked bleak, and he hugged his daughter as if she were some ancient martyr about to be tossed to the lions.

Juliana Applegate clung to her father for several moments, and when she stepped back, her eyes were liquid with unshed tears. She didn't meet Gabriel's gaze.

He couldn't look *that* threatening, Gabriel told himself. Nonetheless, he tried to soften his expression, and he spoke to her gently. But when he escorted her to the hired carriage and she learned that he was riding, not joining her inside the chaise, she looked distinctly relieved.

So much for harmonious family relations, Gabriel thought. This whole thing was doubtless a terrible mistake! And on that cheerful note, they set out for London.

⤞

Sitting in the drawing room, Margery, Lady Sealey, lowered her cup of tea when she heard the thump overhead. What on earth was that?

Listening for more alarms, she waited. A thud followed, and surely that was a muffled shriek? Then the house fell silent again. Fearing the worst—after the last weeks, she found herself inclined toward a pessimistic humor quite unlike her usual serene good spirits—she went to the door and opened it.

Now she heard nothing, but something had caused that uproar. She climbed a flight of steps and turned toward the guest wing and heard the sound of a door closing.

Hurrying her steps, she rounded the corner and found her godson, Sir Oliver Ramsey, emerging from his chamber. His hair was tousled and his cravat in sad disorder.

She paused to stare up at him. His expression looked both guilty and abashed.

"Is everything all right, Oliver?" she asked.

"Yes, Godmother, certainly."

"Did you hear a strange sound just now?"

"Ahhh—what did it sound like?" he asked, his tone cautious.

He was stalling for time, she was sure of it. "A bump and a thud, and then a shriek," she told him, her tone a little sharper.

He shook his head, "I—um—dropped a book. Perhaps I yelled; it hit me on the shin when it fell," he told her. But she made out a sheen of perspiration upon his forehead.

Bless them, men were so transparent, she thought, not sure whether to hug him or box his ears. Oliver was a dreadful liar. "I doubt you could make such a noise. Besides—"

He looked even more anxious. "Yes?"

"Are you aware that you have a scratch upon your cheek?" She frowned at him. "Oliver, you are a dedicated scientist, and I admire you for it. But you are not going to blow up my house again, are you?"

He flushed. "I was fourteen when that happened," he pointed out, his tone as dignified as only a gentleman just turned six and twenty could assume. "And it was only the garden shed, not precisely your house. I have made no such miscalculation since then, I assure you. And anyhow, at present, I am more interested in zoology than in chemistry."

He seemed to think that explained everything. She felt a rush of affection for him and decided to let the matter drop. He had always been a young man of good character, and even if he was hiding something now, she did not believe it could be significant.

She was diverted by the appearance of her butler at the end of the hall.

"You have a caller, milady. Lady Gabriel Sinclair."

"I shall be there at once," Lady Sealey told him. "Bring us a tea tray, if you please. Perhaps you would like to come down and be introduced, Oliver? You might wish to wash the blood off your face, first."

He nodded. "I will do that, Godmother, and join you presently." He disappeared back into his room, shutting the door with haste.

Still puzzled, she made her way downstairs. Then, pushing her own worries away, she entered the large room and greeted her guest.

With her cool blue eyes, classical profile, and fair hair, Psyche, Lady Gabriel, was as lovely as ever, but she also looked anxious.

"Is something wrong, my dear?" Margery asked after a quick embrace, motioning to a chair close to her own.

Sitting down, Psyche sighed. "I have had a most surprising letter from Gabriel. He has found his birth father!"

"Oh, my. It has been a long search. Was it a happy reunion?"

"I'm not sure."

Margery listened with interest as Psyche explained about the injured man living a quiet life in the most barren reaches of Yorkshire.

"And Gabriel is bringing one of the girls—his half sister—back with him."

Even the countess was startled. "Indeed? He must have been quite taken with these new relatives."

"Or else he feels pity for them. They are apparently quite poor, and Gabriel may have felt constrained . . . Anyhow, she is coming. Oh, and no one is to know the true connection. We are to say they are distant cousins, and pray that no one guesses the truth of the matter."

Margery smiled. "That will have all of Society's matrons searching their knowledge of bloodlines in bewilderment. But if you hold firm to your story, you will be able to face them down. You and your charming husband have done as much before. And of course, I will back you."

Psyche flashed her a grateful smile, and the countess patted the younger woman's hand.

Psyche's mother had been one of Margery's dearest friends—one of the few ladies in Society to share her forward-thinking views—and her early death had been a great blow. And though Margery would have felt benevolent toward Psyche because of the link to her late mother, in recent years Margery had found that she loved this young woman for her own sake.

"I appreciate that very much, and so will Gabriel," Psyche was saying. "And I will certainly make this girl welcome, for Gabriel's sake. But I have another problem."

"Yes?"

"Our kitchen maid is ill. At first, I thought it only a slight fever, but the physician says she has the measles,"

Psyche announced, her expression doleful. "She has come out all in spots. And one of the grooms and both housemaids have caught it, and now the latest victim is Circe."

"Oh dear, how are your sister and the servants progressing?" Lady Sealey asked. "The disease can turn quite serious, I believe, if not carefully nursed."

"Yes, and Circe is a terrible invalid, wanting to go back to her easel at once. I'm keeping her in bed with great difficulty, as rest and quiet are essential so that the afflicted can heal. The disease is also most contagious, and I *cannot* bring in a guest at this moment. Even if she has already had the disease as I did as a girl—and I have no way to know—my household is in a shambles! And by the time I received Gabriel's note, they had already departed on the trip south. I have no way to get in touch with him. I suppose I can ask Gemma if she can take in this new relation." Psyche sighed.

Margery thought quickly. "Gemma and Matthew's house is small, my dear, compared to this one. Why not allow me to host the girl?"

Psyche looked up. "Oh, I did not expect such a generous offer, Lady Sealey. I would not impose upon you."

"It is not an imposition," the countess contradicted. "It should be interesting to meet this—ah—cousin of your husband's. And I have my godson staying already; he pretends otherwise, telling me he is in London to pursue his studies, but I know he came down mainly to cheer me after the death of my dear friend. So it will make little difference to my staff."

"You are so kind," Psyche said. "Perhaps in a few weeks everyone will be recovered, and then we can take her back to our house."

"Don't worry yourself any further. Just go home and take care of your invalids," Lady Sealey told her.

Psyche stood and hugged her again.

"You are a jewel," she said. "First, I must visit Gemma and break the news. She has longed to find their father, too. And then I must get back to Circe and make sure she is staying in bed. At least the servants don't argue with me when I tell them to rest!"

"I will send over my own mother's recipe for a healing draught," Margery promised. "But yes, you had better go. When you need a respite from the sick room, come back and see me."

"I shall," Psyche said. "And when Gabriel arrives, I will send the girl on. Poor thing, she must be feeling quite bewildered."

Margery nodded, and they paused as a footman and housemaid brought in tea trays. Next, Oliver, an impressive figure even in the wide doorway, appeared just behind the servants and followed them inside. A gleam of appreciation in her eyes, the maid glanced admiringly up at him, though the young baronet didn't appear to notice.

The countess did notice and she considered her godson's attributes: he was very tall, his shoulders broad, and he had a fine physique. And presently, his face was clean, though the scratch on his cheek was still visible, and his neckcloth neatly arranged.

"Ah, here you are. Psyche, may I present my godson, Sir Oliver Ramsey. This is Lady Gabriel Sinclair," she said, "a very dear friend."

Oliver gave a somewhat stiff bow. She should really have had him to stay sooner, Margery thought. The lad was much in need of a little town bronze. His own mother had died when he was only a boy, and he had spent too much time hidden away in his laboratory.

"How nice to meet you." Psyche returned his bow with a graceful curtsy and offered her hand. "I'm afraid I must cut my visit short today—I have sick at home to tend to—but I look forward to talking to you another day. I understand from the countess that you are a scientist!

"A student of science, only," he protested, but the statement seemed to please him. He touched her hand, couldn't seem to decide whether to shake it or do something more courtly, and released it quickly. "Zoology, especially."

"My father, a noted inventor, spent much time in scientific research. I shall be interested to hear about your studies when we have more time to chat," Psyche said. A hint of mischief in her smile, she added, "I believe you will find London's young ladies also intrigued by—ah—zoology." Then she smiled at them both and took her leave.

Oliver watched her go. "She's very beautiful." He sounded a little stunned and quite unaware of Psyche's implied compliment.

Lady Sealey bit back a smile. "Yes, and she has a charming and most handsome husband."

He nodded. "Of course she would."

"I can introduce you to many young ladies who are beautiful and unmarried, although you have mentioned that you are not interested in matrimony just now," she reminded him, waving a dismissal to the servants.

Oliver colored.

She took her seat again and waved him toward a chair.

He sat down somewhat gingerly, as if afraid his large frame would break the delicate legs of the armchair.

"I'm just not very good with females," he told her, as if confessing a dreadful secret. "I mean, I never seem to know what to say or do. I can handle a microscope or a vial of acid quite calmly, but ladies, especially pretty ones, send me all to pieces."

Feeling more in humor with him, she answered gently, "You simply need practice. Scientific pursuits should not consume your whole attention, you know. Well-rounded gentlemen should be at ease in Society. Besides, you have your baronetcy to consider. I should think that you will want children some day, which means marriage and a wife."

His ready blush came again. "Someday," he agreed. "B-but not just now." He sounded as if he were regarding an imminent appointment with the hangman.

Margery swallowed her smile. "At any rate, you shall soon have someone to practice on," she told him, her tone cheerful. "I don't know if she is pretty . . ." Lady Sealey paused; she could not imagine any relation of Gabriel's being less than handsome! Then she went on. "But we will have a young lady joining us as my houseguest, and I'm sure you will be polite to her for my sake, if not from your own sense of decorum."

"Of course," Sir Oliver agreed, although the teacup in his hand wobbled alarmingly as he registered the news of the additional guest.

This time, she did smile. "It will be good for you," she suggested.

Oliver wasn't so sure. Having a young lady under the same roof would just make him feel more awkward. But he would not have to spend a lot of time with her, he told himself. And anyhow, he had a more pressing problem.

For a moment, he considered admitting everything to the countess. His godmother had been so kind, and he hated keeping secrets from her. It would be the right thing to do. But would she understand? She might be upset or angry with him.

So he managed to drink his cup of tea without upsetting it, chatted politely, and finally excused himself.

Outside, he hesitated again just as a footman, carrying a letter on a silver tray, entered the drawing room. Perhaps,

Oliver told himself, he should just confess the whole thing and be done with it. He waited for the servant to come out of the room and then turned back to quietly reenter.

His godmother sat staring at a single sheet of paper, and the expression on her face made Oliver freeze.

Had she had bad news? Perhaps this was not the time—

Even as he debated, Lady Sealey's features contorted even further. Rising abruptly, she ripped the sheet and tossed the shreds into the fireplace, to be rapidly consumed by the dancing flames.

She stood and gazed down at the fire, and what she saw seemed to darken her usual pleasant expression. Oliver could glimpse only the side of her face, but even that partial view made him feel this was not the moment for chancy confidences.

Retreating, he climbed the stairs slowly. On the landing, however, worry gnawed at him, and he hastened his steps and hurried down the hall, then hesitated again before opening the door to his room. All his senses alert, he eased the door open, then slipped quickly inside and shut it behind him, at once turning the lock.

The housemaids had been forbidden to enter—he knew the servants were buzzing with speculation as to the reason for the strange command—but he couldn't risk anyone seeing his secret. And even the lack of housekeeping attention did not explain the books pulled from the desk and lying here and there on the carpet, the covers tossed about on the bed, or the bite marks on the delicate cane chair.

But at least this time the cage door was still shut and locked, and its occupant was curled up, taking a nap after her rampage through his bedroom.

Oliver sat down on the side of the bed and stifled a groan. What would Lady Sealey say when she discovered he was hiding a, well, a rather unusual female in his chamber? He'd be tossed out on the street, probably, and as for poor Mia, it would be her death warrant.

What was a man to do?

Three

After traveling all day, they spent the first night on the road in a well-appointed inn, where they obtained a change of horses. Juliana had her own bedchamber, and she found that her half brother had hired a private parlor as well, where they could sup in quiet luxury.

Juliana was not accustomed to traveling in such style. Of course, she was not used to traveling, she thought wryly. Except for visiting her married sister, who lived only a few miles away at the squire's manse, or riding her donkey into the village, she had had little chance to enjoy pleasure jaunts.

With the help of one of the chambermaids, she changed into a dinner dress and met her half brother in the private parlor at the appointed hour. The table was already laden with an amazing array of food. So many dishes for just the two of them—she thought of their usual dinner fare at home and realized that perhaps, indeed, her family was poorer, beneath their veneer of gentility, than she had realized.

The inn servant held her chair for her and then offered to serve them. Presently her half brother—no, no, she must not think of him as such, she would slip up and say it aloud. Her newly-found *cousin* made a polite inquiry about her ride in the hired carriage, but he seemed somewhat distracted. Was he regretting his agreement to this visit?

And what on earth would his wife say?

Juliana was already regretting her quick decision. If Madeline had only come instead . . . And as for her unfaithful suitor—well, Juliana didn't want to see him, it was true, but this visit might be even more uncomfortable than meeting Mr. Masham and his new bride. Several times a week. For months to come . . .

She found that her spirits had sunk even lower, and her body had gone stiff with tension. Which was worse, to be forced to go through a sham of offering welcome and hospitality to the newlyweds while all the neighbors watched, or to be away from home and the people she loved, and, most likely, be made to feel unwanted?

She found that the bite of chicken she was trying to chew seemed to grow larger. She swallowed, but it was hard to get the food down. Almost choking, she took a sip of her wine, then glanced toward her host.

Brows knitted, he gazed at the far end of the room, regarding the bureau there as if he wished to run it through. Oh, dear.

"You don't have to do this, you know," she blurted.

He looked at her in surprise. "Is the dinner not to your liking? Shall I order something else?"

"No, no, the meal is delicious and more than ample," she assured him. The fact that she was so nervous she could barely swallow was something she didn't care to share. "I mean, me, this visit. I feel very . . . very awkward, and you must resent having me foisted upon you. I know my father meant well, but—"

The expression on Lord Gabriel's face was hard to read. "If I have given you cause to believe that you are unwelcome, I apologize, Miss Applegate."

Now she felt ungenerous as well as uncomfortable. Juliana wished she had more practice in difficult social situations. At home, where she knew all the neighbors, where she seldom encountered new people . . . She drew a deep breath. She must not allow her new relation to think she was such a craven. Perhaps it was as well to say aloud what they must both, surely, be thinking.

"I feel that you must . . . must blame my father," she said. "For—"

She faltered as she saw that Lord Gabriel's deep blue eyes, in their hue and shape so like her father's and her own, could turn icy cold.

"For having an affair with a married woman?" he finished for her. "For fathering children upon another man's wife, a somewhat inconvenient fact for all concerned?"

Smarting for this disparagement of her parent, their parent, Juliana raised her chin. "I have seen little of Society," she acknowledged, her tone stiff. "But I believe affairs among the Ton, married or not, or perhaps especially when safely married, are quite common."

"Which hardly makes them right!" he shot back.

"Of course not!" She hoped she was not blushing. "I am not condoning such behavior. But I just want you to believe, to consider the possibility, at the least, that my father is not a man, even in his prime, who was in the habit of trifling with ladies."

He gazed at her, too polite to utter his doubts, but she could read them in his too bland expression. It was unnerving to see how much his expression resembled—in that moment—her older sister's, when Madeline was feeling most censorious.

"He fell in love with a lady in a difficult situation," she argued. "I believe his motives were altruistic. And I do believe that he loved her most sincerely. Before they married, he admitted as much to my mother."

The hardness in his eyes softened, and he gazed at her with increased interest. "That must have been difficult for her."

Juliana looked away for a moment. "My mother loved him very much," she said and could think of nothing to add.

Lord Gabriel drew a deep breath. "Perhaps I am too quick to confer judgment," he acknowledged, although his voice was still cool. "I simply think of my mother, unhappy in her marriage, and how vulnerable she was . . ."

"She was also"—Juliana pointed out—"in need of a friend."

For perhaps the first time, she saw him smile briefly. "True."

She could think of nothing more to add, and anyhow, she was afraid to press her luck. Silence hung in the air between them.

At last Lord Gabriel said, "My mother is dead. Your father is an invalid. Whatever happened between them, they alone knew the full truth of it. We'll never know exactly how and why it occurred, and perhaps we should not try. What is clear is that we have a connection between us, and I feel we should respect it."

She nodded, and some of the strain that had stopped her throat eased. "It is kind of you to say so."

"No, it is only proper," he said, and then smiled again. "As incongruous as that word might seem."

She gave a nervous laugh.

"So, if I can do you some small service by showing

you a few weeks in London, it is a small enough thing," he told her.

If he took this view, she could hardly demand to be taken north again, which Juliana realized she had been on the verge of doing. She nodded. "I fear I have not much practice in Society. I shall try not to disgrace you, *Cousin!*"

He grinned at her emphasis on the last word. "I'm sure you will do splendidly."

So they finished the meal in more or less companionable fellowship, and Juliana managed a little sleep in the strange room and unfamiliar bed. The next day, riding once more alone in the chaise, she gazed out the window and watched the countryside as they approached London.

But when they rolled into the West End and she saw the elegance of her half brother's residence, all her nervousness returned. An icy knot seemed to have formed inside her, and when the carriage pulled into a particularly fine square and up to a large and well-appointed house, she shivered, even though the day was mild.

Lord Gabriel had dismounted, and the groom helped her down. She paused and looked up at the door of the house as it opened. A very beautiful fair-haired woman came out, her clothes alarmingly fashionable. Juliana immediately felt dowdy by comparison, dressed as she was in the made-over gray traveling costume which had once been her mother's and the somewhat scraggly shawl that the twins had knitted for her last Christmas.

"This is my wife, Lady Gabriel Sinclair," Lord Gabriel said. "My dear, Miss Applegate, my—ah—cousin."

"I am so happy to meet you, my dear," the vision said. "And I so regret that you cannot stay."

Juliana felt as if she had been slapped. Oh, dear lord, this was her worst fear come true. The ravishing Society beauty did not wish a visit from a relation who was so improperly connected. The trip south should have been delayed until she had been consulted.

Lord Gabriel gazed at his wife in surprise. Juliana could not speak; she felt her cheeks flush with mortification.

"We have several people in the house who are ill with measles," Lady Gabriel explained. "Have you had the disease, my dear Miss Applegate?"

Swallowing her chagrin, Juliana tried to think. "Not that I can recall."

"There! I was afraid that might be the case. So, you see, I must not allow you to be infected."

Lord Gabriel frowned. "What a contretemps. Perhaps Gemma—"

His wife shook her head and gave Juliana a quick smile. "It's already been arranged. Our dear friend, Margery, countess of Sealey, has invited Miss Applegate to stay at her house."

His face cleared. "Ah, good. The countess is a very gracious lady, Cousin. You could not be in better hands."

Juliana wished she could feel as sure. A *countess*? She was to stay with a countess? And one, moreover, with whom she had not the slightest family tie, illicit or otherwise. Oh, good heavens, she had thought her case bad enough already, but this was much, much worse.

"Oh, no, I couldn't presume to accept such a kind offer—that is—it would be an imposition, surely—" she stammered.

Lady Gabriel patted her hand. "It will be quite all right, I promise you. I would come with you, but the youngest kitchenmaid has just dropped a bowl of soup in the middle of the hallway, plus I must check if Circe is drawing under the bedcovers again."

Not sure she had heard this aright, Juliana stared at her almost hostess, but Lord Gabriel had given his wife a quick kiss and was ready to hand Juliana back into the carriage.

Feeling strongly out of place—it was bad enough at any time to have a houseguest foisted upon one, but in the middle of a family illness, it was more than a nuisance—Juliana had no choice but to step up into the carriage and wave good-bye.

"I will come to see you very soon," Lady Gabriel called out, but before Juliana could answer, the lady had turned to hurry back inside.

Surely Lord Gabriel and his family were wishing her to the devil! But they were all of them trapped by the constraints of good manners. Lord Gabriel had agreed to bring her to London, and he could not abandon her. Juliana had agreed, despite her better judgment, to come, and now she could not, as she very much wanted to do, demand to be returned to the North Country.

Oh, hell, what a mess.

Soon the carriage once more came to a stop, and Juliana was not surprised to find this house even larger and grander than the last one.

By this time she would also not have been surprised to find that the countess, too, had some excuse to put her off, but a footman, sublime in purple livery and powdered wig, opened the door for them and offered no resistance to their entry. Lord Gabriel escorted her inside, where an elderly butler, just as well outfitted and even more intimidating, waited.

They were taken up a flight of wide stairs to a drawing room roughly the size of the ground floor of Juliana's family home. Gazing up at the plastered, gilded ceiling high above them, which was decorated with classical scenes, and scanning the elegant silk-covered chairs and settees placed all about, Juliana felt an irrational desire to cast her bonnet aside and run for her life. Who was she to be visiting such a grand lady?

Introductions were made, although she was too flustered to listen closely. She tried to pull herself together and execute a smooth curtsy.

Lady Sealey was as impressive as her surroundings. Her silvery hair was perfectly arranged, her lightly powdered face still handsome despite her years, and her lavender silk gown would have made the twins swoon with envy over the skill of the countess's dressmaker.

Her blue eyes were somewhat faded by time, but they twinkled with wit and intelligence. "Welcome to London, my dear Miss Applegate. Is this your first visit to town?"

"Yes, it is." Juliana tried to keep her voice steady. "It is most kind of you to offer me hospitality."

"Ah, poor Lady Gabriel. I fear she has her plate very full just now, but her loss is my gain. It will be my pleasure to have you."

Juliana, who feared her knees were shaking and hoped that her heavy traveling skirt hid this fact, could think of no good reason why, but it would have been impolite to say so.

Her hostess turned to Lord Gabriel. "I know you are anxious to be home, dear boy, so I will not keep you. Tell Psyche to let me know, when she has the time, how everyone is doing."

He bowed. "I will. Thank you again, Lady Sealey."

Suddenly, her intimidating half brother looked like an old and dear friend. When he took his leave of Juliana, she had to fight to keep from clutching his hand to hold him back. She must have looked forlorn because he smiled at her and said, his voice low, "I will return soon to see how you are."

Then he was gone. Juliana swallowed.

"Would you like to see your room, my dear?" the countess suggested. "You may wish to wash away the dust of your journey. When you feel refreshed, come back down and we will have a cup of tea and get acquainted."

"Yes, thank you," Juliana agreed. So she was handed back to a footman, who took her up another set of stairs and then passed her on to a maidservant in a neat uniform, who showed her to a bedchamber so large and luxurious that at first Juliana felt she must have been taken to the wrong room.

But before she could embarrass herself by uttering such a gauche statement, she saw that her bag had been brought up, and another maidservant was hanging up her gowns in a clothespress. Oh, hell's fire, in this setting the dresses looked even shabbier than she'd realized. How could she possibly go about in any Society, if anyone actually invited her anywhere, when she was going to look like the proverbial country cousin next to all these elegant ladies?

"Can I get you anything, miss?" the maid was asking.

"A brain," Juliana muttered. "I must have lost mine."

"Pardon, miss?"

"Nothing, thank you. You may go."

"Just call if you need anything, miss," the servant told her.

In a few moments, the other maid finished her task—Juliana didn't have all that many clothes to unpack!—and also took her leave.

Juliana washed her hands and face and tried to push her dark hair back into place, then walked to the window and gazed out. She could see a bit of the street from the corner of her window and hear the sound of carriages passing, wagons rattling, horses trotting, voices of many different accents calling to each other—what a bustle!

It was exciting to be in London, she had to admit it. And perhaps she would be able to see some of the sights of the capital before she returned home; after all, it was unlikely she would ever get such a chance again. But as for meeting any marriageable men—in London as in Yorkshire, she felt sure that men wanted wives with property or status or a nice sum invested in the Funds, and she had none of those. Juliana was too sensible to believe in fairy tales. Sighing a little, she picked up her shawl and draped it around her shoulders, then left the room before her nerve failed her.

She walked along the hallway and turned a corner, then paused in confusion. This did not look familiar. Just as she'd decided she must have gone the wrong way, she heard the sound of a door opening, and a muffled curse.

It was a man's voice—one of the servants, perhaps?

She looked back. No, she saw a very tall young man with very broad shoulders, but he was dressed as a gentleman. And he was—what on earth was he doing?

He seemed to be wrestling with a small blanket, which bulged and jumped in odd ways as he carried it awkwardly in his arms. Wondering if it—or he—was possessed, Juliana couldn't keep from staring.

Perhaps she should have retreated to her own chamber, but the sight was too curious. Just as she was about to ask him if anything was wrong, a small form popped out of the blanket and darted off down the hall.

Was it a cat or a ferret, perhaps? It moved so quickly that she couldn't get a good look, her startled glance making out little more than a brown blur of fast-moving fur and skinny limbs.

Her arms filled with a stack of linens, a maidservant came out of a door farther down the hallway. She turned toward them.

The young man exclaimed in concern.

Whatever it was, he did not wish it to get away, Juliana deduced. Or perhaps, he did not even want it seen.

Moving with the same agility with which she habitually made her way across rocky hillsides or boggy moors, Juliana pounced. Throwing her shawl over the small animal, she scooped it up and held it to her chest, hoping that the creature—whatever it was—did not bite.

The shawl wiggled, but she held it firmly until the maid, giving them a curious glance, passed by.

The stranger hurried up to her.

"Thank you! That was very quick thinking," he told her. "Well done, indeed."

He stood close to her, and now Juliana could see how large he really was.

She was tall for a woman, but this man was a young Goliath. She tilted her head back to gaze at his well-made face with its firm chin, strong nose, and handsome eyes of such a clear luminous gray that they seemed to reflect his deepest thoughts. His tousled hair was brown but streaked with lighter strands, and he could have passed for a handsome young Viking if he had been decked out in armor and a leather harness, instead of a well-tailored coat and trousers and a slightly disarranged neckcloth.

Something seemed to melt inside her, and Juliana felt a curious shiver travel all the way down her spine. She realized she was staring and tried to pull herself together. "Not—not at all," she stuttered. "I take it that th-this is yours?"

She looked down to discover just what it was that she held and almost dropped it all when a small brown hand, eerily human-looking, pushed its way out of the knitted bundle.

This was no cat! What unearthly creature had she captured?

Before she could even gasp, a small head, brown and

hairy, followed. It was not the elf she had, illogically, half expected. This was certainly an animal, although the eyes that turned to gaze up at Juliana displayed a disconcerting intelligence inside their round depths.

"Is this a-a monkey?" she demanded.

Four

*T*he large young man blushed, his handsome face turning a rosy shade from brow to chin.

Juliana stared at him. It was an unexpected sight, but it failed to make him either any less appealing or any less sturdily masculine.

He reached for the monkey, but as Juliana loosened her grip, the animal slipped through her hands and somehow sprang instead to his shoulder. Although the gentleman swore beneath his breath and reached at once to grasp it, the monkey didn't wait.

From his shoulder it was only a short jump to the sconce on the wall. The glass shield that protected the candle went flying and crashed into a dozen pieces. Both of them winced at the impact. Now the candle inside the holder wobbled as the monkey gripped it with one hand, and, feet planted easily on the twists of the handsome frame, looked about for another likely perch.

"Mia, come here!" the man commanded.

Ignoring the order, the monkey dropped to swing from the gilded edge of the sconce, almost pulling it from the wall.

The gentleman dropped the blanket he held and hurried to stop the further destruction of Lady Sealey's property. But although he was able to grab the sconce before it pulled loose from the plaster, the monkey had already plunged to the floor and darted off.

The young man ran after the monkey.

Having some idea that it should not be left in the hallway as evidence of the monkey's devastation, Juliana paused only long enough to retrieve the blanket, then she hastened to follow.

Now they were definitely going back in the direction of the drawing room. Feeling a bit like the Pied Piper, or perhaps just one of the rats, Juliana ran faster, trying to catch up. The young man had gotten ahead of her going down the staircase, and she heard him mutter another muffled curse as he pounced but failed, again, to capture the escaped animal. Then he went through a doorway and was out of her sight. She hurried to catch up.

What was he doing with a monkey? She had never even seen a real one before. Did it belong to a circus or a menagerie? What was it doing in a countess's house? Suddenly, she ran smack into the young man, who had stopped without warning.

Juliana gasped at the impact. He was very solid, she thought, all muscle, no fat. Had he lost track of the animal or—

Then he turned, still so close that she was virtually in his arms, and the rest of her thoughts seemed to disappear like smoke up a chimney.

His chest was solid and broad, and his arms, as he caught her before she could fall, were corded with muscle. His hands were large and yet somehow seemed capable of tenderness. Why did she suspect that? It had to do with the way he held her, carefully, as if she were a china shepherdess who might shatter at the slightest mistouch.

Juliana could feel his warmth envelop her. She felt a weakness inside her, a quivering, shivering strangeness that no man had ever in her life induced. And this giant of a man, with his obvious strength and yet at the same time a gentleness in his clear gray eyes, how could he look at her just so, when they had not even been introduced?

"Are you all right?" he asked now.

She found that her mouth was agape and shut it hastily. But still, she could find no words. She nodded.

"I'm very sorry," he whispered. "But I have to find Mia before she does more damage."

Juliana nodded again. The necessity of locating the monkey at once was quite evident. If allowed to roam free, she would have the house down around their ears!

"Has she disappeared from your line of sight?" she whispered back.

He nodded. "Yes. She got ahead of me down the last flight of stairs. But if I could just search all the rooms on this floor—"

A noise behind them made him pause, and he seemed to realize how close they were standing. He stepped back and allowed Juliana to precede him.

And, as improper as all this was, Juliana was chagrined to note that she felt only disappointment at the loss of their closeness. She thrust the monkey's blanket into his hands, and they both faced the sound of the footsteps.

Juliana was alarmed to see that they were almost in front of the drawing room doors. And it was Lady Sealey herself who had come to see who had arrived.

"Ah, there you are, my dear, and you have found Oliver, how providential. But don't linger in the hallway. Come in, both of you, and I will introduce you properly. We have other callers, as well, to add if not sugar at least spice to the day."

Oh, dear. Too distracted to work out what the countess meant by her odd remark, Juliana tried to dust off her out-dated traveling costume, without success. But she had no choice, so she put on a stiff smile and followed her hostess back into the enormous drawing room, with Oliver a few feet behind them.

When they entered, Juliana saw that three women were already seated on the damask chairs.

"This is Lady Pomfrey, and Mrs. Swarts and her delightful daughter, Miss Swarts. Ladies, I'd like you to meet Miss Juliana Applegate, who is visiting from Yorkshire; she is a distant relation of Lord Gabriel Sinclair's. You know my godson, Sir Oliver Ramsey, whom you met last week. Now, take a seat, do. I have rung for fresh tea."

As Lady Sealey performed the introductions, Juliana made her curtsy. The two older matrons responded in kind. Miss Swarts dipped her own curtsy and then smiled up at Sir Oliver and appeared to dismiss Juliana completely from her notice—to Juliana's thinking a perfectly understandable reaction.

Sir Oliver's hands were empty; he had apparently taken advantage of his place at the back of the procession to stash the blanket out of sight before entering the drawing room.

Juliana admired his presence of mind. She took a chair at the edge of the group, and he sat down next to her, a choice which made Miss Swarts frown and slide her own chair closer to the two of them.

Trying to quell her nervousness, Juliana sat up straight and listened to the chatter that flowed around her, ready to respond correctly when addressed. But since the visitors had little to say to her, her powers of polite discourse were not unduly challenged.

While the two older ladies chatted with the countess, and the younger woman smiled and made admiring comments directed toward Sir Oliver, Juliana had more than enough leisure to wonder what on earth she was doing in a titled lady's drawing room in London when she could have been at home, doing something productive like helping Thomas shovel out the stables. This made her laugh at herself, or at least grin.

Sir Oliver glanced at her as she did so, and he smiled back.

This momentary absence of his attention made Miss Swarts frown. "You don't care for the theater, Sir Oliver?" she persisted.

"Oh, no, that is, I like it quite well," he answered, turning back.

"There is quite a good sort of play at Covent Garden just now," she told him. "A little bit of tragedy but not too much, I'm told. Quite a few funny parts, too, if you know what I mean. Mama is thinking of making up a party for next Thursday. Perhaps you would like to join us, Sir Oliver?"

Juliana waited for him to blush, but to her surprise, he did not.

"That's very kind of you, but I fear I may be out of town," Sir Oliver said vaguely. "I shall have to consult my calendar. My zoology studies, you know, take up much of my time. It is a hindrance when it comes to one's social life."

"Is that why you are still unmarried? Such a waste, you know!" Miss Swarts sounded unbearably coy. "All that scientific genius must not be allowed to die with you. You must beget many sons so that you may pass on your aptitude for such lofty intellectual pursuits, not to mention your baronetcy, which is even more important!"

"I suppose that depends on one's point of view," he answered, not meeting her eye and fumbling with his neckcloth.

"Now, Sir Oliver, I know you are not a republican, like one of those dreadful French anarchists!" she answered archly, unfurling her fan and glancing at him over the top of it. "Science is all very well, but an old and respected title is much more important. I have heard that your estate is a handsome one, too."

He didn't seem to be paying attention.

Juliana bit her lip so as not to smile. After listening to them both for only a few minutes, she had the feeling that Sir Oliver was not as keen on Miss Swarts as Miss Swarts was on the young baronet. An attractive brunette, although she had a tendency to pout, as she was doing just now, she had a slightly vindictive cast to her brown eyes. But as Miss Swarts batted her lashes—and they were nice lashes, thick and dark, Juliana admitted, trying to be fair—Sir Oliver stared across the room at a tall cabinet that held a handsome assortment of Chinese vases and urns.

Juliana stiffened. One of the vases had moved. She looked back at Sir Oliver and saw a faint sheen of perspiration on his upper lip. She glanced back at the vase. She had not imagined the shift in position. And now, if she stared hard, she could make out the faintest shadow—and yes, there was the tip of a tail protruding from behind the vase.

Oh, lord.

They had found Mia.

She held her breath. If the monkey pushed the vase off the shelf—

She looked at Sir Oliver, who seemed ready to leap out of his chair. But he had no excuse to dash across the room.

The other visitors would think him mad. Did Lady Sealey know she had a monkey loose in her elegant home? Somehow, Juliana had a feeling that the answer might be no.

What could they do? And why did she feel she should help the young baronet?

Oh, how could she not?

The vase shook again, rocked, but, thankfully, it did not fall.

Abruptly, Sir Oliver stood. "May I take a look at your Chinese vases, Godmother?" he asked. "You have a particularly handsome collection."

Lady Sealey looked surprised, but she nodded. "Of course," she said.

Juliana said, "I should love to admire them, too."

"As would I!" Miss Swarts added, throwing a jealous glance toward Juliana.

Rats. Juliana smiled sweetly at the young lady who seemed to fancy her a rival. As if an impoverished York-shire lass could capture a baronet's hand in marriage! She only wished to aid him in capturing the escaped monkey. She swallowed a hysterical desire to giggle.

And now Sir Oliver had no choice, of course, except to offer an arm to both young ladies and escort them across the room.

It was apparent that Sir Oliver had examined the vases before. He cleared his throat and gave them a brief commentary. "This one is a fine example of the Ming period. You can make out the blue and white pattern and the fine porcelain details, and the piece of porcelain behind it is even older."

Miss Swarts had eyes for nothing except the tall young man beside her. She gazed up at him and batted her fine lashes in double time.

Juliana stared not at the vase but at the shelf. Now the valuable piece of china was motionless again, and she could not see a tail nor any other trace of the monkey. Oh, dear. Had the animal moved on? The creature was as silent as a shadow, and it seemed to move with as little fuss.

She exchanged an anxious glance with Sir Oliver, and she saw the worry in his clear gray eyes.

Where was Mia?

A footman brought in a tray heavily loaded with a silver teapot and clean cups, and a maidservant followed with another tray holding plates of small cakes and sandwiches and other delicacies. Lady Sealey glanced toward them and motioned for them to return to the group.

Reluctantly, Sir Oliver turned, and the two women followed his example. Miss Swarts was eager to take his arm again to sustain her against the perilous trek across their hostess's fine Oriental rug. Juliana lingered for a moment to glance back at the vases, but she still could catch no glimpse of their elusive simian.

When they took their seats, Juliana accepted a cup of the steaming brew, and in a moment, a plate of small sandwiches and cakes. The food was delicious. She ate one of her sandwiches and then nibbled at a raisin cake while she waited for her tea to cool.

"The pastries are delicious," she noted. "Don't you think so, Miss Swarts?"

Miss Swarts ignored her plate as well as the question and smirked up at Sir Oliver. "I seem to have no appetite today. Mama says that a lady must watch her figure if she wishes to be widely esteemed."

"Really? I admire a lady with a healthy appetite," the gentleman said.

Hiding her smile, Juliana sipped her tea. Miss Swarts's

lips curved downward, and her simper now looked sour. Then, about to swallow a bite of cake, Juliana gasped in horror, and the morsel almost choked her. Coughing, she put one hand to her mouth as she set her cup down hastily on a small table next to her chair.

"Are you all right?" Sir Oliver asked in concern.

She couldn't answer, but she gazed toward the oblivious Lady Pomfrey, who—with no regard for her already well-rounded figure or any absence of potential admirers—was rapidly consuming a tidy stack of cakes and sandwiches. Sir Oliver followed her glance.

The lady's handsome plum-colored silk dress had acquired a new adornment. She now sported a slim brown tail which lay just over her left shoulder. Because of the garment's dark hue, Mia's tail was not immediately obvious to the beholder, but sooner or later one of the other guests, or Lady Pomfrey herself, was bound to notice that she had gained a new and doubtless unwelcome fashion accessory.

Now the monkey's ears also could be seen above the back of the settee. Oh, dear!

Sir Oliver stood.

Everyone looked at him.

He hesitated, as well he might. What could he say? Juliana wondered. Pardon me, Lady Pomfrey, I have misplaced a monkey, and it is climbing on the settee just behind you?

Juliana rose, also, and moved toward the low table in the center of their group where the platters of food were set out, not waiting for the footman to pass the food again and not caring if the Swarts thought her gauche.

"These cakes and sandwiches are so delicious," she said, leaning over to select another small cake. "You have the most wonderful cook, Lady Sealey. I vow we have no such delightful treats in Yorkshire."

Her hostess smiled. "Do help yourself, dear child. I'm so glad that you like them. There's plenty here, Oliver, if you would like more, also. I know how hearty a gentleman's appetite can be."

Oliver nodded jerkily. The footman hastened to bring one of the platters to him, which forced the young baronet to sit down again. Juliana firmly held her ground and pretended to look over the assortment of pastries. If they wished, they could think her as greedy as a child in a sweet shop, but it would keep their gaze off Lady Pomfrey.

Apparently just as unpleasant as her daughter, Mrs. Swarts gave a tight little smile. "Of course, on the uncivilized moors of the North you would not have enjoyed the same level of culinary delicacies as do we in town. You poor child, you must feel very fortunate to have had the countess take you under her wing."

"Dear Mrs. Swarts, sadly, civilized behavior is not guaranteed by town houses and excellent cooks. I am the one who is fortunate to have such an engaging house-guest," Lady Scaley put in, her tone steely beneath its usual surface charm.

As if aware she might have gone too far, Mrs. Swarts nodded quickly. "Certainly." But she turned her cold hazel eyes back to Juliana, apparently not finished with her inquisition. "And do tell us, how is that you are related to dear Lord Gabriel, exactly?"

The first comment had caused Juliana to flush. Now she bit her lip as she wondered how to reply to the latest sally. She was spared the necessity by a sudden shriek. She straightened and turned toward the other matron.

Wide-eyed, Lady Pomfrey was staring at her own hand, which she held up before her, as if it might be possessed.

"What's amiss, my dear?" their hostess asked, her silvery brows arched.

"I had a smoked salmon sandwich in my hand," the other lady answered. "I was about to take a bite, and—and when I looked back, it wasn't there!"

The monkey! Mia moved with the speed of an arrow in flight, Juliana thought, almost too fast to see.

"Perhaps you dropped it," Juliana suggested, keeping her tone soothing. She managed not to glance at Sir Oliver, who she knew must be in agony. Since she was already on her feet, it was easy to move toward Lady Pomfrey and make a show of searching the lady's plum-colored lap and the silk upholstery around where she sat. Juliana leaned her other hand on the back of the settee, hoping to shoo the little monkey away before it was seen.

At any rate, no one else seemed to notice a stray simian, although there was no sign of the missing sandwich. By now all traces of it would have been swallowed up by a hungry little monkey.

Lady Sealey motioned to the footman. "Here is a fresh plate with more sandwiches; we have more than enough."

"So strange." Lady Pomfrey shook her head at herself as the servant brought over the plate. "I could have sworn I had that sandwich in my hand."

But just as Juliana thought the danger was past, another screech arose.

"Over there!" Miss Swarts pointed and screamed again. "Oh, what is that horrible creature? I think I shall swoon!"

The footman jerked and let go of the plate of sandwiches. It shattered, the china breaking with a tinkling sound almost unheard as the other women, except for Lady Sealey and Juliana herself, screamed or exclaimed in surprise and horror.

Mrs. Swarts threw up her hands and tossed her cup of tea into her daughter's lap, causing Miss Swarts to shriek all over again as the liquid splashed her.

Sir Oliver jumped back to his feet and ran toward the corner of the room. Juliana saw the moving brown streak and darted toward it, too, not so much to catch it—she knew there was no chance of that—but at least to obscure the other women's vision.

Lady Pomfrey stared down in dismay at the shards of glass that rendered the foodstuffs now forever lost. "Such good sandwiches," she said mournfully.

Oliver pounded after the fleeing animal and disappeared into the hallway. Juliana left him to the pursuit and turned back to the group of women.

"Sir Oliver," Miss Swarts called after him as she shook out her dripping skirt. "Didn't you hear me? I am going to swoon."

"Maizy," Lady Sealey told the maid, who had gone white, "take a deep breath; there is nothing to fear. Bring some smelling salts and a towel for Miss Swarts."

The maidservant gulped but seemed to pull herself together. "Yes, milady." She hurried out.

"Clean up that mess, please," the countess told the footman. "And then see about assisting my godson."

"What was that awful creature?" Mrs. Swarts demanded. "I thought—"

"It was only a mouse, of course," Juliana said, surprised at how level her voice sounded. "Miss Swarts, would you like more tea? It might steady your nerves."

"A mouse? That was not a mouse. It was much too big!" The young lady snapped as she stared at Juliana.

"You would not suggest that Lady Sealey would have a rat in her house?" Juliana allowed her own voice to rise just a little. "What a thing to say to your distinguished hostess!"

There was a moment of silence as that comment sank in. With almost identical expressions, both mother and daughter appeared to digest the possible consequences of uttering such a social solecism.

"No, of course not," Miss Swarts answered as she glanced at her mother. "But it was so big—"

"I admit that in a moment of shock, things can often look larger than they really are," Juliana continued brightly. "Why, when a bee stung one of my younger sisters, she swore it was as huge as a hawk. Papa told her she must not exaggerate, and really, she is quite a sensitive child and she didn't *mean* to tell a falsehood, you know."

"I never exaggerate!" Miss Swarts retorted. "And I am quite sensitive, myself. Mama always says so."

"There, you see, just as I said." Juliana smiled sweetly. "On a susceptible spirit, a sudden shock can create a graphic if undependable impression."

Miss Swarts regarded her with dislike and turned to their fellow guests for support. "Did you not see it, Lady Pomfrey? What did you think?"

"They were such good sandwiches." Lady Pomfrey sighed as she stared at the rug.

"I do apologize for the commotion," Lady Sealey said. "I will have my cook make up more sandwiches, Florence, if you like."

"No, I would not put you to such trouble," Lady Pomfrey said bravely. "But when I call next week—"

"We will be sure to have the smoked salmon, which is your favorite," the countess promised, winning a smile from her friend.

Lady Pomfrey stood. "It has been a most—ah—surprising visit, Margery," she told her hostess. "It was a pleasure meeting your young houseguests. Bring them along to my house party at my estate in three weeks, if you would. We can always use an extra man, especially one so good-looking, and your young lady might like a spin around the dance floor, too."

"That's very kind of you," Lady Sealey said, smiling, even as Juliana felt a flicker of alarm at the offer. The countess rose and walked her old friend to the doorway where they met Sir Oliver returning, his expression grim.

"I'm afraid I could not find—" he began.

"The *mouse*?" Juliana finished for him.

He paused to stare at her.

Miss Swarts made one last try. "Was that monstrosity not too large to be a mouse, Sir Oliver? You saw the oddity, now really!"

"I believe you exaggerate again, Miss Swarts, no doubt due to your delicate constitution." Juliana turned to look at the gentleman and spoke directly to him. "You do not think that the countess has a rat in her lovely home, do you, Sir Oliver? It must have been a mouse we saw. It is the only logical explanation, do you not agree?"

He glanced at her, and she saw comprehension dawn in his eyes. "Ah, no, I do not think that my godmother has rats in her house, no, indeed. But a cat is no doubt in order. I shall see about getting her one right away."

"You're very kind, Oliver, dear," Lady Sealey said, her expression bland.

The maidservant returned with the smelling salts and a linen towel, but Miss Swarts waved away her offered assistance. Pouting, she rose, along with her mother, and they, too, said their good-byes. Miss Swarts's farewell to Juliana was chilly, indeed.

When the Swarts family had departed, Lady Sealey returned to her chair. She motioned the other two to sit down again. She poured herself a fresh cup of tea, then sent the maid away and told her to shut the double doors behind her.

Now the three of them were alone in the drawing room. Juliana glanced at Sir Oliver, who looked uneasy, but neither of them spoke. Silence reigned for a few moments as the countess sipped her tea. Then Lady Sealey broke the stillness.

"Now tell me, Oliver dear, why I have a monkey in my house."

Five

Juliana felt her heart sink.

Sir Oliver squared his wide shoulders and faced the countess with the desperate mien of a captured enemy soldier hearing the firing squad cock their rifles. "Godmother, this is entirely my fault."

"I rather thought it might be," she agreed, her tone dry.

Juliana wanted to interrupt, but since she knew nothing whatsoever about the monkey or how it had come to be in this West End mansion, it would be silly to try to help explain its presence. But she felt for the tall, broad-shouldered young man who looked as guilty as a schoolboy caught smuggling in a stray puppy he'd found shivering in the cold.

She'd done that, too, she thought absently—brought home fledglings she'd discovered in her rambles, baby birds who'd fallen from the nest, when she'd been afraid they'd fall prey to foxes before they could fly safely away. And she had helped Thomas raise many an orphaned lamb whose mother had died . . .

But Sir Oliver was speaking. She pushed the stray thoughts away to listen.

"I do apologize, Godmother. It was very wrong of me not to tell you."

"Indeed, it was," Lady Sealey agreed, her voice stern. "That does not answer my question, however. Wherever did this creature come from? And why is it here?"

"My mentor, the esteemed scientist Mr. Rodney Needham, has instructed me to make a study of the monkey. He gave me this specimen to study. And my first task was to . . . um . . . kill and stuff it."

"What?" Juliana knew she should not have spoken since she had no part in this, but she couldn't help herself. Appalled, she drew a deep breath.

"Um, yes. Then I am supposed to draw a sketch of the body, and then of the head and eyes and ears, and then the digestive tract and lungs and heart and other vital organs, the muscles and sinews and later the bones and skeletal frame and so on." Sir Oliver sounded totally miserable at the thought. He lowered his head and dropped his face into his cupped hands.

Lady Sealey pursed her lips but said nothing. She seemed to wait for Sir Oliver to get his feelings under control.

Juliana was still awash in horror. Remembering her first encounter with the monkey in the hall, her memory supplied a vision of the big eyes of the creature she had held so briefly, the almost human-looking face and the tiny wizened hands.

Kill that strange elfin creature? Despite her struggles, she couldn't be silent.

"B-but how can one study such a mobile little thing if it's dead? It's pure motion if any such exists! Don't you want to see how it moves and thinks and acts and learns?

That kind of antiquated examination seems so—so—so limited, to destroy it so you can see its bones and muscles and the rest. The animal will die in time of natural causes. You can study its frame and inner workings then, you know. Until then, you could learn so much more!"

Sir Oliver raised his head and looked at her, eagerness lighting his expression, his eyes once more bright. "Yes, yes, that is just what I would argue myself. But Mr. Needham will not listen to me! He tells me I am only a green boy to argue with the great minds in my field, and he's quite right. Only, I have become quite attached to Mia, I mean, to the monkey." He looked embarrassed at the admission, although Juliana thought it noble of him. He continued doggedly, turning back to the countess. "And I just couldn't bring myself t-to slit her throat."

"Oh, no!" Juliana cried. "Please, Sir Oliver, please don't kill her."

Lady Sealey smiled faintly. "It seems that imp of a monkey now has two barristers to plead her case. Even if she is not to be sentenced to death, at least do try to find her and get her back behind bars, Oliver, before she dismantles my house completely. I have witnessed gangs of monkeys in Morocco rampaging through the city, and they are strong and fast and destructive. That is quite my favorite Chinese vase that almost took a tumble, you know."

Juliana exchanged a guilty glance with Sir Oliver. The countess had seen the near disaster with the Ming vases? Oh, dear.

"Of course, Godmother," Sir Oliver agreed.

"I will help you," Juliana promised. "I grew up with farm animals all about me, Sir Oliver. I am not afraid of any kind of beast. If you will excuse us, Lady Sealey?"

"Go!" the countess told them. "Every moment that creature is free, I fear for my breakables."

Murmuring her thanks, Juliana hurried after Oliver as he strode out of the drawing room. Without more ado, they set about a search of the house, starting with the ground floor. Juliana was still awed by the size of the house. They covered a small front office, which had little in the way of furnishings, then entered a large music room.

As they crawled on their hands and knees around the legs of the grand piano, trying not to miss any hiding place no matter how unlikely, since the monkey had a penchant for the smallest crevice and cranny, Juliana shook her head.

"I have never seen a house so grand," she admitted to Sir Oliver. "My sisters would stare just to imagine such a magnificent dwelling."

Sir Oliver grinned. "Wait until you glimpse my god-mother's country estate," he suggested. "It makes this place, as handsome and spacious as it is, pale by comparison. You could fit the whole of her London house into the country house's guest wing."

"Good heavens," Juliana said faintly, ducking her head to stare up into the shadows beneath the large instrument. She could make out no trace of the small, mischief-making monkey. "She must be very—" Juliana paused, not wishing to be gauche, then continued, "that is, I know very little about the countess, but she has been so kind to me. I'm so grateful. I suppose you have known her all your life?"

He nodded. "She was of good family herself, of course, the second daughter of a baronet, and her mother and mine were bosom friends. Her first husband had no title, but he possessed a tidy fortune, and her second husband—"

He paused, and Juliana, too, saw the flash of movement as the missing simian dashed from its hiding place behind a music stand and streaked toward the doorway. They both raised their heads, but Juliana forgot to allow for the mas-sive piano just above her. Her head met the edge of its frame with a solid thud. The pain brought an involuntary grunt. Her head spinning, she fell to her hands and knees.

Sir Oliver, who had jumped to his feet ready to run after the monkey, turned sharply back toward her instead, thrusting out his hands to keep his balance. Somehow, his outstretched hand struck a handsome viola which stood propped beside the piano. The stringed instrument tipped over with a jangle of discordant notes.

The sounds seemed to echo in the large room, and Sir Oliver flushed. Looking flustered, he hurried on to her side.

"No, no," Juliana urged. "Do not stop for me, go on."

But despite her protest, he waited to see if she was hurt. "Your head is bleeding," he told her, pulling out a large clean handkerchief. "Here, press this against the wound."

"Oh, it's nothing," Juliana told him, although her head throbbed painfully. She tried to get up, but the room spun around her, and she had to sit down again on the rug. "It was most foolish of me!" She had meant to be of assistance to him, not to slow him down, and now that dratted animal had escaped them again.

He reached to help her up. His hands were so large, but the fingers so well formed, and his grip so strong—she felt a shiver of some emotion she could not identify as he gripped her shoulders, partly lifted, partly guided her easily to the nearest chair. This time, she was not sure what caused the giddiness that made her feel a little light-headed.

"It was not at all foolish. You were simply distracted by the sudden sight of the monkey. If you had not been helping me, you would not have banged your head." Sir Oliver contradicted, his tone firm. "Here, the cut has almost stopped bleeding, but you look pale. Just hold the handkerchief to your head, and do not move; you might feel dizzy for a few moments yet. If you promise to be still, I will go in search of Mia. I will send a maid to help you."

"I promise, now go, please!" she urged him.

Nodding, he made for the door, this time without having any more musical instruments leap into his path. She watched him disappear through the doorway. The music room was large, but without his tall frame, it seemed strangely empty. How had he come to seem such a vibrant and exciting addition to her life so very quickly?

She should not be thinking like this, Juliana scolded herself. She was in London for a brief visit, no more. Sir Oliver was a baronet with important relatives and friends. He must be a most eligible marital prospect; he had no interest—could have no interest—in an impoverished young lady from the north of England. Put such thoughts away from you, Jules, she told herself, trying to mimic the stern tone which she sometimes used on the twins when they were at their most fractious. Not that they ever listened! Unfortunately, her wayward heart showed no signs of heeding her good advice, either.

She'd barely met the man!

Perhaps sometimes that was all it took?

When a young maid came in, Juliana knew that her expression must be dismal.

"Are you all right, miss? Sir Oliver said as you 'ad a small accident?"

"Yes, I banged my head, I'm afraid."

She stood up cautiously and found her giddiness seemed to have passed. "If you would come up to my room and clean the wound? And I suppose I must change my gown for dinner soon."

"Of course, miss."

On the way upstairs, Juliana had another lowering thought. Sir Oliver was not already married, was he? No, Miss Swarts would not be fluttering her excellent lashes so hard at a young man who had a wife. Comforting herself with this thought, and not caring to examine just *why* she found this comforting, Juliana allowed her wounded head to be bathed with cool water, and then, wincing, she let her hair be combed. Next, she washed her hands and face with rose-scented soap, trying to pretend this was not an unaccustomed luxury, and set about looking over her array of tired-looking frocks to see which might be the least out-of-date so that she could change for dinner.

She did not see Sir Oliver again until they all met in the dining room, but she was not surprised to see him looking glum and, when they were all seated, to see him glance her way and shake his head just slightly.

The monkey was still at large. Oh, dear.

Of course the countess's dinner was just as good as her pastry confections and the sandwiches served up with her tea trays. Juliana sipped her excellent turtle soup and tried not to let her worry make even this wonderful delight taste bitter.

There were what the countess had described as "a few" guests for dinner. Juliana thought that if this was a few, she hated to see the countess's idea of a large dinner party. She had no idea who most of the guests were; a stout man with a French accent had the honored seat to the right of the countess, and an elderly man who she'd heard someone at the table mention was a Prussian diplomat sat at her other side. Juliana felt as out of place as her red hen back home would if it had wandered into the duck pond.

She sipped her soup to put off having to make conversation with either one of the men seated beside her. Neither was Sir Oliver, of course. That stalwart young man was seated on the other side, and, being of higher social status, farther up the large table. She threw a quick glance at him, trying not to look as wistful as she felt. For his part, Sir Oliver looked absent-minded and seemed to be paying little heed to the handsome fair-haired lady beside him who was trying hard to engage him in conversation. Sir Oliver's gaze seemed to roam over the sides of the room. What was he—

Of course! The food, the monkey was always drawn to food!

Oh, dear. All they needed was to have the pesky animal pop up and show itself in the middle of the countess's dinner. If that happened, even the magnanimous Lady Sealey might change her mind about the monkey's fate.

Juliana felt her throat go dry; she took another quick swallow of soup. Oh, what could she do? Almost nothing, but she, too, now tried to keep a vigilant eye out for any suspicious movement. And when the young man to her right addressed her, she was so intent upon scanning the corners of the room that she forgot to be nervous about talking to unknown gentlemen at her first London dinner party.

"How do you know the countess?" he asked. "Miss—"

"Miss Applegate," she told him absently. "I am her houseguest."

"Really?" Sounding surprised, he inspected her more closely. She didn't blame him. Her drab clothes and country mouse appearance did not make it likely that she would be befriended by a lady of high degree. "I did not, that is—"

"She has been most kind," Juliana told him. "I came to town originally to stay with Lord and Lady Gabriel Sinclair, but they had measles break out in their household, so Lady Sealey invited me to stay for a time in their stead."

"Lord Gabriel Sinclair?"

"He is a connection of my family," Juliana said, pausing as the footman removed the soup plates. Changing the subject before the tall, slightly built young man could pursue that subject any further, she asked. "And you?"

He preened. "I am Monsieur Andre Dumont. I have the honor to be attaché to the comte de Montaine, whom you see at the head of the table sitting beside Lady Sealey. They are *amis*, friends of the long time. I served my lord at the Congress of Vienna, a most important and history making event, I do not have to tell you! It was the distinguished members of the Congress who endeavored to repair the wounds of Europe after the monster Bonaparte's ravages upon so many countries before his final defeat at Waterloo!"

"Indeed," Juliana agreed, impressed despite herself. "I have read about it. Did you see the kings and princes and famous diplomats who gathered there?"

"Oh, many, many," the young man agreed. "And the social whirl—it was *magnifique*! Did you know that Lady Sealey came to Vienna for several months during the height of the Congress?"

"Really?" Juliana found that she was not surprised. She wondered if there was anything her hostess had not done.

It was soon clear that Monsieur Dumont liked to gossip. He told her stories of Vienna, and of many other exotic and interesting places that he and Lord Montaine had been sent during his lordship's long diplomatic career, about the comte's advantageous marriages, and hinted at his interest in other ladies, too, which surprised and somewhat shocked Juliana, although she gathered that on the Continent, such goings on were commonplace. She thought of her own parents and sighed, wondering if Lady Montaine had viewed her husband's affairs with complacency. She made a note never to marry a Frenchman!

The young man chatted steadily through the courses that followed, so that Juliana barely had the chance to talk to the man on her other side, an unassuming if alarmingly well-dressed young tulip of fashion. The food was delicious, and she soon felt as stuffed as the lobster on the silver plat-ter that made up one of the many side dishes.

And all the while, she watched for any sign of an un-wanted simian, but the china on the sideboard remained still, and the apples and grapes that adorned the fruit trays seemed untouched. Perhaps the shrill clamor of so many voices rising above the clatter of silver and the clink of china was enough to scare the little monkey away.

By the time dinner ended and the countess stood and gazed around the table, collecting the other ladies' atten-tion with a practiced glance, there still had been no sign of Mia. Along with the other females, Juliana put down her napkin and rose. Before she turned away, she met Sir Oliver's eyes for a moment and saw her own relief reflected there; they had been spared one catastrophe, at least. Then she obediently followed the parade of women out of the room and left the men to their glasses of port and their ex-clusively male conversation. Whatever happened now, Sir Oliver would be left to guard the dining table.

The women in the drawing room were somewhat more difficult to handle than her dinner partners had been. Here, amid the delicate silks and elaborate satins of the other ladies' dinner dresses, Juliana's simple faded muslin gown seemed even more out of place. She took a seat at the edge of the group and tried not to attract attention, but one of the younger ladies craned her neck to stare at her.

"I'm afraid I did not catch your name during the intro-ductions before dinner?"

"I am Miss Juliana Applegate," Juliana said.

"You are new to London?" Her expression disdainful, the young lady looked her up and down.

"Yes," Juliana answered, knowing her outdated clothes and unfashionable appearance made that quite obvious.

"I see. I hope you have a pleasant stay," the other woman

said, her tone already bored. She stood. "I must rejoin my mother; please excuse me."

"Of course," Juliana muttered, but the other woman had already turned away. So much for forming a new acquaintance. Two ladies nearby were talking together, but neither looked her way. Wishing for some excuse to escape these supercilious females, Juliana glanced toward the windows, but the draperies had already been drawn. She had no excuse to wander across and gaze down at the street below.

Chatting with an older woman, the countess sat by the hearth. In a few moments, she lifted her head and scanned the room, and in the process met Juliana's eye. She made a small motion, and Juliana realized she had been summoned. Hoping she did not look as forlorn as she felt, Juliana made her way to her hostess's side.

"How are you faring, my dear?"

"Fine," Juliana lied bravely. "Dinner was delicious."

"My chef will be happy to hear that you enjoyed it." The countess flashed her sparkling smile. "Let me introduce you to an old friend. Lavinia, this is Miss Applegate, whom I am privileged to have as a houseguest. She is a connection of Lord Gabriel Sinclair's. Miss Applegate, Lady Worthington."

This lady was short and plump, with graying wisps of hair that strayed from beneath an elaborate headdress topped by ostrich plumes dyed a deep purple. They bobbed and dipped every time she laughed, which was often. "Oh, I just adore Lord Gabriel, he is such a charming, handsome man! You must tell me all about him, and how you are related."

Juliana hoped she had not paled. She could not tell the real story, and it was dangerous to fabricate half truths, and much too easy to be caught out at a lie. And she knew almost nothing about her newly discovered half brother, no, cousin, *cousin*! She threw a desperate glance toward the countess.

"Further, Miss Applegate is from Yorkshire, Lavinia, where you also grew up. You must tell her some of your stories, especially the one about your pony running away with you across the moor and how you became lost for hours and thought you would never find your way home."

"Oh, yes," Juliana seized on this with relief. "I should adore to hear it." She took a seat nearby and settled down to listen to the older lady's stories.

Fortunately, Lady Worthington proved to be easily distracted. The pony story was long and complicated, but Juliana relished every minute it consumed. It finally concluded with the youthful Lavinia's safe return home. "And Papa gave the undergardener a gold sovereign, but he didn't allow me to ride my pony off the grounds again for a whole six months, just fancy!" The peeress shook her head at herself.

To keep the conversation going, Juliana offered a funny tale about her own donkey. This helped elicit other anecdotes from Lady Worthington's childhood, interspersed with many gales of laughter and bobbing plumes.

When the gentlemen rejoined the ladies in the drawing room, Juliana could only throw them a fleeting glance. Sir Oliver's tall, broad-shouldered form stood out from the rest of the men like a magnificent young stallion looming over a herd of, well, donkeys. Her concentration still apparently centered on Lady Worthington, Juliana watched covertly as the young baronet was at once surrounded by no less than three young ladies, all ready to smile and chat and try to capture his attentions, as their doting mamas looked on in approval.

Oh, yes, he was obviously prime marital bait. Sir Oliver looked less than pleased at being the target of all this feminine regard however. He still tended to watch the corners of the room, and once he looked toward Juliana, and they exchanged a brief but meaningful glance. She did not need to speak to him to understand that the monkey was still at large. He also spilled one cup of tea and stepped on one lady's white slippers, but his slight lack of grace discouraged his entourage not at all.

So the evening passed with less discomfort than Juliana had feared. They had no success in finding the fugitive, and she was granted no chance to speak to Sir Oliver again, but she had had little hope of that. Still, by the time the other guests took their leave, Juliana was more than ready to say good night to the countess, thank her again for her hospitality, and prepare to climb the staircase to her guest room.

"Don't worry, my dear," Lady Sealey told her. "I know you may be feeling overwhelmed, but you will adjust. One's first visit to London can be unnerving."

That was putting it mildly, Juliana thought. At least Mia had not put in an appearance; perhaps the monkey didn't like rooms crowded with strangers. On the whole, Juliana thought the monkey had the right idea!

When everyone else had departed, Sir Oliver waited for Lady Sealey and offered her his arm. To Juliana's surprise, he gave Juliana his other arm, flashing her a warm smile.

It was her turn to color as she returned his smile. She was silent as he escorted them both up the staircase, but her thoughts raced. He was a true gentleman, she thought, not disdaining her because of her lack of fashionable costume. He had been so chivalrous when she had hurt her head on the piano. And his kind heart—not wanting to kill the poor little monkey . . .

Yes, they did need to find Mia before she did any more damage. At least they were reasonably sure the animal was not in the drawing room, and the doors had been securely shut so that Mia could not slip back inside.

Tomorrow, Juliana promised herself, she would rise early and help Sir Oliver scour the house. They had to find the monkey, for the creature's own safety as well as to protect the countess's property!

She followed the countess and Sir Oliver up to the next landing, said good night to them both, then made her way to her own room. One of the housemaids was waiting to help her out of her dress, and Juliana washed her face and slipped into her nightgown.

The maid had brought her a cup of tea and a biscuit. "Just in case you might be feeling peckish, miss," she explained.

Juliana thought of the lavish dinner, with so many courses and side dishes and delicious entrees. It had made her own family's dinners look positively meager. She decided that any guest in this household who went hungry would have to have the appetite of a giant boar, but she kept the reflection to herself. "Thank you, that was very thoughtful."

Although the servant was ready to brush out Juliana's long dark hair, Juliana caught the girl in a yawn and sent the maid away to her own bed. "No, I'm fine, away with you."

She wasn't yet accustomed to so much pampering, and really, she could use some time to herself. She brushed her hair as she stared absently into the looking glass above her bureau and thought that she must write a letter to her sister Maddie tomorrow. Already, she had so much to tell her! The journey south and Lord Gabriel's kindness, the measles outbreak, the surprising offer from Lady Sealey, Sir Oliver, the monkey, Sir Oliver again and the guests at tea, Sir Oliver—no, she must not mention the young baronet too often or Maddie would think—

Brush in hand, she paused. Had something moved at the corner of her vision, or was it only shadows from the candle flickering on the table beside her bed? She put down the brush and looked around, but she saw nothing out of place.

Her nerves were as jumpy as a cat's, Juliana told herself. She should drink her tea before it went stone cold. She went to sit on the edge of the bed and picked up the cup, then stopped with it halfway to her lips.

The cup, which had held steaming liquid only a few minutes ago, now was quite dry. And in the china bowl sat a withered leaf from one of the house plants with a small bite mark taken out of its side.

Mia!

Oh, lord, how had the monkey gotten into her room? Had it followed her up, or trailed the maid when the servant had brought in the tea and the biscuit—which was also missing, now surely residing in the animal's always hungry belly?

Juliana dropped the teacup back into its saucer so quickly that it rattled. She stared about her, trying to think where the creature could be hiding. Beneath the bed? She dropped to her knees and peered beneath the frame but the monkey was not there.

The clothespress? She went to it and pulled the door open, but nothing stirred inside, and her faded collection of dresses and bonnets seemed undisturbed. The bureau? Again, the drawers seemed as neat as ever. But where?

Oh, they could not allow the creature to elude them again.

Making up her mind, Juliana went to the bell rope and tugged it vigorously. While she waited for a response, she checked out the room, from one corner to the next. The chest in the corner . . . surely the lid was too heavy for the monkey to lift on its own. Still, she opened it carefully and thumbed through the linens that were stored inside.

When at last a sleepy-eyed maid, her cap rather crooked, opened the door, Juliana hurried to her.

"Please go to Sir Oliver's room and tell him I need him at once!"

"Miss?" The servant gaped at her.

"Sir Oliver, Lady Sealey's godson. Quickly! There is no time to waste."

"But 'e'll be in bed, miss. And tell 'im to come to your—your bedchamber? What will milady say? It ain't proper!" The maid looked scandalized, as well she might.

But Juliana had no time to explain.

"It's not what you think, but it's highly important that he comes, now, at once. Go!" Juliana looked about her, determined not to allow the monkey to slip past and escape into the hallway. "Just give my message to Sir Oliver. He will understand. Now hurry, and shut the door firmly behind you!"

Shaking her head at this unladylike lack of decorum, the servant frowned, but she turned away.

Juliana put her back against the door and watched the room for any telltale movement. If she was very quiet, perhaps the monkey would emerge from hiding. Oh, dear, she should have told the maid to bring more biscuits. The animal was likely still hungry. Unlike Juliana, it had not been sated with savory recipes by the best cook she had ever had the good fortune to encounter.

Juliana folded her arms and tried to breathe lightly. She did not even turn her head, though she attempted to watch the whole room from the corners of her eyes.

Nothing moved. Everything looked neat and tidy. The bedclothes had been turned down for her by one of the servants, the empty teacup with its odd contents still sat on the table beside the bed with a candle beside it. The bureau was neat with another candle and two porcelain figures sitting side by side on top. The empty hearth—it was too warm tonight to require a fire—had a decorative fan to fill the empty space. Juliana could hear her own breath and almost her own heart thumping in her chest, but no other sound.

She looked down. Oh, dear. She was in her nightdress. At least she could put on something. She hurried to the bureau and found a shawl, tying it about her shoulders so that her bosom had another layer other than the thin linen to shield it. She didn't want to look totally unladylike. Then she took up her post once more.

It seemed forever before she heard the small tap at her door. Juliana jumped, then drew a deep breath.

A male voice whispered, "It is I."

"Sir Oliver?" She found she was whispering back.

"Yes."

She moved aside just enough so that she could turn the knob and open the door just a slit. "Come in quickly and shut the door behind you!"

He did not, thank heaven, stand and argue as the housemaid had done while leaving the door dangerously agape. He came inside. Despite his size, he could move with a surprising lightness of foot when necessary. He shut the door behind him as charged, but she saw that his handsome brow was wrinkled.

"This could be taken amiss, you know," he told her. "I mean, your bedchamber, the two of us alone here at this time of night. You are new in London and you may not be aware—"

"I know, I know, but this is important! Mia is here, in my chamber, I am sure of it," she argued.

"How can you be certain?" Despite his caution, his eyes lit up.

She pointed to the teacup.

He moved closer and picked up the china cup. Lifting his brows, he inspected the leaf with its teeth marks. "Yes, definitely the incisor pattern of a monkey."

She nodded. "As I said. I certainly didn't do it!"

"No, I think not. It doesn't match an adult human female's bite marks at all."

"If you think I go around chewing on—" She saw the twinkle in his gray eyes and swallowed the rest of her hasty retort. "Anyhow," she said, instead, "where can Mia be hiding? I've been very quiet, but she hasn't stirred. I wish I had told the maid to bring some more food with which to tempt her."

He didn't answer but reached inside his shirt pocket. He wore only a white linen shirt and his trousers, and he was in his stocking feet, she noted for the first time. He must have been undressing when the maid delivered Juliana's message, and he had taken her "Come at once" quite literally. For some reason, this gave her a thrill of pleasure. Or perhaps it was the glimpse of his chest beneath the half open shirt placket. Hastily, she pulled her gaze away from the sprinkling of golden hair that covered his chest and found he was holding out a handful of biscuits.

"Mia is very fond of these," he said. He put them down on the foot of the bed and stepped back beside Juliana.

She was very aware of him standing so close, and heavens, he was not even fully dressed. She tried not to concentrate on his chest rising and falling. The monkey, she had to think of the monkey. That was the reason, the only reason he was here, she told herself sternly.

"Come out, Mia," he called softly. "Here's a treat for you, my girl."

There were other kinds of treats. . . . The monkey, she reminded herself, think about the bloody monkey . . .

Juliana held her breath.

Then she saw a shadow stir. From beneath the clothes-press, which hugged the floor so closely she would have sworn there could have been no room for even the delicate form of the monkey to hide, the little animal unfolded itself and dashed across the few feet of floor. In a blur of motion it scampered up the bedclothes and grabbed one of the biscuits, crammed the food into its mouth and kept going straight up the nearest bedpost.

Sir Oliver leaped for the monkey.

So did Juliana.

They collided just as they reached the end of the bed. Sir Oliver was built very solidly, Juliana noted, in her last moment of coherent thought. Then the collision sent her sprawling across the bed, dazed, with the wind knocked out of her. Or if not that, if was the fact that Sir Oliver landed half on top of her.

He was heavy. His torso seemingly all muscle, his arms solid and his legs, well, just the thought of his legs made her blush. She felt she must be blushing all over, and she had no voice at all. In fact, she wasn't even sure she could breathe.

Sir Oliver was blushing, too. Almost absently, she noted the rich crimson that shaded his handsome face from the light brown hairline at the top of his high forehead all the way down to his strong cleft chin. As usual, it only made him look more adorably masculine.

But he seemed to notice her with difficulty, and with one arm he pushed himself up so that he hung a few inches just above her.

"Are you all right?" he asked, his voice somehow husky.

Juliana managed to nod.

She had never in her life been so close to a man. Oh, once Mr. Masham—Who? one corner of her mind asked—had leaned close to her when they had been picking wildflowers on the moor and threatened to steal a kiss, and laughing, she had fended him off. In the same circumstances would she put Sir Oliver off? Would she even want to? Or would she put her arm about his neck and pull him closer and press her lips against his own firmly made mouth that looked suddenly so inviting?

Juliana stared up at his face, the squarish contours of his jaw, the sturdy nose, the strong arch of brows, and the honest gray eyes that seemed as clear as untouched sylvan springs. She could lose herself in those eyes . . .

Just now she saw concern in them, and something more. His flush was fading, and her own—oh, who knew. But the warmth in her belly wasn't waning. If anything, it seemed to grow, fueled by his closeness, a small flame that threatened to blossom into a fire that might consume her— burn away all her carefully nurtured precepts of right and wrong.

Maidens did not lie abed with young men and think thoughts that lurked just behind the walls of constraint that Society had built up, brick by brick, through the course of her whole life. So why did those walls now feel as thin as much-washed muslin?

He glanced farther down, and she felt his body stiffen.

Juliana followed the direction of his gaze, and as she saw what he saw, she gasped. She knew she must be flushing once more. The shawl she had donned earlier as a sop to propriety had loosened and been knocked away by the force of their impact. Now her body was concealed only by her lightweight summer nightgown. And her breasts! Somehow, the fire leaping in her belly had sent sparks flying up into other parts of her body, and her nipples, clearly visible through the thin linen, seemed to strain against the fabric, as if they longed for the touch of his hand . . .

Juliana blushed for her own weakness. Yet, if she could have wished it away, she wasn't sure that she would have. Would he move his hand to touch those weak parts of her body which so cravenly called out for his attention?

Sir Oliver drew a deep gasping breath. He leaned even closer, and she could smell his masculine scent, see the faint shadow of blond stubble that shaded his cheeks. She wanted desperately to run her hands along his jawline, feel what a grown man's unshaven cheeks would feel like. She had never touched a man's face, she realized, never skimmed a man's lips with her fingertips. Never kissed a man.

She lifted her face—

Oliver. Her lips formed the word, though she did not say it aloud—

Just above them, the monkey shrieked.

To Juliana's enormous disappointment, Sir Oliver straightened with a jerk, putting an arm's distance between them. He appeared white about the lips.

"I beg your pardon, Miss Applegate. The monkey . . . I didn't mean . . . are you all right?"

The monkey chittered at them from atop the bed. Her small black eyes gleamed, and Mia sounded considerably interested in this human drama. For an instant, Juliana would have liked to wring the creature's neck.

Forced abruptly from her fantasy back into the real world of morals and manners, she bit her lip. Drawing a deep breath, she too sat up, although her head spun and she still felt giddy.

"I . . . my head is a bit . . . I'm only a little shaken, that's all. It was not your fault. It was an accident, of course."

But she found herself looking away and did not meet his eyes. An accident, yes, but one she wished had gone on for a few moments more. Just to touch his lips . . .

Sighing, she remember the eager young ladies in the

drawing room. Who was she to think she could secure such a popular young gentleman's attention? He was only here to recapture the monkey. Remember that, you goose, she scolded herself. And you agreed to help him. The poor monkey shouldn't have to die because you can't keep your head when a handsome young man is around, so mind what you're about!

Wishing she had a more proper wrap to cover her nightgown, she looked about her for the lost shawl and at last espied it on the rug. Picking it up, she tied it firmly back around her shoulders, then folded her arms across her chest and listened to the baronet. He, too, had suddenly become brisk and businesslike.

The monkey was jumping from the top of one bedpost to another and back again, continually eluding Sir Oliver's reaching hands.

"If you stand at one end, and I stand at this end, perhaps we can confuse her."

Juliana obediently moved to the position he indicated, but still, the monkey could not be corralled. Although Juliana put her arms high into the air, and Sir Oliver jumped and swung his big hands back and forth, and once forgot himself and uttered an oath that Juliana pretended not to hear, the monkey remained untouched and even seemed to think this quite a good game. Mia chittered and shrieked and made a fiendish noise, but the beast evaded their clutching hands.

"Damn the silly creature," Sir Oliver said. "Oh, sorry. But it's enough to make a vicar swear."

"I agree," Juliana told him. "She's simply too swift in her responses. What about the biscuits? If we take the rest of them, could we lure her into a closed area and then—do we have anything to use as a trap?"

They both looked about the room, but it was Juliana

who remembered the basket of embroidery silks she had glimpsed in the trunk of linens. She opened the trunk and moved aside the stacks of linens until she located it again, then took out the delicate threads and removed the basket, trying to hide it behind the skirt of her nightgown so the monkey could not get a clear view. Juliana was not sure how intelligent the little animal was, but she saw no reason to take any chances.

She handed the empty basket to the baronet. He put a couple of biscuits into the center and positioned the basket partially hidden behind the chest.

"I don't suppose you have a belt or something similar I can tie to the basket's rim?" he asked.

Juliana looked about the room, then went back to the chest and thumbed through its contents until she came across a thin linen towel. Sir Oliver tied it to the basket and draped it partially over the rim.

Then they stepped back and waited to see if Mia would take the bait. She had been watching them from the top of the bed. Her dark eyes blinked rapidly, and she chattered to herself as if commenting on all their plotting. Did she realize what they were up to?

Mia was not human, Juliana reminded herself. The monkey couldn't know everything! Still, it was hard not to read an uncanny knowledge in those gleaming eyes.

"Be very still," the baronet whispered.

Juliana nodded, moving her head only a fraction of a degree. The monkey swung restlessly from the top of the bedpost, as if wondering about the sudden cessation of activity.

Neither of them spoke. The house seemed very quiet around them. Everyone else seemed to be asleep, the servants in their rooms in the attic or the basement, Lady Sealey in her own chamber. It was just Juliana and the young baronet, as solitary as if they were marooned on some desert island, alone in a tropical sea. She felt the hairs on her arm prickle, and she had to swallow hard. No, no, she mustn't think about how close he stood, or how strange it was to be to be alone in one's bedchamber with a man. She had never in all her life—and yet, it was a glorious, exciting feeling—if only they could be as close as they had been on the bed—their bodies touching, their legs almost wrapped about each other's . . .

At that thought, she felt the strange shivery weakness inside her body once more, and Juliana knew she was blushing. What was this strange effect that he had upon her? Was there something wrong with her? She had no one to ask. At home, she could confide in Maddie, who since their mother's early death was the only confidante she had. But she doubted that even Maddie would know the answer to this puzzle. And could she tell even her trusted older sister that she had stood alone in the flickering candlelight of her bedchamber with a handsome young man only inches away?

It was just because of the monkey, she hastened to remind herself. Yet, did Sir Oliver seem to be breathing faster, and did she detect a faint shimmer of perspiration on his upper lip? Was he thinking of the monkey, or did his thoughts, too, run along other lines?

She jumped at a hair-raising sound.

The monkey had given a sudden shriek, as if taunting them, demanding to know why they stood so still and so silent.

"Hush, Mia," she couldn't keep from scolding. "You'll wake the whole house!"

"Come and have a biscuit," Sir Oliver added. "It's your favorite. Come along, now, that's a good girl."

The monkey hung by one hand from the bedpost and regarded them doubtfully, then dropped to the floor with a speed that dazzled the eye. Then she was off, hurrying across the floor and jumping for the basket—a barely visible streak of brown fur.

The baronet jumped for her, and this time, Juliana knew to hold her position and leave him the space to scoop up the monkey.

"I have you!" he exclaimed with pardonable triumph in his voice. He intercepted the animal in midleap, pulling the monkey out of the air and scooping her into his large strong hands.

"Oh, well done!" Juliana cried.

"There, now," he said, keeping his tone gentle as the monkey chittered, scolding him for such impertinence. "It's all right." He caressed the top of the monkey's brown head, soothing it, and the little animal's cries abated.

For a moment, Juliana felt almost jealous of the monkey, then she pushed aside such an irrational thought.

Sir Oliver was still speaking to Mia in soft tones. "You must go back to your cage, I'm afraid, for your own good. Else you're going to find yourself in real trouble."

"Thank goodness we have her," Juliana said, stepping closer to look down at the small creature and marveling that such a tiny thing, contained easily between the circle of the baronet's two hands, could cause such turmoil. "Mia, you are fortunate to have such a determined champion."

When the baronet looked up at her, she was surprised to see the worry lingering still in his eyes.

"What is it?" she demanded, then only belatedly realized that whatever troubled him might be none of her concern.

"It's only, when my mentor Rodney Needham comes to inquire about my progress, he is going to expect to see—"

"A dead monkey? Oh, no, Sir Oliver, you can't—"

He frowned. "I certainly don't wish to, but—"

"Try to put him off," she urged. "We will think of something!"

She had, she realized an instant later, somehow irreparably linked herself to Sir Oliver and his quest to save the monkey. Would he think her too bold, too forward?

But he was smiling down at her, and the warmth in his gray eyes seemed to flow right through her, like a ray of sunlight on a hitherto cloudy day. Suddenly Juliana didn't care how rash her impulsive commitment might have been. She would have promised her last breath to that dratted monkey if it allowed Sir Oliver to continue to smile at her in such a way. . . .

Then he blushed again. What?

Juliana glanced down and saw that not only had her shawl been pushed aside, but the monkey had reached out with its long spindly fingers and untied the ribbon at the neck of her nightgown. Its placket now gapped open, exposing the curve of her breasts. Oh, dear . . . She felt a prickle of embarrassment, as well as something warmer and more urgent.

"I do beg your pardon," the baronet said, his cheeks growing even redder. "Mia doesn't, that is, she—"

"I know, I mean, she's only a dumb creature who . . . do not think of it—" Juliana tried to reassure him, even as she reached to retie her nightgown.

As if despite himself, Sir Oliver reached to help her. This unthinking if automatic response produced two unfortunate results. His fingertips brushed the curve of her breasts, only for the barest instant, but Juliana gasped. The slight contact sent a shiver of white-hot feeling racing across her entire torso. She had never felt such a sensation, never been touched on her bare skin by a man, and it took her breath.

The baronet jumped back as if he, too, had encountered a raging flame. And he let go of the monkey.

Mia shrieked in triumph. They both exclaimed in frustration.

Sir Oliver jumped to grab the animal before it could escape them again, and Juliana sprang to do the same. Sliding easily around them, the monkey scampered across the floor as if this were some manic game. It headed for the clothespress on the other side of the room.

Juliana made another desperate leap. She could almost grasp the very end of the animal's tail, but it slid through her fingers, and the monkey ran on, unfettered. She wanted to curse. Now she and Sir Oliver both dashed after Mia, but with all their running about, the usually smooth rug had somehow developed a crease. They stumbled over it at almost the same moment and hit the floor with a thud.

Again, they were tangled in a pile of arms and legs. Not sure whether to smile or groan, Juliana wondered if this was in answer to her secret wish?

The monkey shrieked once again and stopped to stare at them, as if even she were perplexed at all this lying about.

The door opened.

Six

*T*he first thing Juliana saw framed above them in the doorway was the countess, in an impossibly lovely nightgown and wrapper, with a lacy nightcap perched on her silver hair. Behind her, garbed in various combinations of nightshirts and gowns and crooked caps and hastily donned jackets and shawls, a mob of servants crowded to see.

Then Juliana noted a streak of brown fur slip past the open door and disappear once more past the assembled legs and on down the shadowy hallway. She groaned.

Sir Oliver swore vigorously beneath his breath.

Juliana would have very much liked to echo his words. Then she realized that not only were they lying in a very compromising position, but her nightgown was still open at the neck, and her skirt had been pushed up to show several inches of bare limbs. She tried to sit up, but found Sir Oliver's legs still lay across hers, holding her down as effectively as bars of iron.

Sir Oliver was blushing deeply. Heaven knew what Juliana herself looked like, with her disheveled clothing and her awkward pose, which was that of a total wanton! The countess would never understand, and she had been so kind. Lady Sealey would likely turn Juliana out onto the street! And Lord Gabriel! Oh, she would be sent home in disgrace!

Juliana felt herself go cold with dread and mortification.

"Godmother, I can explain," Sir Oliver was saying, his voice hoarse. "This is not what it seems."

"I should hope not," Lady Sealey agreed, her voice as steady as her hand that held a candle in a silver holder. "Aside from the fact the two of you have just met, Miss Applegate is my guest and under my protection."

"I—we—were simply trying to catch the monkey."

"I 'eard it called a lot of things, but that's a new one," one of the footmen muttered from behind the countess.

Another servant smothered a nervous laugh.

The countess glanced briefly behind her. "You all know my feelings about gossip," she said, her tone level but firm. "If you are happy in my employ and wish to continue—"

She didn't finish the statement, but she didn't have to.

There were no more comments from the servants, and some of them stood up straighter. The footman who had spoken jumped as one of his fellows poked him in the ribs. But Juliana was still feeling too miserable to take much comfort from his rebuke. She bit her lip.

"It's true, Godmother, I give you my sacred oath," Sir Oliver continued. "The monkey followed the maid up to the guest room, and Miss Applegate summoned me to retrieve it. Miss Applegate realized it was hiding in her chamber when she saw the teacup. We stumbled over each other just now as we tried to recapture Mia. You know how fast the creature is. We were very close to having it, too."

As Juliana pushed her nightgown down to cover her legs, Sir Oliver scrambled up and turned to the table, lifting the cup for the countess to inspect.

Lady Sealey accepted the leaf from the cup and nodded. "And now we have let the animal out again? Oh, dear, that is unfortunate."

"What is it, milady?" one of the maidservants asked in a timid voice. "Is there a wild animal loose in the house?"

"It is a monkey, Gladys, that is all," the countess said. "A very small monkey. Nothing dangerous, but a nuisance, I admit."

"You mean a wild ape, like the man-eating monster what my cousin saw at the amphitheater?"

One of the younger maids paled. The first one shrieked and threw up her hands and fainted dead away.

"Catch her, Donaldson, don't let her fall!" the countess told the nearest footman. "Maizy, fetch the smelling salts for the kitchen maid. It's not a man-eater; it's a very small animal, and most of you will likely never see it. See to Gladys, and then the rest of you, go back to bed. No, one of you bring Miss Applegate some hot tea first, I think she can use it. And mind what I said about gossiping!"

"Yes, milady, I'll see to it." A stout woman, her hair streaked with gray beneath her nightcap, who must be the housekeeper, cast a stern eye on the other staff members and issued orders in a low voice while she bent over the girl who had swooned. The rest of the servants made themselves scarce, the footman who had been rebuked disappearing more speedily than his mates.

Shaking her head, Lady Sealey turned back to the two of them. "Do get up off the floor, my dear," she told Juliana.

Sir Oliver offered Juliana his hand.

Blushing, she allowed him to help her up, then turned

away to retie her gown and find the shawl that the monkey had so helpfully discarded.

"I am so very sorry, Godmother," Sir Oliver repeated.

"I know, Oliver, you never mean to get into scrapes," the countess said, sighing. "Off to bed with you."

"But—" He looked anxiously back at Juliana, who could not seem to meet his gaze. She observed him only from the corner of her eye. She wasn't sure she could look at the countess, either. What on earth could she say, after summoning a young man to her bedchamber? She'd only meant to help, but her actions, when viewed in hindsight . . . Oh, dear, she knew perfectly well what Maddie would say. No conventional young lady would have done such a thing.

And when had Juliana ever been a conventional young lady?

"I will not devour Miss Applegate in your absence," the countess said, her tone astringent. "And I think she will do better without you in her bedchamber."

"Oh, of course. My apologies, Miss Applegate." He gave a stiff bow, then departed.

"No, I mean, n-not at all," Juliana stuttered, hoping he would not think she was offended.

And as he walked away, that thought gave her the courage to at last look anxiously at her hostess. "It wasn't his fault, Lady Sealey. I asked the maid to fetch Sir Oliver when I discovered that the monkey was in my room. I had promised to help, but I didn't think I could do it alone, you see. And it seemed more important to find the creature, even though I knew it wasn't proper to ask the baronet to come to my chamber. Perhaps I should have called for you first, but I was afraid you might be asleep and—I am so sorry! I know I'm not very good at remembering ladylike behavior, but I do apologize."

"My dear, I am not here to scold." Lady Sealey came into the bedroom and shut the door quietly behind her. She sat in the chair beside the bed and motioned to Juliana to sit down on the bed itself. Her tone was kind, more kind than Juliana privately thought she deserved. "It's good of you to want to help my feckless godson. He is strong enough to lift an ox and as brilliant as any scientist in the Acadamy, and despite that, he does blunder into scrapes now and then."

"Oh, no, he's just so kind-hearted. And I don't want to see that poor creature—even though she is sadly mischievous—condemned to death. Her eyes look so uncannily human, or almost so, at least. How could one wish to hurt her? I think Sir Oliver should be commended for his compassion," Juliana said, then wished she had not been quite so fervent in her defense.

Her gaze thoughtful, Lady Sealey searched Juliana's face. "Yes, I see. But as I was about to say, I'm not here to scold, but I must point out, my dear, that unmarried ladies do have to take care with their conduct. Married women and widows have more latitude, but maidens must be circumspect. Society can be quite harsh in its judgment, you know, and I would not wish to see you suffer for a thoughtless action. Since you are in my house, and your brother has left you in my care, I feel I should tell you this."

"Oh." Juliana felt mortified all over again, especially when she remembered her body's unexpected reaction to the baronet's nearness.

"And he is quite a handsome young man," the countess pointed out, her tone gentle, although she looked down at the empty cup and this time did not study Juliana's face.

Juliana had no desire to argue the point. She hoped she had not turned as crimson now as Sir Oliver had done when the door had opened upon them in such an awkward position.

Lady Sealey reached across and patted her shoulder. "Now then, drink your tea when it comes and try to get some sleep. We'll say no more about it. Your visit is just beginning. With any luck, Sir Oliver will track down that troublesome monkey tomorrow, and you'll have more pleasant matters to think about."

But when the countess had departed, Juliana lay back upon her bed and discovered that the only image in her mind was that of the brawny young baronet, and the amazing touch of his hand upon her breast, of how it had felt to have his body so close to her own, and how little of what she had now experienced would be included in her first letter home!

It was perhaps not surprising that she had a somewhat restless night. When she woke, Juliana rang for a maid, who appeared after a longer delay than usual, bearing a tray with tea and toast and ham and poached eggs. The servant looked nervously about as she came in and jumped when the door shut behind her.

"Sorry, miss." She put the tray hastily down on the table beside the bed. "The 'ouse is in a bit of an uproar, what with wild beasts runnin' amok, and all."

"It's only one small monkey," Juliana pointed out mildly. "It might break a piece of china, but it's not going to do you any harm."

"So 'e says," the maid argued, her tone dark. "But what does a man, even if 'e is a gentl'man, know about it? Begging your pardon, miss, but Sir Oliver, 'e's one of those biologisest blokes what cuts up stray cats and takes out their 'earts and livers and put 'em into vats of gin. Me uncle seen such in a traveling show once. A waste of good gin, 'e said!"

Juliana had picked up her fork but now she shivered at the graphic description and put it down again. She wasn't sure she was hungry. Besides, the eggs were hard at the edges and raw in the middle, and the ham was scorched, not at all like the cook's usual adroit touch. What was happening down in the kitchen? Were all the servants terrified by one small mischievous monkey?

She had to go and help Sir Oliver search for Mia! And if the thought of seeing the young baronet again made her smile, that was neither here nor there. She had promised to help him recapture the animal. Just because the image of him warmed her from head to foot—don't be a fool, Jules, she told herself. He's not for you!

And why can't you enjoy the moment, she answered her inner voice. You'll be here for a short enough time. Just cherish the chances you have. . . .

She nibbled on the toast and drank her tea, which today had escaped the ravages of the monkey, and then turned to open the clothespress. Sighing at the sight of the faded dresses, she chose the nearest one and dressed quickly with the maid's help. After washing her face and brushing her hair, she soon was ready to venture downstairs.

She found Lady Sealey in the drawing room, but when she asked about Sir Oliver's whereabouts, keeping her tone as noncommital as possible, her hostess informed her that he had gone out.

"Oh," Juliana said.

The countess smiled at her. "I believe he had a science lecture to attend, and then he was summoned by his mentor, the esteemed Mr. Needham, to discuss the extent of his progress on his studies of the simian."

"Oh!" Juliana said, in an entirely different tone. "We have to find that dratted monkey! I don't suppose—" She paused, but Lady Sealey shook her head.

"No, he has had no luck, although my poor godson was up at dawn tearing the attic apart. One of the servants thought she heard noises over her head during the night. Of course, another maid was sure she detected a rustle underneath the china cabinet while putting away teacups and screamed so loudly that the chef dropped the souffle he was making for my breakfast into the ashes of the kitchen fire. We must find this wretched creature, or no one will ever have anything decent to eat again!"

Juliana flushed and felt guilty, although she wasn't quite sure why. That reminded her of all the things she did have reason to feel guilty about, however. She bit her lip, wondering if she dared ask the countess.

Lady Sealey allowed her a few moments of silence, and Juliana found the courage to say shyly, "My mother died when I was very young."

"That's a great loss for a girl."

"Yes," Juliana agreed, sighing. "My sister tried to mother us all, but she is only two years older than I, and we have no living grandparents, nor any aunts that we are close to."

"So you have had no female relations to guide you as you grew up?" the countess asked, her tone gentle.

"No," Juliana said, grateful that the older lady seemed to understand. "And so I have had no one to ask about certain topics which, which—"

The countess nodded. "I see."

"When I summoned Sir Oliver to my chamber last night, and I know it was most improper, and I do beg your pardon, I will not do it again—" Juliana raised her gaze anxiously to her hostess's face and was relieved to detect no trace of a frown there.

"I was thinking only of the chance to capture the monkey, I give you my solemn oath. Only later when by accident we ended up so close, I experienced the strangest sensations, and my body—my body seemed so aware of—" Knowing that her face was burning, Juliana hesitated. She found it impossible to go on.

She stared at the faded muslin of her skirt but she could feel the countess's gaze upon her. Oh, she should not have considered confiding in someone she had only just met. The countess would decide that she was a wanton, after all. Juliana should have never said a word!

But just when the silence seemed to grate on her anxious nerves until Juliana thought she would scream, she heard a delicate noise. She looked up in disbelief and found that the other lady was chuckling.

"My dear, you are very fortunate."

"What?" Had she not been clear enough in her description? Had the countess not understood the surely abnormal reactions which Juliana had described? Perhaps she was indeed a totally wicked person deep inside.

"I believe you had a healthy reaction to a young man whom you felt an attraction to."

"But—"

"Do you not like Sir Oliver?"

"Of course."

"Do you find my godson attractive?" Lady Sealey smiled.

Juliana thought of his amazing physique and appealing face, and she blushed again. That feeling of warmth that had spread through her, that yearning in her breasts and her belly . . . she could almost feel it again just by picturing the young baronet.

"Then what could be more natural? You like him, you are attracted to him, in mind and in body, just as nature and the good God intended. Your body responds to him when he is so close. Some young ladies do not come to this as easily; they have been too sheltered or too frightened by overanxious mamas or governesses to listen to their own bodies' responses. Even when they eventually become brides, it can be hard going for their husbands and themselves as they seek to recover the natural appetites which have been so long buried."

The countess looked distant for a moment, then she smiled a little, a small smile that widened and left a gleam in her eyes. Somehow, Juliana did not think that the countess had been one of those overly sheltered young ladies.

"However, that does not mean that you can give in to all your feelings, of course. You cannot afford to turn up with child, my dear."

Juliana felt as if she had been dashed by icy water. She gasped, and the lovely feeling of warmth that memories of the baronet had evoked vanished as in one splash. Having grown up surrounded by farm animals, she had no illusions about the mysteries of the relationship between males and females and the resulting appearance of springtime litters. And as for

"No, no," she managed to say. "Indeed, Lady Sealey, please believe me, I mean to do nothing improper."

"I know you don't mean to," the countess told her, her tone still gentle. "But the only danger to having a a healthy response to one another is that response can burst forth, my dear, in delightful but dangerous ways. A mild flirtation is permissible, if one is discreet, but one must not allow it to go too far. Those feelings that have surprised you can swell too swiftly into a torrent of emotion and thrust you beyond the bounds of propriety and well-being. You are in my care, just now, and I must protect you even from yourself, if need be. I certainly owe Lord and Lady Gabriel my vigilance."

"I will remember," Juliana told her.

Lady Sealey smiled at her. "I'm sure you will," she agreed. "Now, something else I have to tell you."

Juliana braced herself for more lectures, even delivered in the countess's exquisite voice, but to her surprise, her hostess went to pull the bell rope. She took her seat again, and when the servant appeared, gave directions to the maid.

Presently, the girl brought up a large parcel wrapped in brown paper.

"This came for you from Lady Gabriel," Lady Sealey explained. "And there is a letter here for you, too."

Mystified, Juliana broke the seal and skimmed the elegant writing inside, all delicate loops and swirls. She scanned the words, then looked up. "She says that she bought these muslins for her younger sister, but that Circe is not allowed out of bed just yet, and she has begged her sister to get these out of the house as the colors seem to taunt her since she's not allowed to paint."

This made no sense at all. Juliana read the line again, but it still seemed to say the same thing.

"Circe is an artist, you see," Lady Sealey explained. "And when one is ill—"

Juliana nodded as if she understood, although she didn't. She read on. "So Lady Gabriel begs that I will make use of them instead, since I had little time to prepare for my journey south and perhaps could use some new dresses." That was the understatement of the century, Juliana thought, thinking of the meager wardrobe hanging upstairs, though she did not voice her thought aloud. "And she will send over their usual seamstress later today to take my measurements so that she can begin work."

They could very well have put these lengths of fabric

aside for a few weeks, for goodness' sake, and wait for Circe to regain her health. Wealthy people were very strange, Juliana thought. She opened the paper and gazed at the folded lengths of muslin: bright blues and clear pink, stripes and sprigs, jonquils and whites with delicate figures, and all with laces and threads and trims to match. They were beautiful; such bounty to bestow upon her so casually. She could not afford so many dresses in two seasons, much less one! But could she accept so much, and then the services of their dressmaker, too?

Juliana put the note aside and touched one of the fabrics, fingering a length of muslin sprigged in a delicate pink, the colors clear and fresh. She had not had a new dress in several seasons. She and Maddy tended to give the new clothes, when there was money for such things, to the twins, who so longed for pretty things. She thought of wearing this lovely fabric . . . Would Sir Oliver think she looked pretty?

She cleared her throat. Her voice seemed to have gotten somewhat husky. "This is very generous of Lady Gabriel. I hope her sister does not change her mind. These are very pretty muslins, you know."

"I'm sure when Circe feels like getting out again, they will pick out a new selection of fabrics for her," Lady Sealey assured her.

Of course they would. They were not light in the pocket, as the Applegate girls always were. Juliana gave herself a mental shake. She was too used to a tight budget and a house full of girls always in need of new clothes. But she was being such a charge upon her new half brother, and she had not meant to be a burden—

"Perhaps I could make up some of the dresses myself," she suggested. "I'm not the best with a needle, but it would save the fees of the dressmaker."

"That's a commendable thought," Lady Sealey agreed. "Of course, Mrs. Whitson, the needlewoman whom Lady Gabriel uses, is a most accomplished seamstress, and in addition, a worthy woman. A widow with six children, she would sadly miss the business if we did not engage her, and this may be one reason Psyche did not wish to delay giving her another commission."

"Oh," Juliana said. There seemed no way to avoid all these wonderful gifts. She could hardly deprive a hard-working widow of a job she obviously needed.

"And that reminds me," Lady Sealey said. "Would you pull the bell rope again, my dear?"

"Of course," Juliana agreed. She tore herself away from the pile of lovely fabrics and went to do as she was requested.

When the maid returned, Lady Sealey instructed the girl to send for the countess's personal dresser and then added another message which Juliana did not hear. She had already turned back to the stack of muslins and trim, dreaming of the dresses which would be created from this bounty, wishing she could send some of them to Maddie. At least the sisters were much of a size; when Juliana returned home, she could share some of these with her sister and the twins, even if she had to take up the hems a bit. . . .

So when the other servant, an older woman with a stern expression, appeared with her arms full of dresses, Juliana blinked in surprise.

"This is my dresser, Adams, who has been with me many years and who helps me to look my best."

The lady's maid allowed herself a moment of obvious pride, then smoothed her expression again just as she smoothed out the skirt of an incredibly lovely silk evening frock as she laid the armload of dresses carefully across the settee.

"We were going through my wardrobes just the other day. I do seem to accumulate a surprising collection of dresses, but I admit that I adore clothes. Still, I do have to make room for the new gowns I have on order from my modiste, and I found a few that I thought you might humor me by making use of? When the dressmaker comes, I think she could adjust the measurements on these without too much trouble so that you could wear them."

She made it sound as if Juliana would be doing *her* a favor, instead of the other way around. The countess was the kindest lady in the world, Juliana thought, or at least she was tied with Lady Gabriel.

Juliana looked down at the dress which lay on top. The silk was the color of a summer sky just after dawn; she had seldom seen anything so lovely. She wondered if it would bring out the color of her eyes, and what Sir Oliver would think if he saw her in it?

She remembered she must say something. "Thank, thank you," she stammered. "You are much too generous."

"Nonsense, I hate to see these wasted, I barely wore them," the countess assured her. "And some of them were too young for me, I'm sure."

The lady's maid looked skeptical. Juliana also doubted that the elegant Lady Sealey had ever made a mistake in fashion, but she smiled politely, and then looked back at the pile of beautiful dresses. She had never imagined she would have such beautiful creations to wear. These were not the work of some provincial dressmaker! She felt she must be dreaming.

"Which reminds me, I have a dinner party planned at the end of the week, so a dinner dress will be useful."

Juliana looked up, and she knew that her expression reflected dismay.

"Oh, not to worry, my child. With the Season over, London is sadly empty. It will be a small affair, nothing to concern yourself about."

For a young lady who had had only the slightest social encounters with small local parties, even a London dinner party was an event to make her nerves jump like the monkey had done last night in her bedchamber.

Which brought her thoughts back to what she should be doing.

Juliana scolded herself for being distracted by something as minor as apparel. But such beautiful garments would distract any woman who wasn't dead, the other part of her brain argued. Still, she must get back to searching for the lost animal.

Lady Sealey did not seem to share her anxiety, however. She had reached across to a pile of mail and lifted a gilt-edged card from the stack to show Juliana an invitation to tea at Lady Pomfrey's house. Juliana nodded, impressed despite herself. She was invited, too—amazing!

As the pile of cards and letters shifted, another piece of mail slipped out, a somewhat grimy note.

The countess's expression changed, and her mouth went tight. She pushed the small piece of mail quickly back out of sight.

Juliana could not fail to note the unusual moment of apprehension, or at least, grim resolution that had crossed the countess's face. She looked away, feeling almost embarrassed, as if she had seen something that she should not have witnessed. Focusing again on the pile of dresses, Juliana pretended to examine another silk evening gown. When the countess told her lady's maid to take the dresses up to Juliana's guest chamber until the seamstress arrived,

Juliana jumped up. "I will help you," she said. "Thank you so much, Lady Sealey. You are being much too kind to me!"

"I am happy to do so, dear girl," Lady Sealey said. She sounded herself again; the moment of strain seemed to have passed.

But now Juliana could detect a small line of tension in the other's forehead that did not seem to have been there earlier. What on earth was the note about, and what was troubling the countess?

Juliana puzzled over the mystery as she and Adams carried the dresses up to Juliana's room and left them on the bed until the seamstress appeared. The lady's maid took her leave, and Juliana lingered a few minutes to examine the dresses in more detail, marveling over the richness of the trim and the softness of the silk. The countess had the most exquisite taste, and, obviously, the means with which to indulge it without stinting. How kind it was of her to share her gowns with Juliana. It made her giddy just to think of wearing such wonderful dresses, and it didn't bother Juliana at all that they were hand-me-downs. She had worn her mother's old clothing whenever the out-of-date garments could be salvaged and made over, and she and her sisters were always passing clothing back and forth. At last she decided to go back downstairs and wait for the sewing woman to arrive. When she reached the drawing room, however, it was empty, and there was no sign as yet of Mrs. Whitson.

Until she arrived, Juliana decided she could start the letter to her sister. Maddie would worry if she had no word from her. Juliana looked about her, then pulled the bell rope.

In a few minutes a maid appeared. "Yes, miss?"

"Could you tell me where to find paper and ink and quills, please, so I may write to my sister in Yorkshire? And has Lady Sealey gone out?"

"No, miss. Milady 'as gone up to lie down. She 'as a bit of an 'eadache, but I'm sure she wouldn't mind you using 'er desk. There's paper and ink and all such stuff in there."

The servant led the way to an elegant French writing desk in one corner of the drawing room and opened the lid, showing Juliana a stack of fine quality writing paper, rougher textured blotting paper, an ink well, an assortment of quills, and a small pen knife to trim them with. The maid lit the wick on a handsome silver wax jack, so that the wax inside would be softened by the time Juliana needed it to seal her letter. In short, she had all that she would need for her correspondence.

"Thank you," Juliana said.

She drew up a chair and sat down, taking a sheet of the paper and admiring the texture. Next Juliana selected a quill and sharpened its end to a keen point, then dipped it into the ink and started her letter.

Dear Maddy,
I have so much to tell you, I hardly know where to begin. I
shall be such a London dandy by the time I return that you
will hardly know me . . .

There was so much to tell that she didn't think Maddy would notice the many gaps in her narrative, the parts that she had to leave out. She finished the first page, blotted it and turned it at right angles to write over her lines to get the most of the space, and then turned the sheet to write on the back, writing as small and as neatly as possible so that the letter would not cost too much when Maddie received it. But Juliana's elbow hit a pile of mail stacked neatly at the side of the desk. It went flying, and one smaller piece fell to the floor.

Oh, dear.

She reached to pick up the paper that had fallen and as she did, she recognized the smudged note that had alarmed the countess earlier and most likely brought on the headache that had sent her up to bed.

Juliana stared at the paper. Before she could stop herself, a few words, scrawled in an unnaturally large sprawling script, leaped out at her:

I know your dirty secret! You will rue the day . . .

Seven

*J*uliana gasped at the ugly words sprawled in the shaky, unschooled hand. Then she refolded the sheet and pushed it back into the pile, straightening the stack and praying her accidental intrusion would not be obvious.

Her thoughts raced. Who could be so unkind? Who would write in such a nasty and, yes, threatening tone to a lady as generous and kind and universally admired as the countess?

Yet, Juliana had no acquaintance in the Ton, had not moved in Society. What did she know of the attitude that prevailed in London circles? Still, how could people not admire and like Lady Sealey? And even if some were jealous of her, even if all of Society were not her close friends, who could dislike her so much? It was impossible to imagine. Who could Juliana ask about this, and could she admit seeing the countess's private correspondence?

Could she tell Sir Oliver, and what would he think of her if she did?

Her cheeks burned that he might consider her impertinent enough to snoop through her hostess's desk and mail. And a hostess who had been so kind to her, too!

Juliana wished she had never sat down at the countess's desk. But she had, and she still needed to finish the letter to Maddie. Sighing, she dipped her quill into the ink and set to work again, trying to stuff all her experiences into the letter and get away from the desk and its contents before she got herself into more trouble.

She finished the page in a rush, sending her love to her father and all her sisters, then folded the letter, wrote the directions on the outside, turned it, and dropped a couple of large dollops of hot wax onto the crease. As she waited for the wax to cool, she extinguished the burning wick. She wanted only to close the desk quickly and put the tempting pile of mail out of her sight.

Because now temptation called to her.

Who could have sent such a dreadful letter? Who could be tossing such beastly words at the countess? Juliana did not, could not, believe that such an attack was warranted. She felt her fingers literally itch to reach for the pile again, to pull out the note, read the rest of its contents and learn more . . .

She picked up her own letter. The wax was cool. She made sure she had replaced everything neatly and then shut the desk's lid, stood, and pushed the chair back into place. Still, she hesitated for a moment, drawn to the threatening note like a child to a sticky bun.

Perhaps it was just as well that a footman appeared in the doorway.

Juliana turned.

"The seamstress is here for your fitting, Miss Applegate."

"Thank you, I'm coming. Can you post my letter, please?" she asked.

He took her letter. She went out to the hall to greet the
seamstress kindly and lend her up to her guest chamber,
where she had her measurements taken. They discussed
how the lengths of muslins were to be made up, and how
the donated dresses from Lady Sealey should be made over
for her benefit. Juliana shed her own worn muslin so that
she could put on a lovely sea green dinner dress they
agreed should fit nicely.

Taking a pin from between her lips, Mrs. Whitson
marked a seam and then stood back to judge the fit. "Fortunately," she pointed out, "the good countess is so slim that
I have only to let out the hem a bit and adjust the seams
'ere and 'ere. This dress needs little done to the trim; the
seed pearls will be just right as they are. On the others,
'owever, I would suggest that we remove the lavender lace
trim on this gray and add pink, instead, for a younger lady.
And on the blue, take off the gray feathers and add white
silk roses to the flounce."

"Whatever you say," Juliana agreed, feeling almost
dizzy at the thought of owning such wonderful apparel. "I
can't wait to see them!"

The other lady smiled. "You're going to look a treat,
miss."

Juliana sighed happily. "It's so kind of the countess and
of Lady Gabriel, too."

"Ah, Lady Gabriel is a gracious lady," the seamstress
agreed, "and 'as been most kind to me, and many others,
too. Did you know she oversees a foundling 'ome? The
poor girls in it are that much better off since she 'as 'ad 'er
eye on the place! And the countess, the good she does to the
poor: I could tell you stories, my dear, not that she would
want me to. An angel, the woman is and that quiet about it!"

And did that sound like a woman who should be receiv-

ing vile letters? Juliana thought again of the note. Yet, perhaps she was making too much of it, she told herself. If the
countess was admired by so many, what was one ill-
natured piece of mail?

When the seamstress had completed her assessment,
and they had agreed on which muslins and which silk
dresses should be tackled first—it was almost impossible
for Juliana to imagine owning so many delightful dresses
all at one time—the dressmaker put them into her large
carpetbag along with her measuring tape and pin cushion
and said a cheerful good-bye. Juliana walked back downstairs with her.

Juliana was pleased to see that the countess had reappeared. Lady Sealey looked a little pale, but not as strained
as she had earlier, so perhaps her headache had eased. Just
before entering the drawing room, the countess paused to
speak to them.

"Ah, Mrs. Whitson, thank you for coming to help us with
Miss Applegate's wardrobe," the countess said now.

Mrs. Whitson dropped a deep curtsy. "Oh, I'm so 'appy
to do it, me lady. These dresses are going to look beautiful
on 'er, if I do say so."

"Can you have a dinner dress ready by Friday? I have a
dinner party planned, and it would be nice if Miss Applegate could have a new gown."

The dressmaker drew herself up like a knight accepting
a challenge from his king. "Of course, me lady. I'll drop
everything else, I will, and get right to it first thing. You'll
'ave the dinner dress by Friday morning, not to worry."

"Thank you." Lady Sealey smiled and gave the footman
quiet instructions to call—and pay for—a hackney for the
seamstress's use so that she did not have to lug the heavy
carpetbag all the way home.

Then she instructed the parlor maid to bring a tea tray and motioned to Juliana to join her in the drawing room.

Juliana tried to thank her again for the dresses, but the countess waved aside her expression of gratitude.

"But why should you not have the use of them, my dear? It will give me much pleasure to see you wearing the dresses. And by the time Mrs. Whitson is done with them, you needn't worry that anyone will recognize them."

So Juliana nodded and followed her into the large room. She sat down in one of the brocade chairs. The countess still looked a bit distracted. Was her head still aching, or was it something else?

They chatted about fashion and the latest styles, which Juliana knew precious little about, until the footman brought the tea tray, and he returned shortly after with the latest mail. Amazing how many postal deliveries London houses received, Juliana thought, but was it her imagination or did the countess stiffen at the sight of the silver tray with its pile of letters? The teacup in her hand paused for an instant, and Juliana thought the countess's lips tightened. Then her expression returned to normal, and Juliana looked quickly away.

A new form appeared in the doorway, and Juliana forgot, for a moment, everything except her pleasure at his reappearance.

"Come in, Oliver, we're just having some tea," Lady Sealey said, her voice calm. "Put the mail into my desk, I will look at it later," she told the footman.

Coming across the room and sitting down next to Juliana, Sir Oliver flashed her a tired smile.

Returning it, she felt a surge of sympathy for him. He looked as if the science lecture had been long and his meeting with his mentor trying. The countess poured him a cup of the steaming brew and passed it to him.

"So, did you have a productive session with Mr. Needham?"

The baronet frowned for a moment. "He is not terribly pleased with my progress, I admit, but—"

Juliana gazed anxiously at him. "You're not going to kill Mia?"

"I can't even find Mia!" Sir Oliver exclaimed, his voice bitter. "I admit, I'm getting tired of making excuses. But you were a great help, Godmother."

Juliana turned to gaze at the countess, wondering what she had done to intercede with Sir Oliver's mentor, but secretly applauding her for doing it, whatever it was.

"He's most pleased to be invited to your dinner party Friday night, so he didn't roast me as much as he would have otherwise." Sir Oliver flashed them both a wicked grin and finished off his tea in one gulp.

Lady Sealey smiled calmly and refilled his cup. "It's nothing, dear boy. Have some sandwiches. I have the cheese and ham that you like."

Mr. Needham was coming to the dinner party? Juliana decided she would have no more qualms about the dinner, and she would do everything she could to be gracious to Sir Oliver's grumbling mentor, anything to help spare the poor monkey.

Now, as Sir Oliver said, if they could only *locate* the poor monkey!

It seemed that Lady Sealey also had her mind on the same problem. "Oliver," she said, raising her silvery brows and fixing her godson with a stern gaze. "I refuse to have my dinner party disrupted by a monkey, or even to have my peace of mind disrupted by the mere possibility. You have a day and a half to find that creature!"

"Yes, Godmother," Sir Oliver agreed. He put down his cup and stood.

"I will help you," Juliana said quickly, and she returned her cup to its saucer, too. "Where shall we search first?"

"I did the attic this morning, without success, and asked the servants to keep the doors closed, so we can but hope that they did," Sir Oliver told her as they went out into the hall. Juliana had to rush to keep up with his long strides. "I suppose we must do the guest rooms again, and then take the house floor by floor."

The problem was, the monkey could just as well be going behind their back. They could search a room or a whole floor and an hour later the moneky could zip back into the room they had just searched if one of the servants left a door open for even a minute. And servants were always moving about the house.

Juliana wondered if they would ever find the creature!

They spent the rest of the day poking through dark corners and beneath beds, looking inside trunks, climbing on stools to inspect the tops of clothespresses, checking out even the smallest spaces where a determined monkey might squeeze herself.

By the time a maidservant came to tell them that dinner was about to be announced, Juliana was alarmed to look down and see that she was covered in dust, and now she had no time to change her dress.

"Oh, dear, I'd better run and at least wash my face and hands," she said. "We don't have guests tonight, do we? I look a fright."

"I don't think anyone is dining with us," Sir Oliver assured her. "And you gained your dust in a good cause. It's very kind of you to help, you know. And I think you look very nice, except for, ah, a smudge just here on your nose."

He reached out to rub the spot off the end of her nose, and she found that his touch made a sudden rush of feeling run through her whole body. She looked up at him with wide eyes, and he paused, his hand just a few inches from her face, looking as if he wanted to touch her again.

She was the one blushing now, and suddenly he had reddened as well. She should say something, Juliana thought. He had only meant to—to—to what? Not only was her voice not working, neither was her brain . . .

And now they heard the butler in the hallway below, and he was announcing dinner, and here she still was, dusty and still in her day dress. Oh, dear.

Sir Oliver stepped backward and lowered his hand. And that was even worse. She felt a stab of disappointment.

"I—that is—y-you were going to wash your face. I shouldn't keep you," he stuttered.

Still unable to speak, she nodded and turned and fled. In her room, she splashed water on her face from her bowl, rubbed her face and hands hastily with her linen towel, ran a comb through her hair, which did little to tame the straying tendrils, and hurried back downstairs, not sure which was worse in the countess's eyes—to come late to dinner or to come disheveled.

Lady Sealey and her godson were waiting in the hall and to Juliana's relief, the countess did not remark on her tardiness nor her appearance. Sir Oliver offered Juliana his other arm, and they went into the dining room. It was only the family tonight, which was a relief.

Dinner was still not quite up to the usual standards of the countess's household. Lady Sealey took a bite of pork and raised her brows. "This is sadly overcooked. Is the cook still seeing monkeys behind every pot?"

The footman who was serving the sauce grimaced, which seemed answer enough.

The countess looked at Sir Oliver. He said, "We had no luck today, but we will keep looking, Godmother."

"My party is tomorrow night," Lady Sealey reminded him, her voice tart.

Juliana thought the baronet winced. "I know. I am going to be sure that all the food in the kitchen and pantries are well secured, and then put out a trap in the attic tonight. I will make a pallet for myself there so that I can be close at hand, in case Mia takes the bait. Perhaps I will have better luck."

"Let us hope," the countess said.

Juliana felt her stomach tighten, and she found it hard to eat her dinner. Not to mention that the food was, as the countess had said, a bit less appetizing than usual.

Lady Sealey put her fork into a serving of raspberry sauce, usually smooth and creamy, and tried to flatten a lump. "My reputation as a hostess is at stake, Oliver. My cook is a bundle of nerves, the maids are breaking china as if they were bulls in the proverbial shop, and I fear that my butler is taking to drink. And as for the footmen, I expect a sauceboat in my lap any night now."

The footman passing the sauceboat fought to control his expression, and Juliana tried not to giggle at the face he made. But really, it was no laughing matter. They simply had to find the monkey!

She looked at Sir Oliver, wishing she could lift the worry she saw in his expression. She knew it was impossible for her to lie, unchaperoned, beside him in the attic to help him watch for the monkey. She would have to hope for the best.

❧

But later, she went to bed still anxious, and it was hard to fall asleep.

When she did at last drift off, it seemed that she had

only just shut her eyes when a sudden crash and a shriek pulled them open again. Heart racing, Juliana sat up straight in bed.

What was that?

Another scream pierced the darkness. Juliana thrust the bedcovers aside, reached for the shawl she had left at the end of the bed and pulled it around her shoulders, then ran for the door. She saw a dim light at the end of the hallway and she hurried toward it. It was the countess's personal maid, candlestick in hand, hastening toward her mistress's bedchamber.

"Where is the countess?" Juliana demanded.

"I heard a dreadful noise. Thumps and bangs, and then a scream. Is it robbers, housebreakers?" Adams replied, her voice thin with fear. "Oh, they must not harm my mistress. I shall throw myself upon them before I allow them to hurt one hair on her head."

Since the dresser was about as big as a sparrow, Juliana made no answer to this but hurried on ahead to Lady Sealey's chamber.

The countess couldn't possibly be sleeping through all this. And indeed, Juliana met her coming out of her bedroom, a wrapper drawn over her nightgown, looking calm but determined and with a candle in hand.

"What do you think it is?" Juliana shivered despite herself.

"Need we ask?" Lady Sealey answered, her tone resigned. "I'm sure it's that dratted jungle creature. We will have no peace night or day until it is back in a cage."

"Oh." Juliana bit her lip, feeling an agony of impatience that she could do nothing. But the scream did not come from the monkey—who had seen it? Probably one of the servants. If she could go—but she could not scandalize the household again by running off alone while wearing her nightgown.

Damn propriety and its awkward rules, anyhow. And where was Sir Oliver?

Two footmen appeared from the other end of the hall, looking faintly ludicrous with trousers pulled up over their nightshirts. One still had on his nightcap, the other had donned his powdered wig, though it sat crookedly on his head. One of them carried a candle, too, the other a stout stick, and they puffed as if they had been running.

"You must go up to the attic and aid my godson," the countess said at once.

"We did, your ladyship, go to the attic, I mean, but 'e ain't there," the first servant said, his voice tremulous. "'Is blankets on the floor were empty. And, and it's awful dark, like, up there."

"And while we was looking about, we 'eard strange thumps, and then some 'un screamed," the second footman added.

"Loud, like—"

"So we thought we'd better come down and see if you 'uns was all right," the second footman finished, still breathing hard and not quite meeting his mistress's eye.

"I see," the countess said, her tone dry. "Your prompt solicitude for my safety is to be commended. But as you see, I'm quite all right, and I did not scream."

They might want to find out who *had* screamed, Juliana thought rebelliously.

Lady Sealey was telling the footmen much the same thing. "Please check on the rest of the servants—" she had begun, when a clump of half-clad females came running down the hall, squealing and clinging together.

"Here, now!" Lady Sealey spoke sharply. "What is it? Stop that noise and speak rationally. Is anyone hurt?"

"'Tis a devil, my lady, Sarah saw a devil, wid 'er own eyes!" exclaimed a maid, who looked a bit devilish herself with her hair pushed up wildly and her eyes wide with fear.

"Nonsense," the countess retorted, her tone stern. "Pull yourself together, girls. Who thinks she saw something? Take a deep breath, stop this silly screeching, and speak slowly. Tell me exactly what you observed."

A girl short of stature, with a face Juliana did not know, perhaps a scullery or kitchen maid, shuddered, her expression hesitant. "I was in me bedroom, and I 'eard an awful noise inside the wall."

Sarah paused for a breath, and the countess waited patiently.

"Then, then I 'eard a scrabbling noise in the fireplace and out popped an imp from the depths of 'ell itself, all black and with red eyes like red 'ot coals! It came scudding across the floor with its wings dragging on the floor behind it, comin' straight for me, trying to steal me immortal soul!" She shrieked again, remembering, and several of the other female servants screamed, too, in sympathy.

"Now then!" the countess said. "You are safe, body and soul, I promise you. It was not an imp or a devil, Sarah. It was only that blasted monkey. Does my godson know?"

"Yes, me lady, 'e met us on the stairs and ran to see the—you're sure it weren't no devil?" Sarah sobbed, and one of the others patted her on the back.

Shaking her head, the older lady looked across at Juliana.

She knew her own eyes had widened. "Mia—she is going through the chimneys!" The system of brick flues that served the many fireplaces in the big house snaked weblike inside the house's walls, and a nimble little monkey would find them a fine highway, now that it was too warm for the household to need any fires regularly, except in the kitchen. Juliana almost groaned. Now what? The baronet would need her help!

She looked at the countess in silent entreaty.

"Oh—" the countess began, then stopped.

A stout figure appeared at the end of the hall, and even Juliana tensed. What on earth?

The gaggle of maids screamed again and clutched at each other for support. One footman lifted his stick, while the other muttered a word Juliana pretended not to hear.

The newcomer's face and hair were covered in black, though she seemed to have made hasty attempts to wipe off the gritty coating, resulting in streaks of a slightly lighter shade. Juliana drew a breath, then released it slowly. Now she recognized the familiar form of the housekeeper beneath her inadvertent disguise.

"Forgive me, milady," the woman said, her voice as stiff as her backbone. "But just as I went to my hearth and bent to look up to see what was making such a racket, a big cloud of soot exploded from inside the chimney and, well, I ended up as you see!"

"Oh, my, how dreadful for you," the countess said, keeping a commendably straight face.

Though she knew it was an embarrassing predicament for the poor woman, Juliana had to bite her lip to keep from giggling. Now, here was the picture of a demon, even if she did have on a most respectable nightdress, buttoned up to her chin and down to her wrists, at least before it had been stained a blotchy black by the accumulated soot of many fires. Even chimneys that were swept regularly were always sooty.

Although having the housekeeper join them should have reassured the maidservants, seeing her turn up in such a state seemed to overset their nerves completely. One maid swooned again, and one seemed to be having a fit of hysterics.

The countess sighed. She turned to her lady's maid. "Get one of my wrappers for Miss Applegate," she instructed.

When the lady's maid returned with a more respectable cover for a nightdress, the countess took Juliana's shawl and gave her the wrap to put on over her nightgown, tying its belt securely herself, and then handed her a candle. "I would send one of the maids with you, but—" Glancing at the sad-looking lot, she shook her head.

"I am needed here," she went on. "I know my godson is a gentleman, in manners as well as birth, so I have no fears for your honor, my dear."

Juliana nodded.

For the first time, it occurred to Juliana that the countess, who always seemed so in command, so serene and so full of energy, was, after all, not a young woman. For a moment her shoulders had sagged just a little, and she looked frail in the flickering candlelight. The veins were blue in her temples, and she looked tired. Had she had any sleep at all? Perhaps more was worrying her than a monkey on the loose and a looming dinner party.

Juliana was going to have to broach the subject of the note to Sir Oliver.

"Go back to bed," she suggested. "Leave the servants to the housekeeper. Sir Oliver and I will find Mia. If she is now covered in soot, at least she will leave a trail."

The countess laughed. "That is true," she said. "I will go back to bed presently. You go and search for monkey prints, my dear."

And, drawing herself up to her usual stately posture, Lady Sealey turned back to the sobbing group of maidservants and the housekeeper, who had run her fingers through her cinder-filled hair until she now resembled a short, stout Medusa.

Juliana did not wait any longer. She sped down the hall toward the back staircase and on to the servants' bedrooms. Where was Sir Oliver?

When she reached the row of small bedchambers, she slowed and tiptoed down the hall, not wanting to scare off the monkey. Most of the doors were open; the servants probably had left their rooms in a rush. She peeked in; the beds had covers thrown hastily back. All of the first rooms were empty of inhabitants, human or simian, and she saw no telltale paw prints as a monkey covered in soot and cinders might leave behind.

Juliana held her candle higher and looked into each room, but no one was there. Perhaps the baronet was ahead of her, already following the monkey's trail. She thought of calling out, but it might alarm the creature. Her light might, too, of course, but she could not grope her way through the darkness, so she had to take that risk. A few candles were lit, here and there, no doubt left behind by the servants, so perhaps the monkey would not be too alarmed by the glow of another candle.

In the next room, but one before the end, she saw it—a line of small black prints on the otherwise clean wooden floor. It was easy to follow the trail over the door, then pick it up again a few feet away and, yes, the monkey had leaped to a table here at the end and gone down a new set of narrow stairs at the opposite end of the hall. Oh, where was Sir Oliver?

The sooty prints, as well as the occasional thin line left by its dusty tail, led to the servants' stairwell, so she made her way there and carefully—this staircase was cramped and steep—wound her way down it, her steps noiseless in her slippered feet. She circled once and then paused.

Several feet below her and crouched in the half-darkness of the stairwell, she saw the baronet, a blanket in his hands ready to throw upon the animal when it emerged. He did not see her; he had eyes only for the steps below him as he waited for the monkey to come forward. Sir

Oliver had put out some pieces of bread as bait farther down on the narrow treads.

And it might have worked, too, Juliana thought. Except that Mia sat upon a cross beam a couple of feet above the baronet's head, silent for once, observing him with as close an attention as Sir Oliver gave to the lower stairs.

What could she do? Juliana bit her lip. If she shouted or even whispered, the monkey would whisk away before Sir Oliver could grab the animal.

Could *she* reach the monkey? Mia was only just below her. But she had nothing with which to hold the creature, and she was wary of being bitten—

Moving very slowly, careful not to make a noise, Juliana set her candlestick down beside her on the step, then untied her wrapper and eased out of the borrowed garment, gathering it into both hands. It took only a minute, and for a wonder, the monkey still concentrated on Sir Oliver and the enticing foodstuffs and had not looked up.

Juliana took one long breath, and then she pounced.

Eight

*I*n her determination not to miss, Juliana put too much energy behind her leap. She reached the monkey before the animal saw her and swooped Mia successfully up into the folds of the linen robe. The monkey gave an angry screech. But then Juliana found she couldn't stop—her own momentum kept her going.

Gasping, she tried to catch herself on the edge of the step, but she couldn't get a grip. Despite it all, she managed to hang on to the struggling monkey, but she could not keep herself from tumbling forward.

She had one glimpse of the startled face of the baronet as he looked up at her in surprise. Then she crashed into him, and they were both falling. The next thing she knew, she was sitting atop his well-shaped form, and he was slipping, too. Now he seemed to have folded in two like a clam's shell, with her tucked neatly inside him. At least she still had the monkey!

Determined to remember what her priorities were, Juliana kept her hold on the animal until they slid to a stop. Then she tried to get up, but she seemed firmly wedged against the baronet's substantial form.

"I'm so sorry," she said. "I seem to be—ah—ouch! That is, I didn't mean to—"

Oliver hoped he had not gone brick red, as he usually did when confronted with a truly beautiful woman. What was it about social encounters, especially with ladies of the more engaging type? Somehow he turned clumsy and awkward as if he were still in short pants, a schoolboy all agape with never the right words to say. And Miss Applegate was surely the most charming and lovely lady he had encountered in many months.

And that was before she had landed in his lap.

This was most improper. Whatever would Lady Sealey say?

He could not help pausing just one more moment to relish the feel of Miss Applegate's warm hips against his thighs, the delightful pressure of her body against his belly—and she was wearing only a thin linen nightdress! If he could lift that light cloth and touch the smooth skin that lay beneath—and what in hell was he doing to think such thoughts about a respectable maiden who would likely faint dead away if she knew the direction his thoughts—and his body—were taking?

Oliver thought he must be blushing even harder, or he damn well ought to be, anyhow, if he had any conscience at all. And hell, his body was going to give him away in other ways, too. He must put her back on her feet and get more distance between them. He tried to move and found that he couldn't pull himself out of the crevice. She had fallen into him and pushed him so firmly into the corner of the narrow stairwell that he was wedged like a cork into a wine bottle. Good God! Were they stuck until some servant could come to help them? They would be the talk of the household once more! What would his godmother say? Oliver bit back a groan.

Juliana stared at the rough wood across from the stair casing. It was that or look into the baronet's face, and it was so close to hers that she did not think she could keep her composure if she looked into his clear gray eyes.

It was unnerving enough to be sitting in his lap, with his legs pushed up so close about hers, holding her almost like a vise, cradling her next to his chest, and except for the distraction of the struggling monkey—she still kept a firm hold on Mia, with both her hands about the bundled up animal—she was intensely aware of his body so close about hers. His legs were corded with muscle, his chest hard and firm, and he put one arm about her. No doubt he only meant to steady her, so that she did not feel even more uncomfortable than she already did.

And if she could not meet his eye, it was only embarrassment, she told herself, nothing else. Nothing like a dreadful awareness that she was clad only in her nightdress, and a thin summer linen one at that, instead of a sturdy woolen winter nightgown. And, oh dear, her body was responding to his nearness again, with that shivery weakness running through her, the ache in her belly leaving her trembling almost literally. She blushed more deeply, hoping he did not notice.

It was all very well for the countess to say that this was a healthy response but what would Sir Oliver think? He did not have to contend with his own body betraying him by—

Juliana paused in mid-thought, suddenly mindful, as their bodies pressed so closely together, of a change where her hips met his thighs. Her belly rippled with the awareness.

Ah, perhaps she had been mistaken . . . perhaps men, too, had bodies which could respond, in what the countess had said was a natural and healthy way to the closeness of a young woman to whom they were attracted? She thought of the reaction of the male animals on the home farm when their females were in season, and then, blushing furiously, tried to turn her thoughts in other directions.

"Did you not know that the monkey was behind you?" she blurted, still not meeting his eye.

"No," Sir Oliver said, his voice sounding strange. He coughed and cleared his throat. "I saw her go down the stairs and then slip out of sight below a step. I thought she was hiding in its shadow. I put the food out to lure her back, and I was waiting to grab her. I cannot think how she managed to double back on me."

He thumped one of the narrow stairs absently as he spoke, and the tread's thud sounded flat. "Unless—" Sir Oliver hit it again with the back of his knuckle. "Unless the imp found a loose board. I daresay the frame of the staircase is hollow, and she simply made her way up the inside. Mia, you imp!"

Juliana thought she must tell the baronet about the maids and their fright, and how one had mistaken a small soot-covered monkey for a devilish apparition, but not just now. It was hard to speak normally when they were forced so close together. And he was barely dressed, she realized; he wore only a linen shirt and his trousers and boots, no neckcloth, no coat or vest. She could see the curve of his jaw and the slight prickling of blond beard where he had not yet been shaved by his valet for the day.

He should have looked uncouth, disgusting even, yet she thought he seemed a magnificent male creature, and again she was aware of how closely she nestled against his thighs, and something inside her belly rippled and her knees felt curiously weak. If she didn't move soon, she might not be able to!

Was the baronet truly attracted to her? It was impossible not to feel pleased at such a possibility. But she still could not look him in the eye, even if her stomach did ruffle with strange waves of sensation. She found that she was breathing faster than usual, and somehow, Sir Oliver seemed to be doing the same.

She bit her lip, and not until the ball of bouncing fabric in her arms jumped higher than usual did she realize that she had almost let go of the monkey. Hastily, she tightened her grip.

"Um, do you have Mia secure?" Sir Oliver asked. Now his voice sounded strangely husky.

Juliana nodded. She did not trust her own voice at all. She tried to clear her throat, then said, in an almost whisper, "I did not mean to fall. I do beg your pardon."

"Not at all. Glad to be of service. I would help you up, but I don't seem to be able to move," he explained.

"Nor I," she agreed.

"I suppose a servant will come along soon," he told her. "Then we will be able to extract ourselves from this corner. It is a bit constraining."

"Yes," she said, wondering why the thought of their release didn't cheer her. Her legs were starting to cramp, but it seemed a small price to pay for being so close to him. But the reminder that their time here was limited gave her the courage, at last, to turn and look into his eyes.

Afterward, she did not remember who shifted closer, or if they both moved at the same time. Only that their lips met as easily as if two magnets had slid effortlessly and inevitably into contact, and his lips were just as firm, just as warm as she had known they would be.

He kissed her, and she clutched the squirming bundle in

her arms and kissed him back, losing herself in the warmth, the sureness, the certainty of his kiss.

His lips were strong, and the warmth of his kiss enveloped her. Juliana felt awash with the delight of his touch. He shifted a little as one arm encircled her shoulder. The other touched her arm, then moved to untie the ribbon on her nightgown.

She seemed unnaturally aware of every faintest touch. The weakness inside her deepened, and the yearning in her belly intensified. If she were not forced to hold on to the monkey, she would have helped him pull open the neck of her gown. Instead she murmured, "Oh, yes!"

This time, it was not Mia's curious little fingers, but Oliver's own who pulled her nightgown open, who pushed the cloth back and slid his hand onto her skin. She felt his light touch like a branding of delicious fire, icy hot, pleasure instead of pain, and instead of sating her hunger, the need inside her grew. She pushed harder against him and felt his tongue slip inside her lips even as his hand gripped her breast. Both sensations took her by surprise, and both were luscious and delectable. She felt that she might melt away, consumed by the flame that leaped inside her, and yet she would not have stopped it if she could have . . .

A minute, an hour, an eternity later, a door banged and footsteps sounded. The baronet drew back.

Juliana sighed in disappointment, then she looked down. To her relief, she still held Mia, who chattered darkly inside the veil of her cloth trap.

With amazing presence of mind, the baronet called down to the servant who was clattering up the steps, "You there!"

Juliana craned her neck to see. She shifted the monkey to cover up the open placket of her nightgown.

It was the first footman. He stopped. Looking confused, he glanced around. "Yes?"

"Up here, quickly."

The footman climbed a few feet, then stopped and stared. "Well, I never!"

"As we were chasing the monkey, we fell down the steps and got stuck—and you're going to help us and forget you saw a lady in such an embarrassing situation, do you understand?" The baronet's tone was firm and even held an underlying sternness that made Juliana's eyes widen and the servant stand up a little straighter.

"Yes, sir, of course. Shall I pull you up, sir?"

"Not yet. First, go back down, grab the first servant you see, and station him or her at the bottom of the steps; tell that person not to allow anyone else to come up, do you understand?"

"Yes, Sir Oliver," said the footman, who obviously didn't.

"Then go to my bedchamber and bring the small cage you'll find there back with you. We will put the monkey securely into her cage, and then you can help us out of this confounded narrow staircase."

"At once, sir."

"And, Gannet, if no one else in the house hears about this, you'll earn yourself half a crown."

"Oh, thank'ee, sir!" The footman brightened and took off at top speed.

Except for Mia's continued scolding, the stairwell was quiet for a moment. Then Sir Oliver drew a deep breath. "I should apologize," he said. "That kiss and, well, I acted improperly. I assure you it will not happen again."

Juliana had just been thinking that such a kiss, such intimate behavior, was the most amazing, delightful occurrence that she had ever experienced. Now the shining glow inside her dimmed, and she wished that dratted footman would hurry up about it. Not sure what to answer, she said nothing and stared again at the wooden frame of the staircase, sure that to look Sir Oliver in the eye would lead to more disaster.

Oliver waited anxiously for her response and was not surprised to receive none. What had possessed him to lose his head to such an extent when she was trapped by the circumstance of her fall and unable to repulse him—she must be horrified at her predicament, perhaps even frightened, and he had not meant to force himself on her. He would not dream of alarming such an innocent young lady, who had just begun to learn about Society and the ways of the world.

But she was so very lovely, and those sweet luscious lips and the way they curved up into that full-lipped smile, and the merry look on her face when she threw him a mischievous glance . . . Oh, stop it, you fool, he told himself. The girl will likely never speak to you again, and here you've gone and scared her to death. She's trapped in your arms and you had to kiss her and caress her like some bloody pirate! And the way she responded . . . Well, perhaps she hadn't been totally repulsed!

He looked anxiously down at Miss Applegate, but she would not meet his gaze. He wished he could take back everything about this final misadventure. Well, perhaps not everything. The feel of her luscious body against his own was so memorable that it would haunt his dreams for nights to come. And if the feel of her smooth breasts and hips and buttocks kept him awake, inflamed his dreams and made his body ache with a longing that he had no way to satisfy, well, it was his own fault. He still had no business frightening an innocent . . . Damn his awkwardness for upsetting her, damn and double damn.

So he leaned his head back against the hard wooden treads of the stairwell and tried not to move beneath her, nor show more than he could help how enticing was the softness of her body against the hard muscle of his own. But still, sweet feminine scents seemed to waft from the nape of her neck as she bent her head away from him. They inflamed his passions even further, and though he gritted his teeth to keep from reaching down to kiss that sweet curve of skin just below the hairline, though he managed not to push her dark strands of hair back from where they strayed, every fiber of his body wanted to gather her closer and never let her go.

Those long kisses, that smooth soft breast, had been just a dip into the vat of temptation, and how he longed to plunge further!

Oh, God, why had she fallen so literally into his lap, waking all his senses to her perfections? He wanted it all now, and he barely knew her. Worse, she barely knew him, and she would be horrified if she had any clue as to what he was thinking.

You must be rational, he told himself. You're no half-wit, no moon calf. You're supposed to be full grown and a gentleman! Yet you can't open your mouth without sounding a fool, you color up like a child when you speak to her, and you've embarrassed her before you've known her three days. What do you expect the lady to think?

Of course she avoids your eye.

He wanted to groan.

He had to do better. He had to convince Miss Applegate he was not witless, not boorish, not the fool he must surely seem to her, and he had to do it soon, before the rest of the male population of London saw what a treasure was about to be dangled before them.

Because he was the one who had to have her!

Juliana kept her gaze fixed on the rough stairwell and bit her lip to keep the tears out of her eyes. The candle she had brought with her was burning low, and it was just as well; she didn't wish the baronet to see her face. Of course he should not have kissed her, should not have touched her—there—but he didn't have to disavow his action with such determination. Had the kiss not pleased him? Had she not kissed him back properly? Well, she hadn't had much practice, hardly any practice at all, if you discounted that time when she was twelve, and the baker's son had grabbed her by the shoulders when she wasn't expecting it and given her a hasty smack, and he'd barely connected with her lips. She would do better with a little practice, she was sure of it!

Her pride bruised as well as her feelings, Juliana held tight to the monkey, whose screeches had at last fallen to angry mutters. She wished she could screech and moan as audibly as the animal; she felt almost as indignant. And Juliana was still just as thoroughly trapped as Mia. What had seemed a delightful position a few minutes ago now felt like torture. Her legs had gone quite numb, and now her back was aching. It occurred to her that Sir Oliver must be in even greater pain. He was bent almost double, and he had her weight on top of his own to bear. Serves him right, she thought, with no attempt at sympathy.

"Hold the monkey," she ordered Sir Oliver, her tone brusque. He put his hand around the monkey in its fabric covering, and Juliana was able to retie the ribbons of her nightgown. Just in time, too.

At last she heard the clatter of the footman returning, and this time he had the cage in his hands. She breathed a sigh of relief. With the footman holding the receptacle, and Sir

Oliver reaching around her to grasp the monkey, they were finally able—with three pair of hands—to thrust a protesting Mia back into her prison. They shut the cage door on her angry shrieks.

"You're fine, Mia," Sir Oliver told the animal. "I'll get you into a larger cage very soon, I promise. For now, however, you cannot continue to terrorize the household." With great care, he double-locked the door, then instructed the footman to set the cage aside, and pull Miss Applegate up.

The servant took Juliana's hands and tugged until at last she broke free of Sir Oliver's involuntary hold and tumbled forward, but her legs were so numb that they would not support her. The footman steadied her, but still, she had to sit on the stairs for a few minutes until she could get the feeling back into her limbs.

"Are you all right?" Sir Oliver's tone was diffident, but he sounded sincere. His gray eyes appeared darker in the dim light of the footman's flickering candle, which he had set down on one of the stair's treads.

She nodded and did not answer. Perhaps, in time, she might forgive him after all. In time.

Sir Oliver also had to be helped up, though the footman staggered under the greater weight of the baronet. They waited a few minutes until strength returned to them both, and when Sir Oliver and Juliana could walk again, Sir Oliver picked up the monkey in her cage, and handed over a coin to the footman.

"You'll get as much again in a week, if there is no gossip," he promised. "Keep an ear out with the rest of the servants and make sure no one is repeating anything that should not be noised about."

"Thank'ee, sir, no one won't 'ear a word, sir," the servant promised. "I'll see to it." He headed off down the hall. With the monkey back in its cage, the baronet had returned the borrowed robe, and she had hastily donned it, so that she was once again somewhat more respectable, but she was still eager to hurry back to her bedchamber and hide herself from curious eyes.

"I will tell my godmother that we have found Mia. Thank you for your help; it was invaluable," Sir Oliver told her, his tone formal.

"You're welcome," she said, her manner just as distant. If he chose to be aloof, she could be cool, as well. "It was the least I could do since Lady Sealey has been so kind to me. Anyone else would have done the same, I'm sure."

Suddenly he was smiling, and the shell of formality vanished as quickly as it had come.

"Ah, no. I cannot imagine Miss Swarts, for example, creeping about the house helping me capture an escaped monkey." His eyes danced with merriment.

Juliana grinned despite herself, then frowned in mock censure. "Are you accusing me of acting in an unladylike manner? That is unkind, sir!"

He took a step forward.

Juliana's frown died, and her heart beat faster. She stared up at him, and something leaped between them—and it all rushed back, the spark of vibrant feeling that seemed to rush over her, the excitement which she had never felt the like of before, and which his mere physical nearness, his presence, his being triggered inside her. She felt a tightness inside her chest and it seemed hard to breathe.

Juliana found that she was gazing up at him and waiting, but he didn't move. He seemed frozen, and once again, the monkey broke the spell.

Mia shrieked.

"I-I had better . . . the monkey, the countess—"

Juliana nodded, just as if his words made some kind of sense.

She took a long breath and became aware that she had been holding it, waiting for him to kiss her again. Damnation! She turned and strode quickly for her bedchamber.

Of course he did not want to kiss her. Why did she think that he did?

Mia was a menace!

After such a troubled night, Juliana slept late, and no one came to wake her. When at last she woke, heavy-eyed and feeling grumpy and low in spirits, she tried to cheer herself with the thought that at least the monkey was no longer a threat to the countess's dinner party.

Oh, heavens, she still had to suffer through the party. For the countess, and yes, for Sir Oliver, too, even if he did not want her affections—and why should she blame him? She was still the impoverished daughter of a worthy but unimportant country gentleman. She sighed. Yes, she would still do her best to be a credit to her hostess and not embarrass her, Juliana told herself.

After she pulled the bell rope for a maid, she washed with the tepid water in her jug. Warm water was a luxury she often did without at home, and the day was temperate enough. She put on one of her muslins, thinking with pleasure of the new gowns that would soon be made up for her.

She paused at the window for a moment. The air that drifted through her open sash felt pleasant, and the street noises that floated up were growing more accustomed to her country ears, the cries of the vendors, the shouts of the drivers trying to make their way through the London traffic, just now even the muffled curses of two ashmen having a dispute whose details Juliana could not make out.

When the maid appeared with tea and a plate piled with

food, Juliana found that, even in a bad mood, she seemed to have appetite enough, so she sat down and ate. At least this time, there was no monkey in hiding to raid her plate.

When she made her way downstairs, the drawing room was empty. Perhaps Lady Sealey was busy with preparations for tonight. Juliana wondered if there was anything she could do to help, or if she would only be in the way. Just as she had decided that she should at least ask, and was preparing to inquire of a servant if the countess was upstairs in her private sitting room, a footman came to the doorway.

"A caller, miss."

Juliana looked up in surprise. "The countess is not here."

"A caller for you, miss. Lady Gemma Sinclair."

Juliana was silent from surprise, but after one frozen instant, she jumped to her feet and gave a credible, she hoped, curtsy.

A dark-haired, blue-eyed young woman, slightly older than Juliana herself, came into the room. She was elegantly dressed in a trim walking costume of gray silk and her hat, a marvelous creation trimmed with ostrich plumes, would have made the twins swoon with envy. Her poise seemed absolute, and her deep blue eyes, so much like Gabriel's— and Juliana's and their father's—were impossible to read.

"W-won't you sit down?" Juliana stammered. "I, Lady Sealey, that is, I'm not sure where the countess is just now b-but I am happy to see you. I am Miss Juliana Applegate."

To Juliana's surprise, Lady Gemma reached across and gripped her hand for a moment before taking a seat. "Of course. I would have offered you my hospitality, you know, after Gabriel and Psyche were so beset with the measles— poor Circe is having a hard time of it, though I think she will recover without any serious complications, and their servants are getting better, too—but Lady Sealey had made her generous offer. She does have ample guest quarters here, so I'm sure you are comfortable."

"It was very kind of her," Juliana agreed. This was her half sister, then. She could not keep herself from staring. The likeness was strong, if one knew to look for it, yet elusive, too. The eyes were the same, but the nose and mouth less so.

What did this somewhat intimidating woman think about having such a hither-to-unknown and impoverished relative thrust upon them? Juliana glanced down at the faded jonquil pattern of her gown, which had seen three seasons and showed it all too well. It was hard not to compare her garment with the fashionable elan of Lady Gemma's attire.

There was a moment of silence. Juliana swallowed, and her mouth seemed dry. "You must think it strange—" she began.

"I suppose—" Gemma started at the same time, and they both paused.

Gemma smiled, which made her seem less awe-inspiring. "I know this is an awkward situation. When I first received Gabriel's letter, I was as shocked by the news as you must have been when you first learned of our connection. The countess has kindly invited me and my husband to the dinner party tonight, so I will see you again later. However, I thought it would be easier for you, for both of us, if I came to call today so that we could meet and talk privately first."

"Oh, yes," Juliana agreed, thinking what a strain it would have been to meet this unknown half sibling for the first time amid a crowd of strangers. "That was most considerate of you. You must feel that—that—" She looked down again at her dress.

"Do you know my history?" Gemma's voice sounded gentle.

Surprised, Juliana looked up.

"I was sent away immediately after my birth, so I never knew my mother. I was raised by a kind lady until I was five, and when she died suddenly, I was dumped into the unfeeling arms of a poorly run foundling home."

Juliana knew that her mouth had fallen open; she shut it hastily.

"Happily, a year later, my—our—father learned of my perilous plight and arranged for me to be taken away to a respectable girls' school where I stayed until I was one and twenty. At that time I received a letter from my mother, and eventually I met my brother, Gabriel, and learned more about my family history, and that, indirectly, led to Gabriel's long search for our real father, and thus to finding you."

Juliana blinked; she was still staring.

"So I have not always had an easy life, either, and you must not think that I am not ready to consider you family."

The gentle voice and clear-eyed gaze had somehow loosened the knot in Juliana's chest. She drew a deep breath, at last, and found that her eyes had dampened. She blinked hard. "That is very generous of you."

"Despite the—ah—unusual circumstances and the mistakes that our parents may have made—and they paid for them, did they not!—we are still related, and as Gabriel has said, we should be as kind to each other as we may. Even if we cannot acknowledge the full connection to the world, we are still kin, and in private we shall know the truth."

Again, she held out her hand, and Juliana reached to clasp it. For a moment, they clung to each other.

If her new half siblings were as generous and as honorable as they seemed, then she was fortunate, indeed, Juliana thought.

They talked for almost an hour. Juliana told Gemma about her sisters at home, about her father, about growing up on the small estate in Yorkshire. Gemma told Juliana more about her own childhood and explained that she planned to travel north to meet her birth father. "I have no memory of my mother," Gemma said, her voice sad. "So it is a great gift that I can now meet and perhaps get to know my father."

Juliana, who had lost her mother too young but retained many loving memories, felt a lump in her throat. Perhaps she had not appreciated her own blessings. Her home might have been less than rich and the dishes on the dinner table few in number, but she had had, for years, two parents present to love her, and Gemma had had none. Juliana's faded dress seemed much less important.

Lady Sealey came into the drawing room in time to smile and welcome Gemma before their visitor said good-bye.

"Forgive me for not being here to greet you, my dear. I've been checking on my cook and making sure that my servants are recovered from their state of nervous hysteria, so that my dinner tonight will be back to its usual standards, now that the monkey that has turned my household upside down has at last been recaptured."

"A monkey? In your house?" Gemma raised her brows in surprise.

Laughing, Juliana told the story of Mia and her escape, which led to too many mentions of Sir Oliver. If she could not totally contain a slight tendency to blush, she tried not to seem too aware of a tendency to linger over his name. It was obvious that he was not interested in her, she thought, feeling a return of her earlier frustration.

After the monkey had been explained, Gemma took her

leave at last, promising that tonight Juliana would meet Matthew, Gemma's husband.

"I'm sorry to leave you on your own so long, my dear," Lady Sealey said, pulling the bell rope and telling the maid who appeared to bring tea.

Juliana realized with a start that she had forgotten to offer Gemma any refreshment. Oh, dear, she would never make a proper London lady. But the countess was speaking to her again.

"Did you find Gemma agreeable?" Lady Sealey asked.

"Oh, yes!" Juliana exclaimed. "She is so kind and welcoming; I liked her excessively! And she is going north next week so that she can meet my father and my sisters. I shall have to write Maddy again."

Lady Sealey poured a cup of tea and handed it to Juliana. "Gemma and Matthew will be at the party tonight. I had a note from Psyche. She doesn't feel ready to leave Circe just yet, but in a week or so, I'm sure you'll be able to spend more time with Gabriel and his wife, as well."

Since she still found her half brother, her titular cousin, intimidating, this delay didn't distress her too much, Juliana thought, though she made an appropriate reply to the countess.

A footman appeared in the doorway. More callers? Juliana swallowed a sip of tea. Now what?

But he spoke to the countess. "A package for Miss Applegate, milady. I have sent it up to her chamber."

"Ah, that will be your dress," Lady Sealey said. "Good. Mrs. Whitson did not disappoint us. You will look lovely tonight, I'm sure."

Her new—well, newly remade—dinner dress, Juliana remembered with pleasure. Oh, how wonderful to have a new dress, and how generous everyone was being to her.

She tried to thank Lady Sealey again, but the countess laughed and shook her head.

"Why don't you go up and have a rest before you change for dinner?" Lady Sealey suggested. "I plan to do the same; it will be a long evening, and we will need all our energy."

Since she had slept late and done little since, Juliana thought she could easily handle a dinner party, even with lots of guests, but she didn't like to point out that she was younger and more vital than her hostess, so she agreed with the proposition meekly. She would have liked to ask where Sir Oliver was; she had not seen him since she had come downstairs today, but it didn't seem ladylike to inquire.

So she went slowly up the big staircase to her bedchamber and unwrapped the dress that she would wear for the evening, and sighed in appreciation of the smooth silk and the new trim that the seamstress had so skillfully added.

She held it up in front of her and stared at her reflection in the looking glass, amazed at the reflection that stared back at her. Who was this young lady whose fair skin and dark hair seemed enhanced by the clear blue of the dress? And her eyes seemed bluer than ever, set off by the hues of the dress. Oh, what a delight to have something so pretty to wear!

Juliana wished all her sisters had such a lovely new treat, but surely, in time, they would also have charming surprises, too, and if not, she would share her bounty with them. So, easing the slight pricking of her conscience that she had been singled out, that she was the first, she allowed herself a few minutes just to enjoy the unaccustomed luxury of a new dress . . .

And when at last she sighed and hung the dress carefully in her clothespress, laughing a little at herself for being such a ninny, she wondered what to do with the hours before it was time to dress for the evening.

She had no desire for a nap. But one thing she needed to do was write to Maddy, Juliana thought. She could tell her about the amazing bounty of her new wardrobe, about meeting Gemma, and about Gemma's plan to come north. Maddy would certainly want to know about that! Maddy would be at work at once, beating their threadbare rugs, setting their maid to work scrubbing the well-worn oak floorboards, while she turned out the sitting room so that all would look as neat and clean as possible before the visitor arrived.

If the countess was in her room, Juliana could slip back down to the drawing room without disturbing anyone and make use of her desk again, with its supply of writing material. Making up her mind, Juliana went out and descended the steps. But when she reached the drawing room and opened the door, she paused.

Instead of dozing comfortably in her bed, Lady Sealey stood at the desk, and her expression looked contorted. Ripping a sheet of paper in two, she tossed it into the desk and banged the lid shut.

Unsure what she should do, Juliana froze. Should she retreat and pretend that she had not seen the countess's moment of rage? Even though she had only known the countess a few days, she had never seen her lose control in such a way.

What was the paper she had torn up? Was it another threatening note? What did it say?

Someone touched her shoulder. Juliana gasped.

"Hush," a familiar voice said. "We will slip away quietly—"

But even as her mind registered the by now well-known

voice of Sir Oliver, it was too late. Lady Sealey looked up and saw them standing in the doorway.

"You may as well come in, children," she said, her voice tired, but once again under control.

Biting her lip, although she had done nothing untoward, Juliana did as she was bid. The baronet followed. They obeyed their hostess's gesture and took seats across from her after she sank down onto one of the silk brocaded chairs.

"Summon the maid and ask for tea, Oliver, if you would," the countess added.

Oliver returned to the bell rope, and, when the servant appeared in the doorway, he made the request, then returned to take his seat.

Juliana stared at Lady Sealey. This time, the older lady's worry was evident, and the lines in her forehead seemed more pronounced.

"What is wrong, Godmother?" Sir Oliver demanded, the concern in his voice easing some of the bluntness of his words. "I know you've had something on your mind for days, and it hasn't just been the wretched monkey. You know I would do anything for you, but I can't help if I don't know what the problem is."

Juliana stood abruptly. "I should probably leave you two alone," she blurted. "You may wish to discuss . . . private matters, and I have only just, that is, you have been so very kind, but I realize I am a new acquaintance, and Sir Oliver has known you all his life. But please do believe that I would do anything in my power to aid you."

Lady Sealey smiled up at her. "Oh, sit down, dear girl. I trust you. You have an honorable spirit, I know that about you already. I am a good judge of character, you know. At least, I have always believed it to be so. I may have made one mistake, sad to say."

Juliana obeyed, and they were silent as she looked off

from them for an instant. Although she seemed to gaze at the far side of the big drawing room, Juliana had the sense that Lady Sealey looked much farther away than that, past years and miles to scenes far distant. Juliana glanced aside to Sir Oliver, who lifted his brows and smiled at her, though his look of concern did not vary.

They both remained silent until the footman brought in a tea tray and set it on the table before them. Then the countess roused herself to pour three cups of tea. Not until they were cautiously sipping the hot brew did she speak again.

"Someone wishes me harm, you see, and I do not know who it may be."

Nine

Juliana almost choked on her mouthful of tea, and Sir Oliver set his cup down so quickly that the liquid sloshed over the rim.

"What do you mean, Godmother? Someone is making threats? Who? What does the person say?"

"I don't mean to alarm you, my dear boy. I speak only in a general way. The threats are vague and surely only metaphorical, and the notes unsigned. I thought it was some wag's silly banter, at first, surely not one of my friends, but the notes kept coming."

"May I see them?" Oliver's expression was grim. He did not appear to think such a missive at all amusing.

"I burned the first ones as beneath contempt and certainly beneath any intelligent person's notice. The most recent arrived today—" She rose and walked over to the desk, opening the inlaid rosewood lid and retrieving the pieces of paper which Juliana had witnessed her ripping. She brought the fragments back to hand to Oliver. He laid them on the table at the edge of the tea tray, pushing aside a plate of sandwiches to make room to put them back into order so that the note could be read. Juliana could not help but eye them, as well.

The handwriting was large, with lots of loops and blotted with ink, and somehow suggested a barely literate hand.

Oliver seemed to think the same. "The author seems poorly educated," he pointed out. " 'You will get yur just deserts!' I doubt he is offering you a trip across Africa."

"Nor a plate of sweetmeats," the countess agreed, her tone dry. "No matter how the writer spells it."

"Do you have any idea who could wish to do you injury?" Oliver asked, cutting to the heart of the matter.

Juliana had been thinking much the same thing, though she would never have had the nerve to ask it. She waited to hear the countess's answer.

The countess sighed. "That's the problem, Oliver. I really don't. Oh, there are jealous cats among the ladies of the Ton, I have no doubt, the occasional matron who envies my dress on a certain occasion or thinks my weekly Salon during the season more prestigious than hers, or a gentleman who thinks I might have spurned his advances—"

At her age? Juliana blinked and hoped she had hidden her surprise in time. Lady Sealey was still very handsome, with her silver hair and high check bones, there was no doubt . . . Juliana put aside her private musing and pulled her attention back to the discussion.

"Perhaps," Oliver was saying, "you would make a list of anyone you could think of who might have a grievance against you?"

The countess grimaced. "I suppose I could, though I can think of few more depressing pursuits. And it isn't as if we expect this person to actually do anything, dear boy. The missives are only a minor annoyance."

Sir Oliver nodded, but his tone was determined. "Yes, but it's just as well to be prepared. How long has this been going on?"

Thinking, she pursed her lips. "At least a fortnight—no, I think it has been more like three weeks."

"Give it some thought, then; you don't have to complete the list this minute."

"Anyhow, perhaps just now you should take that rest you spoke of, before you have to change for dinner," Juliana gathered her nerve to suggest. There was a hint of strain in the countess's eyes that she didn't like, a touch of weariness that one didn't customarily see, and she felt this whole matter was worrying their hostess more than the lady would admit. Who could be comfortable with some unknown menace lurking in the shadows, making vague and ominous threats? Perhaps the countess was not sleeping as well as usual.

"Yes, as I said, you can work on the list later," Sir Oliver agreed. "And, Godmother, remember that we are here and always at your call. You are not alone!"

She gave them her slow smile. It lightened the somber look of her eyes and eased the lines in her forehead that had lately become more pronounced than usual. "You're a dear boy, Oliver, and I thank you both. It was good of you to come and visit in the first place, and I am aware you have lingered mostly to cheer me. I'm sure this is much ado about nothing, but I do appreciate your support. Very well, I shall go and lie down for a while before I dress for dinner. Be sure to put those wretched scraps away so that no one sees them!"

She swept out of the drawing room with more of her usual air of confidence, and Juliana hoped they had provided her with some reassurance.

Juliana turned back to bestow her own smile upon Sir Oliver. "That was nicely done of you! She's obviously more worried that she will admit. Who on earth can be sending those dreadful letters?"

Sir Oliver glanced at the doorway to be sure that Lady Sealey had gone, then shook his head. "I can't imagine. My godmother is never unkind or vindictive, so how she can have made such an enemy I can't conceive."

"Nor can I, though I haven't known her long, of course," Juliana agreed. "Sir Oliver, if it is just a matter of the letters causing her distress, can we instruct the servants not to deliver them?"

"Do you think the servants would recognize them?" He raised his brows.

"The handwriting seems quite distinctive," she argued.

He turned the pieces of the torn paper over so that they could look at the side of the letter where the countess's name and address had been written. Juliana was disappointed to see that the handwriting here was smaller and less individual.

"Maybe not," she said, sighing. "Well, it was a thought."

"A good thought," he said quickly. "But I'm afraid we couldn't count on the servants to distinguish the handwriting. And we can't keep half the countess's mail back! It would be hard even for us to screen all the mail, not to mention quite audacious and impractical, too, with the post arriving several times a day."

Feeling glum at the loss of what had first seemed a promising solution, Juliana nodded. "So we are back to searching for a likely motive for the letter writer, then, which brings us to someone who must dislike the countess a good deal. But she seems such a kind and generous person, so who could have taken her in such aversion?"

Sir Oliver frowned. After a moment, he said slowly. "That may be the hardest part of the puzzle, but we shall have to make an attempt to find out."

Juliana felt a thrill of gratification that he seemed willing to accept her help once again. She smiled up at him, and they talked for a time about what they might do.

She was so beautiful, Oliver thought, her blue eyes the most amazing color, like deep water in a clear mountain lake. For a moment, all capacity for useful thought deserted him, and he simply wanted to lie at her feet and gaze up into those enchanting eyes . . . He swallowed hard and dropped the pieces of the notes he had been holding. As he bent to retrieve them, he knew his face had reddened.

Why did he turn into such a birdbrain around lovely women? How would he ever be able to woo a woman with any sort of charm or polish if he could not conquer this dreadful curse? Bad enough that he tended to flush like a schoolboy, but to drop things, to stutter, to turn all thumbs and left feet when he was in a winsome lady's presence . . . And when he tried to escort a lady for whom he had particular admiration upon the dance floor, he had as lethal an effect as a wooden horse invading Troy—but she was speaking again.

Hastily, Oliver pulled his attention back to the lovely, intelligent, bewitching creature sitting beside him, who gazed at him now with a hint of a question in her beautiful eyes.

"I said, what do you think we should do next?"

"Well—" He reached for his tea cup to give himself time to think, but gripped the cup too tightly. He released it quickly but distinctly heard the thin china clink ominously. Had he broken it? Oh, hell.

She was still waiting for him to answer.

"I think we must observe closely the people at the party tonight."

"Surely you don't think that the letter writer will be one of her own friends?"

Oliver wished he could take back such a hen-witted answer. "No, probably not, but we still might pick up a hint of information. And we must start somewhere."

Happily, she did not point out how foolish this sounded. Instead, she glanced at the French clock on the mantel and, with what almost seemed—he could hope, at least—was a touch of regret, said, "Perhaps I should go up to change; I would not wish to be behind the time. I shall see you at dinner, then."

"I look forward to it," he attempted, gallantly, and then rather spoiled the effect by bumping the tea tray when he rose too hastily, sending the dishes on it rattling and shaking.

She ignored the clatter and smiled at him before she curtsied and departed.

As she walked away, he bowed, managing not to break any more of the countess's china as he did so. When the room was empty, Oliver drew a deep breath, wiped his no doubt flushed face, cursed his wretched fate, and tried to pull his mind back to the question of the unknown letter writer.

Lost in thought, Juliana climbed the wide staircase slowly. No doubt, she should have been putting her mind to the countess's problem, but since she knew none of Lady Sealey's friends or acquaintances and certainly none of her enemies, if any, that seemed a hopeless exercise. So she didn't feel any guilt that her thoughts lingered over the baronet's face and form, and it seemed quite amazing how his appeal continued to increase with their growing friendship. Even his occasional awkwardness or periodic blushes only served to endear him more. She remembered the enforced intimacy of their time on the staircase and smiled to herself. Yes, he had apologized for the kiss, for his intimate touch, but perhaps he had felt compelled to. She was increasingly confident that he was not unaffected by her presence. . . .

When she reached her chamber, she found that one of the maids was preparing a hip bath for her with warm water and rose-scented soap, and Juliana was delighted with such a luxurious treat. She bathed and washed her hair, toweled dry and brushed it out till the dark waves shone with a lustrous gleam, donned her best undergarments, then at last put on the silk gown.

The maid did up the delicate hooks in the back and adjusted the skirts so that they sat just so, and Juliana turned to the looking glass.

She almost gasped. The young lady who gazed back at her seemed a stranger. Certainly Juliana had never looked so elegant. The smooth deep blue silk made a faultless enhancement for her dark blue eyes, and the white lace that edged the bodice and the white silk roses that trimmed the flounce of the skirt were perfect accents.

The maid pulled her hair up and coiled it into a soft loop on the back of her head, and Juliana put in the pearl ear drops that had been her mother's and hung the small matching pearl pendant around her neck. She felt very grand. She lingered for one last quick glance into the glass before she prepared to go downstairs. Would Sir Oliver think she looked pretty? She was human enough to hope he did.

Downstairs, the first guests were arriving and being shown into the drawing room. Normally, Juliana's nerves would be aquiver, but tonight, she was more concerned with the countess. While it was unlikely that the person who had been bedeviling her could be one of her friends, still, Sir Oliver was right, they should take no chances.

So she must keep her eyes and ears open, and with that

to occupy her thoughts, she had no time to indulge in her own nervousness. And besides, she had a lovely new dress to lend her confidence, so this time, unlike the tea party, she did not have to feel like a poor relation. It was a heady sensation!

So she nodded politely when introductions were made, concentrated on remembering names and faces, and made courteous replies to the finely clad ladies in their silks and satins and the proper gentlemen in their dark evening suits and spotless linen who gradually assembled in the drawing room. If there was any hint of animosity for their hostess among the assembled guests, Juliana was not skilled enough to detect it. But she continued to smile and kept her senses alert.

Lady Sealey herself wore an amazing gown of lavender satin trimmed in silver embroidery, with a dazzling diamond choker about her neck and diamond ear drops. She looked as beautiful as ladies a generation younger, Juliana thought loyally, even though she still looked somewhat tired. But the countess smiled and chatted with her guests as they were announced and did not allow anyone else to see that she might be distracted.

Sir Oliver must have come down early. He had been in the drawing room when Juliana came in, although she had not had the chance to speak to him. Still she was pleased that he was taking his role of protector so seriously. As usual, however, while his gaze went often to the countess, his tall form remained surrounded by several young ladies of high fashion and great determination, all chatting and smiling up at him, obviously hoping to capture his interest. So it gave Juliana a no doubt ungenerous but gratifying moment when Sir Oliver firmly parted the circlet of ladies who encompassed him and strode across the room to speak to her.

"Have you heard"—he glanced at the nearest guest, a stout gentleman in a green evening suit, and lowered his voice a little—"anything interesting?"

Juliana shook her head. "No. I do wish I knew what we were looking, or listening, for!"

"I know. It's like the children's game where they put a blindfold on you and let you search through a bowl of dry oatmeal for some unknown treasure," he agreed, his tone glum.

"At least there is no monkey on the loose," Juliana pointed out, grinning. "At least, I hope not!"

A nearby matron gave her a startled look, and Juliana lowered her voice even more.

Sir Oliver smiled back. "No, Mia is quite safe up in my room, and as secure as any Tower prisoner. She should not escape again. I'm taking her down to Lady Sealey's country estate tomorrow. Indeed—"

Looking stricken, he paused.

Juliana turned her head to see what had distressed him. A tall, spindly man had detached himself from a group of gentlemen and was making his way through the clumps of guests to join them. Who was he? Was it because of this man that Oliver's mood had changed?

The butler appeared in the doorway. "Dinner is served, milady."

Oliver gulped.

"Who is he? What concerns you?" Juliana asked quickly, keeping her voice soft because the man was still bearing down upon them. To Juliana's alarm, the stranger paused before them and made a stiff bow.

"If you would do me the honor of an introduction, Oliver, my boy, perhaps Miss Applegate would allow me the pleasure of escorting her into dinner."

Sir Oliver gave Juliana an apologetic glance and dutifully

said, "Miss Applegate, this is the esteemed biologist Rodney Needham."

Juliana, who had been hoping that Sir Oliver would take her in to dinner, since Lady Sealey did not stand on ceremony at her dinner parties, had to hide her disappointment.

The scientist beamed at Juliana and offered her his arm, and she had little choice except to smile politely, throw a speaking glance toward Sir Oliver himself, and allow Needham to guide her into the dining room. Why ever was this man interested in her?

As they joined the parade of couples strolling leisurely toward the staircase and on down to the formal dining room on the next floor, he was speaking. She tried to pull her wits together.

"Are you enjoying your visit to London, Miss Applegate?"

"Yes, indeed," she answered. "Lady Sealey has been very kind."

"You are fortunate to have secured the patronage of such a great lady," he told her. "That is the way Society works, you know; a young person must form a connection with someone higher and more well placed."

"As Sir Oliver does with you?" she was bold enough to inquire. "I mean, since he is lucky enough to have you as mentor as he pursues his studies?"

Mr. Needham had a particularly long neck and rather weak chin, an unfortunate combination. Looking gratified at her remark, he stretched his neck and appeared to preen, which made him look like some type of bird, perhaps a crane, well suited for one of his own studies. Juliana tried not to giggle.

"I admit that I am considered one of the most respected biologists of the day," he said, his tone pompous. "Since Oliver's graduation from university, I am pleased to be able to give him the occasional hint as to the direction his research should take."

Remembering that his last hint had been to murder the little monkey, Juliana lost her impulse to laugh.

Mr. Needham added, "Of course, you have an added advantage, do you not?"

"I do?" Juliana asked, not sure what he implied.

"I understand you are a relation of Lord Gabriel Sinclair?" He gave her a significant look just as they reached the dining room.

Juliana was glad to have the distraction of finding their place cards at the long table, which tonight had surely all its leaves added for the big party. So that was why she was suddenly such desirable company! Of course, she should have realized. To her great relief, she was not seated next to Mr. Needham—she made a mental note to fervently thank Lady Sealey for that small thoughtfulness—so the biologist left her, promising to seek her again out in the drawing room after dinner. Juliana took her seat, hoping for once that dinner was as long and drawn out as any such meal could be.

Since Lady Sealey's cook had apparently been restored to his normal state of competency, and the food and all the courses were delicious, the dinner did indeed take several hours to complete. Juliana chatted with the young men on either side of her, enjoyed the excellent dishes, and occasionally glanced at Sir Oliver farther up the table, aware that he, too, sometimes looked her way. She wasn't sure where Mr. Needham sat and tried hard not to find out.

Since her dinner partners seemed quite inoffensive, and she could not—without serious breach of good manners—speak to anyone else, and anyhow, she had no wish to shout across the table, little could be done on the matter of the letters until the dinner guests returned to the drawing room.

So when the last course was complete and Lady Sealey collected the women at the table with a practiced glance and led them back to the drawing room, leaving the men to their port and male conversation, Juliana was determined to be alert.

Lady Sealey sat in a comfortable chair and spoke with several friends. She seemed to be quite at ease. Juliana drifted among the other women and listened to discussions of fashion and the theater, babies and lovers, illness and bad drains, and other topics of great import, but nothing that denoted any possible threat or any hint of animosity toward their hostess. She hoped to do the same when the men joined them.

But any thoughts she'd had of continuing to casually circulate through the room and listen to the guests chat was circumvented before it had begun by the persistence of Mr. Needham, who once more appeared in front of her, seemingly determined to hang on her sleeve and dog her steps for the rest of the evening.

Perhaps she should have felt flattered; he obviously expected her to feel gratified at his attentions. Instead she experienced a strong sense of frustration. What on earth could the man want from her? Juliana became more and more annoyed. Even if she was supposed to be a cousin of the rich and powerful Sinclair family, still—

After being forced to listen to two long, gory, and much-too-detailed stories of his research on African zebras, Juliana nodded and decided to be blunt, since hints that he might wish to share his expertise with some of the other guests had failed to detach him from her side.

"Are you a personal friend of my cousin?" she asked.

"Ah, I fear I have not yet had the pleasure of meeting Lord Gabriel Sinclair," he told her, managing to make that loss sound like a great deprivation for her so-called cousin.

Juliana wondered if that was what he hoped to gain, an introduction. Somehow, Needham didn't seem like the social climbing sort.

"You must be a great admirer of Lord Gabriel," she suggested, still feeling her way.

"Indeed," he agreed. "I have heard that Lord Gabriel and his brother the marquess are great supporters of scientific research. They have been known to make grants to support studies in the field. My research does not come cheap, you must realize. It is a costly process to capture animals in the wild and bring them all the way from Africa! And since the marquess and his wife are often abroad, it is much easier to approach Lord Gabriel on the subject."

So that was it! Juliana hid her grin. At last. "I will be sure to mention your name to my cousin the next time I see him," she told the scientist, hoping that would convince him to go away.

Unfortunately, her words seemed only to fuel his determination. Needham at once started a long account of his research into the spinal columns of pregnant zebra mares. Two ladies who had wandered into earshot looked at him with horror and retreated at once. Juliana wished she could do the same. She looked around wildly and caught Sir Oliver's eye.

The baronet had been backed into a corner between several potted plants, and three young ladies were waving their fans, batting their lashes and plying him with laughing anecdotes whose details Juliana could not hear. There was much merry laughter from the ladies, but, to her mild surprise, he did not blush. Sir Oliver only smiled politely at the trio.

However, when Juliana threw him a look of mute supplication, he reacted at once. Somehow, he managed to extricate himself from his apparently hopeless entanglement. With a few long strides, he appeared at her side.

Just as Mr. Needham was extracting the brain from its casing and reversing the path of the blood flow—Juliana hoped her excellent dinner did not decide to reverse itself as well—Sir Oliver said, "Excuse me, sir, but Miss Applegate looks flushed; I think she may be too warm. Would you like to walk over by the open window, Miss Applegate?"

"Oh, very much, please!" Juliana answered, reaching to take his arm. "Pray excuse me, Mr. Needham. And I will certainly remember to tell Lord Gabriel about your excellent research."

"Yes, but, I could escort you to the window. Miss Applegate, you did not yet hear about my studies on the zebra's spleen!"

To her enormous gratitude, Sir Oliver had turned, and they were striding rapidly away. Juliana clutched his well-muscled arm and hoped she never again in her lifetime heard mention of a zebra's spleen.

"You have saved my life, I promise you," she muttered. "That man is a menace to a lady's health."

Sir Oliver raised his brows.

"I admire many types of scientific research," she explained, "Just do not tell me about animal dissection after I have just enjoyed a large dinner, I do beg of you."

"I thought you were turning a delicate shade of green."

He did not pause until they stood before the open French windows that looked over the garden behind the big mansion. A light breeze blew, and the feathery touch of the air upon Juliana's face calmed her roiling stomach. She drew a deep breath.

"In fact, I don't really care to hear about it, at all. Please tell me you don't plan to kill Mia?"

She looked up at him. They stood in the shadow of the

draped alcove that housed the tall windows, partially hidden from the view of the other guests. It gave her the tantalizing illusion of privacy, just she and the baronet all alone. His eyes were hard to read in the dimness, his face darkened, but she knew its lines so well by now that she did not need bright light to map it. She had memorized the strong line of his nose, the chiseled shape of his chin with its slight indention, the well-cut lips . . . Something inside her seemed to melt, and she felt the same shivery delight, the sweet ache that his nearness had provoked in her during the bedroom romp and the accident on the stairwell.

A natural reaction, the countess had told her. Natural, was it? Perhaps, but it seemed stronger every time it occurred. How did one deal with it? It was like having a volcano suddenly erupting in the middle of one's bedroom—

She was still holding his arm, and she could feel the strength of him, the firmness of his frame, the solid muscle beneath his warm, sun-bronzed skin. Everything about him delighted her, incited that strange reaction inside her.

Did he feel the same? If they took one step back, they would be out of view of the rest of the room. Was he looking at her as intently as she stared up at him? Did his heart beat faster, too? Did his belly ache, and did parts of him that he barely understood seem to develop new yearnings?

No, men were different, likely men knew all about such mysterious things . . . and now surely he had bent forward. . . .

Juliana lifted her chin, sure that he was going to kiss her—

"Well, really!" a female voice said. "A fine thing!"

Jolted back to reality, Juliana gasped, then turned to confront the speaker. When had she approached them? A handsome woman somewhat past the first blush of youth, she had fair hair and narrow eyes of faded blue partly hidden by spectacles worn on the edge of her sharp nose. Her dress of ivory silk was well made, the neckline higher cut than normal. And she stared at Juliana as if she were a cat who had invaded a robin's nest, and the stranger were the mother robin.

"Pardon?" Juliana said.

"Perhaps you don't know who I am?" The lady stared down at her, or tried to stare down at her, they were much of a height. "I am Miss Stanwood, of the Berkshire Stanwoods, an old and most distinguished family!"

The other woman's tone sounded openly hostile, and she made her announcement as if Juliana should be awed by the name. Was she supposed to drop a curtsy, like a peasant to a queen? What was this about?

"I see." Juliana tried to remember if they had been introduced earlier. "I am Miss Juliana Applegate, of Yorkshire. I am staying with Lady Sealey."

She glanced toward Sir Oliver, perplexed to see that the baronet, who had been quick to come to her aid with the persistent Mr. Needham, now seemed strangely silent. He also had a curious expression on his face.

"Yes, I heard as much, but you are not an old acquaintance, I take it? By contrast, my mother and the countess have known each other since they were girls. My mother would be here tonight, but for the sad fact that her gout is troubling her again. You are fortunate that Lady Sealey is so good-hearted as to have taken you in."

She made it sound as if the countess had rescued Juliana, like a stray kitten, from the gutter. Juliana felt even more irritated. It was bad enough to lose a precious opportunity for a kiss with Sir Oliver, but to be berated by a stranger for no logical reason—

This was so ill-mannered that Juliana was now annoyed

enough to lose her own self control. "I hardly think that is your concern," she said shortly.

"Oh, really? When one finds one's fiancé about to kiss an unknown woman, is that not my concern?"

Fiancé?

Ten

Juliana felt as if she had fallen through the ice atop a frozen pond. If she had plunged into frigid water, she could not have been more shocked, more chilled to her very bone.

Betrothed? Sir Oliver was betrothed to this termagant, and he had not told her?

Time seemed to have stopped. The rest of the party appeared strangely silent. Surely the other ladies and gentlemen still chatted, the stout foreign gentleman who leaned close to Lady Sealey still spoke into her ear, but Juliana hardly noticed the hum of conversation. The room seemed almost entranced, like a storyteller's spinning of some fairy-tale. Far away, Juliana could hear a horse's shrill whinny and a street sweeper's cry.

Beside her, she heard Sir Oliver speak, but it was an incoherent mumble, and she did not make out the words. He cleared his throat and tried again.

"I did not—I have never proposed to you, Miss Stanwood." He looked not flushed as he did when he had colored up in the past in Juliana's presence, just somewhat grim about the lips, but he spoke with determination. "You know that I have not offered for your hand."

Lifting her brows, Miss Stanwood smiled at him and managed to look superior and forgiving at the same time. "I understand your natural reticence, Sir Oliver, and I make allowances for it. Do not distress yourself. I forgive you. However, we do need to make an announcement soon; my mother is beginning to worry."

Juliana felt her head whirl. Were the two engaged or not? "I don't understand. You can't just assume you are betrothed!"

"Of course we are going to be wed. My mother and Sir Oliver's mother always planned it so," the redoubtable Miss Stanwood announced calmly.

"I honor my dear mother's memory, Miss Stanwood, but she died when I was ten years old," Sir Oliver argued. "I cannot take such marriage plans, as you call them, seriously. I was riding hobby horses and you were playing with dolls when my mother joked about such ideas over teacups with your mother."

"Actually, you carried one of my dolls off to Camelot on your noble steed and then rescued her from a dragon, all before tea and biscuits. It was very romantic." Miss Stanwood seemed lost in her memories.

"That's as may be, but we're not ten years old any longer," Sir Oliver pointed out. "And we are certainly not betrothed, so you might as well stop telling people that we are."

"I don't know why you are being so obstinate, Oliver," Miss Stanwood argued. "You know my mother went over our bloodlines, and we would make an excellent match.

Why, my great-uncle and your great-great-aunt are both descendants of Harold the Unready."

"He's not the only one," Sir Oliver muttered under his breath, but the lady didn't seem to hear. She held up one hand and was ticking off other reasons on her fingers why the two of them would make a good pair. She seemed to plan her marriage along the same lines as a farmer charting his breeding stock, Juliana thought, wanting desperately to giggle, partly from sheer relief at learning that the baronet was still unfettered.

"If you are recovered, shall we move back into the drawing room?" Sir Oliver asked her, his tone low.

Deciding with regret that there would be no stolen kisses tonight, since Miss Stanwood seemed determined to remain glued, leechlike, to their side, she nodded. Sir Oliver gave her his arm, offering his other arm, perforce, to Miss Stanwood, and they strolled back toward the rest of the guests.

As they returned to the main party, Mr. Needham was waiting to pounce, and now there were two obstacles to prevent any private conversation. Juliana resigned herself to a tedious evening dedicated to learning many more scientific and genealogical particulars than she would ever wish to know.

If one could only marry Mr. Needham's zebras to Miss Stanwood's ancestors, it would be a much more interesting experiment, Juliana told herself. She made a note to suggest as much to Sir Oliver the first time they were alone; she thought he would appreciate the notion.

Fortunately, Lady Sealey had arranged for entertainment: a young Swiss soprano was to play and sing for them. Chairs and settees had been arranged in a half circle around the pianoforte. Another woman accompanied the singer on a tall harp, and for an hour, the guests were mostly silent as music filled the drawing room.

Juliana sat next to Sir Oliver where she could covertly admire the clean lines of his face. Now and then she was still vexed by the high-pitched whispers from his other side, since even during the musical performance Miss Stanwood continued to offer comments. Sir Oliver looked straight ahead and didn't respond. Juliana thought about what it would be like for any man to be married to such a woman and didn't wonder that his jaw seemed set.

For herself, the singer's liquid notes carried away the last remnants of her shock over Miss Stanwood's surprising announcement. Juliana felt her shoulders relax and her breathing grow deeper and more regular. She could even feel more hopeful about the countess's worrying notes. Surely, they were only someone's idea of a bad joke. Perhaps there would be no more correspondence, and they were all worried over nothing. Who could hate Lady Sealey so much that he would wish to harm her? The countess could be tart if provoked, but she was still a darling.

Mr. Needham sat on Juliana's other side. While he had sufficient good manners to be silent during the music, Juliana knew he only bided his time before he brought up the matter of scientific research again, and his need for funding to support it.

As the singer began her last song, Juliana considered tonight's strange turn of events. What a laugh that Mr. Needham should think she had influence over Lord Gabriel, that polished and intimidating man who was her newly discovered half brother! She hadn't even known of his existence until a few weeks ago. For anyone to think that she would have the nerve to petition her so-called cousin for a stranger and for a—likely—large sum of money was ludicrous.

Mr. Needham would have more luck rowing his own

boat to Africa then waiting for her to ask for a farthing from her noble half brother! Lord Gabriel and his wife had already been so generous and done so much that Juliana would never dream of asking him for more. It stung her pride already that she and her sisters should be on the edge of penury and be unable to do anything in return. So, even if Mr. Needham's cause were the best in the world—and she didn't favor cutting up the poor animals—she would never entreat the Sinclairs for money! Just thinking of it made her cheeks burn. So it seemed that Mr. Needham was destined to be just as disappointed as poor Miss Stanwood, Juliana thought as she joined in the applause for the soprano and her accompanist.

Now the footmen were moving about the room with silver trays, serving wine and tea and small cakes to the guests. Juliana accepted a cup and sipped the hot brew cautiously. It made it easier to delay murmuring a noncommital answer to Mr. Needham's questions about her so-called cousin.

"I'm not sure when I will see Lord or Lady Gabriel again, Mr. Needham," she told him. "Lady Gabriel's younger sister is ill with the measles just now; they are not entertaining or going out."

"But surely the nursery maid can deal with that kind of thing?" Mr. Needham suggested, looking disappointed.

Hardly the compassionate type, Juliana thought. "I could tell them you suggested it," she said dryly.

He seemed to realize he had gone too far. "No, no, that is, I'm sure Lady Gabriel's concern for her sister is most commendable," he corrected himself. "But when you do see them—"

"I will certainly not forget your request, Mr. Needham," Juliana assured him. Whether she voiced it was another matter entirely, but she also did not intend to be pushed into doing something she did not wish to do.

"You will remember about the spinal column research, and the brain, and the spleen—" he went on.

"I will certainly remember the spleen," she assured him, looking about for Sir Oliver and hoping for a way out of this tortuous conversation, which seemed likely to stretch on into the next century. "You do not have any tea. Pray, do stop a servant and refresh yourself with a cup."

"No need," the scientist told her. "But—"

Since she could not get him to stop talking, Juliana herself turned away and after searching through several clusters of guests found Sir Oliver similarly encumbered with his would-be fiancé, Miss Stanwood. She already had a teacup in hand, but sadly, it impeded her rapid-fire chatter not at all, although she waved it about with such abandon that a few drops had splashed onto her high-cut ivory-colored gown. After a time, Juliana noted, Miss Stanwood's high-pitched voice seemed to take on the annoying cadence of an insect's hum.

Sir Oliver looked increasingly grim.

The monkey had been much less annoying.

Juliana tried to think of a diversion. She spied a large box of chocolates sitting on a side table; surely Miss Stanwood liked chocolates. With her mouth full, she would have to be silent for a moment or two.

"Would you like a chocolate, Miss Stanwood?" Juliana lifted the gilt box and offered the candy.

Miss Stanwood paused in midsentence, and for a moment, her chatter stopped. The look of intense gratitude that Sir Oliver directed Juliana's way was reward enough. She met his glance with an answering twinkle of her own as she allowed Miss Stanwood to select two large, shiny, glazed chocolates before setting the box back on the table.

Another guest drifted closer and looked over the selection of sweets; the box had apparently just been opened.

This lady, a sweet-faced matron in puce green, chose a cherry dipped in chocolate and nibbled on the outer layer, trying not to get the sticky chocolate on her fingers.

Less fastidious, Miss Stanwood tossed both candies into her mouth and munched. At least, Juliana told herself, the lady would surely be silent a minute or two, but to her surprise, Miss Stanwood opened her mouth almost at once.

And shrieked like an angry peahen.

Juliana jumped in surprise. What was wrong?

The rest of the company in the drawing room fell silent, and the other guests turned to stare in their direction.

"What is it?" Sir Oliver demanded.

"It—a terrible taste—and my mouth and throat are on fire!" Miss Stanwood moaned, and indeed, her face had taken on a darkish tinge. "You have poisoned me!" She threw an accusing look in Juliana's direction.

Pale with fear, the matron who had nibbled on the chocolate-covered cherry spat out the confection into her handkerchief.

"It is she," Miss Stanwood said again, glaring at Juliana. "She is jealous of your affection for me!"

"Miss Stanwood, be sensible," Sir Oliver told her. "Miss Applegate would do nothing to harm you. Here, sit down," He took Miss Stanwood's arm and helped her to the nearest settee. To the closest servant, he said, "Fetch Lady Sealey's physician, at once! And put this box of chocolates into my room and make sure no one else touches it."

Now the countess herself cut through the crowd of whispering guests. "What has happened, Oliver? Is something amiss?"

He nodded toward Miss Stanwood. "She ate two chocolates from what appears to be a new box of candy. I have had the servants take it away so no one else is imperiled. Almost at once, Miss Stanwood felt her mouth and throat burn, and she feels very ill. I have sent for your doctor. This lady ate one piece from the same box. Do you feel all right?"

The matron was holding her own throat as if in sympathy, but she drew a shaky breath. "I believe so."

"Sit still, Amelia, just in case," Lady Sealey said, her voice concerned. "And you, child, tell me what you are feeling."

"Oh, it's dreadful," Miss Stanwood whispered, and indeed, her voice sounded hoarse and her lips seemed swollen. "My stomach is on fire. . . ."

The countess looked grim. "Come away into an anteroom. Oliver, support her, please. Miss Applegate, you can aid us, too, if you would."

"Of course," Juliana said, coming quickly to Miss Stanwood's other side.

Lady Sealey gave rapid instructions to two of her footmen, and followed as they helped the unfortunate Miss Stanwood into a more private room, where servants brought her a basin in case of nausea, and she was allowed to lie down on a chaise.

"I am going to give you something to bring up this substance, which is trying to destroy your body, before it can be totally absorbed and do its worst," the countess said. "I once encountered something similar in Europe. My maid is making up a draught right now which had very good results for me, and I believe it will be just as effective for you."

Juliana felt genuinely frightened now as she watched the young woman on the chaise. Lady Sealey unhooked the back of her gown and loosened her stays; the younger woman's breathing was growing more difficult, and her complexion looked mottled. Was Miss Stanwood going to die before their eyes? Despite the shock she had given Juliana with the so-called engagement, she did not wish the young lady such a terrible fate!

Then Lady Sealey's dresser came at a run, carrying a pitcher with a noxious-smelling, milky-looking mixture, which the countess poured into a goblet and held to the young woman's mouth.

"You must drink this, my dear, all of it."

At the first taste, Miss Stanwood tried to protest. "We should wait to see what the doctor says," she sputtered. "This tastes awful."

"I know," the countess agreed. "But it will save your life, my dear. You must trust me, or else, what on earth will I tell your mother? The doctor will only advise bloodletting, and anyhow, I do not think we have the time to wait for him."

Miss Stanwood gazed up at them with eyes already sunken, but at this none too subtle hint, she took the goblet and drank, and when the countess refilled her glass, she drank the next one, too.

"Oliver," the countess said, looking up at her godson. "I suspect that Miss Stanwood would not wish you to witness what comes next. Perhaps you would like to go and make my apologies to my guests?"

"Of course," he said, taking the countess's hand and pressing it for a moment.

"You may go, too, if you wish," Lady Sealey told Juliana.

Juliana shook her head. "I know the servants are loyal, but you may need my assistance," she suggested. "And I have aided my younger sisters when they were ill. I will stay."

"Thank you, my dear," the countess said.

As she knelt beside the chaise, ready for the difficult hours to come, Juliana gazed up at Sir Oliver, who paused for a moment in the doorway to look back at her. His expression was bleak. He caught her eye, and she knew he must be thinking the same as she.

Who had poisoned the chocolates? And, of course, the other obvious conclusion—surely they had been meant for Lady Sealey.

⌘

The night was long and difficult, and not one that Ju-liana would later recall with any pleasure. They were fortunate, the doctor told them when he arrived, that Miss Stanwood was by nature of a strong constitution and still hale at seven and twenty years.

What if it had been Lady Sealey who had eaten the chocolate? Juliana thought often of that possibility during the small hours of the night, as she wrung out cool cloths to lay on the ill woman's forehead and washed her face gently, listening to her moan between bouts of retching.

A woman who was older, more frail, less able to fight off the poison, might not have survived its effects, even after taking prompt action to purge it from her system. As it was, Miss Stanwood was fortunate that the countess knew the right steps to take. Someday, Juliana thought, she must ask Lady Sealey when and why she had once been poisoned. . . . Or perhaps not. Maybe Oliver knew the story.

The countess's physician was a sensible man who did not, after all, suggest bloodletting, but approved of Lady Sealey's antidote. He stayed with them to watch over the afflicted young woman, though there was little more to do except wait out the night and determine whether, once her stomach had emptied itself of all its contents, she could recover.

"It's all to the good that she ate the adulterated sweet on

top of a full stomach," the doctor told them. "The poison did not have as much of an opportunity to be absorbed into the body as quickly. Once she does stop retching, she must drink as much liquid as we can get down her, because she will be vastly dehydrated. We must not let her become parched. Her blood could weaken, and that would be highly dangerous in itself."

The countess nodded. She looked very tired, but none of them could persuade her to go to bed.

Miss Stanwood's mother was bedridden with gout and unable to come to Lady Sealey's home to sit with her daughter, but the countess sent her hourly notes of reassurance, and footmen ran back and forth carrying missives between the two women.

When the first pink fingers of light streaked the sky above the London rooftops, Miss Stanwood's painful paroxysms had at last ceased, and she had fallen into an uneasy sleep.

"Allow her to rest for a couple of hours," the doctor said. "Then we will start to ply her with nourishing liquids."

Heavy with fatigue, Juliana nodded. The poor woman on the bed looked wretched. Her complexion was as pale as the sheets she rested on, her eyes were still shrunken and her lips almost blue, but the doctor seemed sure she had a good chance at recovery. Juliana only hoped he was correct.

Lady Sealey went off to write one more note to the widowed Mrs. Stanwood and then, she promised, she would continue on to her bedchamber.

Left alone with the sleeping woman, Juliana slumped back against the small chair she had drawn up next to the bed—they had early on, after the dinner guests had all departed, moved the patient to one of the guest rooms—and allowed herself to shut her eyes for a moment.

She drifted into sleep. Someone touched her shoulder, and she jerked awake, surprised to see by the sunlight that time had passed.

"Is she worse?"

"No, she has had some heavily sweetened weak tea and was able to keep it down, a good sign, the doctor says. In another hour we will try beef broth." Sir Oliver smiled down at her. "It is time for you to go to bed, Miss Applegate."

"No, indeed," Juliana argued. "I promised Lady Sealey I would stay. It was the only way I could get her to nap, and she must get some sleep. She's exhausted."

"As are you, and since no one would let me stay in the sickroom last night, I have slept. I will sit with Miss Stanwood, with one of the maids here to help and provide female assistance. You go to bed; I can see how weary you are. You were a great help, and it was most good of you to sit up all night with a woman you don't even know."

It had not seemed unusual at the time, Juliana thought. Lady Sealey had needed assistance—her guest had been threatened—and of course Juliana had responded. Somehow, the countess seemed like family, much more so than Lord and Lady Gabriel even, although to be fair, she had not yet had a chance to spend time with her newly discovered half brother. Still, it was curious how life was. She couldn't begin to explain it, certainly not now, with her brain clouded by lack of sleep.

"You won't leave?" she blurted and then blushed, not even sure what she had meant by such a strange—and surely brazen—request. But now they knew that the evil they feared was real, and not just a matter of vague threatening letters. And no matter how short a time Juliana had known the countess, Lady Sealey was as dear to her as the grandmother she had never been privileged to know.

"I will be here when you wake," Sir Oliver promised, as if it were not at all an unusual petition.

So, before she got herself into more trouble, Juliana gave him a quick smile and departed, and later she hardly remembered the walk to her own chamber. She managed to get out of her dress, one of her old muslin ones, since early in the night, the countess had ordered one of the servants to bring her a replacement for the silk dinner dress in order to protect it from the worst of Miss Stanwood's illness.

Juliana washed her face and hands and then fell into bed. Neither the sunlight shining through the windows nor the street noises drifting up from the square could keep her from drifting at once into a dreamless sleep.

When she woke, it was well into the afternoon. She still felt less alert than usual, but she went to her china bowl and splashed water on her face, then rang for a maid and donned a clean dress.

"Have you heard how Miss Stanwood is doing?" she asked the servant.

"I 'ear she's stronger, miss," the serving girl told her. "She's 'ad tea and soup and 'er color's less peaked. 'Er poor mother's feeling much 'appier, too, the countess says. And if I may say so, miss, it 'twas that good of you to sit up with 'er and 'elp out the countess!"

"I was happy to do it," Juliana assured her.

Lady Sealey had a loyal staff, no doubt of that. Still, Juliana was almost surprised to see how quick the servants were, now, to spring to her assistance. They seemed much impressed with Juliana's support of the countess.

The maid had also brought up not one but two letters that had come from Yorkshire from her sisters. Before she left her room, Juliana broke the wax seals and skimmed both quickly to see if all was well at home.

Maddy had written:

> *Tuesday: I have little news as exciting as all your Lon-*
> *don jaunts to tell, my dear sister. Father is well, or as well*
> *as usual, and so am I. Thomas has the last of the beets*
> *dug. The twins are still away, drawing out their stay at*
> *the squire's estate; I fear that Lauryn is too lenient with*
> *them, and the squire—always one to enjoy a pretty face,*
> *much less a pair of identical ones—indulges them, too,*
> *but I will not scold from a distance. For one thing, it does*
> *no good!*
>
> *There is little news to report in the neighborhood except*
> *that a widow of small independent income, a Mrs. Barlow,*
> *has moved into the old Arrington cottage. The neighbors*
> *are gossiping, as little is known about her past, but she*
> *seems a most genteel, pleasant sort, a lady by all appear-*
> *ances, and I see no harm in her.*
>
> *I am scrubbing out the best chamber for our guest.*
>
> *Friday: Oh, now I do have important news—Lady*
> *Gemma has made her appearance! She will stay a week,*
> *and I find her most pleasant! She promises to be a cher-*
> *ished half sister, indeed. And she was most affected by her*
> *first meeting with our father—*

The other letter, with lines much less even and many
more blots and exclamation points, was from the twins:

> *Oh, Juliana!*
>
> *London! How could you go to London without us?*
> *Have you been to the theater or met any eligible gentle-*
> *men? What are the latest styles in bonnets? Are the London*
> *gowns too, too elegant? If you bring us any gifts, do re-*
> *member my favorite color is coral—and did you hear*
> *about the mysterious new neighbor? They are saying she's*

*not a widow at all, but a paramour of Bonaparte himself!
But I don't think she's handsome enough for that . . .*

Your own Ophelia.

Dearest Big Sister,
*Pay no attention to my twin. The new widow is too bor-
ing to be a retired . . . well, you know. And we're being really, really good. Lauryn is too kind to us, and the squire is
a dear. And don't hurry home, enjoy your visit with our
new cousin, but bring back lots of gossip. We want to hear
all about our new relations.*

Your loving sister, Cordelia.

Juliana scanned the pages quickly, then put the letters
aside for more careful reading later, feeling duty bound to
check on their invalid without delay. On her way to the sickroom, Juliana encountered Sir Oliver in the hall. Pleased to
see him, she paused, but he seemed to be on his way out,
and he stayed only long enough to bow over her hand.

"I have an errand to run," he told her. "I will be back in
time for dinner."

"Of course," she agreed.

Had he really stayed at home just because of her child-
ish request? Remembering it made her feel silly, and yet it
warmed her inside that he had taken her plea so seriously.

Juliana went on to the sickroom and was not surprised to
find Lady Sealey there, checking on Miss Stanwood. The patient was dozing, but the maid's report seemed correct. Her
color was much better, her eyes less sunken, and her breathing seemed normal, so Juliana could see why everyone felt
optimistic, including, the countess assured her, the doctor.

"I believe we were able to get enough of the poison out
of her in time," Lady Sealey told her, keeping her voice
low as they stood in the doorway.

"She's very lucky that you knew what to do," Juliana said.

The countess sighed. "I fear she would have been luckier not to have been in my house last evening."

Not sure how to answer, Juliana bit her lip.

Confident that Miss Stanwood was strong enough now to leave in the housekeeper's supervision, Lady Sealey sent Juliana to change into her new dinner gown and they both came down to dinner at the regular hour. The table had been reduced to a much smaller size tonight, but, to Juliana's surprise, four places were set, and there was one guest.

Sir Oliver had returned, and he had brought Lord Gabriel with him.

Eleven

Her half brother bowed over Lady Sealey's hand, then gave Juliana a courtly bow. She was annoyed to find herself still somewhat flustered by her awe-inspiring relative, but she did her best to execute a graceful curtsy.

"How is Lady Gabriel and her sister?" she asked as the servants served the first course.

"Circe is holding her own, but Psyche doesn't feel ready to leave her just yet," Gabriel told them. "However, when Oliver told us about the disturbing incident that someone inflicted upon your poor guest, Psyche agreed I should come along and do what I could to help."

When their plates were filled, the countess dismissed the footmen so that they could talk in relative privacy.

"I understand the poor girl is recovering?" Lord Gabriel added in a low tone.

"Thank heavens," Lady Sealey agreed. "Who could have done such a thing, I have no idea."

"But we are going to find out," Sir Oliver said, his tone firm.

Lady Sealey sighed and nodded.

"Did you ask about the box of chocolates? I assume that the countess did not buy the sweetstuffs in a shop?" Lord Gabriel asked.

"No, indeed," their hostess agreed. "I had never seen the box before yesterday evening."

"That was my first inquiry," Sir Oliver told them. "The first footman said it was delivered by a young boy; there was no note. The footman assumed it was a gift from one of the countess's friends. He put it into the drawing room. One of the maids opened the box before the guests arrived. Miss Stanwood was the first person to eat from it."

After she herself had encouraged the other lady to do so, Juliana remembered, her heart sinking at the thought.

"Apparently all the chocolates were not poisoned; another guest had no ill effects. Perhaps it was too much trouble to poison all the pieces?" Lady Sealey suggested. "My unknown enemy doesn't seem very thorough."

"Was there anything different about the pieces of chocolate that *were* poisoned?" Sir Oliver asked.

"I asked Miss Stanwood last night which pieces she chose," Juliana said. "She picked out the almond creams, with nuts on top, which are her favorites."

Lady Sealey stared at her. "They are my favorites."

The others were silent for a moment. "Not a coincidence, I think," Lord Gabriel pointed out, his tone grim.

"And it speaks of someone who knows you fairly well, Godmother," Sir Oliver added.

Lady Sealey pressed her lips together.

Sir Oliver gave the countess a steady look. "I believe we are going to have to pursue that list of people who might fancy that they possess some grievance against you. Have you given the question any thought?"

The countess sighed. "Of course I have, Oliver. It's just so disheartening to think that someone I considered a friend, or at least a friendly acquaintance, could secretly harbor such enmity for me. I shall be looking twice now at every old friend I see."

Oliver's expression was sympathetic. "I know it's not pleasant to consider such thoughts, but it is necessary. It's more than just nasty letters now, Godmother."

Lord Gabriel added, "We cannot stand by and allow someone to do you harm, Lady Sealey. You have always been there for us in the most difficult times, and your support has meant more to us than you know. And now, when your life is imperiled, we would do anything in our power to keep you safe!"

Juliana nodded her agreement.

She thought she saw an answering glint of moisture in the countess's eyes. The older lady blinked and raised her chin, but she kept her voice steady.

"With such friends as these, how can I have anything to fear?"

So, with their encouragement, Lady Sealey delved into her past, trying to think of possible enemies who might have reemerged with still simmering grudges.

"There was the Tuscan ambassador who thought that I encouraged his wife to leave him . . . merely because he beat her regularly. I did, of course, and she was much better off, I must say. No, he died ten years ago when a jealous husband killed him in a duel." The countess stared into space, then paused as the servants returned to serve the next course.

For a few minutes they exchanged only pleasantries as new dishes were brought in.

Juliana wondered what on earth the countess's servants must think of this odd dinner. But perhaps they were accustomed to unusual behavior; hadn't they just put up with a ravaging monkey hiding in the big mansion? Juliana turned her attention back to the countess, after the footman departed.

"Then there is the baron von Greft, who was one of my second husband's most implacable enemies, and he is still alive, I'm quite sure. Plus, he is in England. I heard from Lady Alverston that he has come over from Prussia a few months ago, something about consulting with a banker about his investments in English shipping."

Lord Gabriel looked thoughtful.

"And this is perhaps far-fetched, but I heard gossip recently . . ." Lady Sealey hesitated, and frowned down at the untasted sweetmeats on her plate as if she disapproved of their honey sauce.

"We need to explore any possible suspect," Sir Oliver reminded her.

She grimaced. "I was told that Lady Rives still holds me in great dislike. She, ah, thinks that her husband and I once shared a brief assignation. Whether she would go to such lengths as poisoning a box of chocolates over her suspicions, I have no hint."

She gave a delicate little shrug, but did not, Juliana noticed, deny the charge.

Lord Gabriel looked thoughtful. "They say that poison is often a woman's weapon," he pointed out. "Can you think of anything else, no matter how far-fetched? We are searching for ideas, remember."

"Other than that, I have rejected a few gentlemen's propositions in my time, but that would hardly be grounds to incite an attempt at murder." The countess's lovely brows arched at the insanity of such a thought. "Or, as unlikely as it sounds, I suppose this attempt could be connected to certain delicate diplomatic missions abroad that I have undertaken in the past for our government. But even now, I cannot give you details about that, my dears."

"If that should be the case, our task would entail finding some unknown paid assassin and could be almost impossible." Lord Gabriel looked grim.

Juliana felt her heart sink. She glanced at Lady Sealey and saw an answering bleakness wash over her face for an instant before her lips tightened, and her usual resolute expression returned.

"That does not mean that we are giving up, needless to say," Sir Oliver put in.

"Of course not," Juliana added, then blushed a little, not sure what, if anything, she could do. But it was hard to sit here and be silent when she felt that the woman who had been so generous to her was threatened.

Lady Sealey smiled at them all. "Thank you," she said. "Your loyalty means a great deal to me."

"I have some contacts in the banking community," Lord Gabriel said, somewhat to Juliana's surprise. The countess nodded. He went on, "I shall check out the baron and see what I can discover. How can we get close to Lady Rives?"

"I shall see what I can do," Lady Sealey answered. "If she is still in London. Only a scattering of people are, since the Season is over. But we shall see."

They talked a little longer over their cheese and fruit, then Lady Sealey and Juliana retired to the drawing room. The two men came almost immediately to join them, and again, they discussed what precautions might be taken. Obviously, any future deliveries to the house would be closely scrutinized. A guard dog had been purchased, and the big bulldog was allowed to roam the ground floor of the house during the hours of darkness. Sir Oliver suggested that they also engage several Bow Street Runners to watch the house, but Lady Sealey shook her head at that idea.

"On this quiet square they would stand out like one of your African elephants in the midst of a herd of Yorkshire sheep, dear boy. I think, for now, we have done as much as we can do."

And on that note, Lord Gabriel took his leave. They walked out into the hall with him and found the first footman holding the leash of the bulldog, a large canine with a pushed-in face, who regarded them all with a perpetual scowl.

Lord Gabriel bent to hold out his hand to the dog so that it could sniff it and learn his scent. "Just in case we have any more midnight adventures," he pointed out, his tone wry. "It would be good for your guardian to know who is friend and who is foe."

Lady Sealey laughed. "Yes, indeed. Although if so, this time I do hope no one gets shot." She and Lord Gabriel exchanged a look of understanding, as if they shared a private jest.

Juliana glanced at Sir Oliver, but he seemed as thoroughly in the dark as she was herself. Just how often did the countess have these adventures? What a life she must have led!

When Lord Gabriel had gone, the rest of them also retired for the evening. Juliana could tell that, try as she would not to show it, the countess was concerned. Juliana herself felt increasingly worried.

She exchanged a look with Sir Oliver when he bowed, first to his godmother, and then to Juliana as they said their good nights.

"Try not to worry," he said, his tone low. "We will keep up our guard."

Grateful for his presence, she smiled at him, and the

answering gleam in his clear gray eyes warmed her. It was only friendly reassurance, she told herself, as she climbed the staircase, reluctant to leave him and yet unable to make an excuse to stay behind, unchaperoned.

Upstairs, she went with Lady Sealey to check on Miss Stanwood, whom they found sleeping peacefully. The head housemaid was to sit with her through the night, so Lady Sealey continued to her own chamber and Juliana to hers.

When she opened the door, the room felt familiar to her now, and it was hard to remember how brief a time she had been in London, or how strange it had all appeared when she had first arrived. Lady Sealey seemed so much like family, despite their short acquaintance. It was illogical, but since when did feelings need logic to drive them?

Very soon, a housemaid brought warm water for her bowl. Setting down the ewer, the servant unbuttoned the back of Juliana's dinner dress and brushed out her hair, then departed. When Juliana had washed and changed into her nightgown, she got into bed. But instead of lying back, she sat up against the pillows, thinking hard.

Could they narrow the suspects enough to find who had sent the letters and the poisoned chocolate? No one must be allowed to harm the countess. Just considering another and more successful attempt to harm the older lady made Juliana's stomach clench.

They couldn't permit it!

But it was so hard to pinpoint an unknown villain; it was like trying to strike out at a shadow! Juliana swallowed, trying to force back her frustration. At least she was not alone. Lord Gabriel was with them; she had less of a sense now of awe and intimidation when she thought of her half brother. Instead, she felt reassured by his obvious intelligence and determination. And there was, of course, Sir Oliver, whose steady character and warm dependable kindness was the most appealing part of his personality, as enticing as his good-looking face and strong, well-built form—

She pulled her thoughts away from areas they had no business going, such as how it had felt to lie against him when she had fallen into his lap in the stairwell, forced so close to him that she could feel every response his body made . . .

Turning and pounding her pillows with a force that sent several feathers flying, Juliana curled up in a half circle and tried to compose her thoughts for sleep. And a certain young baronet who could so easily make her pulse race and her belly tighten had no business interfering with her attempts at slumber.

Waking early the next morning, Juliana blinked at the sunlight which slipped past the draperies, not sure about the sense of urgency that hovered at the edge of her mind. Of course—the recent poisoning, the unresolved mystery; so much still to do and learn. Juliana rose and dressed. Two new muslins had arrived from the dressmaker, and it was a rare pleasure to try on a fresh new day dress, its pattern bright and unfaded. She chose a blue sprigged gown, then pinned up her hair in a simple twist, not waiting for a maid to help her. She was eager to be downstairs and see what was happening.

She found that Lady Sealey was astir, as well, and already clad in her hat and gloves to go out. The doctor had come to check on the progress of the invalid and had apparently announced her well enough to be sent home in Lady Sealey's carriage.

"Mrs. Stanwood has been anxiously awaiting her return," Lady Sealey explained. "As a mother would, of course. I'm riding with her and taking two footmen to help her in and out. Be sure she doesn't fall, Thomas, she's quite weak, still."

Juliana watched the procession come down the staircase. Miss Stanwood wore a day dress which her mother had sent over and was wrapped in a warm pelisse and supported by two stalwart servants. Her face was pale, but she looked much better than she had the night of the poisoning.

"I hope you are soon back to normal, Miss Stanwood," Juliana called.

The afflicted woman simply gave a feeble moan and didn't answer, saying instead, "My head aches."

Lady Sealey told her, "It will be only a short ride, then you can lie down again, dear. And the doctor will come by your house this afternoon to check on you. Now, into the carriage with you."

The countess followed them out, and Juliana went on to the dining room. She had finished a plate of ham and eggs and poached salmon when, to her secret delight, Sir Oliver appeared.

"You have missed Miss Stanwood," she pointed out. "She has left, in Lady Sealey's carriage and under the countess's supervision, for her own residence. The doctor says she is much improved."

"Jolly good," he said, nodding. "And I'm glad you're up. Would you like to ride to the coast with me?"

She blinked in surprise. She would gladly ride to the moon with him, Juliana thought, but she knew more than to blurt out such a sentiment.

"I mean—" He was blushing again. By now, Juliana was no longer surprised to see the waves of crimson wash over his face. Instead, she found it endearing. "I mean to say, I have to take the monkey down to Lady Sealey's country estate, which is only a couple hours' drive, and two of the housemaids will join us, as well, so we will have an—um—chaperone, so to speak.

"My godmother will soon be moving to her country house for the rest of the summer. London gets very hot and dusty, you know, and it's much nicer in the country. So she's starting to send the servants down."

When she hesitated, he added, his tone anxious, "It would be a nice drive, lovely day. And from there, I need to go on to the coast to see about picking up some new animals. And we will take one of the maids along, too, of course."

Juliana felt her heart sink. "I'm sure it is a good day for a drive," she told him, her words coming slowly, "and yes, I'd love to go with you. But by the time Lady Sealey moves her household to the country, I will probably have removed to Lord Gabriel's house, or even perhaps have returned to Yorkshire. I was never meant to be here at all, you know." And no matter that she felt strangely disconsolate at the thought.

Sir Oliver's face seemed to go even redder. "Ah, as to that, I had a word with Lord Gabriel last night, when we were alone in the dining room."

Juliana looked at him in surprise.

"I suggested that having you here, keeping company with my godmother, I mean, is perhaps a good thing just now . . . another lady, that is, not just a servant." He seemed to be having a hard time getting the words out. "She's quite fond of you, I know, however, I really should have asked you first before I took the liberty of suggesting that you stay—"

"No, no," Juliana assured him. "That is, as long as I can be of help I am delighted to stay here."

"Oh, good," he said, and some of his high color ebbed. "I have already extended my own visit. I came originally to cheer her after the death of her friend, when I saw how downcast she was. And, of course, I could not leave her now, while she is in danger."

Juliana smiled, and the world itself seemed to brighten. "I can be ready in five minutes."

He grinned. "I will send round for the carriage. Good thing the countess keeps two in town."

Also a good thing it was roomy, Juliana thought when they were all inside. The maids' wicker hampers had been tied on to the back, Mia's cage was sitting carefully on the seat, and since the maids eyed the simian with alarm, it was Sir Oliver who shared the seat with the bulky cage.

This left Juliana squeezed into the opposite seat with the two maids, one of whom was slim but the other was a round girl of a goodly girth. Oh, well. Juliana would have preferred sitting this close to Sir Oliver, but at least she could glance at him often. Conversation was almost impossible, as Mia's shrieks and angry chatter were too loud for anything but a shout to be heard above.

"She's annoyed, you see," Sir Oliver tried to explain, in a bellow. "She's been cooped up for several days. I have a much larger confinement area for her at the estate; she'll be happier there."

A good thing, if it stopped this racket, Juliana thought. She tried to answer, but her words were drowned out by the monkey's whoops.

"What?" Sir Oliver shouted back.

The two maids put their hands over their ears.

"She's eating one of your buttons!" Juliana pointed to the monkey. The creature's small hand had slipped through one of the cage's openings and pulled an enticing brass button off Sir Oliver's well-tailored coat.

Judging by the baronet's expression, he swore briskly as he tried without success to retrieve the button. This time, it was just as well that the rest of the carriage's occupants could not make out his words.

Looking distinctly smug, the monkey shrieked in triumph and continued to bite on its brass prize.

With such antics to put up with, the ride seemed longer than it probably was, but by the time the sun was high in the sky, they had reached the countess's estate.

The two maids rolled their eyes in relief as they stepped down from the carriage. Juliana couldn't blame them, her head was pounding, too. But the slimmer maid had agreed to ride on to the coast with them, after Sir Oliver had promised faithfully that the monkey would not accompany them.

All three females went inside, two heading below stairs, no doubt to share the hair-raising tale of their perilous ride with a demon monkey with the rest of the staff; Juliana was taken away by the under housekeeper to another spacious guest chamber where she could wash the dust off her hands and face, remove her hat, and comb her hair, then come down for a light luncheon and cup of tea.

By this time Sir Oliver reappeared and sat down for a bite, which ended up being two large slabs of ham, a considerable quantity of roast beef, half a loaf of bread, and a quite moderate serving of gooseberry fool.

He told Juliana that Mia was happily swinging through the wooden poles of a much larger enclosure.

"And quiet, at last?" she asked, as she took a bite of roast beef.

"Well, no," he admitted, taking one last bite of the gooseberry sweet. "But her shrieks are happy ones, this time."

Laughing, Juliana hoped, for the servants' sake, that the monkey's new home was a good distance from the house.

She went up to don her hat and gloves and summon the maid, who had made her own refreshment below stairs, and they set out again with a new team of horses.

"What kind of animals are you picking up?" Juliana asked, looking about her. Between the maid and the two of them, there was not much room for animal cages. Any extra passengers would have to be small ones. "A dormouse?"

Sir Oliver grinned. "I'm not bringing them back myself. I'll arrange for a cart and oxen to bring them on. They'll be much too big and too heavy for a carriage. I just want to check their condition and well-being before I pay for their shipment. They've come a very long way and sometimes the poor beasts die on the ship coming over from Africa."

"Oh." Juliana readjusted her mental images quickly. "You're not talking about an, an elephant, are you? I've seen pictures."

He looked mischievous. "No, not an elephant. We didn't have that much money. That's one reason why Mr. Needham would love to enlist the patronage of Lord Gabriel or a wealthy backer like him. No, there are several mammals on the list of beasts we are hoping to acquire, and I'm not sure exactly what has come, but we'll soon find out."

Juliana was happy just to be near the baronet. And as the carriage spun along on the highway, the young maid, worn out by the morning ride with the noisy monkey, soon blinked and yawned and her eyelids drooped.

Watching green fields slip by and farmers busy in their fields, Juliana looked over at the young servant, whose eyes were closed, her head back against the squabs, dozing quietly.

She looked to the side, and Sir Oliver met her gaze.

Juliana smiled at him, but her pulse quickened. Just for a few precious moments, they were, for all practical purposes, alone.

"It seems very quiet, now that Mia is no longer traveling with us." She kept her voice low so that she didn't wake the maid; no point in disturbing the girl, she told herself.

He grinned. "Shall I arrange for more monkeys?"

"Oh, no, that's not necessary," she answered quickly "But I do hope that the new animals you acquire are not as adept at escaping their cages as Mia was!"

The baronet laughed.

Just then the carriage swung wide to pass a lumbering slow-moving hay wagon she could glimpse through the chaise's window. The maid slid a little on the other seat. Juliana paused to make sure the servant didn't wake. The girl sighed, but then she seemed to sink back easily into sleep.

Juliana could have caught herself by clinging to the edge of the seat. If she had been paying closer attention, no doubt she would have. And if she had, she would not have slid into such close vicinity with Sir Oliver.

So it was a shame, indeed, she hadn't been paying closer attention. But now, now her thigh pressed against his, their two limbs separated only by a few thin layers of cloth, and his was so hard and firm and somehow warm that it was, doubtless, the reason that hers felt warm, too, that her body felt suddenly warm all over.

She felt a dizzying rush of heat from deep inside, and it stirred feelings that threatened to overwhelm all rational thought. She didn't want thought, she didn't want logic or reason—need stirred, and it moved her; she wanted it to move him, too.

When Juliana looked up into his clear gray eyes, she found them too honest to allow her to hide behind such a ruse. She had never played such games in her life; she really couldn't start now.

So she simply stared up into those clear eyes and allowed her own to show her growing awareness of him. She saw the spark leap inside him, too. And the heat that flowed between them grew.

Oliver leaned closer.

She put up one hand to lightly touch his chest, to stroke the fine woven linen of his tailored jacket, then moved it higher still, past his neckcloth, to dare to touch his chin, the adorable small cleft which looked as if a thumbprint had been left in its firm molding. She could not imagine a better made chin, or better eyes, or better—he was leaning closer.

He put both of his hands—such strength he had in his hands—on her shoulders, holding her as if she were a delicate, precious thing, and the contrast between the power of his hands and the care with which he gripped her stirred something deep inside her.

He was going to kiss her.

She lifted her face, waiting for the touch of his lips—

The carriage hit a hole in the road and bounced sharply, rocking and swaying. The maid shifted and gave a strangled little cry. Sir Oliver dropped his hands and moved farther away, turning to scowl fiercely at the far window of the carriage.

Juliana thought she might weep from frustration.

The serving girl rubbed her eyes and sat up straighter to peer out the other window. Sir Oliver folded his arms. The silence inside the carriage was tense.

Juliana thought she would have preferred the monkey's interruptions!

⚬⚬⚬

When they reached the port, Juliana was more than ready to climb down from the carriage and stretch her cramped limbs and stiff body. The maid looked weary, too. It was not the servant's fault she had to play chaperone, Juliana told herself. Amazed at the chaotic yet purposeful bustle of the docks, she looked around her.

The piers smelled of brine and dead fish, and the strong breeze that skimmed the shifting water also carried exotic aromas of cargoes that had journeyed here from far-flung countries. Teas and spices, silks and muslins, china and now even strange animals, all of it brought to England's door by the greatest sea-going fleet in the world.

The harbor was crowded with ships and boats of all sizes, the masts bobbing and shifting like a forest of leafless trees, and the docks were packed with merchants and seamen, travelers and vendors, government officials and even— Juliana eyed a woman with a very low-cut gown, then looked away hastily as a sailor paused to leer at the female and leaned over to grab her half-naked breast—women of the street.

Although he was eager to inspect the animals, Sir Oliver offered to procure some refreshment for them first, so they went into an inn and took lukewarm tea and biscuits. Then, feeling refreshed and almost as curious as the baronet, Juliana, with the maid behind her, walked with him through the busy docks to locate the ship carrying his precious cargo.

When they found the *Merry Marmot*, which floated a little way off the dock while its sailors plied smaller boats back and forth to unload its cargo, Sir Oliver hailed one of the sailors.

"Where is your captain? I have some important property aboard your boat."

"'E's on board, mate." The man hardly paused as he wrestled a large barrel up to the dock and rolled it across the uneven boards warped by exposure to sun and saltwater.

"I shall have to go out on one of the boats." Sir Oliver took a moment to speak quietly to Juliana. "Perhaps you should wait here."

Juliana inspected the balding, sun-burned crewman man-handling the cask farther down the dock and turned her head as another seaman paused to stare boldly as her.

Sir Oliver turned to give the man a hard look, and the sailor walked on.

"That is, I will take you and the maid back to the inn and engage a private parlor where you can wait. Perhaps I should not have invited you to come. I thought it would be a diverting trip."

"No, it was a lovely excursion," Juliana assured him. "But, really, I would feel safer if I stayed with you. Let me go to the ship with you."

"I don't know," he began, then glanced up at the sun, and pulled his pocket watch out to look at the time. "We don't have time to debate the question if we wish to be back be fore dark. Very well. Let's go to the boat. I must look at the animals, if, hopefully, they have survived their passage. Then I must pay the captain and make arrangements for their cartage to Lady Sealey's estate."

He returned to the sailor, and this time, by the simple expedient of taking out a large coin and holding it up at eye level, got the man's complete attention.

So very soon, Juliana had her first experience of making the tricky climb down to a large dingy, after first hiking up her skirts—and knowing uneasily that every seaman within viewing distance was certain to be eyeing her exposed legs with appreciation! But with the baronet's help she made it safely.

They'd had an unexpected complication. The young maid had had hysterics at the very thought of getting into a boat and had had to be left behind. Worried about her safety on the docks, Juliana had almost stayed, too, but the appearance of one of the dock police had offered the chance for an escort. Sir Oliver had tipped the man to escort the serving girl safely back to the inn to wait in a private parlor for their return,

Juliana clung to the side of the boat as they were rowed to the ship. The sea spray flew into her face, and the cold wind threatened to snatch her hat away. She pushed her hat pin in more firmly and retied her ribbons, but although her heart beat faster, she found the experience exhilarating. The boat rocked as it met each cresting wave, dipping and then rising. It was a curious motion, quite different from riding her donkey. Yorkshire seemed as far away as China!

She glanced across at Sir Oliver and saw that he was grinning at her. She smiled back.

"Shall we continue rowing and journey right on across the ocean?" he asked, his tone mischievous.

She laughed. She was chilled right through. Her face felt damp and sticky from the sea spray, and tendrils of hair clung to her cheeks, but she didn't care. What an adventure this was! Her family estate in the North was inland, and she had seldom traveled far afield. She had a dim memory of once glimpsing the ocean as a child, but she had never had the opportunity to venture out on a boat. On impulse, and before she considered how improper it was, she held out one hand to the baronet, not even caring about the crewmen behind them, who were bent over their oars.

Sir Oliver clasped it and squeezed her fingers lightly. His clear gray eyes, much the color of the harbor water, twinkled. He seemed to sense her enthusiasm.

"Thank you for inviting me to come," she told him. "It has been a lovely trip. I do hope your animals have fared well."

He looked sober for a moment. "As do I!"

As the small boat cut through the waves, they neared the ship, and she had to release his hand. Now she negotiated the rope ladder again, but she was learning the trick of it, so her heart did not pound in her throat quite as much, and she pretended not to see the sailors' grins around her as she brushed her skirts back into place once she got to the top.

On the deck of the ship, the captain, a burly man with a pockmarked face, waited to greet them. Had some kind of signal passed ahead of them? At any rate, Sir Oliver quickly explained what he was seeking.

"Your animals are in the hold, sir. Lost the antelopes afore we got past Gibraltar, didn't seem to like our 'ay— too moldy, may 'ap, but not a total loss as they made a right tasty dinner." The man actually licked his cracked lips at the thought.

Juliana gulped. The captain had several missing teeth, and his breath was foul even from a distance.

"But we still got most of the big 'uns, so you should be proud." The man walked a little away, gesturing as he spoke, and Sir Oliver followed, offering Juliana his arm.

Determined not to be left behind, Juliana took long strides. The captain led them down to the dank, dark interior of the boat, where puddles of water lay in the corners, and Juliana was sure she heard the scuttle of rats moving away in the shadows. It smelled incredibly vile, and she took a handkerchief from her reticule and held it to her nose.

She shuddered. Poor beasts, to have to spend weeks in such dreadful confinement. She was sure that Sir Oliver would provide more healthful surroundings in the English countryside. It would not be their native Africa, of course, but she hoped they would be happy.

"Take care, lady, that one is said to throw its spines," the captain called over his shoulder. "Ne'er saw it do it, myself, but we kept it shut up, just in case."

Startled, Juliana looked into the large crate next to her and saw a monstrosity of an animal, at least three feet tall, shaped like a giant hedgehog, only thinner, and with long sharper spines covering its strangely shaped body. The nose on the massive head was long and pointed as if some unearthly force had pulled it forward. What—

"It's an anteater," Sir Oliver informed her calmly. "And I don't know that the spine throwing has ever been substantiated."

The captain rolled his eyes. "The natives say so, don't they?"

"Where did you find enough ants to keep it alive?" Sir Oliver asked, voicing the question that Juliana was thinking.

"Didn't," the captain said cheerfully. "But it turned out to be right fond of the termites in the ship's hull; probably bought us another three voyages, that hell's spawn did."

"Useful," Sir Oliver agreed.

Still, Juliana backed cautiously away from the crate until she bumped into another wooden cage.

Something growled, a sound as deep and low-pitched as thunder in late afternoon.

Jumping back, Juliana whirled to see what new beast she had awakened.

Between the cracks of the wooden cage, two gleaming eyes watched her.

Twelve

Juliana licked her lips—or tried to—but her mouth seemed suddenly dry. The eyes were slits, catlike, and she felt like a mouse must feel when the kitchen cat unfolds its limbs ready to pounce.

Nonsense, it was in a cage, she tried to tell herself. She was quite safe.

Her mouth was still too dry to speak. She put out one hand, hoping that Sir Oliver had not moved too far off.

Her fingertip brushed his sleeve.

Thank God!

"It's all right," he said, and he put one arm about her shoulders.

Juliana found she had been holding her breath. She inhaled at last, almost choking on the fetid odors of the ship's hold.

"The cage is secure, but all the animals are half dead from sea sickness and poor diet. I have arranged to have

them brought up and sent to land. I will have carts ready to
bring the cats and the others to Lady Sealey's estate."

Cats? There was more than one? She was happy to leave
these wild animals behind. A mischievous monkey on the
loose had been one thing, but a big jungle cat with a preda-
tor's wild eyes was quite another!

He guided her back to the upper decks, and Juliana
hoped he could not see how weak were her knees, or how
her legs trembled beneath her. She could barely climb, and
she almost fell once, caught by Sir Oliver's strong arms.

He held her close for a moment.

Juliana was glad the captain had preceded them.

She could rest against the baronet's broad chest, shut her
eyes and relish the feel of his arms about her, the firmness
of his body beneath hers. But only for a moment, there were
too many seamen about to smirk and make lewd comments.

Sighing, she forced herself up the rest of the way. At least
on the deck of the ship, a breeze stirred the air, and she could
breathe more easily. Sir Oliver paid the captain for his shipment, and then they were rowed ashore. Here the baronet
made arrangements for the animals to be brought on, and
they returned to the inn.

Sir Oliver insisted on delaying long enough for Juliana
to have a glass of wine and some food, although she was
worried now about the daylight waning.

"There will be a half moon tonight and few clouds," he
assured her. "We should have no trouble getting back to the
estate, even if we don't make it all the way to London."

However, to her disappointment, Sir Oliver hired a
mount for the return trip, so that she and the maid rode
alone inside the carriage. With fewer passengers, the vehicle could make better time.

But she missed his presence and his quiet conversation.
With only the maid for company, and the serving girl was

silent as the carriage rattled along, Juliana gazed out the window at the passing landscape until twilight obscured her vision. It hardly mattered. She realized she had no idea what she had been observing, at least, nothing beyond how well Sir Oliver sat the rangy gray he had hired from the inn and how handsome was his profile against the passing greenery. . . .

The moon had risen, and with its silvery light and the faint glow of the carriage lanterns they finished the last few miles of their journey. Juliana was glad to see the large brick front gates of Lady Sealey's estate come into view, and even the serving maid, trying to hide her yawn behind her hand, perked up. The carriage slowed to enter the drive, and the coachman clucked to his team.

When the carriage rolled up to the front of the big house, a footman hurried out to let down the steps. He helped Juliana down, and she was surprised to see the countess herself come out to greet them.

"Lady Sealey, what are you doing here?"

"I suspected my godson had been too optimistic about covering so many miles in one day, my dear. I thought it would be better not to abandon you here with only a skeleton staff. I cannot treat my guests so shabbily," the countess told her, smiling easily.

Juliana hoped the darkness hid her blush. She had just been wondering if she and the baronet would eat dinner alone, and if he would take the opportunity to take her hand or steal a kiss when they sat in solitary splendor in the drawing room after dinner.

Perhaps the countess knew too much about natural urges! Young ladies were to be chaperoned at all times, and Juliana supposed it was just as well. Where their "natural urges" might have led her and the baronet, if left unaccompanied, she couldn't have said.

At least Lady Sealey didn't scold Juliana for wanting what she could not have.

Smiling, her hostess sent her upstairs. "Wash off the dust of your journey, my dear, and change for dinner. We will dine fashionably late. I know you must be exhausted, but you'll feel better once you have supped."

Juliana admitted to feeling fatigued. She climbed the staircase with slow steps and found one of the estate's maids waiting to help her. When she returned, she saw that Sir Oliver had changed, too, and looked neat and even more handsome in his evening clothes.

He offered one arm to the countess and the other to Juliana so she had an excuse to lean lightly upon it, which lifted her spirits. Perhaps they were not alone, but she could still touch his firmly muscled arm and smile up into his clear eyes, and somehow, she did not feel half so weary.

After another good dinner—the countess had high standards when it came to cooks, Juliana thought—she followed the countess to the drawing room, though with a private sigh at the thought of the private tête à tête she could no longer look forward to, and very soon Oliver rejoined them.

He was full of high spirits as he told his godmother about the new animals he had acquired.

"Oh, my heavens, Oliver, and you are bringing these savage beasts to my quiet estate?" Even Lady Sealey looked alarmed. She sat up straighter and regarded her godson with narrowed eyes.

"I will take the greatest care, I give you my word," he vowed. "These are not monkeys, with clever little paws so much like hands which they can use to unlatch their own cages. These are cats, big cats, I grant you—"

"Yes," the countess put in. "Very big cats with big claws and big teeth, I have no doubt!"

He grinned reluctantly. "That is true."

"And they must require a great amount of food," she suggested.

"Yes, but you have an abundance of deer in the park, and I will hire some village men to hunt for venison, if you do not object," he suggested. "And if the cats need more, I will see to their needs out of my own purse. The beasts will not be a burden on you, Godmother, until I can move them to my own estate."

"It is not my purse that I fear could be ravaged, Oliver dear."

Lady Sealey raised her silvery brows in mock censure, but Juliana could tell she found it hard to deny Sir Oliver anything when his good-looking face shone with such enthusiasm.

As for her, she shivered, remembering her close up look into the cat's eyes; the big animal had a ferocity about it that anyone had better respect, she thought. And she would prefer to respect it from a very healthy distance!

"I have hired carpenters and set them to work building suitable enclosures so that by the time the cats and other creatures arrive—" Sir Oliver began, always prepared to argue the case for his animals, when a footman entered carrying a silver tray. The baronet paused.

"There are more?" the countess asked. "I hope there are no elephants, dear boy, or African rhinos?"

She turned her head as the servant paused at her side. He had grimaced in dismay at the mention of elephants, but now he appeared impassive once more.

"A letter for you, milady."

Lady Sealey's face smoothed into an imperturbable mask, but Juliana could not hide her own alarm. Even from where she sat, she could make out the sprawling, ink-blotted script and the coarseness of the paper, so unlike most of the countess's other correspondence. No, not another abusive letter!

"Thank you," the countess said, her voice quiet. She took the note, and no one spoke until the footman had left the room.

Then the countess unfolded the sheet.

"What does it say?" Sir Oliver asked, keeping his voice low.

Lady Sealey scanned the page, then tossed it to him. "The usual. I am not fit to live, and the writer will see to it. I should flee the country and never show my face again, and so forth."

Juliana swallowed hard. "Who knew that you were here?" she asked, hearing the hollow note in her voice.

"What?" Both the others looked at her.

"Who knew you were about to come out to your country estate?" Juliana repeated.

Sir Oliver pressed his lips together, and Lady Sealey nodded in understanding.

"Of course. I made the decision to come only this afternoon."

"How the hell—oh, sorry—how did our would-be killer have the chance to know that you would be here and not at the London house?" Sir Oliver looked genuinely alarmed. "Godmother, we shall have to engage some Runners, after all. I like this not at all. It must be someone very close to you. You don't think one of your servants—"

"Of course not!" The countess looked offended at the thought. "I'm sure my staff is loyal, and they have all been with me for some time."

"You would vouch for all of them with your life? Because that is what you are doing, you know," the baronet pointed out, his tone gentle. "You are certain that there is not one who could be bribed?"

She hesitated, but after a moment shook her head. "No, but there is someone else. You remember the list of suspects we discussed?"

"Yes?" Sir Oliver said quickly.

Eager to hear, Juliana leaned forward.

"I asked Lady Rives to tea," the countess told them.

Juliana looked at her in surprise, and Sir Oliver shook his head. "And she came? You should not have been alone with her! The danger—"

"The servants knew she was there. I doubted she would attack me in my own drawing room," Lady Sealey pointed out, her tone dry. "No, I was not sure if she would come, but she did. She would not pass up the chance to slash me with her dagger-sharp tongue. She still hates me, no doubt about that. But as she took her leave, Oliver, she saw the servants putting my bags into my carriage. That's the point. She knew I was going somewhere, and it would take no great imagination to guess that it would be to my country estate."

"In that case, I think that we must return her call right away," Sir Oliver said, glancing at Juliana, who nodded in agreement. "Tomorrow, after we return to London."

They talked a while longer before going up to bed. The countess wanted to burn the unpleasant note, but Sir Oliver overruled her. He put the dirty little sheet inside a larger sheet of paper and placed it in an inside coat pocket.

"You never know," he said. "We might wish to have a sample of the handwriting later."

"Just keep it out of my sight," Lady Sealey told him.

Juliana gazed at her hostess in concern. Now it was the countess who looked fatigued; this ongoing threat was taking its toll. They had to find the answer to the hidden threat and disarm the would-be assassin so that they could ease the countess's anxiety!

When she said good night to Sir Oliver, he bent to kiss her hand, and his touch seemed to linger. The warmth of his lips against her skin sent a shiver racing up her arm. The longer they stayed under the same roof, the more she seemed to be aware of his presence. Perhaps it was a very good thing they had a chaperone tonight who was more effective than a few servants . . .

Juliana looked up into his eyes, and the awareness in their depths made her blush. He felt it, too, that spark that jumped between them whenever they were close. Heavens, whenever they were in the same room!

What was she to do?

Concentrate on the danger to the countess, she told herself sternly. She had no right to think of frivolous yearnings when someone as dear as Lady Sealey was in danger. So, although she smiled up into his eyes, she made herself curtsy and murmur only a polite good night. Indeed, she could say little more while under their hostess's watchful eye.

She climbed the staircase just behind the countess and tried to think about bitter women who could nurse grudges for years. But a certain tall young man was the image that lingered in her mind and stirred her blood so that sleep came too slowly . . .

She woke early, rang for a maid and dressed in her worn traveling costume, the one that had been made over from an old outfit of her mother's. But even so, when she came downstairs, she found both the countess and Sir Oliver were up before her. It seemed that all three of them were eager to return to London and find some answers to this puzzle. So after she'd consumed a cup of tea and a plate of ham and sliced venison, they were soon on their way. The second carriage followed behind them, with the countess's dresser.

Sir Oliver rode again, this time on a mount of his own, and Juliana discussed with Lady Sealey what actions they should take. Then, when the older lady fell silent, Juliana's thoughts returned, as they always did, to the young man who rode only a few feet beyond the carriage window.

She watched him ride. He seemed almost a part of the

horse, so well did he sit the copper-colored gelding. His firmly-muscled thighs gripped the sides of the horse, and his back was straight, his chin up. He moved in concert with the horse's gait, and the rhythm was a natural one, not imposed upon the animal, but seeming to blend with its normal stride. For an instant, Juliana thought she envied the horse, moving beneath the baronet's easy control, then she blushed, thinking how foolish such a thought was.

And when the fast-moving hooves of the team that pulled the carriage threw up a rock that startled a bird in the hedge, and the creature flew up almost at the gelding's feet and set it rearing, Juliana gasped for the baronet's safety. But he pulled the steed easily back to order. His hands gripped the reins with such strength that it seemed a simple matter to control an animal weighing hundreds of pounds more than its rider. When his mount settled, snorting and shaking its head, Sir Oliver patted his horse's neck in reassurance, rubbing the coarse hair. The coachman slowed the carriage, too, to be sure that all was well, so Juliana could lean back to watch him.

How would it feel if those same hands stroked her body the way he gentled the horse, she wondered, fascinated at the same time she blushed at her own thoughts. If, beneath her gown, beneath her shift, he ran his hands along her arms and stomach and thighs . . .

Oh, lord help her, she was turning into a total wanton! How had this happened?

Juliana bit her lip.

She became aware that the countess was watching her. Juliana flushed even more deeply, hoping that her disgraceful thoughts were not imprinted upon her forehead.

"What's wrong, my dear?" Lady Sealey asked. "The baronet is unharmed. He's a fine horseman."

"Oh, I know," Juliana agreed, her voice faint. "I just—"

"You are having problems?"

How could she admit what disreputable problems she was having, Juliana wondered. She looked away from the countess's searching gaze. But perhaps it was indeed written on her face.

Lady Sealey sighed. "You are blessed and cursed, my dear."

"What?" Juliana jumped and turned back to meet the older woman's glance.

"You are one of the rare women who can truly know love. Many women never experience—in all their lifetime—the depths and heights you will attain, dear girl; so in many ways you are blessed, as are the men who will be fortunate enough to be chosen to be your partner."

Wide-eyed, Juliana stared at her hostess. Whatever she had expected to hear, it wasn't this.

"At this same time, it's a curse. You will find it harder than average to control your needs, and there are times, of course, when they must be controlled, reined in. Neither moral strictures nor fear of public disgrace can prevent the emotions and physical hunger you feel, but they can be contained, and if necessary, you will do it. Your body yearns for him, does it not?"

It *was* obvious, then. Oh, dear. Juliana knew that her cheeks were burning, but it was a relief to admit it. She nodded.

"We are not beasts, my child, no matter what that savage Rousseau writes." Lady Sealey dismissed the Frenchman with one flick of her fan. "We, of course, are English, and we control ourselves, though only—I admit—when necessary."

She smiled suddenly, and Juliana saw an unexpectedly wicked gleam in the older woman's eyes. Not sure what to respond, Juliana was silent.

"And as an unmarried lady, you must control yourself now, and I, sadly, must admonish you to do so, for your sake, and to observe my responsibility to my good friends the Sinclairs," the countess explained. "This does not mean that I do not feel for you."

Juliana met Lady Sealey's smile with one of her own. She felt at ease again, though she could not have explained just why her embarrassment had ebbed, only that she knew, on a level deeper than words, that despite their difference in ages the other woman did understand and that she, too, had felt similar urges, fought similar battles with her body's longings and the need to hold them back. Or sometimes, perhaps not hold them back!

Had the countess really had an affair with Lady Rives's husband?

And was Lady Rives now ready to murder her over the old grievance? Juliana sat up straighter as the carriage bounced over a pothole. Outside the vehicle, she could see signs of the approaching city. Perhaps soon they would have some answers.

They approached the quiet square where sat Lady Sealey's handsome home. The carriage pulled up to the front door. A footman hurried to help them down as Sir Oliver dismounted. Juliana waited for the countess to be helped out, then she followed.

In the front hall, she took off her hat and waited for Lady Sealey to greet her butler. Sir Oliver joined them, and the footmen brought in the baggage.

"We will have a cup of tea, change clothes, and then set out for Lady Rives's house," Lady Sealey announced. "You may bring a tray to the drawing room," she told the butler.

She headed for the big room, while Juliana exchanged a resigned glance with Sir Oliver. Neither of them could convince her that it might be better if they went alone.

"She may be a killer," Sir Oliver said again when they were all seated in the drawing room.

The countess waved aside his concerns. "I am the one returning the call, dear boy. She doesn't even know you. You might not be admitted."

"But—" he argued, pausing when she put up one hand.

"You have heard the saying, 'Save your breath to cool your porridge'? You know you are not going to change my mind, Oliver. So I might suggest that you do, or at least to cool your tea."

Grinning, he shook his head, but he added, "You must take this seriously, Godmother. Murder is not a jest."

"I never suggested that it was," the countess agreed, and indeed, her blue eyes were cool and seemed to be looking far beyond them.

So, an hour later, they set out again. Lady Rives's house was not as large as the countess's home, but it was a handsome one.

The door was opened by an elderly butler, a tall thin man with oily hair who looked as if a good puff of wind might blow him away.

He took their cards and went away, then returned very shortly, and despite Juliana's private doubts about their welcome, they were shown in.

The house had a curious stillness about it and seemed pervaded by a sickly sweet smell, like preserved violets left too long under glass. The drawing room held chairs and settees with gilt-colored feet shaped like dragon claws and a red lacquered Chinese cabinet which held colorful china figurines.

Startled, Juliana blinked at the unusually vivid background that almost obscured the small woman who sat in the chair before them. Dressed in a silk gown of puce and gold lace, she was as round and smug-looking as the gold-colored statue of Buddha, which sat nearby on a side cabinet.

Lady Rives, apparently.

"Lady Sealey, what a surprise," the small woman said in a pinched voice. "I had no idea that my company was so indispensable to you. I rather thought we had said everything that was to be said yesterday."

"You did, at any rate," the countess answered, her tone calm.

Although they had not been invited to, she sat down gracefully in the nearest chair, and Juliana and Sir Oliver, after a moment's hesitation, bowed and curtsied and followed suit. There was no point in standing like supplicants in front of this woman.

"This is my godson, Sir Oliver Ramsey, and my young friend, Miss Juliana Applegate. We have a few questions to ask you."

"What on earth could you wish to ask me? Whether I objected to my husband's affections being trifled with?" The woman's laughter, high-pitched and shrill, was even more unpleasant than her voice. "You should know the answer to that, Margery."

Oliver winced at the sound, and perhaps at the implied criticism, as well.

Feeling anger spark inside her, Juliana pressed her lips together.

"If there had been any genuine affection, I should not have dreamed of trifling—as you put it. Your marriage was a business arrangement from start to finish, Louisa. Perhaps I took pity on your husband. Or perhaps we were simply friends who enjoyed an occasional amiable conversation over a glass of wine.

"At any rate, you were busy with your own affairs and

wouldn't even have noticed our supposed liaison if you hadn't tried to balance *amours* with no less than three lovers at once and been dumped by two of them in the middle of the biggest ball of the Season."

"That's not true!" This time, Lady Rives's thin voice rose to a virtual squeak. "I was the one who chose to end those flirtations."

"It was simply bad timing, no doubt, when Lord Montaine walked in on you dawdling with the marquess's son in an anteroom of the palace at Vienna. And the child was only fifteen, I might add."

"He was a sweet boy and very fond of me!" Lady Rives protested, a flush of anger mottling her round cheeks.

"His father, who was also your lover—your bed had barely cooled from his exertions—was not pleased."

"A mere bagatelle." She tossed her head, but her hair, which lay so heavily upon her low forehead that it seemed plastered with some kind of hair cream, did not move.

"And you are still angry over such an old grievance?" Sir Oliver asked.

"I have the right to be!" the woman snapped. Her breathing was too rapid, she was still flushed, and she fanned herself rapidly.

They all watched her and waited, and presently some of the redness in her face faded. She drew a deep breath.

"If your conscience is bothering you, Margery, and you are waiting for me to forgive you, you are wasting your time!"

"That is not the purpose of my errand, Louisa." Lady Sealey's voice, which had never sounded so pleasingly mellow, was controlled. "My conscience is easy enough. I am in no need of absolution from you, thank you."

"We might suggest that murder carries its own penalties, however, and they are more weighty than those of an overburdened conscience," Sir Oliver pointed out, his voice stern.

The somewhat gaudy fan that Lady Rives had been cooling her cheeks with paused in mid-motion.

Juliana heard the small snap as a rib of the fan broke. Perhaps the woman gripped it too tightly.

"M-murder?" Her dark eyes widening, their hostess stared at them. "Don't be ridiculous."

Juliana would have sworn she was sincere. Lady Rives might be spiteful and small-minded, but a murderer?

"Perhaps I am mistaken," Lady Sealey murmured. She rose and glanced at the other two, who followed her example. "We shall not trouble you further, Louisa. I'm sure you have a busy day planned."

It was a relief to turn away from Lady Rives and leave the house with its showy gilt and Oriental trappings. Despite the surface brightness, the mansion had no heart. It seemed to reflect its mistress, both encased in a dreary tedium of unchanging malice.

Yet Juliana heard a steady tapping as they walked away from the sitting room. Glancing back over her shoulder, she saw that—with the aid of a walking stick—Lady Rives had risen. The woman rapped on the hardwood floor with a restless energy that belied the inertness of her pudgy body, and her eyes gleamed with spite.

Perhaps she was not as taken aback—or as innocent— as she had seemed.

Thirteen

The next morning Juliana found herself waking early, and she came downstairs even before the countess.

When Lady Sealey entered the dining room, Juliana was sitting at the table, sipping her tea and nibbling on a piece of ham.

"Did you not sleep well, my dear? You look pale this morning."

"Tolerably," Juliana lied. "But I'm concerned about you. That woman, Lady Rives, I do not have a good feeling about her."

The countess smiled faintly. "Louisa is so full of venom she will choke on it one day. But I don't think she has the wit to concoct a plot against me."

"So you don't think she's the one who poisoned the chocolates?"

The countess filled a plate from the sideboard and then took her seat at the head of the table, nodding as the footman brought her a steaming cup of tea. She waited for the servant to step back before she said quietly, "I cannot be sure, of course. Poison does seem to be in her style."

"You see!" Juliana exclaimed. "I think—"

Someone appeared in the doorway, and she paused, but it was the familiar tall form of the baronet. She flashed him a smile. He made quick work of piling a plate with meat and bread and puddings and then joined them.

"But you must take more care. Don't you think so, Sir Oliver?" She appealed to the baronet for support.

With his mouth full of cold beef, he could only nod.

"I don't trust that woman at all." Juliana had described her last impression of Lady Rives in the carriage coming back to the house yesterday, but she told them again, and she shivered, remembering.

The sound of the stout woman tapping her cane on the polished floor, like a spider biding its time in the center of its web, had inserted itself into her dreams last night, and she could still hear that ominous tapping. She shuddered again.

Swallowing, Sir Oliver cast a sympathetic glance toward her. "Don't fret," he told her. "We will keep a close eye on the house and on my godmother."

"You're not going to hire Runners, Oliver, you know what I said about that. They will stand out like a cuckoo in a field full of larks!" Lady Sealey shook her head.

"We're not staying in London. In the country, we can be more mindful of any strangers who lurk nearby. Besides, within a few days, I shall have beasts which shall make much more effective guardians than any mere watchdog!"

Despite the gravity of the situation, Oliver looked mischievous.

Remembering the savage glare of the big cats, Juliana couldn't hold back a giggle. If any hired assassin came for Lady Sealey, she would be glad to loose the jungle cats on him!

"But we have a guest, Oliver. What a way to treat her, shuttling her off when she came to see London!" the countess objected.

"I don't mind; we must keep you safe!" Juliana began, but Oliver interrupted.

"You said yourself, London is hot and dusty, and the Ton have already begun to leave for the summer."

"But there is Lady Pomfrey's house party and ball only a few weeks away, and she is north of London. I promised her we would be there!" Lady Sealey looked distressed. "You know I would not break a promise to a friend."

Not even over the mere matter of a still-to-be-identified killer, Juliana told herself, biting back a rueful smile.

"Very well, we will return to the vicinity long enough to attend Lady Pomfrey's ball," Sir Oliver agreed, grinning. "Are there any other social engagements you are committed to? Events important enough to risk your life for?"

The countess threw back her head and gave her hearty laugh. "Only a few dinners and a tea party or two, and you're quite right, Oliver. They're not worth exposing myself for. I will write notes begging off. You're being sensible, and I know it. I simply hate that some faceless villain can make me change all my plans and feel like a cowering poltroon!"

"You are no coward, and never have been," Oliver told her, leaning across the table to lift one of her hands and kiss it gallantly.

Juliana nodded her agreement. "No, indeed!"

Lady Sealey sighed. "I am not so sure. If I could only do more to unmask him—or her!"

The footman appeared in the doorway again. "You have a caller, milady. Lord Montaine. I have shown him to the drawing room."

"Goodness, the day is slipping past." The countess glanced toward the French clock on the wall. "I am coming. Tell my dresser to start packing my wardrobe, please, Thomas. Finish your breakfast, children, then you had better do the same."

Juliana watched her go, then turned back to look at Sir Oliver.

"Nicely done," she muttered.

"What?" His expression was innocent, but his eyes glinted.

"You can be very persuasive when you wish," she told him. "Lady Sealey is fortunate to have you looking out for her interests."

He smiled, and she felt the warmth of it flow through her. She carried the glow with her as she went up to pack her own clothes. Since her garments, even with the addition of her new clothes, took up much less space than those of the countess, her task did not take long. She had almost finished when a maid came to find her.

"You have a caller, miss," the girl said.

"Me?" Juliana looked up in surprise.

"Yes, miss, Mr. Needham to see you," the maid said, her tone innocent.

Juliana suppressed a groan. Oh, not again. How could she convince the enormously tedious scientist that she was not a certain warranty for a large donation from the wealthy Sinclairs? But since she could not be rude to Sir Oliver's mentor, she paused in her packing.

"I'll finish that up for you if you like, miss," the girl suggested.

"Thank you," Juliana said. "That would be very nice."

Glancing into the looking glass without really seeing herself, she patted her hair absently and made her way downstairs. Where was Lady Sealey? Oh, good. Thankfully, she found the countess also seated in the drawing room, pouring out tea for their visitor, so Juliana didn't have to face the ze-bra man alone. Putting on a polite smile, Juliana made her curtsy to Mr. Needham.

"Good day, Miss Applegate," he said, with slightly too much enthusiasm. "I am delighted to see you again, and in such good spirits, too. After the sad accident that occurred, I was worried about your condition."

"I am in good health and spirits, sir," she told him, won-dering if he realized what he had somewhat awkwardly im-plied. "My hostess is taking the very best care of me, I assure you."

The countess gave her lustrous laugh as she passed him a cup of tea. "Indeed, I do not poison all my guests, Mr. Needham. You may drink your tea without any worry."

His long face turned slightly purple. "No, no, I did not mean to imply, that is, a sad accident, I am sure. I-I-I mean to say—"

Juliana took pity on him. "Yes, we are all puzzled as to how it might have happened. As a scientist, Mr. Needham, do you have any theories?"

"Eh?" He took a big gulp of his tea, as if determined to show that he had no suspicions of Lady Sealey, and almost choking on the hot liquid, coughed until he rattled his teacup.

Leaning away from him—she had on one of her new frocks—Juliana waited for his paroxysm to pass.

"Ah, no, not really," he said at last. "Perhaps the choco-late had simply sat out in the sun too long and had gone naturally sour. I mean, if the box had been carelessly han-dled. These delivery boys can't be trusted—"

So much for scientific minds, Juliana thought, nodding absently as he continued to talk. Soon enough he came to his real mission, but before he'd gotten well launched into another explanation of his research and his dire need for more funding, the butler announced more visitors, and this time it was a pair that Juliana had met before, Mrs. Swarts and her charming daughter.

Miss Swarts grimaced as she entered just behind her mother, apparently about as delighted to see Juliana as Juliana was to see the two women who had called the first day she had come to Lady Sealey's house, the day the monkey had first run amok in the countess's household. Remembering the so-called "rat" in the drawing room, and the commotion the beast had caused, Juliana swallowed a smile.

Introductions were made, and Mr. Needham bowed to the newcomers.

"But where is Sir Oliver?" asked Miss Swarts at once, her voice plaintive and her handsome lashes fluttering.

"I'm not sure," Lady Sealey admitted. "I believe he had some important errands to run, something to do with his studies, or he would have been here to greet his mentor."

"And other important visitors!" Miss Swarts pointed out.

Her mouth drooped, and she threw herself into a chair, apparently prepared to pout for the entire visit. But since she couldn't admit that seeing the baronet was the real reason for her call, and since her mother could only glare at her—not scold her daughter in public—and since Lady Sealey, though she watched skeptically, could not point out that no one really wanted them there, they all prepared to spend half an hour muttering polite lies.

And no one could say, Juliana thought, that she had not learned a great deal about Society during her visit to London!

Juliana was struck by an idea. While the two newcomers were served with tea and cakes, she leaned closer to Mr. Needham and spoke quietly into his ear.

"You must be sure to speak to Mrs. Swarts about your research, Mr. Needham. I hear she has an interest in such scientific matters, and Miss Swarts is, I'm told, quite an heiress, although she doesn't like to talk about her wealth."

He brightened at once and as soon as he could, shifted his seat to sit closer to the mother and daughter.

When he moved farther from Juliana, Miss Swarts flashed her a triumphant glance as if reveling in some victory. Juliana tried to look cast down, but again, she had to press her lips together to keep from smiling in relief. You can have him with my blessing, she thought, and his zebra spleens, too!

She saw Lady Sealey's eyes twinkle and knew that the countess had not missed the small byplay. Keeping her expression bland with some effort, Juliana was content to sip her tea, nibble on a small cake, and allow the scientist to pester Mrs. Swarts and her daughter with tales of his research and the many valuable discoveries he had made about zebras and their vital organs.

And although the afternoon threatened to stretch on forever, even zebras run out of spleens in time. At last Mr. Needham took his leave, followed closely by Mrs. Swarts and her daughter, both looking slightly greener in complexion than when they had arrived.

Juliana spoke nicely to them, and the footman hailed them a hackney to send them home in. The door had hardly shut behind them when Sir Oliver appeared in the doorway of the drawing room.

"Any tea left?" he asked.

"Oliver, you really are a reprobate." The countess frowned at him, but her lips softened into a smile almost at once. "You know perfectly well they all came to see you."

"Yes, but I've been quite busy, really, going over plans for the animal enclosures. And if I speak to Needham, he'll just want to know if the animals have been dissected yet, and Jul—Miss Applegate is not in favor of that project." He threw her a quick glance, coloring again as he spoke.

Juliana felt a rush of pleasure. "Thank you for considering my wishes," she told him. "I still think you can learn much more by watching animals that are alive and healthy, truly I do!"

He grinned at her, then turned back to the countess. "And as for the other ladies, well—"

She waved aside his words. "You don't have to make excuses there, dear boy. Any man in his right mind would avoid the Swarts females." She poured tea for him and handed him the cup. "Here you are, somewhat lukewarm, but unless you wish me to call for a new pot—"

"No, no, this will do nicely," he said, taking a gulp, and unlike his mentor, swallowing it easily. "I'm parched. Will you be ready by three, Godmother?"

She looked at the clock on the mantel. "I believe so. I shall go up and confer with my lady's maid. Are you ready to leave, Juliana?"

"Yes, Lady Sealey," Juliana was glad to answer. "Maizy finished the last of my things when our guests started arriving."

"Good, then I shall tell my coachmen when to bring the carriages around and see that my notes go off to my friends." Lady Sealey rose with her usual easy grace and headed for the doorway.

Juliana knew she had announced her own departure, but she lingered for a moment, watching the baronet drink his tea. "I'm glad she has you," she said without thinking. "I mean, with this threat hanging over her, she needs someone to look out for her. I know her friends are faithful, but family is important, too, and you are that to her, I think."

"I hope so!" he agreed. "And it's been good of you to be so loyal to her, too."

He reached for her hand again, but somehow managed to upset his teacup. At least it was empty, and it only spun a little on its base, rattling with the clatter of fine porcelain. The baronet flushed, and Juliana bit her lip.

One moment he was so sure and so masculine, and then he had a moment of clumsiness, like an overgrown puppy. Sometimes, she wished—

"I suppose I should go make quite sure that all my things are packed," she said slowly.

Nodding, he didn't quite meet her eye.

She turned and walked out of the room.

<hr>

*The drive down to Lady Sealey's country estate was un-*eventful. Sir Oliver rode, Juliana sat in the first carriage with the countess and her dresser, and another carriage with more servants followed, with another hired vehicle bringing up the rear with yet more staff and more baggage.

When they arrived, the countess went inside and supervised as the lighter bags were untied from behind the carriages, and the trunks unloaded from the cart. Then, after they had all had a cup of tea, Lady Sealey went upstairs for a rest.

A footman approached Sir Oliver and spoke quietly.

"Oh, well done. I'll be there right away," the baronet responded.

Juliana looked up.

He grinned at her. "Perfect timing. My animals have arrived! Do you want to see?"

She needed no further invitation. Hurrying to keep up with his long strides, she followed him outside and around to a paddock at the rear of the house, well past the kitchen gardens and the pastures, where a large double pen had been constructed. She was glad to see that the enclosures looked sturdily built of wood and stone on all sides, even the roof. Even so, she hoped they would hold up to the teeth and claws of the fierce creature she had glimpsed in the ship's hold.

At the side of the enclosure, a cart pulled by oxen had been backed up to its double door. Two burly men stood ready to release the traveling crate's occupants. As they prepared to loose the crate door, a roar from inside seem to shake the cart, and even the stoic oxen stamped their feet and lowed.

Juliana gasped. Two of the grooms from the stables, who had followed them, apparently curious to see the new arrivals, retreated hastily.

"I would stay back from the enclosure," Sir Oliver told her, his voice calm. "They have had a long journey, and they have been confined more closely than they can like. I doubt their temper is very happy just now."

"I doubt it is," she agreed, amazed that he could sound so calm. She also stepped back from the cart to stand behind a small oak tree where she could still easily see the beasts that would emerge from the crate. She wished Sir Oliver would not stand so close, himself. But the baronet only leaned down to pick up a stout piece of wood, then he checked the door of the enclosure again and nodded to the head cartman.

The man, a burly Scot, gulped audibly and then eased the door a foot forward.

The animal inside waited no longer. Sliding out the narrow opening, it bounded forward straight into one side of the enclosure, as planned. It jumped once against the wooden bars that framed the long enclosure, a pair of stout pens made wide and long for the cats' use. Juliana held her breath. But the strong oaken poles, braced at key points by copper joints, held against its assault, and the big cat fell back against the grass.

Snarling, its gold and black irregular spots outlined by the green English grass, it turned its head and glared at them, as if asking who had dared to take such a beast out of its exotic home. Its eyes were dark and fierce and wild, and when it shrieked again, ears flattened against its head, Juliana held her breath. It was primal but magnificent.

The servants who were watching gasped, and a milkmaid screamed when she saw what manner of creature had been brought on to the estate.

"Quiet!" Sir Oliver commanded, his voice sharp. "Don't upset them."

"Don't upset *them*?" Juliana muttered, grinning despite herself.

The second cat followed just behind the first, fortunately also into the first enclosure, and again, the stout wood bars seemed strong enough to hold. The door was slammed shut and the heavy bolt wedged securely.

The big Scotsman wiped his brow with a dirty kerchief and breathed a sigh of relief, and Sir Oliver moved closer to hand over his pay and offer him and his mate commendations.

The cats prowled up and down and stopped to touch noses for a moment, then continued to explore their new home, sniffing at the grass and small bushes much like the house cats they resembled slightly in form, if not in temper.

In a moment, Juliana realized that Sir Oliver had come to stand beside her as he eyed the fluid beauty of the beasts. "What do you think?" he asked. "They are a little underweight, but they do not seem to have suffered too much from the sea voyage. I hope the anteater and the snake arrive tomorrow in as good shape."

"Snake?" Juliana tried not to shiver. She returned her gaze to the animals in front of them, watching the muscles slide beneath the burnished hides. The cats were indeed a little thin from their long journey, but hopefully they would soon put back the weight they had lost. Now she watched as they paused long enough to lap up fresh water from their drinking trough. They were entrancing to watch, and the crowd ogling them grew larger as more and more of the staff came out to see the strange new arrivals.

"They are amazingly beautiful," Juliana observed, "although I would not want to meet one alone in the darkness! What are they called?"

He chuckled. "They are leopards," he said. "They range over much of Africa, and they are meant to be wild—that is how they survive. We can expect no less of them. Ah, I see the hunters I sent out returning with the cats' first meal. That will make our guests happy." He strode toward the hunters to supervise the feeding.

Juliana saw that, indeed, two of the local villagers were trudging up the path with big bloody slabs of venison slung over their shoulders. Scenting the meat, the cats let out more of their deep roars and moved to the end of the enclosure to pace up and down.

At the sound of the cats' howl, the female servants screamed almost in unison, and most scurried away toward the house. Juliana decided to follow, not sure she wanted to watch what was sure to be a messy meal. She rather doubted that anyone had instructed the big carnivores in the finer points of dining etiquette!

In front of her a grasshopper sprang up from the tall grass. She dodged its erratic leap and paused long enough to glance back at Sir Oliver. He had shed his coat and rolled up his sleeves. Now he aided the men in the tricky feat of maneuvering the venison through an opening in the barn, managing to allow the cats to grasp the venison with their claws and teeth without also capturing the captors' hands.

His arms were corded with muscle and his expression clear and confident. How could he face wild beasts with certainty and yet overturn china cups and color up when faced with ladies at tea?

He was a paradox, that was clear.

Yet he still made her heart beat faster. Shaking her head at herself, Juliana headed toward the house.

⤳

Seated in front of the large mahogany desk, Lord Gabriel Sinclair felt a dull ache like a band around his head. The air in the room was stuffy and overheated. London itself felt hot and increasingly oppressive, the air gray with coal dust. He and his family would have already left for their country estate, except for the commission he had accepted to help Lady Sealey pinpoint her secret adversary. Because of it, and also because Psyche wanted to give her ailing sister a few more days before putting her to the stress of a carriage ride, they lingered. So he had taken advantage of the delay to make additional inquiries.

So far, this interview had been singularly unhelpful.

Ignoring the headache, he raised his brows and turned his look of polite skepticism on the banker behind the desk. At one time in his life Gabriel had survived as a gamester, and he was adept at reading an opponent's reactions in the small movements of his face and body. So, although Mr. Bartlett tried to maintain a bland expression, the twitch in his left eye, the nervous tremor in his hand, and the tightness of his throat that made his voice rise a little too high told Gabriel much more than the other man would have wished.

"You understand that I cannot reveal our client's business arrangements. It would be anathema to our bank's reputation if I revealed confidential information." The man cleared his throat and tried to face Gabriel with a look of confidence, his fingers laced together as he rested his clasped hands on the polished desktop.

"Of course," Gabriel agreed politely. "I would expect my own place of business to treat my affairs with the same discretion, so I commend your caution. I would not wish you to impugn your bank's reputation, or, even, perhaps, its future."

A definite hit. Blinking, Mr. Bartlett almost cringed. He reached for his handkerchief, then paused and replaced his hand on the desktop. Now he had a beading of perspiration on his wide forehead.

"I am glad that you understand. Otherwise, I would certainly wish to help you with your inquiries, Lord Gabriel. But my hands are tied."

In fact, his hands twitched as he spoke, and one bead of moisture ran down his forehead and slipped along his cheek. The banker blinked again and tried to ignore the sweat that popped out now in bigger droplets.

Gabriel gave the man his lazy smile and stood. Best to leave before the man melted away before his eyes. He had what he'd come for. "Then thank you for seeing me," he said easily, and gave a slight bow and was out the door before the bewildered cit would do little more than stammer.

It was easy enough to work out what the banker could not come out and say. The bank had lent Baron von Greft money, a sizable sum, and now they were worried about getting it back. Was his credit not good? Had they heard more about him since the first transaction?

Gabriel would have to do more digging. He would call on

some of the agents he had used for work on the Continent in other delicate cases. The problem was, they didn't have much time. The danger for the countess existed now, dammit!

At least there was the hint of a motive, to Gabriel's mind more urgent—if von Greft was in need of funds—than an old feud with the countess's late husband. And his need for money was surely more compelling than Lady Rives's resentment over an old love affair. Although how harming Lady Sealey would profit the baron Gabriel couldn't see. If they could find a way it would, however, that would go a long way toward establishing the identity of the villain. Therefore Gabriel would keep working . . .

The very idea of anything happening to Lady Sealey made Psyche go pale with horror, and Gabriel would be deeply grieved, too. The countess had known Psyche and her sister since they were small and had been especially close to them since their mother's early death. And she had been a true friend to Gabriel and Psyche both ever since his highly improper debut into Society.

Remembering, he grinned. A strange impostoring, that, and the biggest gamble of his life, but it had won him Psyche, his soul mate, so he had never regretted it. And Lady Sealey had stood by them. No, they would not allow anyone to harm the countess!

With that resolve, he strolled out onto the dusty London pavement, shook his head at a boy trying to sell him a sugared fig from a pushcart, and headed for the next name on his list.

Juliana wondered if anyone in the house slept that night. The big cats shrieked at irregular intervals throughout the hours of darkness. The first time she heard one of the leopards cry, she jumped in her bed, awakened from a sound sleep. It sounded like the scream of a tormented soul, and the thought made her shudder. At least *she* knew what it was. She hoped the villagers in the next hamlet knew where the unaccustomed noises came from, or the more superstitious among them would be out scouring the forest for werewolves and witches' covens!

By the tenth scream, she had given up any fanciful comparison and was simply pulling the pillow over her head to try to block out the ear-splitting noises. Even knowing how deeply Sir Oliver cared about his new acquisitions, she felt a strong sense of, well, annoyance. Couldn't he collect quieter beasts, like, say, butterflies?

Giggling a little at the idea of the tall, broad-shouldered Sir Oliver jumping about in a field with a butterfly net, some of her anger faded, and Juliana at last drifted back to sleep.

When she woke late in the morning, she rose and washed and dressed and then went downstairs. In the dining room, she found Lady Sealey, looking a bit pale, drinking a cup of tea. She had a plate in front of her, with the remains of her breakfast.

"There you are, my dear. Did you get any sleep at all?"

"Some," Juliana said. She filled a plate from the sideboard and accepted a cup of steaming tea from the footman, then sat down and looked over a letter that had been forwarded from Lady Sealey's London address. It was from the twins.

Ophelia wrote:

Darling sister:

 Did you buy us any presents yet? Remember that I have a fondness for coral beads. Are there any parties at all going on at this time of year? I do hope so, for your sake! You might mention to our cousin that he should be sure to invite my twin and me during the Season! You didn't hear of any contretemps in the shire, did you? If so, I assure you, we had no hand at all in it!

And Cordelia wrote:

If Madeline says the to-do was our fault, be assured it was not. If the victor's daughter had not come early—

Juliana sighed and put the letter aside for later, just as Sir Oliver appeared behind her. His hair was tousled and his face slightly flushed from the sun. He had obviously already been outside, no doubt checking on his cats.

"Good morning, Godmother, Miss Applegate," he said, his tone cheerful. "A lovely morning. You must be sure to go for a walk."

They both regarded him, the countess without a smile.

"Oliver, did you hear your beasts last night?"

"Ah, yes," he agreed. "They are definitely nocturnal, don't you think?"

"Everyone in the household can attest to that," Lady Sealey pointed out, her tone acerbic. "Our breakfast toast is burnt, the eggs underdone and the kippers scorched, all because the cook has had no sleep. Two of the maids had hysterics in the middle of the night, sure that the devil had come to collect them for their sins, which they confessed in enormous detail to the housekeeper, who as a result has taken to her bed this morning with a sick headache. So if your bedchamber is not cleaned, that will be the reason."

"Oh, don't mind about my chamber, it will do just fine. And I'm truly sorry about the disturbance." Sir Oliver gave her one of his disarming grins. "I'm sure the cats will settle down in a day or two. At least I hope so! I suspect they're still adjusting to the change in surroundings. I'm doing all I can to make them feel at home."

"Ah, yes. We certainly don't want to make them feel unwelcome," the countess agreed, dryly.

"I knew you'd feel that way." The baronet picked up a piece of blackened toast and lathered it with butter. Chewing on it and ignoring the worst of the charred edges, he explained his theories about the cats' piercing screams. "They may be calling out to others of their kind, you see. Or possibly establishing this as their territory."

"I doubt there will be any more leopards abroad in the English countryside to dispute it," Juliana noted. She hid her grin behind her napkin and tried not to dissolve into a fit of giggles as the countess frowned. The baronet seemed quite oblivious to the fact that the rest of the table was not as enamored of his beasts as he was. "One of them seems somewhat tame, I was surprised to see. I wonder if she has been in a circus? Not what I had in mind but—"

The footman standing beside the sideboard smothered a yawn, and the baronet continued. "Still, the other cat is savage enough, so at least one of them has come straight from the jungle." He went on about his cats.

Juliana took a bite of her eggs. The countess was correct. The food was not at all up to the household's usual standard.

But Sir Oliver was so happy that Juliana found her own indignation over her troubled sleep had faded. This was what marriage to the baronet would be like, she thought, wild animals from God knew where disturbing one's peace, and servants who needed soothing . . . She flushed and looked down at her own plate. She had no business at all thinking such a thing! When the time came, Sir Oliver would marry someone of his own station and wealth. So although Juliana might enjoy sharing his conversation and his unusual passions for exotic beasts, that was as far as their connection would go.

No longer feeling an inclination to laugh, she ate her

breakfast slowly, and the quality of the food was not what lightened her jaw.

After the meal, the countess asserted that she was going back to her room for a nap.

"If these infernal beasts sleep during the day, I must likewise take advantage of the opportunity!" she announced, her tone grim.

"Jolly good idea," the baronet agreed. "I'm going back to the enclosure to check on them. Would you like to walk out to see them, or do you need a rest, too?" he asked Juliana.

She felt at once quite wide awake. "I would like some air, thank you," she said. He offered his arm. With a small thrill she put her hand in its crook, delighting in the firm feel of it, and they strolled toward the front door. He paused there, however, and waited as she sent a servant up to her room to fetch her hat and gloves.

When the maid returned, she had brought not just the bonnet and gloves, but an extra item. "The sun is bright today, miss. You might also like a parasol," the serving girl said. "So I fetched this for you."

"Oh, thank you. That was clever of you." Juliana accepted the maize-colored parasol. When they stepped outside, she opened it and tilted it to shade them from the hot sunshine.

"A pretty trifle," the baronet said, although he had to stoop to avoid it hitting his forehead.

She laughed and tilted it back so she could see his face. "The countess was kind enough to make me a gift of it when we visited one of her favorite shops on Bond Street. I admired it in the window. It was very kind of her, but she's like that. We must keep her safe, Sir Oliver."

Sobered by the thought, she gazed up at him. He looked back at her, his clear gray eyes as serious as her own.

"Don't worry, we will," he told her. "I haven't forgotten

the danger. I have servants on the watch at the edges of the estate, and I have received two letters from Lord Gabriel about his inquiries since we came to the country. He is investigating von Greft. I have a Runner watching the movements of Lady Rives. We are not being lax, I promise you."

Reassured—his preoccupation with the big cats had indeed made her wonder if he had forgotten about the danger of the unnamed letter writer—Juliana nodded.

They walked toward the cat enclosure. Today there was no crowd of servants observing the animals, and the path was empty except for the two of them. The midmorning sun felt warm against their backs, and a haze of golden light hung over the meadows that sided the enclosure, like a halo swung low around the world.

It was a peaceful scene. Juliana was about to remark that surely even the leopards would settle down and relax under the spell of such a day when she saw the cats' pen ahead of them. The animals were out of sight inside their shelter, apparently napping peacefully.

"Really," Juliana muttered. "I think we should pound on pots and try to wake them. Let's see how they like it!"

The baronet chuckled.

He checked that the cats had an ample supply of fresh water and that the door to the pen was securely locked, then they turned and strolled back toward the house. In a dip of the path, they paused to look over a colorful patch of daisies.

Juliana shut her parasol and gathered an armful of the wildflowers to take back to the house. Sir Oliver helped her pick the flowers.

She chatted about the cats, then about the difference in the flowers which grew in the south of England as opposed to the moors of Yorkshire, and though he listened and smiled, for once, he could think of nothing to say.

As Juliana wrapped a length of long grass around the flowers to hold them loosely together until they reached the house, he simply watched her, enjoying the unusual moment of solitude, just the two of them.

He was mesmerized, once again, by the sweet symmetry of her face, the beauty of her delicately wrought features, and he couldn't seem to look away. He'd never been able to linger so long and so close to her before without something interfering, and it was intoxicating, like standing over a vat of the sweetest wine while breathing in its heady fumes. He felt a little drunk, simply on her presence.

She paused to look up at him, and they stood, only a few inches apart, and this time she said nothing, only meeting his glance, her eyes going wide.

Her lips were half open. Her teeth were well formed, and he could glimpse just a hint of her soft pink tongue within; for some reason, it tantalized him. She licked her lips, and he wanted to taste them. A gnat brushed her cheek, and she waved it away. He wanted to capture those fingers and kiss them, one by one, then run his lips along her cheek, her jaw, her throat with its pale line of delicate skin that would ripple with sensation—he was sure of it—and make her gasp deep within her throat.

And he could do more, oh, yes, much more, and she would love every moment of it, he would make sure of it, just as sure as weeks, months of study of what she liked, what she enjoyed, could assure him. . . .

He had devoted himself to many much more mundane subjects. Just now he only wanted to study Miss Juliana Applegate and find what made her smile with pleasure, shiver with delight, gasp with ecstasy. And if she moaned a little when he touched her in her most private place, if he put his hand just there, where no man had doubtless ever placed his hand before—

She stared up at him almost in alarm.

"Sir Oliver? What is it? You look . . . is something wrong?"

He smiled at her and wondered what she had glimpsed in his eyes. Perhaps he had looked, for an instant, as wild as the cats. "No, something is quite right," he told her and knew his voice was husky. "However, I fear that I am going to kiss you."

Her eyes went even wider.

He thought perhaps she drew back for an instant.

If she was frightened, if she objected, he could not, in good conscience, force her into something she did not wish; he would not frighten her again.

But she said only, "And when will you know for sure?"

Grinning, he bent forward and touched her lips, at first tenderly, gently, then with increasing force. But she met his pressure with her own, delighting him, sending the blood roaring to his head, and he felt his pulse racing. He pulled her even closer, and this time she did push him back.

Chagrined, he released her at once, but she said only, "You are crushing the flowers!"

"Oh," he said.

She tossed the flowers aside and pulled him back to her, and this time she put her arms about his neck, and they came together in mutual need, mutual desire. And he found he was kneeling over her, pushing her back against the soft long grass, and he had one hand upon her breast, touching the softness of it even while he kissed her mouth, her cheeks, her throat, ran his other hand through her hair, and in a moment he caught himself reaching to pull up her skirt—

Abruptly, he pushed himself away.

He knew that bemused look in her eyes, knew she was too lost in a fog of desire to stop him. He could have her totally if he wanted. And he wanted her, oh, God, he wanted her. But he couldn't do it like this; she was too innocent and too unknowing.

"Juliana, my darling—" he said, then had to clear his throat. "We, I—"

Blinking at him, she drew a deep breath. From somewhere in the distance, a dog barked, and it caused one of the cats to roar, suddenly, from inside their shelter. Juliana shivered, and she seemed to remember where they were. She looked around, sat up. "Oh," she said. "Someone will see us."

"No, it's all right," he assured her. "No one is here. But I think we should go back to the house."

Blushing, she straightened her gown and tried to push her hair back into place. It had somehow come down from its neat twist. Had he done that? He tried to help and seemed to only make it worse. She took out her pins and pushed it back into place as best she could, then put her hat back on her head and picked up her parasol. The flowers that had been crushed by their mutual embrace were beyond redeeming. Quickly, they picked a new bunch, then made their way back down the path.

Miss Applegate didn't speak, and Oliver didn't, either, but he watched her covertly, hoping that she would not hate him for again losing his resolution. But as they reached the big country house, she looked up at him and smiled, and his heart lightened.

When they entered the front door, they found the elderly butler with his collar on upside down, the footman still yawning as he accepted the flowers to put into water, and an even more unwelcome surprise in the drawing room. Without really discussing it, they had planned to walk on past and go up to their chambers to change. But as they passed the wide doorway, someone called out, "Sir Oliver!"

The familiar shrill tone made the baronet freeze in his track.

Juliana gasped and turned to see who occupied the big room.

Lady Sealey was sitting in her favorite chair, and across from her—

"Miss Stanwood!" Sir Oliver stared at the new arrival, as transfixed as if she were also some exotic creature just off the boat from Africa or the Far East.

"Oliver, dear!" the lady in question responded quickly. "I knew you would be relieved to see me looking so well."

"Ah, of course, that is, I mean—"

"We are very happy to see you looking so much recovered," Juliana put in, taking pity on the baronet's obvious consternation. "We didn't expect to see you here, however."

That was an understatement. Wild cats were nothing compared to the enforced company of Miss Stanwood. And as a house guest, day and night, impossible to avoid? Horrors. No wonder that the baronet had gone pale.

Lady Sealey threw him a sympathetic glance. "Do sit down, children. Yes, my dear friend Mrs. Stanwood thought that some country air would help her daughter complete her recovery, and Lord Montaine was kind enough to run Miss Stanwood down. I invited him to stay, as well, but as he saw that my household was, ah, in some disorder, he very courteously declined." She shook her head as she poured two cups of tea for the newcomers and then found that the sugar bowl was somehow empty.

"You will have to drink your tea bitter today, Oliver," she told him as she offered him the cup.

"A fitting punishment," he muttered, gulping the liquid down.

Juliana tried not to giggle as she accepted her own teacup from the countess.

"I went outside to find you, but you were not in the garden," Miss Stanwood told the baronet, somehow making the comment sound like a complaint. "Perhaps you and I could take a turn in the garden, Sir Oliver. I am supposed to be here to enjoy the fresh country air, you know."

"Ah—" He hesitated, picking up his teacup again and looking as if he would like to hide behind it.

"And you don't seem to mind escorting Miss Applegate," Miss Stanwood added, her expression twisting.

"We were not in the garden," he explained, a hint of desperation in his voice. "We were simply checking on my cats."

"Oh, yes. I understand you have collected more of your so interesting animals. Perhaps you would be good enough to show them to me, Sir Oliver. You know that I share all of your interests! A wife should always support her husband's hobbies."

"Hobby?" Looking indignant, Sir Oliver raised his brows. "If you think that my study of zoology is a *hobby*, Miss Stanwood—"

"I really think you should take a rest first, Miss Stanwood," the countess interrupted. "You have just arrived, and the trip down from London must have fatigued you. We must not allow you to overtax yourself; you have barely recovered your strength. What would I tell your mother if I did not take the best care of you?"

Miss Stanwood frowned, but Lady Sealey's gaze was firm. "I'm sure that Miss Applegate plans to take a short rest, as well. We often do in the afternoon."

Obedient to the countess's obvious hint, Juliana nodded. "Of course," she agreed. "I was just about to suggest it."

Looking sulky, the newest arrival gave in. "Very well," she said. "But not for long. And when I rise, Oliver, I shall expect you to escort me for a leisurely stroll around the estate to see your excellent collection of exotic beasts."

"A rest sounds just the thing for you, Miss Stanwood," the baronet said, not meeting her eye. His teacup clattered as he put it down too quickly. "I shall leave you ladies to your respite."

Standing, he bowed and retreated, with more than necessary haste, for the doorway.

The countess rose, as well, and the younger ladies followed her example. Miss Stanwood hurried to grab a word with Sir Oliver, and the countess put out a hand to stop Juliana and speak softly to her.

"Are you all right, my dear?" Lady Sealey murmured. "You have a leaf in your hair."

Juliana patted hastily at her disordered hair. "Oh, we, ah, were picking some wildflowers."

After Sir Oliver made his escape, the countess collected both of her young female charges and led them up the staircase. She left them on the next landing and went to her own bedchamber. Still looking sullen, Miss Stanwood made her way toward the guest room that had been assigned to her.

Juliana headed for her own chamber. She was in no mood for a nap, but she certainly needed to change her dress. A glance into the looking glass sent her to the bell rope, but she hesitated, hating to ask the servants to prepare a hip bath after their disturbed night. She would have to make do with a wash in her bowl, using the tepid water from her ewer.

When she had washed, Juliana sat down in her shift. She found that the maid, by now familiar with her habits, had brought up writing materials and put them in the bureau in her room, so she wrote short notes answering Maddie and the twins' last letters, keeping the references to Sir Oliver's animals short. She did not want to alarm Maddie, nor cause her sisters or father to worry.

Then, when Juliana judged that enough time had passed, she put on a fresh gown, though not one of her new ones. If they were going back to see the cats again, she would not end up with grass stains on her skirt. She picked up her parasol and hat and gloves and made her way quietly downstairs, but any hope of evading Miss Stanwood soon proved elusive.

Their newest houseguest was sitting primly in the drawing room, hands folded on her lap as she watched the front hall. When she spied Juliana, the young woman jumped to her feet.

"Ah ha! There you are. Trying to sneak outside with my fiancé again, no doubt, and without inviting me along, if you could manage it!"

"I beg your pardon?" Juliana said stiffly, pausing in the wide doorway. The fact that she would willingly have done just that made it a trifle hard to sound indignant, but she gave it her best effort.

"You needn't bother to sound so innocent!" Miss Stanwood continued, her voice even shriller than usual.

"I thought you said a young lady modulated her tone?" Juliana asked. "The servants are going to hear you, so do hush. Lady Sealey will not be pleased if you make a scene."

"A *lady* also does not roll around in the garden with a man," the other struck back. "Do you think your disgraceful appearance earlier was not noticed? You had grass stains on your skirt, for pity's sake, and leaves in your hair, and that is more than disgraceful! I'm surprised the countess has not put you back on the street where she found you!" Miss Stanwood took several steps closer.

"She did not find me on the street!" Juliana felt her palm

itch and had to take a deep breath to keep from slapping the smug expression of superiority off Miss Stanwood's face. "You'd best mind your fishwife's tongue!"

"Ha! You're worried about the servants hearing my comments? I imagine your disheveled condition is the talk of the servants' hall by now!"

"You should not pass judgment when you have no idea what you are talking about," Juliana snapped.

By now they were standing barely three feet apart. And, oh, hell, the countess's butler had appeared in the hallway.

Biting back the rest of the words she wanted to hurl at this silly woman, Juliana fell silent.

"A likely story—" Miss Stanwood began, then paused.

"Miss Applegate, I have a message for you from Sir Oliver," the butler said, his expression impassive. This time, he had his collar on the right way up. Perhaps the household staff was getting back to normal, Juliana thought. For the sake of their dinner, she did hope so.

"Yes?" she said, but was drowned out by Miss Stanwood.

"A message for her? He would not be leaving messages for her, how improper! He would leave messages only for his fiancée, for me!"

"You are *not* his fiancée, Miss Stanwood. Sir Oliver has said so! How many times must he repeat it?" Juliana interrupted.

Collins ignored the newest houseguest as if she were a buzzing gnat. "Sir Oliver said to inform you, Miss Applegate, if you decide to walk toward the animal enclosure, that he has gone ahead to take some further examinations of the cats."

"Thank you, Collins," Juliana told the butler, pleased that her preferred status with the staff as Lady Sealey's protector seemed to be intact.

Miss Stanwood's scowl had overtaken most of her face.

"You are going to walk to the animal enclosure? What about me? Sir Oliver was supposed to escort me! I have been waiting simply ages for him to come down."

What had he done, gone down the back staircase? Or simply gone out earlier and never come in at all?

"I'm sure he will, later," Juliana said, not quite sincerely. "If you will excuse me, however—"

"No, I will not. I'm going with you," the other young woman announced. "If you persist in sneaking about to see my fiancé behind my back, I shall at least go along."

Juliana wanted to grind her teeth. "He is not your fiancé, and I am certainly not sneaking about!"

Fourteen

They argued all the way out of the house and across the front lawn.

By the time they had circled the house, Juliana had pointed out that Miss Stanwood had no business making comments about other young ladies about whose past and family history she knew nothing.

Miss Stanwood had observed that the Stanwoods of Berkshire were a most distinguished family and their descendants could make comments about anyone they wished.

Juliana had noted that making barbed comments about a lady of good character showed a certain lack of intelligence and refinement on the part of the commenter.

Miss Stanwood had observed that the Stanwoods of Berkshire were a most distinguished family and never showed a lack of refinement, and, by the by, that dress Miss Applegate was wearing was sadly faded.

Juliana replied that the dress Miss Stanwood was

wearing was sadly overtrimmed for a country walk, and her headdress, with its three long dangling ostrich plumes, might well scare the chickens out of laying.

Miss Stanwood replied that the Stanwoods of Berkshire were an old and most distinguished family—

"And no doubt have the most distinguished chickens." Juliana finished for her, absently.

In the midst of this pleasant conversation, Juliana realized that there was now no chance of another tête à tête with Sir Oliver. Instead they would have an awkward threesome with this silly creature. Perhaps they could feed her to the cats. This unlikely and certainly un-Christian plan nonetheless made her smile.

As they approached the cat enclosure, Juliana put one hand to shade her eyes and looked about her for any sign of the baronet and his cats.

At first she could make out neither.

Then her eyes narrowed. She could see Sir Oliver, standing just outside the enclosure holding a string with a piece of cloth attached and dangling his makeshift toy near the head of a yawning cat. The enormous animal was inside the bars, stretched out upon the grass. The tall man seemed almost insignificant when compared to the great cat. He was facing the cat, looking away from them and didn't appear to observe their approach. He had no reason to turn, and likely, he would not notice them watching him unless they made a commotion. He seemed very close to the big animal, even with the bars separating the two. Juliana hoped he knew what he was about.

"Oh, dear lord," Miss Stanwood said, horror in her voice. She had come up beside Juliana and she stared at the scene before them. "Whatever is the dear baronet doing?" She drew a deep breath, as if to scream.

"Do not shriek!" Juliana warned. "If you startle the cat,

it will overset Sir Oliver's experiment, whatever it is. And there is another cat, too. The other beast must be napping in the shelter. I cannot see it. But still, we must not disturb them, and we must not make any sudden or loud noise. The big cats startle easily, the baronet says. No doubt that is why he chose to come alone."

"He should not have! He should at least have brought several male servants carrying guns and whips and clubs!" Miss Stanwood announced, sounding genuinely concerned, though she did keep her voice lowered. "How does he know the bars will hold against such monstrous creatures?"

For once, Juliana thought, they were in agreement. She didn't really think the cats could burst through the sides of the pen, but still, they were unnerving to observe, expecially the first time one saw them.

The other woman continued. "He could be injured, and then how will we ever be able to have children, heirs to his estate and title?"

For an instant, the image this naive observation conjured up was so dreadful that Juliana did not know whether to whoop with laughter or blush, but she shook both emotions away. And as she turned her head to hide her expression, she lost all desire to laugh.

"Miss Stanwood," she almost whispered. "You must be very careful not to scream."

"Did I not just agree to be quiet?" the other replied, sounding offended. "I am not simpleminded!"

"I know, but you are about to get a shock. You must also not run. I think they might chase you if you run. You must walk slowly and follow me. We shall walk toward the house."

"But I came here to watch the baronet! I don't believe you are really leaving. You just want to trick me and come back and have him to observe all alone. It is a stratagem."

Juliana bit her lip. "I am walking toward the house. You must do the same. Walk, don't run. And do not scream."

Miss Stanwood turned, no doubt to deliver a biting comment, but her words faded, as did the high spots of color on her cheeks. Not only did she not run, she seemed rooted to the spot.

Somehow, one of the leopards, with its sleek gold-colored skin and mottled black patches, had escaped its pen. Looking as large as a mountain, it stood barely three feet away and regarded them with mild curiosity.

Juliana moved very slowly, not quite meeting the cat's amber gaze, sliding toward the house and an elusive hope of safety. "Follow me," she repeated, her voice very low.

Miss Stanwood seemed turned to ice, and her face was as white. She didn't move.

Sighing, Juliana paused. She sidled back to grab hold of the other woman's hand, which felt cold to the touch. When she tugged, Miss Stanwood came all of a piece, like a china doll. Juliana thought she would fall, but in a moment, the other found her footing, though she stumbled a little along the path. With painful slowness, they tiptoed toward the front of the estate.

The big cat followed.

They had traveled only a few feet when Miss Stanwood stumbled again, and the cat seemed to regard this as an invitation to pounce. It bounded forward, almost touching her feet.

Miss Stanwood opened her mouth.

Desperate to avoid the coming scream, which she was certain would incite the cat to attack, Juliana threw her hands around the woman's mouth to muffle the sound.

Licking a red tongue over long, slightly yellowed teeth, the cat watched.

Miss Stanwood sagged against her, and Juliana strug-gled to stay erect.

"Don't you dare swoon!" Juliana hissed. "You're too heavy. I can't hold you up. I will be forced to let you drop, and the cat will eat you!"

Miss Stanwood muttered a furious reply, which, fortu-nately, Juliana could not make out, as she still had the other woman's mouth covered. But Miss Stanwood straightened, and Juliana was able to take a deep breath.

"I will remove my hands, but you must be silent!" she whispered. "For all our sakes, can you hold your tongue?"

The other woman nodded.

Juliana dropped her hands.

Miss Stanwood's expression was sulky, but she made no outcry.

"We will try again," Juliana whispered. "If we must make a run for it, go for that oak tree."

"I cannot climb a tree!" Miss Stanwood looked aghast at the very idea.

"When the alternative is being dinner for a wild beast, you might find yourself surprised," Juliana predicted. "And I will give you a hand up."

"We could shout for Sir Oliver," the other suggested, a gleam in her brown eyes that Juliana disliked.

"Yes, and if we startle the cat, we will be mincemeat be-fore Sir Oliver can take two steps, and we shall put him at risk, as well. That's a lovely plan," she pointed out, her voice sharp. "Well worth the loving concern of a female who claims to care for the baronet!"

"I do care—"

"Keep your voice down!"

The cat's ears pricked, and its eyes were focused on them. Was it crouched to spring?

Juliana felt a trickle of perspiration run down the center of her back, and Miss Stanwood paused, going pale again.

They were both silent for a moment. Then, when the cat's interest seemed to subside, Juliana tried a small step forward. Then another.

The cat turned its head and watched a butterfly flitter past.

She took another step.

The cat lunged.

"Run!" Juliana said. It had meant to be a shout, but it came out a small sound. Perhaps she was too intent on running. The oak tree lay ahead, but the cat was so big, its legs so long, the tree seemed an impossible goal to reach. Now the cat was upon her, and she winced, expecting sharp teeth and slashing claws, but instead it whirled, knocking her down.

She hit the ground, rolling painfully across the grass, then scrambled up as she heard Miss Stanwood cry out behind her. Juliana managed two more strides.

The leopard sprang at her again, neatly knocking her once more off her feet. Then, instead of diving in for the kill, it darted away.

Was it playing with her, like a cat with a mouse?

Not only did she sting in several places from new scrapes and bruises, Juliana felt an unexpected twinge of wounded pride.

"I am not a mouse, damn you!" she snapped, suddenly furious at being treated like a dumb beast's plaything.

When the big brute made its next run, at the last instant she twisted back and stamped her foot almost in its face.

Startled, the cat recoiled.

Behind her, Miss Stanwood gasped so loud that she sounded like a kettle on the boil, whistling for tea.

Juliana fled once more for the tree. In another moment she had jumped for the lowest branch and was struggling higher.

"Wait for me, wait for me," Miss Stanwood wailed.

Juliana looked back.

The proud descendant of the Stanwoods of Berkshire could, it turned out, climb trees after all. Dropping her embroidered shawl, she had managed to grab the lowest branch, but she hung there until Juliana dropped back to pull her laboriously farther up.

The leopard bounded after them, but it paused to examine the shawl. With much sniffing and pawing, it settled down to chew on the silk.

Panting and pushing, Juliana got Miss Stanwood about halfway up the tree, where they stopped to rest on a sturdy branch.

Thinking of the baronet, she glanced back at the animal enclosure. Yes, she could still see him, but the same reasoning prevented them from shouting for his help. If he came closer, he would be in danger, too. She would not see him injured if she could do anything to prevent it. And so far, they were still in one skin.

Although Juliana could not think of one good reason why.

And having acquired several more bruises and scratches to get Miss Stanwood into the tree, Juliana drew a deep breath. The woman she had saved sat squeezed onto the limb beside her and at once found fault with her rescue.

"Now we are trapped. We should have continued toward the house," Miss Stanwood announced.

Juliana pulled a blade of grass out of her hair and didn't bother to answer.

"You were making good progress, you should have continued. You needn't have waited for me."

"I wasn't waiting for you. The bloody cat was knocking me all around the field!" Juliana retorted. "Why it didn't just snap my neck and be done with it, I have no idea!"

Miss Stanwood shivered. "Still, if you had kept running "

"There"—Juliana pointed—"is the path to the house. If you would like, I can lower you to the ground and you may proceed to fetch help."

Looking offended, Miss Stanwood fell silent, thus proving that not all about the day was a hopeless case.

Perhaps, eventually, the cat would tire and go back to the enclosure, Juliana told herself. And then what, attack Sir Oliver? She did not like the direction of that thought in the least!

Perhaps a servant would come and find them and—no, the servants and the villagers, both, were now avoiding the whole area around the animals' enclosure, and Sir Oliver had encouraged this sentiment.

Which made her wonder, now that she had a moment not actively devoted to simply staying alive, how one of the cats had gotten out? Surely Sir Oliver had not been careless about the enclosure door? He would not be so foolish!

She became aware that Miss Stanwood might come from a most distinguished family, but she had surely the sharpest elbows that Juliana had ever encountered, and she had shared a bed, at one time or the other, with most of her four sisters.

"Mind your elbows!" she muttered.

"But it's eating my best shawl!" Miss Stanwood complained.

"Be more worried about what it wants to eat after the shawl is gone," Juliana answered, with little sympathy as she rubbed her aching shoulders. It was not Miss Stanwood who had been bowled across most of the meadow.

"Oh, good," Miss Stanwood said. "Sir Oliver has seen us."

"Oh, no!" Juliana said, at almost the same time. It was true. The baronet hurried across the grass, and the cat below turned to watch him approach and took a few steps toward him.

"No, no, stay here, we are your prey," she called down to the cat.

"What?" Miss Stanwood protested. "No! He is a man. Let him deal with the beast."

"He has no weapon. What do you expect him to do? Wrestle the animal with his bare hands?" Juliana demanded.

The leopard snarled again, stretching itself and reaching its front limbs once more high up the tree, clawing the bark. Juliana pulled her feet up beneath her and held her breath until the leopard dropped back to the ground. It turned and paced up and down on the grass, then, limping just slightly, it ran a few feet away, twisted and, before she could grasp its intent, loped toward the tree and dashed up the trunk straight towards them.

Gasping, Juliana put both arms around the bole of the tree and held on tight, while beside her, Miss Stanwood clutched her and shrieked.

Below, the baronet ran for the tree.

"Don't!" she called, afraid he would run straight into the cat.

And, indeed, as Sir Oliver tossed a stick toward the animal, who shrieked in protest, the cat managed only to climb a few feet up the tree before falling back. It was at least seven feet long, more than the length of a man, and it could easily touch past the low branch that Juliana had had to jump for.

But it was too heavy for the first limb to bear its weight. The limb bowed beneath the cat's massive body, and something about one of the paws—

"I believe it has a crippled paw," she said, keeping her

voice low. "Perhaps it has been injured at one time. I think, I hope, it can't climb. But take care, Oliver!"

The baronet had to sidestep hastily to avoid being square in its path.

And he had no more makeshift weapons.

The cat growled and showed those too-long fangs once more.

"Oh, heavens!" Miss Stanmore wailed.

"Don't talk!" Sir Oliver advised. "Your voices seem to excite it. It must be the higher pitch of a woman's voice or—or I don't know what. But better if you are mum, I think."

That was all very well, but he was still vulnerable. One less able paw would not keep the cat from raking its claws or biting off his handsome face! And there was the other beast who perhaps might slip out of the enclosure at any moment! If this one had gotten free—

The big beast now watched Sir Oliver, a low rumbling sound coming from deep in its throat. It walked a few inches closer.

The baronet backed up slowly, circling behind the low branch of the tree.

If she distracted the cat, Juliana thought, he could jump for the branch. "Get ready," she said, keeping her tone low. "Hie, you!"

The cat turned its big head, eyed her, decided she was safe enough, apparently, even if she was the preferred catch of the day, and returned its gaze to the baronet.

"Fickle, are you?" Juliana said, offended. She raised her voice. "Here, I'm speaking to you, Sir Cat!"

This got her another long look, but still the leopard didn't move from its too close contemplation of its earth-bound prey. The baronet needed more room to make his leap. Juliana glanced at Sir Oliver and saw that he understood, though the wrinkle in his brow showed his concern about her taunting the cat.

"I refuse to be ignored!" Juliana told the animal. She looked about for a branch thin enough to break off and found a twiglet, which she managed, after some tugging, to separate from the tree. She leaned over—

"For God's sake, don't fall, Juliana!" the baronet begged her.

Her given name on his lips made her heart jump a little, in quite a different way than fear of the cat had done. Nodding, Juliana tucked the sensation aside to savor at another, less perilous time. She held onto the trunk with one hand and with the other tried to wave the twig at the cat. But it wasn't long enough, and the beast ignored her.

Of course! She had the parasol.

She retrieved it from the branch where she had hooked it earlier to get it out of her way and waved it at the cat.

This time, the creature looked up.

Encouraged, Juliana waved it back and forth like the pendulum of a clock. The cat turned and walked back to see what this curious annoyance might be.

Sir Oliver took a step closer to the tree limb.

The cat turned its head and stepped back.

Biting her lip, Juliana pulled her last trick. With a practiced flick, she opened the parasol. The colorful maize silk blossomed like a large flower.

Startled, the cat perked its ears, and it made a low noise deep in its throat. It sprang for the new prey.

At almost the same time, Sir Oliver jumped for the branch.

By the time the cat had the parasol in shreds and was happily chewing on the frame, its teeth filled with shreds of silk, Sir Oliver had climbed to safety and sat squeezed beside Juliana on the one branch tall enough for safety from the cat but still strong enough to bear their weight.

"A clever ploy," he said. "Sorry about your thingamajig, though."

"No matter," Juliana said, though she glanced at the remains of her pretty gift with a moment of regret. "Better the parasol in tatters than your skin!"

But in pulling up Sir Oliver, she'd forgotten to keep an eye on Miss Stanwood, who was trying to move closer to the baronet.

"You cannot sit next to my fiancé," the woman said.

"Take heed," Juliana cried.

"Watch out," the baronet said at the same time, but it was too late.

Miss Stanwood lost her balance.

"No!" Juliana tried to grab her, but it was too late.

With a muffled shriek, the other woman slipped down the tree, grabbing at branches as she fell. In one last accomplishment, she pulled the baronet with her. She hit the ground in a cloud of dust and greenery. He landed with a thump.

"Are you hurt?" Juliana called down. "Oliver?"

His eyes were shut, and Miss Stanwood, too, seemed too stunned to answer.

Were they both dead? Juliana put one hand to her mouth in horror.

The cat stood and ambled over to investigate, as if sure that this time, its prey would not run away. Nor did either of them appear ready to flee. Miss Stanwood, at least, could speak, though her body looked crumpled, and she seemed barely able to lift her head.

"Oh, help! I am injured," she whimpered. "My shoulder is on fire."

Sighing, Juliana made ready to descend. Please, let Oliver be all right, she thought. And yes, the irritating Miss Stanwood, too. She couldn't sit here and watch even the distinguished and unpleasant Miss Stanwood be devoured. It appeared that if one was to be eaten, they all would go down the cat's maw together.

But as she was about to swing down to the next branch, Juliana hesitated, not sure if she would incite the beast further if she jumped down now.

Face pale as mountain fog, Miss Stanwood looked already half dead with fear. The leopard loomed directly above her. Its teeth bared, eyes wild, it looked surely as menacing as anyone's worst nightmare. Frightened, Juliana waited, trying to think what she might do to draw it away from its two helpless victims.

The cat opened its big mouth and leaned forward. Juliana gasped, and Miss Stanwood muttered what might be a prayer and squeezed her eyes shut.

The cat took a mouthful of ostrich plume from Miss Stanwood's hat, which had slid to the side of her head. And another.

Juliana exhaled slowly. "It's Jezebel," she said aloud.

Miss Stanwood opened one eye. "Are you insulting me? I'm about to die, and you must make rude comments at such a time?"

"No, the cat. It's Jezebel. Sir Oliver has named them. He said she is tame, or a little tame. Perhaps we can lure her back into her cage."

Juliana made a rapid descent down the tree, no longer caring about startling the cat, who drew back, but kept its grasp on its newest prize, the hat itself which it had pulled off the protesting Miss Stanwood's disordered hair.

Juliana paused only long enough to help Miss Stanwood lean against the trunk of the tree, which she did with a maximum of martyred protest, then turned her attention to Sir Oliver, who seemed to be stirring.

"You are jolting every bone in my body!" the other lady complained. "My shoulder is in agony! And if the other joints are not damaged already, you have no doubt broken them."

"Then you'll have to wait for more able assistance," Juliana said. "I have to see about Sir Oliver."

"But what about me?" Miss Stanwood objected.

"Sit quietly and I don't believe Jezebel will bother you. If she gets tired of the hat, give her another article of clothing," Juliana advised.

"And when I'm quite naked, what then?"

But Juliana didn't wait to answer. She knelt beside the baronet. To her great relief, he had opened his eyes. He blinked several times, then tried to sit up.

"Slowly," she told him, but he gritted his teeth.

"There is no time to waste," he argued. "I must check the door of the pen."

Juliana thought she must have paled. "You don't think—"

"How did this cat get out?" he pointed out. "When I saw you in peril, I rushed over and left the other cat still inside its pen. We must keep it there. Even if it is tame, too, or somewhat tame, I've seen no evidence of that—"

"Oh, good God," Juliana said, her voice faint at the thought of the second and even bigger leopard also free of its cage.

A bit unsteadily, Oliver got to his feet. They walked a few paces until it appeared that they would not tempt Jezebel into another game of chase and knock down the lady. Fortunately, Miss Stanwood's ostrich plumes seemed to be appealing enough to keep the cat's attention, so they hurried on to approach the cats' pen.

As they neared it, Juliana got a view of the door, and she felt her heart come up to her throat. The big double door hung ajar. Someone had unbolted it.

"Oliver—" she breathed.

He started to run. From inside the barred enclosure, the bigger animal watched them. It seemed to suddenly realize that freedom beckoned. It loped toward the door. It was a race, and the reward might be their lives. Even from here, Juliana could make out the cat's amber eyes watching them. Suddenly, the cat's mouth opened, and its sawing roar seemed to shake the ground.

She trembled.

The baronet called, "Go back, Juliana, while you still can!"

Instead, she ran after him. Outside the pen, a patch of bloody ground showed where venison had been cut up for the leopards' last meal. Pausing, Juliana picked up a scrap of meat, hoping to distract the big cat. She hated to touch the bloody bones, but this was no time to be finicky. Picking up a scrap of meat, she tossed it into the pen, hoping that the leopard would stop to investigate.

For a moment, the big cat slowed. In that space of time, Oliver gained a few paces toward the door. But he was still suffering the effects of his fall, and he seemed to move with terrifying slowness. The cat was not going to wait.

Desperate, Juliana ran for her life.

"Juliana, no!" Oliver shouted when she passed him.

But her hands were outstretched. She touched the barred door, pushing it forward, but it was heavy and seemed to swing so slowly . . .

The cat come roaring down upon her, its big face rushing at her, mouth wide, teeth bared—

Time seemed to slow—

A raking pair of claws caught her arm—

Streaks of white hot pain—

Juliana screamed.

Sir Oliver grabbed her. He tried to put himself between her and the cat, who snarled and reached for her again. Pain throbbed, yet one part of her mind felt numb. How had it gotten there so quickly?

Slashing and leaping, the beast was a whirl of gold and black motion, too fast for Juliana to bring into focus. The world was a blur, a roaring, shouting blur.

Oliver pulled her back, but not before the brute grabbed a bite of her skirt. It pulled most of it away to shred in its long teeth. When the muslin ripped into tatters, the cat took another bite, closer to her skin. She could feel its hot breath. Her skin crawled in fear. She couldn't seem to breathe.

With her gown in its mouth, the brute jerked her forward. Its strength was overwhelming. For an instant she thought she was falling straight into the leopard's maw.

But Oliver wrenched her away from the cat's grip. She clung to him. The beast clawed at the man, this time, slashed down his leg, ripping his leather riding boots.

Oliver kicked the cat in the nose. They fell sideways.

Looking almost as offended as a person, the big cat roared and stepped back. Oliver slammed the door shut and pushed the lock into place.

The cat threw itself against the door.

Juliana breathed again. Oliver put an arm around her and drew her away, holding her tightly against him. They watched the barred door shake, but it held, once, twice, again. The cat roared. The heavens seemed to echo with the sound. Again it roared and attacked, then turned, its whole body sulky. It stalked over to gnaw on the scrap of meat and bone that Juliana had tossed—it seemed hours ago.

She twisted to throw her arms about the baronet's neck. "Oh, you are alive. I am so thankful!"

"Only thanks to you," he told her, his voice somber. "Are you badly hurt, my dar—that is, Juliana, Miss Applegate?"

She so much preferred to hear her given name on his lips, but she smiled at him, not quite brave enough to say so. "My arm hurts," she admitted. "But what about you? Your leg?"

He glanced down at his trousers and the ruined boots that the cat had slashed. "Not too bad, I think, but we need to get your arm bandaged. You have a long scratch, and both of us need our wounds bathed and seen to."

"Yes, and poor Miss Stanwood," Juliana remembered belatedly. "She has some injury from her fall. Let us get back to the house."

"Ah . . ." Sir Oliver hesitated. "As to that, we have a problem."

For the first time, she looked about her. "Oliver, we are in the animal pen!"

Fifteen

"How did this happen?" Juliana demanded.

"There was no time," he said simply. "We had to get out of his reach—he knocked us to the side and I slammed the door. We are on the other side of the double cage."

"But can the leopard get to us?" Juliana asked with horror.

"No," Oliver told her, his tone reassuring. "I built these as two separate enclosures, in case the two cats did not get along. The only door between them we just bolted shut."

"Thank God for that," Juliana muttered. "But, what shall we do? If no one comes—"

"I have instructed my hunters to return at sunset with another supply of venison. So at the worst, we will be released then."

"Poor Miss Stanwood. If she decides she can walk, she might return to the house and then someone could come looking for us," Juliana told him. "Can you see her? She was sitting with her back against the oak tree."

He craned his neck to look in the direction of the tree. "She appears to be lying down," he reported.

Juliana stood on tiptoe. It was hard to see the prone figure. "Oh, is she all right, do you think? Heaven forbid, Jezebel did not attack her after all! She is not . . . dead, do you think?"

He narrowed his eyes, and she waited anxiously to hear his next words.

"She appears to be asleep. As is the leopard, a few feet away," Sir Oliver reported. "But I can distinctly see her chest moving, so, no, I do not think Miss Stanwood is dead."

"She just went to sleep?" Juliana blinked.

"She had a long drive this morning down from London, then a brisk walk, and a frightening experience with the cat, though nothing compared to what you have endured," he added. "And she is barely recovered from the poisoning, you must remember."

Juliana put aside any worries about Miss Stanwood. "Who could have unlocked the door and released Jezebel, Oliver?"

He frowned. "That I would give a great deal to know. I checked it this morning, but I admit I did not when I arrived an hour ago. There seemed no reason. And I have men on the edges of the estate to watch for intruders. Who is doing this and why?"

She looked at him. The elusive poisoner? But how? Was the villain truly a whiff of smoke, to move about unobserved, unstoppable? She shook her head and looked down at herself, for the first time observing the wretched state she was in.

She was a disgrace! Her clothes had been mostly torn away—she was half-naked. She should have been blushing, ashamed to show herself to anyone. But really, what choice did she have?

Sir Oliver seemed to follow her thoughts. "I have a box of supplies on this side of the pen," he told her. "I have some blankets."

She followed him past a hedgerow and found a crate, which yielded several clean blankets. She wrapped one around her shoulders, and he spread one on the ground for them to sit on. The animals had spent little time on this side of the enclosure, and the grass was clean and free of the musty scent of the cats. And, to her surprise, he brought out some clean linen cloth and two large bottles of brandy.

"To clean your scratch with," he explained. "And my foot."

She saw that his boot was ruined, but at least it had taken the brunt of the cat's attack; otherwise, he might have lost his foot! As it was, he had several cuts that he washed with the liquor and bandaged. Her own arm was doused with the fiery liquid, then also swathed in clean cloth.

It stung, and Juliana blinked back a few tears.

"I'm sorry," Oliver told her. "I didn't mean to hurt you."

"It's all right," she assured him. "It's only a scratch, really, and we could have been the cat's meal!" For some reason that struck her as funny, and she laughed a little wildly. Yes, a fine pair they were, coming so near to being a jungle brute's dinner!

A half-naked pair they were.

"I think that you might need some of this to settle your nerves," the baronet said.

Juliana felt insulted. "I am quite calm," she told him. But a little sip of the brandy might not be such a bad idea. She took one swallow, then coughed. She was not accustomed to such strong liquor. It burned its way down her throat, all the way to her stomach. But in a moment she did seem to feel calmer, and the ache in her arm seemed easier.

"Thank you," she said. She took another, then another. "It does help," she suggested, in a voice that seemed rather faint.

The baronet nodded. He took a gulp of the brandy, too, then took another long drink before he put down the bottle.

"In fact, I'm thirsty as hell," he said aloud.

"And we've had no tea," Juliana agreed.

They both took several more drinks.

He had a fine chest, Juliana thought, a bit abashed to see a grown man so unclothed. She was fascinated to see the sprinkling of dark blond hair that covered the upper part of his chest, just the right amount, she thought. Any less, and he would look too young. Any more, and he would have looked like, well, one of his beasts that he collected in these cages . . .

They were in a cage, of course, but that did not mean that they should act like dumb animals! Did shedding one's clothes remove the veneer of propriety that Society bestowed?

What on earth was she thinking? Juliana shook her head and regretted it at once. Whether it was the wounds she had endured, or the difficult encounter with the cat, or the small amount of liquor, somehow, her head seemed buzzing with strange thoughts and feelings.

And she was acutely aware of the man sitting on the grass next to her. He was so broad of shoulder and so tall and his skin so warm—she didn't even have to touch it to know, though she ached to. She wondered if village maidens ever glimpsed him as he roamed the moors and mountains spying on animals or watching lairs . . . saw him and

longed to join with him in some sylvan glade like nymphs
and satyrs at play in classical tales . . .

Juliana found she was intensely jealous of any female
who might have had the chance to see Sir Oliver . . .
Oliver . . . at work, unconscious of her gaze upon him . . .

Of course, she could see him now.

Could she touch him?

She put one hand on his arm.

The baronet jumped to his feet.

"I beg your pardon?" she said, her tone dignified.

"I think," he said, "I shall walk a little way and see if I
can spy any farmers in their fields."

"An excellent notion," she said, although her heart sank.
If any farmers had the bloody nerve to be working in their
bloody fields today, she would tell them exactly what she
thought of such impertinence. Today was a day only for the
baronet and for Juliana. After all, they had come within a
hair's breath of dying, of being food for that bloody cat.
Should they not celebrate their amazing delivery? Should
the baronet not be made to see the amazing logic of this?

Should she not be the one to make him see it?

Obviously so.

Juliana stood, with some difficulty. Her legs seemed a
little unsteady, despite the wonderful clarity of her thoughts,
and she followed Oliver toward the right side of the enclosure. They were surrounded by hedgerows, just here, but
there were no farmers within sight, and nothing else to be
seen, really. In a moment, Oliver came back inside their little patch of grass, where the blanket lay, and their quiet
corner of secluded meadow stood.

"No one is there," he told her.

Juliana was pleased to know there was some justice still
in the world.

He passed her the bottle of brandy, and they drank again. Not much was left in the bottle.

She leaned against him. He felt wonderfully strong and solid.

"Oliver," she began, then paused. "The world is tilting."

He caught her before she could fall and lowered her to the blanket.

"My dear Miss Applegate," he began.

"You called me Juliana before," she complained.

"You were about to be killed before," he pointed out. "It didn't seem the time to stand on propriety."

"And now is?"

He looked over her half-naked body, her bandaged arm, and drew a deep breath. "My dear Miss Applegate, I have done you enough harm today. I cannot take advantage of your vulnerable position—"

"Oh, piffle," Juliana interrupted. She put her good arm up to capture his head and pulled it closer so that she could kiss his lips.

He was still with surprise at first, and then he kissed her back, gently for a moment, then hard with a surging passion that was all any woman could have wished for.

Juliana shut her eyes and let herself luxuriate in his embrace.

A moment, a lifetime, later, he raised his head. "Juliana, you don't know what you are risking—your good name, social ruin and disgrace, and more. When a man and woman come together—"

She opened her eyes and blinked at him. "Are you going to instruct me about biology, Oliver? I know I haven't studied science, as you have—"

She paused to kiss his chin, that adorable cleft that she had been longing for simply ages to touch. She saw his mouth quiver, so she kissed his lower lip again, then rushed on before he could argue further.

"But I grew up in the country, with animals all about. My father is an invalid, my mother is dead. I worked on the farm side by side with the servants. There was no one to tell me what was improper. Believe me, I know all about calves and lambs and how they are engendered. I assume it's not that much different with men and women."

He seemed surprised into a laugh. "I am being compared with your farm's bull and ram?"

She grinned up at him. "Serves you right for inflicting your bloody cats on me! But, in fact, Oliver, while I'm sure it is most unladylike to admit it, you have given me the most amazing ache in my belly—"

She saw a new fire leap in his clear gray eyes, honest eyes, he had, always, and the last doubt inside her relaxed. At least he was not indifferent to her. She had not thought so, not after their earlier encounters, but still, it was a relief to know for sure.

Still, he shook his head. "That doesn't mean that we can act on what we feel."

What *we* feel. She glowed inside.

"Oliver, by all rights, we should be dead. We're alive, by some miracle, and—"

He was shaking his head.

"No miracle—through your amazing courage," he told her.

"It was for you," she told him simply.

"And now I must say no, for you," he told her. "And I must ask you not to touch me, because, Juliana, if you do, I will very soon not be able to stop myself. I have my limits, you know. I am aching for you, as well."

Smiling, she reached up to him again and drew him gently down for another kiss.

Groaning, he came, this big giant of a man who had the strength to break her grip ten times over.

Still smiling, she kissed his lips, tasting the saltiness on them, lingering to savor their firmness and their warmth. When his tongue pushed through her half open lips, she could make out the faint taste of the brandy and detect a deeper warmth which tantalized her. She kissed him back, eager to share this enticing new pleasure.

He ran his hands over her back, barely covered by a few remaining tatters of cloth, then his hands moved down to cup her buttocks and pull her closer.

Delighting in his touch, Juliana shivered. Her whole body seemed alive with new sensation. The grass was cool beneath the blanket, but his hands were so warm, and his body, hard against her own, rigid with muscle. She pressed herself against him. She felt as if the cat had stripped away, not just the layers of clothing, but layers of society's stratified dictates, centuries of rules and shalt not's, prohibitions against such a natural and delightful response.

The countess had said something about natural responses. . . . But just now, Juliana couldn't remember what it was. . . .

Oliver groaned, deep in his throat, and his mouth slipped down to her jawline. Juliana gasped; her skin was so sensitive there, and his lips on her skin—such feelings he evoked! For a moment she simply lay still and allowed him to kiss her throat, to follow his lips with soft strokes by his fingertips, then to kiss the base of her neck, and then to slide down farther to the last vestige of her gown.

He pushed it away and kissed the rising swell of her breast. And all the other sensations paled to nothing.

Juliana's eyes widened. This was a whole new continent. Like the explorers who had chanced on the New World when sailing for the Spice Islands, she felt a surge of both surprise and glee. What was this?

But before she could assimilate these feelings, he had cupped her right breast in one large hand, and Juliana found her whole body tingling from his touch. At the same time she tensed in anticipation—waiting—somehow knowing that even better things were in store.

He touched the tip of her breast, oh, so, gently, with his fingertip.

She gasped.

He ran his finger over the nipple, teased it, petted it, and Juliana watched with awe as the nipple rose and hardened, as her body responded to his touch. Such magic this was, strange earth magic, primitive and wild. This was indeed outside the province of Society's rules. She had been right, after all. Some things were meant to be left fierce and untamed . . .

And then he bent his head and put his lips on her breast, and Juliana gasped at the delicious pleasure that shot through her. And unexplainable though it might be, not just her breast throbbed with pleasure, but a deeper ache in her belly now begged for attention. She pushed her body closer to his, asking for more, yet not sure exactly what the more would be.

"Oh, dearest," she whispered. "Yes, yes."

He kissed her nipple, ran his tongue along the tip and the edge, suckled it softly, and she trembled from the ripples of pleasure that his mouth induced. When he moved away, she made an inarticulate sound of protest, but he only switched to the other side, where, indeed, her left breast strained for its own pleasuring. He pushed the tatters of her gown down so that he could bend over it and kiss a slight scrape on the breast left by her struggles with the cat. He kissed that nipple, too, kissed and suckled and kissed again until she moved beneath him in wordless response. But even as her joy mounted, the ache inside her grew. She could not have explained it, but somehow, Oliver seemed to realize her frustration.

She put both her hands around his neck and pulled him to her, kissing him with a hearty abandon she would not have guessed she was capable of. Any shred of the proper lady had been ripped apart during the cat's attack and left behind in their rush for safety. This Juliana felt almost as feral as the cats themselves, and just now she felt no obligation to adhere to ladylike standards.

She wanted this man. She would have him.

So she kissed him again, harder, and she pressed her body closer. But now what? It was all very well to talk about farm animals, but she was no ewe, and she had no clue how a man and a woman proceeded, so she held herself close and waited for Oliver to guide her.

Her body ached for his touch.

He slid one hand behind her back and loosened the few remaining buttons; mostly they came away in his hands and what was left of her gown slid away. She was left quite naked, lying on the blanket in the warm sunlight, her fair skin mottled by shadows from the high passing clouds. She felt curiously dreamlike, like some Greek nymph seduced by a visiting god. Nymphs in those classical tales tended to come to bad ends, one part of her mind warned her, but she refused to listen. She felt one with the warm earth, and her body hungered for the fair, hard-muscled man who leaned over her. They could have been one of the world's first couples, having just survived early predators, now alone on a sunny Greek isle or a cold Norse peninsula.

Just the two of them . . . and that was all she wanted.

Now his hand moved to trail lightly across her stomach. The skin there fluttered, extra sensitive to the slightest brush of his fingers, and when he slid his fingers lower to brush the dark curling hair at the base of her belly, Juliana inhaled sharply. The ache inside her had intensified, and he had barely touched her; this was another secret place, then, holding promising treasures ready to be explored.

From the way Oliver smiled down at her, he knew just where to delve. He bent to kiss her lips, softly, then more firmly.

"Are you sure, sweet Juliana?" he whispered.

She was sure that if he stopped now, she would die. She pulled him back for one more hard kiss, and then put her arms about his neck and pulled his whole body closer, wanting him, wanting it, wanting him to do what it was that men did, but above all to quiet that ache that lingered in her, that deepening hunger that threatened to pull her down into the earth unless they answered the primal call.

"I want you," she whispered back. "Yes, love."

So he kissed her once more, then paused long enough to shed the rest of his tattered clothing, and position himself over her, and she saw—her eyes widening a little—just what a man looked like with nothing at all to hide him. He was, as in his hands and feet and all of him, a large man.

But the need inside her was great also, so she shut her eyes for an instant. Then, too curious to not look, opened them again. She couldn't keep from tensing as he lowered himself to push inside her.

But he shook his head and ran his hands along her belly once more. "Be easy, my love," he told her, his voice soft. "Easy is better."

She wasn't sure what he meant, but the touch of his fingertips on her belly sent the ripples of sensation flowing back over her body. Her tautness eased as he remained poised over her, and her apprehension subsided a little. The good feelings returned, and he stroked her stomach for several minutes until she moved restlessly, ready for something more. He slipped his fingers down between her legs.

It was a good feeling, but like nothing she had ever felt before. For an instant she moved away, uncertain about such a sensation, but he approached the secret place again, slowly, and she allowed him to find that sensitive spot, and lead her back to such a moment of—oh, heavens! What was that sharp feeling? A pleasure almost too deep for joy.

Again, she inhaled, and he leaned forward and kissed her cheeks, her eyelids, her mouth. "Don't worry, love," he said, speaking against her lips.

"But so . . . so much," she tried to explain. "Such a big . . . an overwhelming—"

He caressed her and she moved beneath his hand, all of her body feeling the streaks of pleasure, of ecstasy that flashed through her being.

And now he lowered himself inside her. He was so big that for a moment she felt afraid of the newness of the sensation, and she stopped, but he kissed her again, stroked her face and the sides of her curling hair and in a moment he slipped farther in until there seemed an obstruction.

What was wrong?

He pressed forward, and she felt a slight pain.

"Oh!"

He kissed her quickly. "I'm sorry, love," he whispered into the damp hair that curled against her cheek.

"It's nothing," she told him. And indeed, compared to the pleasure she had enjoyed up to now, it had been a small pang. She should not have expected lovemaking to be total satisfaction, Juliana told herself. And the part of her mind that was still slightly woozy from the brandy nodded wisely;

she remembered seeing sometimes balky ewes, and said to herself, Well, no wonder.

But compared to the intense pleasure that had come before, a pang or two was nothing. Juliana reached up to pull her lover back into her arms. She was more than ready to continue.

He kissed her again and then slipped farther inside her and began a gentle rhythmic motion. To her surprise, this time, it didn't hurt at all.

In fact, it felt amazingly good. This time, the ripples of pleasure grew and like the circles left behind by a rock tossed into a pond, fled outward over every inch of her body. Pleasure, pure and clean and healing, after the hurts left behind by the cat. Now it was only joy, only the shared pleasure, the rising mutual ecstasy of two people easing each other's pangs and fears and sharing the wonder of being alive and whole under a blue English sky.

They were young and in love and tomorrow they could, would, must do this wonderful thing again.

Juliana had never known so much happiness. She laughed aloud in wordless delight.

Oliver kissed her feverishly on the face, the neck, on her breast, then he continued to rise and fall above her, and she arched her back to meet him and to match his rhythm. They were life at its most primal level, joy in the making. It was so simple, this lovemaking, that she wondered that it had seemed a mystery. It was so intensely joyful, so sweet, so good, that the only mystery was that people ever did anything else . . .

He was moving faster now, the sensations growing. It was like fire and ice flashing across her skin, and she almost couldn't breathe. The feelings Oliver induced inside her were so deep that Juliana thought she would swoon. This was the opposite of pain, as deep but more intense, a joy that spiraled and pulled her forward rushing into joyous release. Waves of feeling raced through her, lifted her, made her gasp and surge into his thrusts, made her meet him with a passion that was every bit as wild and free as his.

He pushed deeper, and she gasped with the intensity of her feeling, wondering if her soul had detached from her body, floating across the meadow like a dandelion's sepal caught by the wind, able to look down upon them both and smile at the coupling of two bodies and spirits in such loving union, while her body rippled in endless rhythms of pleasure, caught in an age-old dance of mutual delight.

And then someone cried out, or both, and she pulled him closer, even as he groaned aloud. And she felt him spasm inside her, pull her tighter, and she wondered if they could meld together and become one body. . . . But now he had pulled her close, and she lay her head upon his chest. It glistened with a light sheen of perspiration, and she knew she, too, was damp with the result of their frenzied lovemaking, strands of hair stuck to the sides of her face.

His eyes sleepy, he kissed her cheek, and smiled. "You are quite incredible, my Juliana," he whispered into her hair.

Juliana smiled back, reaching up to touch his chin, stroke its cleft, then lie her head against his chest, savoring the warmth of his skin, and shut her eyes in total contentment.

~⊱~

She dozed. She woke to find herself curled inside his arm. She ached all over, both from the rigors of the fight with the cat, and in other places where she had never had soreness before. The cat's scratch was one thing—her arm ached again. But the other . . . the other had been well worth it, she thought, tingling a little just to remember the extraordinary sensations they had shared.

He was sleeping, too. She lifted her head very cautiously to study his face. She felt a sense of ownership, a proprietorship that their physical joining seemed to have bestowed upon her. Perhaps it was an illusion. She had no idea if men felt the same way about such unions, yet how could they not?

She thought such lovemaking was bloody marvelous!

Just the recollection of what they had shared made her blood stir again, and she traced her fingertip down the curve of his firm jaw, touched once more that adorable cleft in his chin. Perhaps if she woke him, he would want to try it one more time. There was another hour or more till sunset—

Then she heard a scrap of voices and she stiffened. Oh, hell!

"Oliver!" she said. "Someone is coming."

He blinked and opened his eyes. Looking at her, he groaned.

Juliana, who had been about to offer him a kiss, recoiled. That was not the greeting she had expected. Was it possible that he regretted their wonderful coming together?

"Get behind me!" he urged her, feeling about them for any scraps of her clothing that might be salvaged.

She understood. Sighing, she helped him gather up what they could find of their tattered apparel. Society had lowered its iron dominion upon them once again; they were no longer free, paradoxically, trapped in the animal enclosure.

What on earth would the countess say? How could Juliana face her kind sponsor? Would she guess what had occurred, would anyone? For the first time, Juliana felt a genuine qualm. And what about her formidable half brother, Lord Gabriel; did he have to know? Oh, heavens. Biting her lip, she tried to put on the shredded remnant of her gown. She must conceal at least part of her nakedness.

Sir Oliver tried to help her and at the same time pull on what was left of his trousers. So, standing barefoot on the grass, it was thus, wearing only a few rags and with a blanket wrapped around her, looking more desolate than the poorest beggar on the London streets, that they greeted the two hunters who walked up with bloody slabs of venison slung over their backs.

Eying the meat with interest, Jezebel followed behind them a few paces.

Sir Oliver stepped in front of her. "Hallo there!" he called to the men.

"That you, sir?" the first man asked, staring. "What you doing inside the cage?"

"Of course it's me. We have met with an accident with one of the cats and are lucky to be alive. Let us out of the enclosure, and one of you run to the house and get more blankets. Our clothes have been shredded, and we are both scratched up. And Miss Stanwood is hurt. She's across by the large oak tree. Tell the butler to send at once for Lady Sealey's physician."

"We saw Miss Stanwood already, sir. John 'as gone to the 'ouse to tell 'em to fetch 'er."

"Good. Then let us out, and you can put Jezebel back inside and give both the cats their nightly food and water."

"Jezebel, sir?" The first man looked back and his face paled. "Bloody hell."

"She won't attack. Just move slowly and lure her inside with the meat." Looking white with fear, the man obeyed.

Juliana heard the click of the lock with mixed feelings. Of course she wanted to be free again, and yet, what a wild and unfettered time they had shared! She tucked away her memories of their incredible afternoon to be savored privately.

Sir Oliver had one of the men offer his coat to her so

that she could cover herself with something more than the blanket.

"Thank you," she told the villager, and she also murmured her thanks to Oliver. But he would not meet her glance. Hurting a little that he did not turn to face her, she pulled the rough woven coat about her shoulders.

"I shall set a guard on the animals night and day," Sir Oliver said, his tone grim. "I'll have no more tricks with escaped cats. Until we know who our secret villain is, I'm taking no more chances. I'm sure the countess will agree with me."

He left one of the hunters on duty at the entrance and arranged for one of the others to come back at midnight to relieve him, then they walked back toward the house.

By the time they arrived, Miss Stanwood was being tended to by the countess, the butler told them, until the doctor arrived.

"He'll be here soon, Sir Oliver, miss," the elderly servant said, staring at them as if they were ghosts. "Would you like some brandy, sir, or some tea, miss? Shall we help you up the steps, miss?"

"No, thank you, I can walk." Juliana tried to speak a few private words to the baronet, but again, Sir Oliver did not turn to meet her gaze. Servants buzzed about them, agog at their ragged state, and the baronet spoke to everyone, it seemed, but to Juliana.

Sighing, she gave up and took the opportunity to slip up the staircase to her room. She asked the maid who followed her and who stared at her with wide eyes to prepare a hip bath. When the servant left the room, Juliana glanced at herself in the small looking glass on the bureau.

She really couldn't fault the servants for their astonishment. Her clothes were the merest rags, and she was covered in dirt and grass. At least any evidence of their vigorous lovemaking shouldn't be detected, obscured as it was by their rough and tumble escape from the big cat.

Love—

She felt a little lost inside. True, the baronet could do little to show his feelings with servants and villagers all about, but he had not even glanced her way, shared a special smile, nothing.

Did he not share her emotions about their incredible union? Did it mean nothing to him? She felt betrayed.

"Don't you want to put on your wrapper, miss?" the maid asked.

"I'll just get it dirty," Juliana said. "I'll sit here with the blanket until the bath is prepared."

So the servants brought in the hip bath and filled it with warm water, and when it was ready, she discarded the last bits of her ruined dress. She remembered how Miss Stanwood had called it faded. That seemed a dozen years ago!

She stepped into the bath. Sighing at the enveloping warmth of the water, she leaned back and allowed it to caress her aching body. Her many cuts and scrapes stung a little from the touch of the water, but still, it felt wonderful.

She soaked herself, rubbed her body with rose-scented soap, washed her hair and rinsed it with the maid's help, then stood and dried her body with a linen towel and wrapped herself in a clean robe. Finally, she washed her injured arm one more time in fresh water, wincing at the pain of the scratch.

Later, the countess knocked at her door and brought in the doctor to see her. He examined her arm and cleaned it yet again, as Juliana gritted her teeth, then bandaged it neatly.

"You two are lucky not to be inside that beast's stomach," he observed. "Such a notion, to bring such savage beasts into England. Can't think what the baronet is about!

And now I shall inspect his foot, so he shall have his time to groan, and serve him right."

Lady Sealey shook her head. She sent the doctor on to his next patient, guided by one of the footmen.

"My godson should be hung up by his heels for collecting such dangerous creatures," she said.

"I don't blame Sir Oliver," Juliana told the countess quickly, hoping that she was not angry at him. "Truly, I don't."

"Then you are very forgiving, my dear," the other lady replied.

"How is Miss Stanwood?" Juliana asked, hoping to change the direction of her hostess's thoughts.

"She has a broken collarbone, the doctor says, painful but not serious. She will have to lie in bed for some time to allow it to heal. No more climbing about in trees." The countess's tone was serious, but her eyes glinted with laughter.

Juliana had to smile. "She was not much in favor of climbing them today, but the presence of the leopard persuaded her."

"Yes, I gathered as much." This time Lady Sealey smiled, too. "She has had some laudanum for the pain; would you like a spoonful?"

Juliana shook her head. "It makes one dreadfully woozy."

The countess nodded. "And it can quickly become a dangerous habit. You're wise, my dear. Then perhaps a small glass of brandy, to help you nap?"

"Oh." Juliana remembered the brandy she had sipped from Sir Oliver's bottle and its unexpected effects on her inhibitions.

Lady Sealey wrinkled her forehead. "Is something wrong, my dear?"

"No, I mean, I don't know." Juliana hesitated and battled an irrational desire to burst into tears. If Oliver had simply spoken to her, looked at her, given her a special smile. If only she knew how he felt. . . .

And what if they had made a baby? Could you do that, coming together only once? She had been so smug with her smatterings of farm girl knowledge, when in truth, there was so much that she didn't know.

And would the countess despise her when she knew the truth? Should Juliana despise herself? She felt her eyes fill.

"Would you like to talk about it?" Lady Sealey asked, her voice kind. "You've had a very difficult day. The attack by the cat—"

"Oh, that." Juliana waved the near fatal assault aside as a negligible thing. "No, it's not that."

"Then, perhaps being trapped in the enclosure?"

Juliana was silent.

"Oliver is usually a very courteous gentleman. I hope that he did nothing that offended you, nothing that you disliked?"

"Oh, no," Juliana blurted. "Of course nothing that I disliked—" Then she stopped, aware that her cheeks were aflame. And then the whole story tumbled out.

The countess listened without interrupting, and not until Juliana's spate of words slowed did she dare glance up at the older woman to see if her expression revealed disgust or anger.

Juliana was relieved but surprised to see only a slight smile on the countess's lips. The other lady made no comment at all on her charge's behavior, saying only, "Are you concerned my godson will not do the honorable thing?"

"What is the honorable thing?" Juliana retorted, and this time, she was the one who sounded tart. She knew the answer, of course. She sighed. "Offer marriage, because he has despoiled a young lady of good family?"

"And why should he not?"

"Because he did not have to seduce or persuade me! If anything . . ." Her words slowed for a moment, and this time she looked down, rubbing the coverlet of the bed between her fingers. "I think I may have persuaded him!"

"I doubt he took much persuading, my dear," Lady Sealey replied, a twinkle in her blue eyes.

"Yes, but I do not want to marry him because he feels duty-bound," Juliana confessed.

"Because you do not love him?"

"Because I do," Juliana said, her voice barely audible. "And to bind him to me in such a way, surely, he would hate me for it!"

"I see," the countess said.

And Juliana thought that perhaps she did. So she gained the courage to look up again. "Is it possible that I could be with child, after only one—one time?"

The countess raised her silvery brows. "I fear it's quite possible, my dear. When was the date of your last courses?"

Juliana told her. They sat together and talked about female things, and about how one might reduce the chances, just slightly, of becoming a mother before one wished, if Juliana had known enough to plan ahead. But she had not, of course, so it was all moot.

"And none of this is certain," the countess told her. "Which is why intimate contact, before one is safely wed, is so risky, my dear. And I doubt you would be willing to send a baby—if one should ensue—away to be raised by someone else."

Such a thought had not even occurred to her. Juliana felt her heart contract. Give up a child that Sir Oliver had fathered? A child who might bear its father's face, his gray eyes or tall form? No, indeed. She would take the child and go away herself, first, live in a cottage under a false name.

Indeed, she would have to do just that, or bring ruin on her own family and all her sisters. They would never find a husband, either, if her own disgrace became public knowledge.

"Oh, dear." She put her hands to her face. What had she done?

"Now, do not despair yet," the countess said. "But I do think you should have a serious talk with Sir Oliver."

Juliana nodded, but her spirits were still low. She had placed him, and herself, in an intolerable position. Even if he offered marriage—and how could he not—she would never know, now, if he truly loved her!

When it came time for dinner, Juliana found she was not at all hungry, and the thought of sitting at the dinner table facing Sir Oliver on the other side, and finding that he still avoided her gaze, looking away so as not to meet her eyes . . . just thinking of it made her cheeks flame. No, she could not!

So when a maid came to see if she felt like coming down or preferred a tray in her room, Juliana thankfully asked for a tray. She lay back in bed and was more than glad to sip the hot tea and eat a few bites off the plate of food when it arrived. Somehow, she had no desire for wine or sherry.

The maid returned shortly to take away the tray, and the countess herself came to check on her before bedtime.

"You are a little warm, my dear. Do not exert yourself. I do not wish to see you feverish," Lady Sealey told her, looking worried.

"It's nothing," Juliana predicted. "I'm just very tired."

The next day, Sir Oliver sent up word that he would like a few words with her, in private, if she felt like coming down to the library.

Juliana gripped her hands together and told the maid, whose own eyes were sparkling in anticipation, that she didn't feel up to coming downstairs just yet.

The maid blinked in disappointment.

"Oh. Are you sure, miss? He'll be disappointed!" She blushed at being so forward. "At least, I should think he will be."

Juliana wished she could be so sure. "Tell him I'm very sorry, b-but I'm not ready to come downstairs today."

And for the next few days, she kept to her room, feeling no interest in rejoining the company in the rest of the house. She heard household chatter from the maids who were happy to linger and share the gossip below stairs. Miss Stanwood was also abed and complained mightily to any servant who had the misfortune to deliver her a meal. Sir Oliver spent most of his time in one of the small barns that he had converted to his animal shed, with that imp of a monkey, a large tank of fish that were all colors and sizes, and a dreadful snake that was as big around as a small tree.

The servants had all gone out to see the snake, and it had caused the kitchen maid to faint dead away. Juliana remembered the kitchen maid. She fainted dead away at the slightest provocation, as Juliana recalled.

But mostly, the snake just lay around and didn't do much of anything exciting, so the servants had given up visiting. The big cats were still being guarded night and day, and there 'ad been no more life-threatening escapes, the maid told her.

Twice more, Sir Oliver sent her a message by one of the servants, and twice more, Juliana refused his request. How could she answer the "honorable proposal" she feared he would make, when she had not yet decided what an honorable answer would be?

She had written an anguished letter to her sister Maddie, and she waited anxiously for the answer. When it arrived and a maid brought it up with a steaming cup of tea and some freshly made scones, Juliana gave the girl a smile and could hardly wait for the servant to leave the room before she ripped open the folded sheet.

But the short note was not what she had expected.

If you are with child, Jules, or think you might be, you would be a fool not to marry him. If nothing else, think what you owe to the child. Would you make the baby a bastard?

That was all, except for a scrawled signature.

Juliana stared at the words. Her sister Maddie, usually so gentle and understanding, didn't understand at all. Of course, Juliana was thinking of the child, if there was one, and she would never discount the effect on its future . . . but there were other things at stake, too.

Feeling disappointed and almost angry, she ripped the sheet into small pieces and tucked it inside one of her carpetbags, so that none of the servants would see it. Then she paced up and down in front of the bed, feeling like a prisoner in the Tower.

Two days later, Juliana found that her courses had started.

She went to her bureau to get the necessary stuff, but she found that her hands were shaking, and she felt light-headed. She had to sink down upon the cool wooden floor.

She was shaking with relief and also, a curious disappointment.

There would be no child. No baby with clear gray eyes and his father's firm chin . . . She had almost been able to picture a small boy with a face not quite as strongly cast as the baronet's. But of course she was happy that she had been spared the potential disgrace, she told herself, really, she was. This time, their wild lovemaking would bear no fruit, no life-changing evidence of their mutual lack of fore-sight.

She knew now that she would not be punished. And yet, one part of her mind pushed away the hard word; it had been so glorious, so uplifting, so mutually freeing and pleasurable. Why did Oliver seem so reluctant to acknowledge how glorious and grand and lovely that sharing of love had been?

There seemed only one painful, terrible answer.

He must not love her after all, or at least, he did not love her enough, not enough to make up for her lack of fortune, her lack of dowry . . . Perhaps in the intervening days since his passion had cooled, he had talked to Lady Sealey, found out from her or even from Lord Gabriel about her father's penury and her many sisters . . .

It didn't matter. Her heart would break when she said good-bye to him and returned to Yorkshire, but she would do it.

Or she could pretend that she was still not sure about the baby, some devil whispered into her ear. Why, she could have accepted him yesterday, married him quickly, and then—

Then he could have hated her at his leisure.

No, she would hear his proposal now and tell him he needn't bother, and she would go away with her pride, at least, intact.

For as much as her damned chilly pride would be worth.

So she stayed in her room for several more days until her monthly cycle had passed, but still her thoughts were as dark as the lowering clouds outside that seemed to touch the horizon. On the next morning she rose and washed, ate a few bites from her breakfast tray, then put on one of her new muslin dresses, did her hair as neatly as she could, and wrapped a rather threadbare shawl about her arms. The skies outside looked gray, and she felt cold inside. She came downstairs, ready to confront the baronet, but instead she came face-to-face with the countess's butler, his expression concerned.

It jolted her; he never showed his feelings.

"What is it, Collins?" she asked before she thought. "Is the countess all right?"

He nodded. "She 'asn't come down yet, miss. But this 'as come, another one, and, and it's from the village, miss."

He held out the wrinkled sheet of paper with the by-now-familiar too-large handwriting, his elderly face contorted with worry. He had figured it out, then, that these were the letters that made his employer tense with anxiety. How long had he known? Then she realized exactly what he had said.

"What do you mean, from the village?"

"The London stage 'asn't come in yet, miss. The letter 'ad to be written right 'ere in the village. Whoever sent it, 'e's miscalculated, this time."

Madame X was in the village? Juliana felt her heart beat faster. This was more important than confronting Sir Oliver about his lack of fidelity, which was hardly going to change in the next hour. "I'm walking to the village, Collins."

"Miss, you mustn't go alone," the servant told her, sounding apprehensive again.

She nodded. "I shall take the largest footman with me," she agreed. Lady Rives, if it were her, was short and elderly, but sometimes hatred gave people unusual strength. So far the would-be killer had operated more from guile and trickery than brute force, but still . . .

Thomas the footman was summoned, and with his escort, Juliana set out at a smart pace. There were only two inns in the village that had rooms to rent; neither were large or really suited for gentry, but if an elderly lady was staying in either, it would be known. And Juliana meant to find out.

When she approached the hamlet, she slowed, finding that she was breathing quickly, and gave herself time to catch her breath. She had hurried her step, and she needed to look as normal as possible. No need to give away her knowledge that this might be important information that she sought.

The first inn had no visitors except the landlord's own mother-in-law, the man told her cheerfully. "But ye can take her with ye, if ye wish, miss, and a good riddance, too. Afraid your friend ain't showed up as yet."

"Thank you, sir," Juliana told him, her tone polite. "I will check back, later." She ducked beneath the low door-way and made her way up the street to the larger inn at the other end of the street.

Here she asked about a lady from London, and again she drew a negative response. "No ladies," the woman with the sprigged apron told her as she swept the wood floor.

Juliana was about to turn away in disappointment when the woman paused with her broom, adding, "Only the gen-t'lman, this week."

Juliana hesitated, wishing she had not been so specific in her question. "Perhaps my friend's husband has come ahead. Is he here now? Could I speak to him?"

"I think Mr. Brown 'as gone out, miss," the landlady told her. "But if ye 'as a card, I could leave it in 'is room; it's just at the 'ead of the stairs, like."

"Oh, that's a good idea. I'll just run up and push it under the door," Juliana said brightly. "And not put you to the trouble."

Before the woman could protest, Juliana turned and ran up the wooden staircase. Alone on the landing—she had

left the footman on watch outside on the street—she put her
ear to the oak door and listened, but heard no sound from
inside the bedroom. She tried the doorknob cautiously, and
it turned, she slipped inside, her heart beating loudly.

An elegant street coat had been tossed across a chair,
and a pair of well-cut boots sprawled on the floor. A gentleman of fashion was staying here, that was certain. Who
was he, really, and had he any connection to the threatening letters, or was his presence here only a coincidence?
Hoping that the visitor didn't return too soon, Juliana
looked about her. The top of the bureau held ivory-backed
brushes, a well-worn copy of Rousseau—why did that ring
a bell?—and several documents. Juliana glanced at the
door, which she had left slightly ajar.

Her nerves ajingle as she listened for any hint of a foot-
fall, she hesitated, then touching the first roll of paper gingerly with her fingertips, she smoothed out the heavy
paper, trying to see what the document might be.

But her curiosity was left unquenched. The paper was
covered in intricate script; the words were in a foreign
tongue and told her nothing. An ornate gilt seal was affixed
at the bottom. Juliana stared at it, frustrated by her inability
to decipher the words on the page. What on earth?

Then she heard sounds on the stairwell. Gulping, she
rerolled the paper and replaced it on top of the bureau, as
close as possible to how it had been lying. She slipped out
the door and pulled it quietly shut. Yes, someone was
climbing the steps! She looked about for a place to hide,
but there was nothing but the bare landing.

She had no choice. She would have to brazen it out and
go back down the narrow staircase. There was no flight going any farther up. They were already beneath the roof, as
it was. Drawing a deep breath and trying not to look guilty,
Juliana faced the stairs and started down.

Sixteen

Juliana tried to stare straight ahead, but it was a nar-row staircase. It was impossible to avoid the eyes of the stocky man in the dark suit, and she knew his features were familiar. But who was he?

To her horror, he paused and did not make way for her to pass. Unless he stepped aside, she did not think she could brush past him.

"Were you looking for me, Miss Applegate?"

"Ah, no?" She felt herself flush, and she tried her best to look innocent. "I'm afraid you have me at a disadvantage, sir."

"Quite possibly," he said, his tone dry. He had an accent, she noted, and she had seen him before, she was sure of it, but she could not place a name to his form. She had met too many new faces in the last weeks since she had come to London, and just now, with her pulse racing, her wits seemed to have gone all ajumble.

He put one hand on her arm, and she thought he would

force her back up the stairs. Her mouth went dry. Should she scream, and would anyone hear, if she did so?

Then the staircase went even darker, and she saw someone had stepped in front of the bottom of the stairs, blocking the faint sunlight.

"You coming along now, miss? They'll be wantin' us at 'ome."

"Yes, Thomas, thank you, I'm just coming," she managed to answer.

To her intense relief, the man let go of her arm, and she hurried past him. The footman stepped aside and followed her back out the door.

"I 'ope that wasn't too forward, miss," the servant said, his mouth pursed with worry. "But you took such a long time, and I was afeared—"

"Oh, Thomas, that was excellent, you may have saved my life," Juliana told him, her heart still beating very hard. "Or perhaps I am just—just agitated over, well, I don't know. But we must go and speak to the countess."

"Yes, miss," the footman agreed, obviously relieved to be returning to the estate. They walked rapidly back, taking the short cut across the fields, and once they arrived, Juliana thanked the footman again, then hurried up to find the countess.

Lady Sealey was in the drawing room, where Juliana poured out a tangled tale so confused that the countess had to bid her to sit and drink some tea and start over before she could make head or tales of it. So Juliana did as she was told and, more slowly, told her about the mysterious man with the familiar face, and the document with the foreign inscription and the impressive seal, and the unnerving encounter in the stairwell.

"Perhaps he was simply annoyed that I was snooping in his room," Juliana said now. "He called me by name, so he certainly knew who I was. But perhaps I have made more of it than it was, I simply don't know. I did feel there was something about the look in his eyes; it was so cold!" She shivered as she remembered. She glanced up to see that the countess appeared very grave.

"I do not wish you to go out past the estate's boundaries again alone," Lady Sealey told her.

"But I did not; I took the footman with me," Juliana pointed out.

"I know, and that may, indeed, have saved your life," the countess said, her tone sober. "I shall see that he is rewarded for his quick thinking."

"Then do you suppose this is the villain who may have been trying to—" Juliana stopped, trying to fit it all together. There were still too many parts of the puzzle missing. "But I don't understand."

"Tell me about this document you saw. Did you recognize any words at all?"

Juliana shook her head. "I'm sorry. I think it was in German, but I'm afraid I didn't study it as a girl."

"Did you see any names, my dear?"

"Oh." Juliana considered, shutting her eyes and trying to visualize the paper. "I did, in fact. Marie Alexanderine, I think, and Hapsburg. Yes, I think that's right."

She opened her eyes to see that the countess was staring at the far end of the room, but she seemed to see other sights even farther away. "What is it?" Juliana asked. "Does it mean something?"

Lady Sealey looked grim. "It occurs to me that the comtesse did not much like clams."

"What?" Juliana stared at her in bewilderment.

"Never mind; I'll explain later. Just now, I have some letters to write, my dear. Perhaps you would send our helpful footman to me. I have some instructions for him."

"Of course," Juliana agreed.

She went outside and told the butler to send in Thomas. Then she started for her bedchamber, but paused, remembering that she had set out originally to conduct her interview with Sir Oliver. It would be painful, and there was no use postponing it another hour.

She should have asked the butler if the baronet was still in his animal barn. Oh, a silly question; she was sure he would be. She was tired and strangely drained by the frightening encounter in the village, but she did not wish to put this off any longer.

She turned and headed for the side door.

In the drawing room, Lady Sealey *gave instructions to* the footman when he appeared and added some quiet words of praise which made the young man glow. Once Thomas had gone out again, she sat down at her desk and dipped a pen into her inkwell. She had filled two pages with her fine, flowing script when the butler appeared in the doorway.

"A caller, milady," he said. "Lord Montaine."

So Lady Sealey put down her pen, and covered the letter with a sheet of blotting paper. She rose without haste and made a graceful curtsy.

"Greetings, Bernard, I thought you had gone back to London. Have you returned to the country already?"

"How could I stay away?" he said, coming into the room to bow over her hand. "Your beauty and grace always draw me back."

His bow was deep, and she had only a brief glimpse of his dark eyes. He pressed his lips against the back of her hand. But she found that she did not care for the feel of his lips against her skin—did he sense her stiffening?

When he straightened, he was frowning. "I have courted you for longer than I usually devote to any woman, Margery. Yet you have still not allowed me close to you. Why do you allow me to dangle at arm's length like some callow youth, my hunger still unslaked?"

She sat gracefully in a damask armchair, deliberately passing up the settees, forcing him to choose a chair, as well, and sit at a distance. She took her time answering, as if she chose her words carefully. "Some things cannot be rushed, Bernard."

"And some things should not be delayed overlong. You are no ingenue, Margery, with a dozen suitors to choose from. It's time." A hint of cruelty in his voice, perchance.

"True enough, Bernard. Nonetheless, I am quite particular about the men I take to my bed. Perhaps I have made my choice." She met his eye and did not flinch from the sudden anger she saw there.

He stood. "In Vienna, the young count of Tisza told me that you said you had never slept with a man who did not desire a return to your bed."

"That is true, although they were not always granted the favor. And I should not have told him that; it was boastful, and not very well done of me to say so, but he had made me angry."

"And you granted that pip-squeak your favors, and not me!" the comte almost shouted.

"I gave him nothing, actually," the countess told him, smiling a little. "Is that what aggravates you, Bernard? No, he was annoyed, too. And as for you, I understand you are planning a marriage, so how can you have your mind on me, my dear?"

His face stilled, suddenly, and his eyelids dropped to hide the dark pupils with their betraying spark of danger.

"Where did you hear that, Margery? You must have misunderstood. I am only recently widowed."

"Yes, I know, but I am sure it was you they spoke of. One of the younger daughters of a well-connected Austrian house, I believe? You always do marry well, do you not, Bernard? Even though your poor wives do not seem to be granted a long enough time to enjoy their connubial bliss, dying too soon of childbirth or of other, ah, health problems."

He glared at her. For a moment the air in the room seemed taut with emotion, then she looked away, and he pressed his lips together.

"It happens to many women."

"So it does," she agreed. "A sad thing."

He stood and came closer to her chair. "I fear—"

Margery tensed. The anger in his eyes was a live coal, as hot and as dangerous as any spark that flew wide of the fireguard. She reached for the small table next to her chair, and a china dish clattered to the floor, smashing into pieces.

A figure appeared in the doorway—not the frail and elderly butler, but the footman.

The comte froze.

It was Thomas again, with his tall frame and plain, intelligent face. He waited, his expression impassive.

"Well?" Lord Montaine demanded, looking from her to the servant.

Margery raised her brows. "Are you leaving so soon, Bernard?"

He frowned, but he had no power to send her servant away. Scowling, he gave a jerky bow and stalked out of the room.

Aware for the first time that she had been holding her breath, Margery inhaled and felt the dampness on her brow.

"Thomas," she said, "be sure that he is not admitted again."

"Yes, milady," the footman said. He turned away.

She drew several deep breaths, and when she thought she could stand without trembling, she returned to her desk, took her seat, and set about finishing her letter. She had several people who needed to be informed.

And she never heard the footstep behind her or sensed a presence until the blow caught her on the back of the head.

～

*Juliana made her way quietly out of the house and to-*ward the back of the estate, to the stout wooden barn which Sir Oliver had taken over for his own use and where she was sure, from the servants' reports, she would find him.

The low-slung door was ajar, and she went inside without knocking. Clad only in his shirt and trousers and neckcloth, the baronet bent over a large cage which seemed to hold nothing but a twisted greenish-gray log. As Sir Oliver lowered its top carefully onto the cage, she saw with a jarring shock that the log moved very slightly.

She drew a deep breath. It was a snake, the most enormous one she had ever seen!

At the slight sound, the baronet turned.

"Miss Applegate! Are you feeling better?"

Flushing slightly, she remembered that she had been, officially, unwell. Recovering from her mishap with the cats, the household had no doubt been told, not aching from a broken—or at least thoroughly fractured—heart. She found she could not quite meet his gaze.

"Yes, thank you," she said. She thought of her body shedding its monthly flow. "I am quite myself again."

"You look pale," he said. "Come and sit down. I believe we have something we need to discuss." His words were solicitous, but his tone very formal, and he still did not meet her eyes.

Damn and blast! Did he really think she wanted to trap a husband this way? He appeared about as willing a suitor as a man with a pirate's sword to his back making the walk down the plank to his watery grave.

Sure now that she was making the right choice, she bit her lip. Strange that her certainty lifted her spirits not at all.

The baronet cleared away a strange assortment of books, vials, and drawings from a wooden stool and motioned her to it. Just as he did not meet her eye, he did not seem to want to take her arm.

She thought of the intimacies they had shared during their one wild sweet hour of lovemaking. And now he would not even touch her hand? Somewhere beneath the searing hurt, anger stirred. She pushed it back and waited for him to begin.

He seemed to have trouble finding words. She refused to help him. Juliana dropped her eyelids and stared at the dirt floor while he paced up and down in front of the larger of the two fish tanks that took up most of the back wall. Small fish of assorted bright colors swam busily behind him, heeding this human drama not at all.

"Jul—Miss Applegate, it is only proper that I—"
Proper?

"When two people, that is, when a man and a woman—" He paused his pacing and wiped away a bead of sweat from his forehead. The air inside the barn seemed close and musky with the smell of animals. The monkey's cage was on the other side of the barn, cloaked just now by a large cloth.

"We should wed," he said flatly.

"Such a romantic proposal, sir," she murmured. "I am quite overwhelmed."

It was his turn to color. "I beg your pardon. It is only—"

"You may save your breath, Sir Oliver," she interrupted. "There is no child."

"What?" He stared at her.

"You are the zoologist," she said, impatient with his slowness. "I am not with child. You need not propose marriage, when it is so obviously not to your liking."

"I see."

She lifted her chin, ready to refute his protestations of propriety or affection or both, but he was silent. Would he give up so easily? Well, then, she had obviously made the right choice! But she felt a singular anguish deep inside, and she would have hurried out of the barn and ended this painful interview here and now except that her knees felt strangely weak. If she stood, she was afraid she might fall.

"It will be for the best, I think," the infuriating baronet said.

Juliana struggled to keep her expression composed and her voice level. "Oh, yes. You will marry someone of your own rank and of greater wealth than I can provide—"

"I don't give a tinker's damn about wealth—" the baronet interrupted, his voice suddenly rough. "You are too good for me, Juliana."

This was so nonsensical that she gazed full at him for the first time. "Too good?"

Was he making sport of her? She wrinkled her nose at him. It was bad enough that he would make such little pretense at wooing her, but then to jest at her expense. He had not seemed a cruel person before!

Perhaps he saw the hurt in her eyes because he suddenly took a step forward and took both her hands in his own. "You must believe that, Juliana! I have not had an enormous experience in lovemaking, nor have I wooed a long list of women, but truly, I have never experienced what we shared that day, despite such unpropitious circumstances. You were, you are, the most amazing woman I have ever encountered! So free and so open, so aware of her own responses and of mine. It was an extraordinary encounter. I shall never forget it!"

"Yet you have no desire to repeat it," she pointed out, trying not to sound as angry, or as confused, as she felt.

"Are you mad?" he muttered. He traced the outline of her lips with one fingertip, and inside her belly, the fire leaped, full blown, into a small but steady flame. "Of course I want to, but—"

Juliana drew a deep breath. He was not indifferent to her! He had felt both passion and emotion during the time they had shared; he had not forgotten her so easily. The anger, the hurt began to ease.

"So why . . ." she began, then hesitated.

"But you were giddy with relief that day, and more," he told her, though she saw that he was breathing more quickly now. He reached to touch her cheek, but dropped his hand at the last moment and stepped back again. "We had just escaped an almost certain death. Worse, I gave you strong drink, trying to dull the pain of your wound. I didn't reckon with the fact that it would affect your judgment, and I should have. You were not responsible for your decisions that day, my dear—I mean, Miss Applegate."

"Foolishness," she argued. "Do you think that I would have made any other choice?"

He shook his head. "You are a respectable young lady. Ladies do not fling themselves into . . . into . . . well, not into bed, we had none at the time, but into compromising positions with—"

"With the man they love?" Juliana suggested politely.

He blinked at her. "You couldn't!"

"Why not?" she asked, dropping her shawl to the ground. The air felt warmer, much warmer, and the anger inside her had disappeared. He might, at times, appear gawky, shatter china, and stumble over his own feet, but he was also just as magnificent as she remembered.

"Why shouldn't I love you? Why shouldn't I respect your mind, admire your kindness, your intelligence, your dedication to research? If you have no admiration for me—"

"You know better!" he protested. "Miss Applegate! Juliana, you know that any rational man would worship the ground you walk on!"

"So you show your admiration by spurning me?"

"No, my darling Juliana, I just know you deserve more! I'm a clumsy wretch, and you're a goddess, dammit! You're warm and intelligent and brave, and when you make love, good God, you should be a queen! At the least, you should marry a duke!"

"I'm not"—she pointed out—"in love with a duke. And how do you expect these other noblemen to be aware of all my, as you would have it, outstanding attributes? A lady can hardly trumpet the fact that she's, ah, gifted in lovemaking. I'm not supposed to have experienced the act at all."

"Well." Looking stubborn, Oliver refused to admit the validity of her argument. "They will be overcome by your charm, that's all. You'd only have to smile at them, and they will be smitten."

The absurdity of his logic made her bite back a smile. But it seemed to suggest that someone was smitten, and the insanity of it made her heart lighter than it had been in days. She smiled fully at him for the first time.

"Why shouldn't I have enjoyed what we had shared together?"

A faint sheen of perspiration shone on his forehead, and his white linen shirt stuck lightly to his broad shoulders and well-muscled forearms. She remembered the way his arms and chest looked when they were bare.

She wanted to see them again. She wanted to touch them. There was a hunger inside her, and it was growing. She reached behind her to unbutton her gown.

He inhaled once, sharply. "What are you doing?"

"You suggested that I was not responsible for my actions, that day in the animal enclosure?

"Yes," he told her. "I cannot hold you to—to—"

"I am quite sober, now, Oliver," she told him, jerking at the last button and forcing it out of its buttonhole. "Are you expecting any of the servants?" She slipped one arm out of her gown and lowered it off one shoulder.

Watching her as if she were as fascinating as one of his giant snakes, he shook his head.

She pulled one arm out, then freed the other of the clinging cloth. She could be as alluring as a jungle cat, she told herself. The baronet had not blinked.

"You mustn't—" He sounded hoarse.

"This is my choice, Oliver. My freely decided, rational, sober choice." She unbuttoned her skirt and pushed the waistband down.

She saw his body's reaction, despite his effort to maintain a somber face. He might frown, but the rest of his body betrayed him. She pushed again at her skirt, but it seemed to snag in the back on one of her stays. "You could help me, you know," she pointed out.

She turned, and she was pleased to see that he moved quickly to free the piece of cloth and to slide her skirts down to the dirt floor so that she could step free of them. He unlaced her stays and helped her shed the rest of her undergarments, then ran his strong hands up and down her back until she shivered with delight.

She turned quickly back into his arms.

He pulled her close and kissed her hungrily. His arms

were so strong, his lips so hard and firm, she fell into his embrace like a lost soul who at last finds its way home.

"I thought you didn't care," she said at last when he finally stopped kissing her.

"Oh, Juliana," he said. "I thought I would die, I've wanted you so badly. And I thought you were unhappy, and you would not speak to me. I was ready to cut my damn throat, thinking I had made you so miserable. Don't ever stop talking to me again!"

He kissed her again, possessing her lips as if he would make up for every day, every hour they had been apart. Juliana put her arms around his neck and pulled him even closer, loving the feel of his lips, his tongue as it probed gently, returning the pressure with her own.

Then she reached to untie his neckcloth, pulling at the white linen till it unwound. She tugged at it until he coughed and she saw that she had half strangled him. Then, laughing, she let go and allowed him to loosen it, then she uncoiled the long length of cloth. He ducked his head so that she could pull it away and then drop it, too, to join her own pile of clothing.

Next came his shirt, which Oliver shucked over his head, then his trousers, and undergarments, stocking and shoes, which he seemed to shed in record time.

And at last they were both naked, again, as they had been in the enclosure. She ran her fingers over his chest, touching the light golden hairs, watching him inhale. Her touch did affect him. The thought made her smile. And it made the ache inside her grow, the hunger for him. She ran her hands farther down his chest to his belly, and he gasped and grabbed her hand.

"Not yet," he said. "We're not rushing it, not today. This is for you, my delicious, ultimate, and most exquisite female, my own Juliana!"

He leaned forward and kissed her neck, and the soft skin beneath her chin sent thrills of sensation through her. Juliana sighed with pleasure.

He wrapped his arms about her so that she could lean against him and focus only on the pleasure he was giving her.

Oliver moved to her shoulder, cradled her inside his arm, and stroked the soft skin till she shivered. Then he bent his head and kissed her breast, moving his lips around the soft rising flesh, kissing every inch of it, until she grew so impatient, her need so great, that she moaned aloud. Only then did he take the nipple gently inside his lips and kiss, suckle, run his tongue over the tip, the sides, easing it till it rose to meet his tongue and strained for more of his touch.

Juliana felt the fire inside her grow, the need deepen. The ache in her belly intensified, and she pulled him closer.

"Oh, Oliver," she whispered. "I want you, my love."

His grin was impish. "Soon, my darling, my perfect woman, soon." He turned to the other breast, which also yearned, and kissed it, fondled it gently, touching the nipple until Juliana moved beneath him, eager for more. This breast, too, responded, and the nipple hardened, and she felt the rhythm already building inside her, as if her body instinctively knew and awaited its partner.

Knew its other half, awaited its completion.

"Oliver!" she whispered.

He stepped away for a moment, and it was all she could do not to cry out in protest. Instead, she watched him pick up a blanket and throw it over a clean pile of hay. Then he returned to her, bent, and lifted her easily into his arms. She felt as light as thistledown.

Lowering his head, Oliver kissed her again. Juliana put one hand behind his neck and kissed him back with all her heart. His lips were so warm and so firm, he understood her needs, the longings of her body, the wishes of her soul.

And she only wanted to make him happy. Well, perhaps she wanted to be happy, too!

When he lowered her onto the blanket, she lifted her arms to him, and he leaned quickly down to her, ready to slip inside her, and Juliana was ready, more than ready. She lifted her hips slightly, without being told, and allowed him to slip himself inside her. She was already damp with need, and even large as he was, he had no problem fitting inside her. She wrapped her legs about his hips, when to her surprise, they rolled slightly on the blanket and she found herself on top.

This was another adventure. She knelt over him, pushed him more deeply into her and arched her back, watching as he grinned.

"That's my girl," Oliver breathed.

It was easy enough, Juliana found, delighted to see that she could control it, too, this dance of passion, and it seemed to feel even more sweet, more intense. Joined this way, he seemed to touch her in just the right places so that her pleasure deepened, and she could hardly bear the intensity of her joy. She moved over him, gasping with the pleasure it brought, and they slipped almost at once into an easy rhythm, as elemental as the earth's oldest song.

The waves of pleasure were almost overwhelming. Juliana could barely breathe, the joy was too much, too strong, but she took deep gulps of it, feeling a bit like the fish she could see past Oliver's head. She was swimming, too, swimming in joy, pushing her way through a current of passion, following his lead through rapture, from one moment of spiraling pleasure to another. In and out, deeper and farther, every movement touched another chord of feeling and answered a need she was only still learning that she had.

And she moved with him, held her head high, threw her shoulders back, smiled down at him for a moment, then stooped to kiss him, then lifted her head again, and he ran his hands up to cup her breasts and tease the nipples with gentle strokes while she gasped and moaned aloud.

She took his fingers between her lips and ran her tongue along each one, and he groaned, too. And all the while she rose and fell above him and answered his promptings almost before they were made. Their easy dance was as natural and as free and as wild as any ballet performed deep below the sea by any fierce finned pair darting their way through a watery courtship. They moved together, joined in passionate union, and with every stroke, the joy grew, and the rings of pleasure intensified, till Juliana thought she might explode from sheer sensation.

Now Oliver put his hands tightly on her hips, holding her close, and their rhythm grew so wild and so hard that they slid further down the blanket to the harder ground. It was against the hard clay floor that the last strokes of their union were struck. And then they came together, her thoughts flew away, and there was only feeling, sensation, joy. . . . And it all rose, spiraled, joined, and they were one, merging, joining, flesh and flesh, joy and joy, soul and soul . . . and someone cried out as she/they erupted into glorious passionate freedom.

And then he held her against his damp chest, and she found her cheeks were damp, too, whether from perspiration or tears of release, she didn't know, only that life had rarely been so joyous, and that no one was so precious as this man who held her close, his heart thudding against her ear.

He kissed her, kissed her eyes, cheeks, and mouth, and they lay wrapped together while time floated by, and Juliana allowed her eyes to close. She felt as if they floated together, like the fish in the tanks behind them. Perhaps she dozed, she was so sated in body, so blissful in mind, that it was impossible to say.

But after a time, the monkey suddenly shrieked. The cloth over its cage seemed to have slipped, and Mia could now see them clearly.

"No, you cannot come out and play just now," Oliver told the little animal, his voice drowsy.

He leaned up on one elbow and kissed Juliana's cheek. "She may hear servants moving about outside the barn. Perhaps we should dress, my love."

Juliana stifled a groan. She hated to move, much less to pull on her clothes. But she knew they could not lie about like lotus eaters forever. She pulled him back for one more kiss, then sighed and sat up to feel about for her discarded shift.

While she dressed, Oliver stood and walked over to speak quietly to the monkey, reaching inside the cage to calm the simian with a treat of sliced apple. But for some reason, the little monkey continued to scream.

Goodness, it was warm inside the barn. Juliana wiped her forehead. Perhaps now that privacy was no longer needed, they should open the big doors at the end of the building. She looked toward the other end and stiffened. They were not alone.

"Oliver!" she said, her tone low.

He turned, but not soon enough.

The man who stood in the shadows held a pistol, and it was pointed at Oliver's broad chest.

Seventeen

"*ou? I did know you, then!*" Juliana said. "*But—*"

"Of course you know me, you ignorant child," the man from the inn said "You can stop pretending; you are a dreadful actress. You know that I am Lord Montaine, an old acquaintance of the countess."

He smiled, but the humor did not reach his eyes, which were dark and as flat and cold as an underground stream. She tried not to shudder.

"If you had not intruded, my dear, you would have been much better off," the man's somewhat high-pitched voice continued. The hand that held the gun appeared steady, and his jaw was set. "You and your lover here obstructed my intentions too many times. Appearing at the inn and seeing the marriage contract was the final straw. All I wished to do was to frighten a certain lady into retiring from Society, so that she did not suggest any awkward questions— or inquiries—about my late wife's death. I was afraid my wife, the stupid cow, had confided in her, you see. Margery has that unfortunate effect on females; I have seen it happen before. I thought that if I got close to her I could find out, but—*non;* it was not to be." Lord Montaine frowned.

Juliana thought of anecdotes the countess had told and snatches of past conversations drifted into her mind. Montaine's wife had died suddenly, she remembered. Murdered at his hand? And he had hoped to seduce the countess? That had been an egotistical plan. The countess would not be so easily fooled by such a cold-eyed and hard-hearted man. But now·what?

Juliana stepped closer to Oliver. Would he dare to shoot them both? Did he really think he could get away with a double murder? He had apparently gotten away with everything else he had done, so perhaps he did.

"I don't think that was all," Oliver answered, his own voice quiet but level. "I think you were hoping to alarm her enough that her heart might fail beneath the pressure. But you underestimated her. I should have thought you would have known her better. And we could hardly stand by and do nothing while she was terrorized by anonymous letters."

"She's only a female!" Montaine flashed back, but then he paused and inhaled sharply.

"As your poor late wife was only a female?" Juliana asked. "The woman you murdered? And what will happen to the woman you are planning to marry, this time? When you have spent her dowry, made enough use of her family connections? Will you dispose of her, too?"

The man's dark brows twitched, as they had in the inn when he had come upon Juliana, slipping down after she had seen the documents. "It hardly matters now," he said.

Beside her, Oliver tensed, but Montaine seemed to detect his intentions. The barrel of the pistol shifted its deadly aim until it pointed straight toward Juliana.

"Do not move, monsieur," the comte said, his voice cold. "Unless you wish the young lady dead."

Oliver froze.

"Turn to face the other wall, *s'il vous plaît*."

Really frightened now, Juliana bit her lip. The other man tossed her a length of rope. "Tie his hands behind his back. And do not try to leave them too loose. If you play games with me, I will simply shoot him. I cannot leave the two of you free to cry alarm upon me before I have fled the country!"

A small whisper of hope sounded in the back of her mind. If he really meant to leave them bound, she was willing to endure discomfort as long as Oliver was not hurt. Juliana took the rope and wrapped it around the baronet's wrists as directed.

Montaine came closer to watch. When she had knotted the rope, he nodded. "Now, you, put your hands also behind your back—*vite*, quickly."

She did as she was told, wishing she could grab the gun, but certain she would not be fast enough. She felt the rough touch as another piece of rope was wrapped around her own wrists and tugged much too tight.

Then, she was shoved hard against the baronet so that they both staggered and fell to the hard-packed earth. The diplomat tied them to one of the metal stakes that had once been used to tether animals, binding them in place. Then she heard the footfalls as the comte ran out of the barn. The door slammed shut behind him.

"Are you all right, Oliver? I'm sorry, but I didn't want to see you shot!"

She tried to turn enough to see his face. Her cheeks were damp with perspiration, from nerves, she thought, as well as the warmth of the air. And what was that smell?

"He doesn't mean to let us live, Juliana," Oliver told her. He was trying to get to his knees, an awkward business without his hands to help him, but in a moment, he managed it, though the shortness of their tether gave him little enough room to move.

"What? But he didn't shoot?" Lying on the ground, she stared up at him.

"No, a bullet in our bodies would leave evidence of murder. The ropes will burn."

Burn? A dreadful suspicion searing her mind, she managed to twist her head to see the far side of the barn and the wall which held the only doors—the only way out of what would soon, she saw with a sinking heart, be their deathtrap.

The barn was aflame!

Juliana gasped and managed to struggle to her knees. But that was not an improvement. The air already seemed thick. She coughed sharply.

"Keep your head low," Oliver advised. "That man is a snake. No, he's not good enough to be a snake! Snakes are more honest!"

He turned his back to her again, and for a dreadful moment, Juliana thought he must blame her for putting them into this terrible predicament. But then she saw that he was holding out his bound wrists to her.

"See if you can loosen the knots."

She had to turn, too, as her hands were tied behind her own back, and her fingers were rapidly going numb. Montaine had pulled the knots so tight that the rope bit into her skin, and she was losing the feeling in her fingers.

She wiggled her fingers, desperate not to lose all sensation, and tried to feel her way along the knots that she had tied, it seemed, all too well. Why had she believed Montaine? Because he had appeared very serious when he'd pointed the gun. Sick at heart, she pulled and prodded at the ropes around Oliver's wrists.

And with every passing minute the air became thicker, grayer with smoke, and she coughed and choked as it became harder and harder to breathe. The foul air would kill them, she thought, long before the flames reached them. At least, she hoped that were true. She could hear the crackle of the fire now, feeding eagerly on the wooden sides of the barn, and she shivered from fear.

Why hadn't the servants noticed? Had the count injured some of the staff? Or was it just that the baronet's animals had become so unpopular that none of the staff came to see the creatures now unless they had to. And the cloudy gray day would make trailing smoke harder to detect, if the wind was blowing away from the house itself.

No doubt Montaine had taken all of this into consideration. Damn the man! If he got away with this, he might accomplish his original goal and finally destroy the countess as well. Thinking of Lady Sealey's dismay if her godson and her friend died in a fire of mysterious origins—she would not easily accept that it was an unfortunate accident, not after all the other unexplained events—Juliana gritted her teeth and redoubled her efforts with the ropes.

But it seemed hopeless.

"Can we pull the stake out of the ground?" she suggested.

"I doubt it. They were put in very deep and used to tether horses and cattle, both stronger beasts than mere men," he told her. "But it occurs to me—see if you can reach your hand into my trouser pocket."

Mystified, she did as he asked. Despite her bound wrists, she was able to slide two fingers into his pocket and fish out a bundle of keys. "This?"

"Yes. Now, you have the better angle. Swing them into Mia's cage."

She would have demanded a reason, but it was all so patently hopeless. Juliana gritted her teeth, tried to guess how much effort was needed, since she was doing this backward, so to speak, but it was a bit like the game she had once played with the stable lads, tossing horseshoes over her shoulder, until Maddie had caught her and scolded her for unladylike behavior and forbad her to continue.

Except this time she only had one chance.

She let go of the keys and prayed as they flew through the air. "Did they reach the cage?" she asked, hearing the jingle as they fell.

"Yes!" he said.

In the background, Mia's shrieks, which had risen to a shrill crescendo, paused. Juliana heard the rustle as the monkey went to investigate, and then the series of metallic clinks as the little animal picked up the keys.

"Does she know what to do with them, and which key will open her cage?"

"Oh, yes!" Oliver assured her.

Sure enough, within a few endless minutes, the clever little beast had reached around the side of her cage and fitted the key into her lock, opened the door—no wonder she had gotten out of her cage in the countess's town house—and was scampering across to join them.

She looked proud of herself. For once, Juliana quite agreed.

"Good Mia," she cooed. "Clever little monkey."

Mia chirruped, skipping up to sit on the baronet's shoulder. Now she looked about her, sniffed the air, and scolded them both for allowing the barn to turn into such a smoky mess.

"Yes, Mia, I know," Juliana told the little animal. "But unless you can untie us, I don't know what we are going to do about it. You'd better find a way out. Go get help, if you can."

But the monkey clung to Oliver, and when Juliana tried again to unravel the knot, Mia slipped down the baronet's arm and observed the procedure with interest. Working blind, Juliana thought this must be an impossible task if there ever was one. Peeking over her shoulder now and then, she felt the sweat roll off her face and wished she could wipe it away. She wished she could just see the damned knot, and then at least—

She jumped.

"What is it?"

"I felt . . . I felt small fingers on mine. I believe that Mia is taking an interest in the puzzle," she said slowly. "I think—I think I shall let her try it and see what happens. She can hardly do worse than I have, and perhaps she might do better."

She couldn't see his face, but she knew that he tensed, hoping against hope, as she did, that the animal's natural curiosity might prove to their advantage. Breathing in short breaths, turning her face against her shoulder to shelter her mouth and nose against the sweaty cloth of her dress, Juliana tried to peer over her back and see what the monkey was doing.

"I think she has loosened the rope a little, clever Mia, clever girl!" His voice sounded thick. He was straining, she thought, against the ropes. A pause as he grunted, and then—then he exclaimed in satisfaction. "One hand is free!"

Turning, he yanked at the ropes holding the other hand prisoner, then, when it gave way, Juliana felt him pull sharply at her own bonds. In another minute, she was also liberated. She had to rub her smarting hands to get the sensation back into her numb fingers.

Then Mia shrieked in protest.

To Juliana's surprise, the baronet thrust the monkey into her arms.

"Hold her fast," he commanded. "If she goes to the rafters now, she will suffocate."

Juliana glanced above their heads, and her heart dropped. It was true, the smoke that gathered at the top of the barn would stop even the agile little monkey from escaping out of any stray hole beneath the rafters. But surely, now that they were untied—

She turned her gaze toward the doors, and she gasped, choking a little when she inhaled too much smoke.

The fire made a rampart of leaping, swirling flame. They might be free of their tethers, but how could they get past the flames?

It was a solid wall of dancing fire, yellow and red, scarlet and crimson and gold, deeper hues than she had ever seen in a hearth fire, nothing like the small simple flames kept under control behind screen and fire irons. This fire had no boundaries, no one could stop it, and like some pagan god let loose at last from its shattered urn, seemed determined never to be governed again. No one would contain it. The noise it made grew louder, louder than any bonfire she had ever heard, attacking her ears as the heat pulsated against her skin. And still the fire danced and leaped, exultant in its own unstoppable power.

Fear stirred inside of her as she watched, a deep horror born long ago in ancestors too ancient to remember, a fear primal and unthinking. . . .

And still the fire leaped and spiraled, hypnotic as it gyrated with its own terrible, lethal beauty, as if inviting her closer, inviting her in. The heat of it was enough to make her want to slink back, but they were almost against the far wall already. She could feel the intense warmth pressing on her skin and knew that her face and arms had already reddened from its touch, and soon blisters would pop out on their skin. And then—

Panic stirred inside her

"Juliana," Oliver said. His voice was quiet but calm. How could he be calm?

"Juliana, do you trust me?"

With great effort, she turned her head to look at him instead of at the flames. His face was blotched with marks of dried sweat and dark from the smoke. His once-damp hair still stuck to his head, but his gray eyes were clear and lucid and steady. She had never seen him look so handsome. She saw love in his gaze and an unflinching courage.

"I trust you—" Her voice was a frog's croak, her throat as dry as the smoke in the air. She swallowed hard and tried again. "I trust you with my life."

He nodded. "We have to go through the fire."

And while she allowed the words to sink in, he moved with swift sure steps—why had she ever thought him clumsy? picking up his discarded neckcloth and soaking it in a pail of water that sat beside the snake's pen. Then he picked up the wet length of linen, kicked open the door to the pen, snatched up the pail and poured the rest of the liquid over the reptile as—with startling swiftness—it glided out of the cage and away into the smoke, even as Juliana blinked in surprise.

He came back with the wet linen and wrapped it around Juliana's face and head. "To protect you," he explained. "Hold on to the monkey and grip my hand with your other hand. Whatever happens, do not let go and do not stop."

Her mouth very dry, she nodded.

She was beyond surprise now. So when he bent and ripped off her skirt, leaving her almost naked below the waist, she didn't even protest. Dimly, she remembered stories of women dying terrible deaths after their clothes had flamed up like torches when coals popping out of fire-places had lit their skirts afire. And she tried not to look again at the wall of flame they had to pass.

And then, still moving very fast, Oliver turned to the fish tanks behind them. Before Juliana could even fathom his actions, he picked up—grunting from the weight of it—the largest tank. The poor dead fish were already floating on the top of the water as he poured the liquid over Juliana's head.

The monkey she clutched to her chest shrieked in protest as it cascaded over them.

She shut her eyes and tried not to swallow the fishy-smelling torrent. For a few seconds, it cooled her, then al-most at once, the heat from the fire began to dry her drenched clothes and body. Oliver was doing the same thing to himself with the smaller tank.

"Now!" he said. He held out his hand.

She put hers inside it. They ran toward the flames.

❦

Afterward, she remembered: glaring unfocused images so bright they seemed burned into the back of her eyes, like walking into the sun itself; light so intense she could see it still behind her closed eyelids—heat so strong her skin ached with it—pain intense and sharp—screams from a throat too dry to utter a sound; and—just as they seemed to see hope of blue sky ahead—a sudden rumbling as a flaming beam fell towards them, and she knew they were doomed—

But once more Oliver thrust her aside, sprang between her and danger, his broad frame protecting her. She cried out, afraid for him. But though he fell to one knee, and she pulled at him, he stumbled to his feet again, and they lurched forward—

And always—always he gripped her hand—and she held on for dear life   literally   for her life

And always he was there—

And she held on—

Held on for her life—

Held onto his hand—

And the run through the fire took forever—

Took seconds—

Took forever—

And then they fell into cool air—

Into shouts—

Into reaching hands—

Into air so cool, so blessed that it felt like a light rain upon her scorched skin. . . .

A chain of servants and villagers passed pails of water, from hand to hand, not to quench the barn itself, which was beyond saving, but to keep the fire from spreading.

And Oliver was there, pulling off the burnt bits of linen from about her head, all that was left of the neckcloth he had wrapped about her face to shield her. Juliana saw that bits of her scorched hair came with it; she must look a sight. But savoring the miracle of being alive, that both of them were still alive, she hardly cared.

Mia chirruped feebly from her arms, and when Juliana looked down to see how the poor thing had survived their run through hell, the little animal raised its head—it also looked patchy, with bits of hair gone—and scolded them both thoroughly.

"'Ere, miss, I'll 'old the demon monkey," Thomas the footman told her, grinning.

She handed the simian over, and sighed when she looked at Oliver, seeing the burns on his face and arms and shoulders. "Are you all right, Oliver?"

"Nothing that won't heal," he told her. "We are lucky to be in one piece."

"Only thanks to you," she said. "You were magnificent!"

"As were you and Mia." He grinned.

"If the monkey was helpful, I take back everything I've ever said about her," a familiar voice added.

Juliana turned to see Lady Sealey shaking her head at both of them, her expression stern, though Juliana suspected the countess was only trying to control her relief. And—

"Godmother, there's blood in your hair!" Oliver pointed out.

"Oh, dear, that bandage keeps slipping." Lady Sealey patted her head and dismissed the problem as a minor detail. "Never mind. My physician has been sent for, and he can redo it; I'm afraid that devil Montaine slipped back inside, despite my servants' best efforts, before he attacked you. But they did not give him enough time to finish the job thoroughly, thank heavens. The good doctor must see to your burns, first. Let's go back to the house, at any rate."

"Are we sure he is no longer on the estate?" Oliver demanded, looking about as if he might hope to face down the villain on the spot.

"I should only wish. I'd like to feed him to your cats myself!" Lady Sealey retorted. "No, I sent out a search party, my dear, but they have found no trace of him. I suspect he is on his way posthaste to the coast and a waiting boat. My letters will follow him, so I would not repine. His late wife had important relations. That is why he married her, after all, and when they hear what I have to say—"

"But can it be proved?" Juliana worried.

Lady Sealey gave a twisted smile. "My dear, the Austrian Secret Police will not care about gathering evidence sufficient to prove a court case. I think you will find that our Lord Montaine may also meet with some, ah, bad luck before much time passes."

Even though she knew that the man deserved such a fate, Juliana shivered. They walked slowly back toward the house, and she leaned close to Oliver's comforting presence. And finally she noticed that his other arm hung limp. She remembered the falling beam that had come close to crushing them during the run through the flames, and how he had taken the glancing weight of it upon his left side.

"Your arm!" she said, stopping in her tracks. "Oh, Oliver!"

Lady Sealey at once paused, too. "What is it, my dear? Is your arm hurt?"

"Probably broken," he admitted, his forehead creased with pain. "But we shall see to it presently."

"The first thing the doctor shall examine," the countess decided.

"No, your head wound first," her godson contradicted.

"Oh, that; a mere bagatelle," Lady Sealey declared.

They argued all the way back to the house, where they found that the surgeon had just entered the big front hall. He paused in the act of handing his valise to the butler and stared at them. Juliana realized that they were all a sight to behold. She and Sir Oliver were black with smoke, their clothes in tatters. Oliver's left arm hung limply, and the countess's face and silvery hair were streaked with dried blood. They looked like survivors of some private war!

"I think I shall simply take up residence here, countess," the man said, his tone dry. "It would save us all time. Now, who is the most pressing patient?"

"Lady Sealey," Oliver told him.

"My godson, and then Miss Applegate," the countess spoke at the same moment.

The doctor raised his heavy brows. "Bring hot water and soap and clean linens for bandages," he told the butler. "We shall, all of us, be upstairs in the countess's chambers."

And he led them up the staircase.

⟳

Lord and Lady Gabriel, and Lady Sealey, too, offered to host the wedding in London, and while Juliana was tempted, very very briefly, by the thought of a grand London wedding, she knew what she wanted the most.

So she rode back to Yorkshire in Lord Gabriel's best carriage, this time with Lady Gabriel, as well as a stack of *Goddard's Lady's Magazine*s on the seat beside her, so that they could consider designs for not just her wedding dress but a whole trousseau. And there would be, of course, new dresses for all her sisters for the wedding. The twins would be beside themselves with joy, Juliana thought happily. This would bring them home from the squire's manse, at last, and even Maddie would smile! And if Lauryn had ever felt strained over the difference in circumstance between her in-laws and her own father's situation, perhaps this would relieve her feelings, too.

The second carriage that followed them now had such a supply of silks and satins, and muslins and hats and veils and trimmings as well, garnered from the best warehouses in London, that all the Applegate girls could exclaim to their hearts' content, selecting their favorite designs and colors. Juliana smiled just thinking of it. There had been a lively argument as to who should pay for her new wardrobe.

Lord Gabriel had tried to claim the honor. "Since we

have yet to have the reward of Juliana's company, I think it's the least we can do," he had said.

"But she has saved my life, really," Lady Sealey had pointed out over tea as they had all celebrated the pair's provisional betrothal. Oliver still had to post up to Yorkshire to formally ask her father's permission. "I should so much enjoy the privilege. I haven't designed a wedding in years!"

"But she's my bride—" Oliver had begun, but the others had frowned him down.

"Your time to spoil her will come soon enough," Lord Gabriel had said, grinning.

Who had won the discussion, Juliana wasn't even sure. She and Oliver had wandered off to the side of the room, on the pretext of examining those Chinese vases once more. This time there was no monkey to threaten the priceless works of art, as Mia was still in the country, and they could hold hands and put their heads close together and imagine how the honeymoon would be spent. Sir Oliver was talking about the Greek isles.

Juliana had discovered that her husband to be had a most prosperous income and a handsome estate of his own. She would have lived with him in a peasant's cottage, but since she knew he would continue to import Lord knew what kind of beasts, it was just as well, she supposed, Juliana told herself.

She glanced outside the carriage now and smiled as she looked over his broad-shouldered figure, riding easily just beyond the carriage. He saw her scrutiny and waved, and her heart contracted with love. She lifted her hand in answer, and her betrothal ring, a handsome square-cut diamond surrounded by sapphires, flashed in the sun.

Had she ever been this happy?

When they stopped for the next change of horses, Lady

Gabriel went inside the inn and up to the private parlor Sir Oliver had engaged for them. Juliana made to follow, then waited for her fiancé's escort.

He took her hand and kissed it. She clung to him. There were still healing scars on the sides of his face, and his left arm was still in a sling, but he was so much improved from the smoke-covered, singed figure that she had been so glad to see in one piece the night they had fled the fire.

"Does your arm pain you?" she asked. "Perhaps you should come inside the carriage for a time?"

"I will be so frustrated by the presence of a chaperone, that I think riding, with all its jolting, is preferable," he told her, grinning. "We cannot wed soon enough, my love. I still rue the fact that we did not buy a special license instead of waiting for the bans to be read."

She laughed. "I could not explain the haste to my father, dearest. I'm afraid he might not understand."

"Or worse, that he might," Oliver suggested. "And note that we cannot keep our hands off each other!"

And despite the stable lad who was leading the horse away and the chambermaid shaking out her dustmop from an overhead window, who grinned as she paused to watch them, he bent to give her a hearty kiss.

TURN THE PAGE FOR A PREVIEW OF NICOLE
BYRD'S NEXT HISTORICAL ROMANCE . . .

*N*o one seemed to even notice their plight, much less Ophelia's calls.

Cordelia—who had taken the measure of this London neighborhood long ago—did not waste her breath on cries for help. Poorly dressed passersby averted their eyes, and no one seemed to take note of a mere case of kidnapping. No, no one would help them here. She and her twin would have to look out for themselves.

Oh, why had they come to this miserable city! Kicking and punching, Cordelia fought for her life, sure that if these two villains succeeded in parting her from her sister, she might never see the light of day again. After an evil assault, her throat would be cut and her body thrown into the Thames, or else she'd be taken away and given over to some living hell of a brothel, and even if she had the chance to escape, she might be too wounded in body and spirit to seek out anyone who knew her—

She fought harder.

She kicked the first man in the groin with her heavy boot and was gratified to hear him grunt in pain. But although she clawed next at his face, the man—wiry though he might be—was stronger in the arms and shoulders than she. Despite her efforts, soon he was pinning her arms back against her body.

"No!" Ophelia shrieked from just beyond. "Help, we must save my sister!"

She threw herself upon the first man, trying to pull him away from Cordelia. But the assailant tossed her off as if she were as light as the merest autumn leaf, then the second man punched her in her stomach, causing her to fold in two and collapse onto the street.

With no help at all, Cordelia bit back a moan of despair. The men were scrawny as ill-fed roosters, but there were two of them, and they knew every trick. Although she bit and kicked and scratched and pummeled, they pushed her arms down, evaded her feet and pulled her steadily toward a twisting alley. Stunned and helpless, Ophelia lay still in the dirt, and no one else was here to care—

"Got spirit, this un 'as," the first man muttered. "I should get extra blunt for such a wildcat."

"Yeah, be sure to tell Madam Naja that, won't ya," the other man answered, curling his lips. "I bet she'll be right struck."

They chortled, their breath rank upon her face.

These words were so ominous that, terrified, Cordelia was spurred to a last burst of furious energy. For a few moments her struggles kept them all rooted to the pavement as she fought with every ounce of her strength. But again, the men, through sheer brute force, pushed her hands down and forced her toward the next alley with its denser shadows. Cordelia thought she could glimpse inside the blackness a future too appalling to imagine.

Perhaps she should try another tack. Cordelia shut her eyes and let her body go limp.

"Eh, she's swooned. 'Bout time, too, the little hellcat. You pick up 'er feet and we can make better time," the first man ordered his henchman.

To her disappointment, the other man still held her firmly by the upper body. But as the first villain bent to take hold of her legs, she lifted her feet and kicked him hard in the stomach.

"For Ophelia—" Cordelia muttered, then turned her attention to wrestling loose of the other assailant's hold.

She almost did it.

But the first thug recovered too quickly, and the second man would not let go, although he puffed at the exertion as she pulled against his grip, swearing as she kicked his shins.

"Od's bod, that smarts, that does. Have do, girl!"

"I got 'er!"

The first man had recovered. Now he held a compact but nasty-looking bludgeon in one hand, and his expression was ugly. "Don't like to mar the goods, as it were, but sometimes, we got no choice, eh, Dinty?"

"Don't kill 'er, mate, or we won't get nuttin' for our pains. I got bruises from this 'ellion, and I want me coppers for 'er," the smaller man argued, although he eyed the weapon with resignation.

Cordelia's eyes widened, and she held her breath as the ruffian raised the club. Waiting for the blow to fall, she was so focused on the weapon in the man's fist that she hardly noticed the newcomer come up from behind until he hooked the man's feet out from under him and sent the villain crashing to the ground.

The club fell on the man's own shoulder instead of upon Cordelia's head.

The ruffian shouted in surprise and pain, but the newcomer gave him two quick jabs that seemed to put him rapidly out of the fight. Then—before the second villain, too startled by this interruption to do more than stare, had moved—Cordelia found the newcomer's strong hand gripping her upper arm and his steely gray eyes assessing the situation.

"I would suggest that you unhand my cousin," the stranger said. He had handsome if somewhat rugged features with a firm jaw and arching dark brows.

Cousin?

The smaller thug stuttered. "I—I got a knife, gov," he said. Fumbling in his ragged clothing, he pulled out a blade about six inches long.

Cordelia, who had enjoyed the briefest taste of relief, now held her breath again.

"Oh, come," the stranger said. "How uncivil." Dressed in fashionable evening clothes, he lifted an ebony walking stick.

The second thug chortled, and even Cordelia swallowed hard.

"You gonna bow to me, next?" the man sneered. "Should I run away screamin' in fear or drop 'ee a curtsy, like?"

The newcomer twisted the top of the cane and pulled out a thin, silvery blade. The ruffian's laughter stopped abruptly. He swore again, then suddenly released his grip on Cordelia's arm and pushed her toward the new arrival.

Afraid she would be skewered like a roasted piglet, she exclaimed involuntarily. But the stranger lowered the thin sword in time. Cordelia found herself propelled into his arms as the second thug took to his heels and disappeared down the twisting alleyway.

For a moment Cordelia thought she might swoon for real.

But it would be a shame to waste the touch of his hand on her arm, or the feel of the other arm that now wrapped

itself—he had slipped the long blade back into the walking
otiok around her shoulders. He felt firm with muscle, like
a weapon himself, ready to protect a lady alone in an alien
and dangerous city.

You don't even know this man, she scolded herself. *Have
a care, Cordelia, remember your common sense!*

I know he has come to my aid, she answered herself, *at
a time when I was never more in need*. The fear had been so
deep—and her peril so real—it still lingered in the back of
her mind, leaving her knees rubbery and her limbs strangely
weak.

Finding it a little hard to take a breath, she clutched at
the coat fabric that covered his well-muscled chest.

"It's all right," he murmured into her ear. "Take long
breaths, slowly. I know you've had a shock. But you are
safe, now."

Unable as yet to command her voice, she nodded. She
clung to him, feeling more secure inside his arms than she
had ever felt in her entire life. She might have felt this protected as a child perched on her father's knee, but this man
was not in the least fatherly, and what she felt, standing so
close, inhaling the masculine scent of him—clean linen
and the faintest hint of male skin, perspiration and soap in
a somehow pleasing mixture—was nothing like what a
child would feel. . . .

Surprised at the feelings inside her, Cordelia found she
was blushing, and she looked away from the cool eyes that
seemed to see too deeply inside her. And yet—

"It was you!" She stood up straighter inside the circle of
his arms, and even the realization that shocked her did not—
she only realized later—make her break out of his hold.
"You're the man we saw trying to break into the theater! Are
you a thief, sir, an ordinary house breaker?"

He lifted those dark arching brows. "So it appears. And you cried out for the crowd, alerted them to my presence. They would have shouted for the Watch, tried to have me charged and strung up, leaving me both poorer and with my neck in certain jeopardy."

She felt a ridiculous urge to protest. "But—"

He ignored her interruption. "Under the circumstances, do you not think it noble of me to save your honor, perhaps your neck, too, regardless that you so recently put mine at risk?"

He lifted one hand and touched her neck lightly, just beneath her chin. His fingers felt so warm against her skin that she shivered, and while she should have been shocked, she was still trying to cope with his shocking declaration.

His odd-colored eyes were mocking, and his tone . . . seemed to be mocking, too, she wasn't sure. But he sounded like an educated man, a gentleman. How could he be a thief? Yet they had seen him at the window of the theater. He didn't argue with her label nor claim not to be a thief. And if he were, how could she in good conscience associate with such a man?

Yet how could she not be grateful to a man who had just saved her from such villains? And he held her firmly but so gently, and his face—it really was very handsome—and his form was so good, his nearness caused a strange weakness inside her, and his touch on her skin sent ripples of awareness through her whole body, causing a curious thrill all the way down to her belly—

She blushed even more deeply. "Yes, I must thank you for your fortuitous rescue, sir. We would not have been here at all, it was just that my sister was determined to have her chance to go on stage—oh, heavens, my sister!"

They found Ophelia moaning and holding her stomach.

Cordelia helped her up, disturbed to see that the future Toast of London's Stage still looked green and had to cling to her sister in order to stand.

"Are you all right?" Cordelia asked, remembering how weak she herself had felt.

Ophelia tried to nod. "And you?" she asked, her voice barely above a whisper. "Those awful men—what—"

"This man—I—I'm afraid I don't know your name, sir?" She almost hoped that Ophelia would not realize just who their Good Samaritan was and, in fact, at the moment, her twin did not seem inclined to stare closely at his face. Besides, it was now so dark in this back lane that it was hard to see anyone's features closely. Cordelia had heard that the more prosperous parts of the city had modern gas streetlights, but this lane showed few lights of any kind, and the ones she had glimpsed were old-fashioned lamps with oil wicks, and even they were few and far between.

The stranger gazed about them. "We had better be on the move, ladies, this is not a prosperous neighborhood, and there are worse than those two thugs about," he warned.

At his warning, Ophelia turned even paler, Cordelia thought, though it was hard to tell in the darkness.

"Do you have someone to stay with, an address I can escort you to?" he asked.

The girls looked at each other.

"Surely you didn't come to London without a friend or relative to take refuge with?" He sounded incredulous, and well he might, Cordelia thought, her spirits sinking even lower.

"You expected to present yourself to the manager of the Malory Lane Theater and obtain a position at once?"

"I am, sir, a fine actress!" Ophelia straightened her shoulders, regardless of her powdered gray hair and black weeds, which he could not see anyhow.

"Really? And just where have you played, my dear?"

Bristling at the intimate tone—but then, he thought he was talking to an actress, not a lady, so what could she say—Cordelia bit her lip as she waited for her twin to reply.

Ophelia hesitated.

"I thought so. It's not that simple, my innocent country miss, and Mr. Nettles, the manager of the theater, will eat your liver for dinner and have the rest of you, body and soul, for dessert, if you don't look out. It's not just plays that he makes his blunt off of, you see, and a couple of pretty young things with no one there to protect you—you'll be grist for his flesh mill, I'm afraid."

Cordelia had been following behind the man, eyes down as she tried to see the rough stones of the pavement, clutching her sister's hand so that Ophelia did not disappear again, and for a moment the meaning of their rescuer's cryptic words eluded her. Then Ophelia stopped abruptly and she, too, paused as their meaning became clear.

Join the ranks of the demimonde? Good heavens!

"Never!" Ophelia declared, lifting her chin, her voice carrying her usual theatrical flourish. "I would never do such a thing—surrender my virtue for common coin? Never!"

"Certainly not!" Cordelia agreed, with less drama but a firm tone.

"Indeed?" She could hear his skepticism. "Your sense of virtue is commendable, but an empty belly has vanquished many a conscience 'ere now, I fear. Come along, you don't want to be lost in this neighborhood."

They ran to catch up. The night air was damp, and they had to almost hug the buildings to avoid the occasional carriage that went by. In the vehicles' carriage lights, she could see that fog was forming.

It seemed that they walked a long way, and Cordelia's imagination, never as wild as her sister's, was nonetheless working just fine. Where was he taking them? To his own rooms—they could not stay with a man, a perfect stranger, much less a man of ill repute, a thief, even if he had saved them from kidnappers and—likely—white slavers.

Yet, even if she demanded that they be taken to a reputable hotel, she was not sure that any hotel in this run-down part of town would be safe, and even if such a thing existed, she was not sure they had enough money left to pay for two people's lodgings.

Oh, they should not have spent their coin on that hackney, drat Ophelia's ambitious schemes, anyhow! Their coach fares south had cost more than they'd expected, and then there had been meals along the way—they should have just gone hungry and saved their money. Remembering meals of overdone mutton and stringy chicken, she swallowed. Posting houses dreadfully overcharged travelers who had little choice in venue, but going without meals had been surprisingly hard to do when one's stomach was empty. She thought of his warning and sighed again.

Frowning, Cordelia considered their current situation. At least she had a last desperate card up her sleeve. Lord Gabriel Sinclair, their newly discovered half brother, might still be in London. He would surely lend them enough money to get them back home to Yorkshire—at least if she could convince her sister to go! Even Ophelia must see that she had tried to get an audition and what more could she do? She could not condemn herself and her twin to starvation and death on the London streets. Enough was enough!

After all, they had almost been abducted over this foolish scheme of hers! Cordelia was no longer in humor for indulging lifelong dreams, even for a beloved sister, not when it led them into such perilous straits.

But where was this man taking them? How long would they trek through the dark?

"Need a good time, gov?" a female voice inquired out of the darkness.

Cordelia jumped. They were approaching a rare streetlight, and she saw the woman standing at the edge of the small circle of yellow light, her face rouged and her dress low-cut. Oh, heavens, it was a streetwalker.

She felt Ophelia shiver.

"No, thank you," the man who led them said, his tone polite.

"Guess not, you already got a damn 'areem," the prostitute said as she made out their shapes in the growing mist. "Lawd, 'ow many women you need, gov?" Her laughter faded behind them as they walked on.

Where was he taking them? She should not have told him that they had no family here.

"We have a half brother who is a lord," she said, her voice a little too loud.

"And I am a gentleman of means," he agreed, in his usual sardonic tone. "But taking two young ladies home with me could cause gossip. For tonight, you should be safe where we are going."

But they only had his word for that—the word of a stranger.

"What shall we do?" Ophelia whispered.

Cordelia wanted very much to box her twin's ear. "I don't know!" she answered, keeping her voice low. "We can't sleep on the street. We don't have the money to try to locate our half brother tonight, if he's even in London. This plan was madness, Ophelia, didn't I say so!"

Ophelia grabbed her hand in a fierce grip. "Run!"